I am HER…

Sarah Ann Walker

DEDICATION

This is dedicated to those of you who I love. You know who you are
because I tell you and show you enough (I hope.)
And to Jakkob.

CONTENTS

ACKNOWLEDGMENTS

Thank you...

I would like my son Jakkob to know that he is *by far*, the greatest blessing I have ever received. Jakkob, you are the joy, and the love of my life, and I have nothing in this world which does not begin and end with you. You have been the most beautiful gift of love, in this life of mine.

I would like to thank my husband James Freeburg for giving me his support and patience while I wrote this intense vision of mine. Thanks also for the awesome book cover, its perfect!

Thank you to my parents, but especially to my mom Annie, who always told me I should do this. There! I finally did something you told me to do!

To my sister Brennah; I think you're gonna love him even more.

To Paola, 'my person', if you will. Shy of helping me bury a body (ha ha), I know I can tell you and ask you anything without fear of judgment or repercussion. Nearly twenty-five years is a long, *long* time to put up with me, and it says a lot about your love, and the depth of your friendship. So thank you, *sincerely.*

To *my* Stephen; I want you to know that you were always a very important part of my life growing up. You were my very own '*Mack*' for years. And for that, I thank you, and I miss you.

Finally, I want to thank everyone else who have supported me during this new adventure of mine. Things have been a little difficult for me in the last year and a half, but there were a few people who came forward and championed me when I was lost. Thank you to those family and friends who loved me throughout. And thanks Mme. Tara for being such an awesome Cheer-leader!

I hope you like it!
Sarah

P.S. **Don't cheat!** You'll find out soon enough.

"Porphyria's Lover"
by Robert Browning

The rain set early in tonight,
The sullen wind was soon awake,
It tore the elm-tops down for spite,
And did its worst to vex the lake:
I listened with heart fit to break.
When glided in Porphyria; straight
She shut the cold out and the storm,
And kneeled and made the cheerless grate
Blaze up, and all the cottage warm;
Which done, she rose, and from her form
Withdrew the dripping cloak and shawl,
And laid her soiled gloves by, untied
Her hat and let the damp hair fall,
And, last, she sat down by my side
And called me. When no voice replied,
She put my arm about her waist,
And made her smooth white shoulder bare,
And all her yellow hair displaced,
And, stooping, made my cheek lie there,
And spread, o'er all, her yellow hair,
Murmuring how she loved me--she
Too weak, for all her heart's endeavor,
To set its struggling passion free
From pride, and vainer ties dissever,
And give herself to me forever.
But passion sometimes would prevail,
Nor could tonight's gay feast restrain
A sudden thought of one so pale
For love of her, and all in vain:
So, she was come through wind and rain.
Be sure I looked up at her eyes
Happy and proud; at last I knew
Porphyria worshiped me: surprise
Made my heart swell, and still it grew
While I debated what to do.
That moment she was mine, mine, fair,
Perfectly pure and good: I found
A thing to do, and all her hair
In one long yellow string I wound

I am HER…

Three times her little throat around,
And strangled her. No pain felt she;
I am quite sure she felt no pain.
As a shut bud that holds a bee,
I warily oped her lids: again
Laughed the blue eyes without a stain.
And I untightened next the tress
About her neck; her cheek once more
Blushed bright beneath my burning kiss:
I propped her head up as before
Only, this time my shoulder bore
Her head, which droops upon it still:
The smiling rosy little head,
So glad it has its utmost will,
That all it scorned at once is fled,
And I, its love, am gained instead!
Porphyria's love: she guessed not how
Her darling one wish would be heard.
And thus we sit together now,
And all night long we have not stirred,
And yet God has not said a word!

Sarah Ann Walker

Introduction

Yes, I'm awake. Yes, I can feel you.
Oh god, *here we go...*

Touching my hip, Marcus nudges my back with his erection. Kissing my neck, he pulls my hair behind my ear and whispers, "Good morning. I really want to..."

"Um... now?" I ask.

Taking that as my yes, Marcus pulls my pajama bottoms lower, pushes me to my back and strips my bottoms off completely. Gripping my breast rather hard, he moves between my legs.

Trying to push inside me, he murmurs, "Oh honey, you're so tight... I can't fit. My penis is too big." Uh huh. That's it. It's not the fact that I'm half asleep, and *dry as a bone.*

"I'll get the lubricant." And reaching to the bedside table, I pull the lubricant free and try to hand it to him. When he looks at me with disgust, I huff quietly and spread the jelly on myself.

"I know you think it's gross, but without it you rip me open..."

Smiling, because of his *sexual prowess* Marcus enters me quickly. Pushing inside, he groans loud and long.

Thank god for time. I love time and I love numbers. With time, I know how long something painful will last. With numbers, I have a finite timeframe. Therefore, I know this won't take long and it won't be *that* painful.

Starting a quick rhythm; Marcus lifts his arms to my sides and thrusts hard. I feel nothing. I know he's inside me, but I'm numb. There is no pleasure. There is nothing. I'm not even here.

Five minutes later, Marcus asks, "Are you almost there honey?"

"Yes... *almost*," I smile. And closing my eyes, I begin to pant loudly, swivel my hips, arch my back, and grab his arms.

At least now he asks me that. He acts like he cares if I have an orgasm. He didn't ask or care for the first 4 years we were together. He still doesn't *actually* care, but at least he asks me now. That's something.

"Oh, oh... *Marcus...*"

"That's right, honey. Go ahead." Thump. Thrust. Thump. Oh god, my uterus *loves* this... Lifting my hips, I scrunch up my face, stop breathing, and groan.

"Yes..." he groans as well.

And then it's done. Three more thrusts and he erupts inside me. Less than ten minutes of my life and I'm free for another couple weeks, maybe even a month if Marcus is stressed out or busy at work.

Yes... *I'm free.*

Rising from the bed, I smile at my husband, and enter our ensuite bathroom, as he lies back down to recover from our *love-making.*

Showering quickly, I touch myself and feel swollen... but mostly, I feel numb and slightly bruised down there.

Marcus means well, but he has mistaken hard thumping with sexual pleasure. I wish I had time to use my shower head, but Marcus wasted *those* six minutes of my life. No release for me this morning.

==========

Thirty five minutes later I step out of the bathroom, hair dried, make-up applied, wrapped in my towel. Marcus is waiting for me, fully dressed.

"Is that what you're wearing today?" He asks, while staring at the outfit I planned still hanging on my closet door.

"Yes. *Why?*" Instantly, I'm filled with insecurity. What's wrong with my clothing?

"Oh, nothing. It's just you always wear black. I know you wear black to hide your big thighs and butt, but you would look good in some color too, honey." My face drops. My *big butt and thighs...?* "Oh... don't be so sensitive. I don't mind your body, I'm used to it. Oh, come here..." And walking to me, Marcus tries to strip me of my towel.

Pulling away, I turn my back on him and walk toward my clothing. As if I'll ever be naked in front of him, or *anyone else* for that matter.

Pouting, I say, "I'm not fat. I'm not skinny, but I'm definitely NOT fat. I'm curvy. I'm shapely. I really am..." *God,* am I trying to convince my husband, or *myself?*

"You are such a prude. Lighten up, honey. It's not like I haven't seen your body naked in the last six years." Huh? *When?!* Was I *conscious?*

Smiling, Marcus walks over to me, kisses my forehead, and leaves the room chuckling to himself.

I am NOT fat. I LIKE wearing black. I am NOT a prude.

God, I *hate* Monday mornings.

PART 1

SICKNESS

MONDAY, MAY 23

CHAPTER 1

Arriving at work, I'm greeted by all the women in the lunchroom. Kayla is shocking *and* enlightening everyone with her "hot new screw" details, as she calls her latest sexual conquest from the week-end before.

Kayla doesn't care what anyone thinks about her. She doesn't care if the rest of the women trash her behind her back. She doesn't care that she's never invited to meet husbands, or that she's never invited to private dinners. She doesn't care if she sounds trampy. Kayla is the happiest person I know. *God,* I wish I was Kayla.

Walking toward me, Kayla asks, "Hey Sweetie, how was your week-end?"

"Not as good as yours sadly," I grumble.

"Yeah, well, after all the fabulous sex was over, I was alone last night, and you were with your wonderful husband. Who has it better?" *Who indeed?*

Looking at me closely, she asks, "What's up? You seem kinda off this morning."

"Oh, nothing. I had to fuck my husband this morning, but at least I'm free from doing it again for a few weeks..."

Wow! Kayla is stunned by my statement. *I'm* stunned by my statement!

"Ah... *Sweetie?* You don't say the f-word," she says as she bursts out laughing.

Stunned at my words and my behavior, I suddenly laugh too. I laugh so hard my stomach starts knotting and my eyes fill with laughter tears. I might not swear *out loud*, but I definitely say bad words in my head. *So there!* I'm laughing on the edge of hysteria, watching as Kayla changes from amused to concern within seconds.

Pulling me down the hall to my office, Kayla closes the door, releases my arm and asks, "*Seriously.* What's wrong? You're acting really weird Sweetie, and I don't like it. Are you okay?"

Kayla's looking at me so sincerely, I feel twisted because I want to talk. I actually *want* to tell someone what I feel. I want to tell her... *but I can't.* I don't do that. I don't confide. I don't vent. I don't share. I don't trust anyone, ever.

"Nothing's wrong. I was just being silly. You say the f-word all the time... I was just trying to keep up," I say with a grin.

Looking at my face, I can tell she doesn't believe me. "Are you okay? Is something wrong with Marcus? Did you have a fight?"

"No. We're fine." I exhale. "Everything's fine. Nothing's wrong, I promise. I was just being silly." I am so uncomfortable with the way she's looking at me right now. "Honestly, Kayla... I'm good. But I really need to start calling the Accounts Managers. I'll see you at lunch, okay?"

She looks at me closely and smiles, but I see it doesn't touch her eyes at all. God, I *hate* that look.

I like having Kayla in my corner at work. She's always there to protect

me from an aggressive jerk on the phone, or from an unreasonable Accounts Manager who resents me asking about his expenses. Kayla can talk to anyone. She *always* talks to everyone. I don't talk to anyone. I don't talk to my husband. I don't talk to Kayla. I don't have a single close friend. But it's okay, I like alone.

Suddenly, I'm so scared of losing Kayla; I grab her wrist and beg, "Are you mad at me?"

"Fuck no! Why would you ask that? I'm just worried about your near-psychotic break five minutes ago... But seeing as you never have them, and I do all the time, I'm willing to let this one slide..." And smiling once more, Kayla leaves my office. "See you at lunch Sweetie," she yells from down the hall.

==========

Dropping my purse behind my desk, I plop down into my chair. *Ow.* My body is sore. It must be from all that lovin' this morning. Yes, the passionate loving I received from my passionate, loving husband.

I wonder if I placed a blow-up doll in the bed while he slept, if he'd notice the difference while 'love-making'. Grinning, I can't help thinking maybe I should buy the blow-up doll just to freak him out. Then again, I'm sure they don't make blow-up dolls that are fully clothed *in black,* to hide their *big thighs and butt.*

Just forget it. Marcus is nice, if not clueless. He loves me. He just doesn't really see me. But at least I have him, though I'm still kind of alone... *with* him.

Exhaling, I turn on my computer and wait. Wishing I had grabbed a coffee, before Kayla *escorted* me to my office, I start pulling out the expense reports I have to look over this week. It's the twenty-third with only six more workdays left for me before the thirty-first, to close out the month and to issue the check run. Now, the phone calls begin.

Asking Accounts Managers to hand in their expenses by the twentieth of every month should be easy. *Jeez...* It's not like I change the date every month. It's the twentieth. It's always the twentieth. It has always *been* the twentieth; whether there are 30, 31 or even 28 days in the month. Why do they make every month so difficult? I don't understand.

The women are pretty good. With a few exceptions from the more creative women, I usually have all *their* expenses by the TWENTIETH. The men? *Forget it.* I can't understand them. The men want to be paid for their expenses. They freak out and scream at me, if there's an expense missed or denied. Usually, the men know what they're getting back within one dollar, give or take, but somehow, they can't remember to actually hand in, fax, mail, or email their receipts and expense reports to me *BY THE TWENTIETH* of each month.

I don't understand men. I've never understood men. Men like me. They have always liked me. I am cute and pretty... to men. Apparently, I have a 'Hey, can you be my big brother?' sign on my forehead. Men have always kind of wanted me, but they only ever *talked* about wanting me,

they didn't actually ever *do* anything about wanting me. Marcus did though.

Marcus talked *and* acted. Marcus wanted me *because* I was cute and pretty and smart. Marcus told me after our engagement that he could have had a sexy, beautiful, out-going wife, but he preferred to have someone like me, because he likes stability, and therefore, he wouldn't worry about cheating from a wife *like me.*

I remember wanting to tell him I had been cheating on him since the day we met, but I was too afraid he'd simply laugh and not believe me, rather than being outraged by my alleged infidelity. *That* would have been humiliating. *I could cheat...* but no one would believe it of me, so what's the point?

Once my computer is ready, I search incoming emails. Yes! Two more expense reports. Come on. Come on. *Damn.* I still have to call four Accounts Managers. This is going to be a worse Monday than I thought.

After entering and logging the newest receipts and the two latest expense reports, it's almost 12:30. I've been stalling. I don't want to make these calls. I hate making these calls every month. I hate it. I start getting anxiety by the eighteenth of every month, because I know there will be phone calls to make after the TWENTIETH.

Kayla suddenly knocks on my partially opened door and peeks her head in. "Hey crazy-lady, are you ready for lunch?"

Smiling, I yell, "Hell, yeah!"

Stunned again, Kayla bursts out laughing, as I grin.

"That sooo doesn't work for you. If *I* said that, it would work. I've got the whole trashy, sexy, dirty-girl thing going for me. You, however, have the whole *virgin-sacrifice* thing going for you. It just doesn't work. I do appreciate a good swear word every once in a while from you though."

Rising from my chair, I grab my purse and wish I *could* have the whole 'dirty-girl' thing going for me. I wish I could be like Kayla. I wish my husband could make love to me the way Kayla's men make love to her. I wish I knew *how* to have hot steamy sex. I wish I even knew what hot steamy sex *was...* but it's never going to happen for me. Forget it.

===========

Lunch is okay. Kayla tries to ask again what's bothering me, and again, I tell her I was just being silly. I can tell she doesn't believe me, so I ask about her 'hot new screw'. And after a thirty minute *graphic* rundown of events, I'm blushing and she's laughing. Kayla is *awesome.*

How the hell can she do those things? Why would she even *want* to do those things? I would die of embarrassment, and I would hope to die quickly.

==========

Back at work after lunch, I pull up my contact lists. Most of the Accounts Managers have their own Receptionists, and I usually get along okay with them because they understand I'm just doing my job. It's only after they can't get answers from their bosses, that the mean, often rude, Accounts Managers call me... *and the hell begins.*

I can't understand why the Accounts Managers do this. The expense report is generic. It's always the same. Just like the TWENTIETH of each month. Nothing changes. Fill out your mileage. Fill out the clients you 'wined and dined'. Fill out the products you picked up for your potential and/or existing clients. Fill out any 'incidentals'. Give me the receipts. It's always the same. It is *exactly* the same every month. I never change the report. I never change the due date.

I never change.

Okay. Pulling up one particularly obscene jerk, I make the call. When his Receptionist answers, I ask in my best, most non-confrontational voice if she has all the expenses and receipts ready to send over to me, 'at her earliest convenience'...*of course.*

"No," she replies.

"Ah, will you have them ready soon? I know Mr. Craig is busy, but there are only six days left to process his expenses." *Jerk.*

Giggling, Tamara says, "Um, Mr. Craig was fired on Friday, so I'm not really sure how to get the expenses from him. He was fired right after I left for the day." Why is she *giggling?*

"Oh. Okay. That creates a whole lot of issues. Did his Supervisor state to you how and when his severance was going to begin?" Damn. This is going to get messy for me, I know it.

"No. I just met his replacement an hour ago over lunch, so I don't really know anything yet. Z says he'll contact all personnel with any updated information he figures out. He says he'll be going through all Mr. Craig's reports, and he'll be asking me to help catch him up. Z wants to take this slowly... so he can fill Mr. Craig's shoes *properly* and *efficiently.* I can ask him to call you if you want." Tamara sounds almost giddy. *Why?*

"Um, does *Z* have a last name? I would like to establish contact with him without calling him 'Z'." Who calls himself 'Z' in Corporate America? Is he for real? What an *idiot!*

"His last name is Zinfandel-ike the wine. So he goes by Z. Isn't that cool?" Uh huh. What the hell? Zinfandel, *like the wine?*

"Don't you mean Zinfandel, like the, ah, *Zinfandel?*" I ask.

"What? Oh, yeah... Mr. Zinfandel like the Zinfandel. I get it. Anyway, I'll give him the message that you called. Thanks, Babe." And she hangs up.

Zinfandel? *Zinfandel?* Mr. *Z?* That's it. I lose it, and laughter pours out of me. I can't help it. Tamara sounded so excited about her '*Zinfandel-like the wine.*'

What does someone named Zinfandel even look like? I can't stop

laughing. Why is this so funny? *Shit.* I've got to stop this. Maybe I *am* going crazy. Oh! Maybe I'm *already* crazy. That would be better. *Being* crazy is infinitely better, and *cooler*, like a good Zinfandel, than merely *going* crazy.

==========

Around 3:30, another email comes in with the expense report attachment. I really like this man- Michael Devon. He is late every single month, but he's always so apologetic about his lateness, I just can't be annoyed with him.

Usually, he gives me a charming made-up story about rescuing trapped orphans from a burning building, which sadly delayed his report. Or once he told me about his unexpected trip to the African Serengeti, and how as much as he tried to complete his expense report on time, the Tour Guide wouldn't let him use the fax machine from the touring bus.

He is always funny, and I almost hope each month he'll be late, just so I can talk to him for awhile. Usually, I sit and listen to his elaborate tales, 'umming and ahhing' during appropriate pauses, while his story becomes more and more incredible and elaborate.

By the end, when I laugh and ask him to please send me the reports immediately, he asks me to come work for him, 'to keep him in line' as he states it. Always, I tell him his tardiness would drive me insane, and therefore, for my mental health, I must sadly decline his offer of employment. And each month our conversation ends the same...
I thank him for his time, he laughs and says, "I'll talk to you around the twenty-fourth next month," and I laugh when he hangs up.

See, I can have fun. I'm not always so serious. I'm not always so reserved. I'm not always so *invincible.*

============

By 5:30... I'm done. Number crunching and receipt preparing have made my eyes hurt, and my brain tired. I can't wait to go home.

I know Marcus will be late. He's always very late on Monday nights. Marcus likes to stay late on Mondays to catch up on all the work he could have been doing over the week-end, if he hadn't been stuck at home, with me.

Of course, he would never say something so heartless, but the message is always implied. Marcus enjoys working week days. Marcus *tolerates* being married to me on week-ends. He is actually a much better husband to his career than he is to me. But at least he's nice and stable.

Grabbing my purse, I remember Mr. Zinfandel and smile. That sounds good right about now. I think I'll stop for a bottle at the grocery store on my way home.

============

Reading in my sunroom, with a glass of Zinfandel in my hand, I finally relax. Its 8:30 and I settle into my newest raunchy novel. I love this author. She is absolutely *filthy*. Kayla should write a novel about her sexploits. God, Kayla's novel would be a best-seller at porn conventions.

I'm alone with my book, and no one knows that I'm reading this filth, yet I still blush and shimmy in my chair constantly. I'm always so afraid Marcus will sneak up on me and see what I'm reading. I can just imagine the look on his face. *Oh, the horror!* Actually, I think I'm more afraid he'd think I want this kind of dirty sex with him. Ugh. *Never.*

He is lovely, and a catch by most women's standards, but hot in the bedroom, *he is NOT.* I don't think Marcus has ever been kinky or dirty or wild in bed, at least he's never been with me. He did tell me once about one of two girls he dated in college who was pretty '*kinky*'. Afterward, he stated, she was *clearly* not marriage material, and I had nothing to worry about. *Yeah... like I was worried.*

By 10:30, I'm tired- *really* tired. I think the Zinfandel did me in. Marcus still isn't home, and I'm relieved. I feel a little keyed-up after reading my dirty book. Maybe I could slip into the shower for a few minutes. My shower-head has brought me some pleasure over the last two years, but standing, I realize I have a 'zinfandel buzz'. *Shit.* How much did I drink anyway?

Staggering to the kitchen, I see the bottle has less than a glass left. Giggling, I figure it seems a waste not to finish it. So after pouring myself the last glass from the bottle and hiding the bottle far back under the sink, I slowly move, *unsteadily,* to my bedroom. Once in my room, the thought of a shower seems like too much work on unsteady feet. I'm really, *really*, tired anyway.

Moving to my bed, I crawl in, turn off the light and sip my Zinfandel. This feels so strange, almost exotic or something. Maybe I'm an alcoholic? Maybe I'm a closet drunk? Maybe...? *No.* Drinking once every 2-3 months hardly qualifies me as an alcoholic. Oh, well. Being crazy AND a drunk would be too much for Marcus and my parents to handle anyway.

Sitting the wineglass on my bedside table, I decide to sleep. I'm *so* tired tonight, it's weird. Usually, sleep is a longtime coming, but not tonight. Tonight, I can feel the pull immediately. If I close my eyes, I'll be asleep within seconds. Thinking about sleeping usually keeps me awake, but not this time. This time, as I close my eyes...

I'm done.

==========

Kayla is stroking my back and kissing me gently on the lips in my bedroom. What the hell *is going on?*

"Relax Sweetie. We're okay. I won't hurt you. I promise. Just kiss me."

19

Shocked, I stagger back a step.

"No. I can't. I don't think of you that way Kayla. I'm sorry. I'm married."

"Okay. It's okay Sweetie. Just touch yourself, and let me watch." *She says while smiling at me with pity all over her face.*

"What? No! I can't do that. Please stop this. Why are you here, anyway? You* never come to my house.*"

"I'm here for you. Just touch yourself. I promise I won't touch you. I just want to watch as you pleasure yourself."

What the hell *is she saying? Kayla isn't gay, is she?*

"Um, Kayla... I'm not gay. I don't want to be with a woman. I think you're great, but I don't want to be with you."

"Always so polite," *she smirks.* "Sweetie, I'm not gay either. I just want you to get off... that's all. I figure, I could tell you what to do... you know, what will work for you. Just go ahead and touch yourself. I promise I won't touch you. You can do it. Put your hand on your pussy, and start feeling..." *I gasp. God. That is such a* gross *word. I hate it!*

"I don't want to. Honestly. I know how to do it. I don't need you to show me. Why are you doing this?" *I ask, horrified.*

"Oh, Sweetie... I'm not trying to freak you out. I just think you need to relax a little. I know a good orgasm can help me stay calm for days. Please try... for me?" *She begs with a pout.*

I almost start laughing at the expression on her face. Kayla's pout is legendary. Kayla can get anything or do anything, when she throws that particular pout out there.

"Kayla, you're nuts. I'm not touching myself in front of you. I'm not even sure why you're doing this, but it's gross. I'm not going to masturbate in front of a colleague."

"A colleague? That's it? That's all I am to you? A colleague?" *Kayla actually looks really upset. Shit. Is she mad at me?*

"Kayla. You are* more *than a colleague, but I'm still not comfortable touching myself in front of you. I don't do that with anyone. I don't even really do it by myself. It's just not my thing. I don't really feel it when I've tried, okay? Please Kayla... Don't be mad at me..."

"If you don't touch yourself, and have an orgasm, than I can't be friends with you anymore. I'm sorry, but I need you to do this. You* need *to have an orgasm. I'm telling you. I know. You'll feel much better. What if I turn my back? Will that make it easier? Will you do it then?"

"Ah, okay. Turn around please. But you can't tell anyone... Ever. Promise me."

What the hell *is going on here? Am I officially insane? I must be...*

"I promise, Sweetie. This is just between you and me. I swear."

I can't believe this. Shit. What do I do? What should I do? Just do it. She's not looking. Do it! Loosening my pants, I slide my hands down my underwear. What now? Okay, rub my clitoris. Uh huh. No feeling at all. Nothing. Rub some more. Nope... still nothing.

"Wet your fingers, Sweetie. It'll feel better when you touch your clit." *I flinch at the sound of the word. 'Clit' sounds as bad as 'pussy'. I hate both those words.*

Wetting my fingers, I start to rub against my clit-ORIS... Nope- I can't say

20

it. Um, there is a little feeling, but not much. My vagina feels kinda full though. Ow! *What's going on?!*

"*Kayla. What's happening...?*" *Why does this hurt...? Holy* SHIT!

"*Kayla?* Kayla, from work?" Marcus grunts.

"What's happening?" I murmur. Waking a little more... "What are you doing?" I gasp.

Shit. Marcus is having sex with me. *Dammit.* I'm not ready. I'm so dry it hurts.

"Marcus? Marcus, please stop so I can get some lube. Marcus, *please?*" Thump. Thrust. Thump. Marcus continues. Thrusting into me, he isn't even acknowledging me.

Am I Here? Can he even *see* me? Thrust. Thump. Hold breath. Groan. Marcus explodes inside me. *Oh. My. God!*

"Sorry, honey... but you asked for it. I can't believe you were *masturbating* in our bed. Why didn't you just tell me you wanted to have sex again? After this morning, I thought you were all sexed-out from your orgasm, but you could've asked..." Marcus says, as he pushes off my body. He looks totally grossed out by me.

OH MY GOD! Am I even here? Can he even *see* me? Am I asleep still? *God...* I hope I'm asleep.

"Good night, honey. I don't *mind* having sex with you, especially if you're talking about another woman, but you just have to ask me, and I'll try to do it with you, okay?" Kissing my forehead, Marcus rolls onto his side away from me. "But you don't have to *masturbate*... It's just gross," he sneers, with his back turned to me.

Staring at the ceiling, I am completely lost. I feel suspended between wake and sleep. I know I'm awake, but I wish to god I was still dreaming. I wish I had never wakened. I wish I didn't know Marcus had touched me.

What's going on? Why am I thinking about Kayla, and being wretchedly screwed by my husband? I know I'm bleeding a little *down there*, but I'm too tired to shower.

I think I'm totally losing it. I'm losing it for sure, and closing my eyes... *I'm lost...*

Tuesday, May 24th

CHAPTER 2

This morning begins like any other, except Marcus has decided he wants to talk to me- I can tell. Marcus is watching my every move, like he's looking for an opening. I hate his eyes on me. I hate when he watches me. I hate the *feeling* of being watched by him.

"What is it Marcus? What do you want to say?" I ask rather sulkily.

"Nothing. I was just curious why you wanted to think about Kayla while we were making love?"

"I didn't *want* to. It was just a dream. It's not like I can control them," I state rather matter-of-factly.

"Yes, I know. But do you *want* me to be with you and Kayla?"

"Oh god, no! Why would you think that?"

"It's nothing. You just seemed *really* into it last night, and I want you to know that it's okay with me if you want us to be with Kayla. She's really hot. I'd like to have a threesome with her... if *you* want."

Oh. My. *God.* Is this happening? I think I'm going to lose it here. *Too late-* **Snap.** I've lost it.

"*Seriously?* She's really HOT, huh? You would be *okay* with a threesome, if *I* want!? You think I was really *into it* last night? Marcus... I. Was. Asleep! I wasn't *into it;* I barely knew what was happening. I drank a bottle of Zinfandel last night, and was almost in a coma when you were '*making love'* to me. I'm glad it was *so* good for you, but it wasn't all that great for me. It was quite painful, and I'm pretty sore this morning. But I'm glad it was soo good for you, it usually is good for *you* ONLY, isn't it?" I scream. *Dammit.* Did I just say that? Here we go...

Marcus looks like I hit him. Stumbling backward rather dramatically, he's got his 'how can you be so cruel, to someone as good as me?' face on. *Shit.*

"Marcus...?" I whisper, but he just shakes his head and walks out of the room.

Okay... *great!* How long will he hold this over my head? How long until the little wife is forgiven? How long until we can go back to the way things *should* be... according to Marcus, my parents, and just about everyone else we know? How long do I tiptoe?

===========

Arriving at work, I'm already exhausted. If it wasn't the twenty-fourth, I might have taken one of my many banked vacation days, but it's just not a good idea. I still have over thirty expense reports to finalize and approve before Monday so the checks can be issued next Tuesday morning.

Kayla pokes her head in my office to say hello, and I blush immediately. Trying to look busy at my computer, I smile and nod as she asks if we're meeting for lunch. *Damn.* I hope I can make it through lunch with *Hot Kayla* without blushing the entire time.

Once she leaves, I try to focus on the reports, but I keep seeing Marcus' face. He looked completely shocked by my words. Does he honestly believe his five minutes of thumping into me as hard as he can, is great love-making? *Honestly?* Forget it. There's nothing I can do right now about my husband, so I may as well do my job well- it's about the only thing I never fail at.

Checking my emails again, I see one more expense report in my inbox. Yes... only one more to hunt down. Once I enter this newest report, I still have to research the claims of all the last fifteen or so. I was lucky this month because a few of the Accounts Managers actually sent them in early, so I could start some of their claims last week.

==========

When my phone rings, I try to focus...

"Good morning..." but before I can finish, I hear my boss grunt.

"Good morning, Sugar. Can you come on up to my office? We have to discuss this month's expense reports."

"Ah, of course. I'll be right there, Sir." Gulp. What does *that* mean? He never wants to discuss the reports until after I have completed, approved, and submitted them.

Leaving my office, I pass Kayla talking to one of the outside Sales Reps. She's flirting, and talking, and pouting. Oh. My. *God.* He is *doomed.* Laughing to myself, I continue on my way upstairs. Kayla is truly amazing at everything she does, flirting included.

Knocking gently on Mr. Shields' door, I brace myself for the Texan. Mr. Shields is gruff, big, and very intimidating. Why are all heads of large companies from Texas? I think even Kayla watches herself a little around Mr. Shields.

"Come on in," he bellows.

Entering the room, I'm once again shocked by the sight of him. Mr. Shields screams inflexible and forceful. He's like his own tornado... all you can do is run, find cover, or get out of his way when there's a storm in the office.

"Good morning, Sir. Can I get you anything?" *Like a coffee? Some antlers to wall mount? A small village to pillage?*

"No, I'm fine. Thanks, Sugar. Take a seat."

Sitting in front of his desk, I can *feel* Shields' eyes all over me. Looking over his head slightly, I don't make eye contact, I just pretend to. No eye contact is safe. I don't blush if there's no eye contact. I absolutely HATE eye contact with anyone.

"Look, Sugar. I need you to be really thorough on the expenses this month."

Shocked, I nearly yell, "Oh, I'm *always* thorough." *Shit.* Where is he going with this?

Waving his hand to comfort me, Mr. Shields responds, "Oh, I know that. It's just I need to tighten the belts a little for the next quarter. After purchasing the warehouse and machinery in Phoenix two weeks ago, we need to buckle down for a while. I know you do a good job. I tell everyone about the Little Sugar in Payables. I know how tough you are on some of the more creative, *bullshit* claims, but I'm just asking, *between you and I,* if you could look into some of the larger claims a little more closely."

"Okay sir. Is there any Accounts Manager or claim you have in mind?"

"*Between you and me...?*" When I nod emphatically, he continues. "Okay. Well, we just fired Craig, so if you could wait a little to process any claims he puts through, that'd be helpful. And could you watch Devon? I think he's screwing with his personal expenses, and claiming them as work expenses..." *Michael?* Oh, I like him. Please, not Michael. "...And that Lisa bitch from Denver. I think she's been using her hotel expenses with her lover, and claiming them for the Denver Petrol Reps. She's kind of a slut, but I've met her wimp-ass husband, so I don't really blame her for screwing around... I just don't want to *pay* for it." *Bitch? Slut?* Oh my *god...*

"Um, okay. I'll look carefully at all the claims again. Is there anything else, Sir?" Please god, NO. *Get me out of here!*

"Nope. That's it. I expect to see your reports on Monday before you issue the check run. Unless... *you* want something from me Sugar...?" Pause. What does *that* mean?

Blushing, I rise from the chair as he stands- always the gentleman... *Not.* Mr. Shields is huge. Even with my heels, I'm only about 5'6. What is he, *like 6'4 or 6'5?*

"Okay. Good. Thanks, Sugar. You just let me know if I can do *anything* for you..."

Smiling as I turn, I practically run from his office.

What the hell was *that?* As if I would ever need anything from him. He's huge. He would crush me for sure. He's not a good enemy to have though. I hope I didn't offend him when I left. I gave him my best smile, so I hope I didn't make him mad at me.

Why does everyone call me names? Does anyone even *know* my first name? Does anyone know me at all? I wonder sometimes if *I* even know me.

==========

Returning to my office, still visibly shaken, the phone rings, and in a moment of complete *insanity* I answer... "Good morning. Sugar, Honey, Sweetie, Babe, here. How can I help you?" *Oh. My. GOD!* WHAT HAVE I *DONE?!*

"Well, good morning, Sugar, Honey, Babe. How are you this morning?"

Shit. He forgot *Sweetie.*

"Oops, I forgot Sweetie. Please forgive me," he says with a laugh.

For a moment there is only silence... and then I just burst out laughing. Trying to calm myself, I'm mortified, but the laughter won't stop. I'm trying. I'm really, *really* trying, but I simply can't stop. This is so embarrassing.

Hearing a low laughter on the other end of the phone, I try to shore up my reserve, but I just can't do it- nothing is working. Every time I almost stop laughing, a giggle escapes, and I start laughing again.

"Please... forgive me. It's been a long... d-day," I stammer through my laughter.

"No problem. It's only 10:45, and already a long day for you...? *Clearly,* you need the laughter. This is Mr. Zinfandel. I'm new to the New York...." but he pauses, as I gasp.

Laughter erupts from me all over again. Mr. Zinfandel? *Mr. Z?* I can't stop laughing. Gasping for breath, I try even harder to stop.

"Mr. Zin-Zinfandel... I drank you last night." *Oh. My. God.* Did I just say that? WHAT HAVE I DONE? *AGAIN?!*

I think I'm nearing hysteria. I can't stop laughing. Oh, please make this stop. My breath is hitching. My stomach is killing me. My head is pounding. But I just can't stop laughing. And my laughter sounds all weird and distorted or something. I don't even really sound like me anymore.

"Just breathe. I can hear you panicking. Breathe slowly. Come on, just breathe slowly for me..."

Closing my eyes, I listen to his voice. He sounds so lovely, and confident. He's probably never had a panic-attack in his life. He's probably always so together and sure of himself. I wonder what he looks like.

Slowly, after minutes have passed, I open my eyes and see Kayla in my office leaning against the door. *Shit.* How long has she been here? Smiling at her, I realize I'm still breathing slightly erratically, and I must look crazy.

"*WHAT THE FUCK IS GOING ON?!* The whole office can hear you laughing!" Kayla yells at me.

Jumping at her words, I quickly cover the phone, and try to focus on her as my breath hitches.

"Nothing's going on. I'm f-fine Kayla. I'm talking to the new Accounts Manager out of New York... Mr. Zin-Zinfandel." *Ooops.* A little giggle escapes.

I try to clamp down on the laughter. Shaking with the control I'm trying to hold over my body, the laughter is threatening to erupt again.

Walking over to my desk, Kayla rips the phone from my hand, as I stare at her in shock.

"Mr. Zinfandel. I do apologize, but we'll have to get back to you shortly. We have an unexpected meeting beginning now. Again, I apologize, but... Oh! I see. Yes, she's alright. *I'm sorry?* Yes, I'm going to take care of her..." *Take care of me?* What the *hell* is she talking about?

Trying to grab the phone away from Kayla, I stand as she glares down

at me and continues. "Thank you, Mr. Zinfandel. Oh, *Z?* Yes, alright. Much better name, anyway. Prevents all us lushes in Chicago from falling off the wagon after speaking with you..."

I can hear his rumble of laughter through the phone. Kayla is giving him her best smile. And though he can't see her, you can almost hear her seductive smile through the phone.

"Apologize for my behavior..." I whisper, but Kayla just looks down at me and ignores me.

What is she, like *5'10* or something? Why does she even *wear* high heels?

"Z, I do apologize for this outburst. It's been a long day, and she rarely laughs so consider yourself lucky..." Kayla adds grinning at him through her voice.

I think I'm going to die. Could this be any more embarrassing? Can I go home? I want to go home now. I want to go to sleep, and never wake up.

==========

"Sweetie. What the *fuck* is going on with you? And DON'T say *nothing.* I know you, and there is definitely *something* going on," Kayla practically snarls at me.

But she doesn't know me. No one knows me. *I* don't even know me.

Exhaling, "I'm fine. Honestly, Kayla. I just got the giggles. Everyone gets the giggles. That's all." I flash my best, most innocent smile.

"Yes. Everyone gets the giggles from *time to time,* but not you. I don't remember ever hearing you even laugh before. What *IS* it? Just tell me. Maybe, I can help."

Kayla isn't going to stop. Kayla is going to continue her interrogation. She will continue, because she can. She is Kayla, and Kayla *always* gets what she wants.

Without thinking, I scream, "I had a dirty dream about you last night! Well, kind of dirty I guess. We didn't actually *do* anything, but apparently my husband thought I was turned on in my sleep, and the next thing I knew he was *making love* to me while I was in a near coma from a bottle of Zinfandel..." Breaking out into laughter at the name, I continue. "...Marcus was quite turned on, by the way. He offered up his services. He is *willing* to have a threesome with you and me, because you are *Hot Kayla.* So if you're into a 'five minute man', thrusting his penis into your uterus hard... Marcus is your man. However, I did mention that sex wasn't very satisfying for me, so he's probably going to ignore my existence for the next two months or so, maybe even *during* the threesome. But if you're interested, I'll be sure to tell him- he probably wouldn't be quite so mad at me anymore, if you're game..."

Breathing hard, almost choking on my nausea, I close my eyes and hear him deep inside me.

"*Breathe. Come on, Sweetheart. Just breathe slowly for me...*"

God, his voice was lovely. He sounded so dark and silky. I try to picture him in my mind, but all I see is darkness.

Slowly opening my eyes, I look up, and realize Kayla is wiping mascara from my cheeks. She looks very concerned, and tender toward me. Embarrassed, I pull the tissue from her and begin cleaning my own face. Was I crying? *Doubtful.* It must have been the laughter.

"You're going home, Sweetie. And I don't want to hear it. Grab your purse. I'll tell everyone you had a family emergency and we should expect you back tomorrow. That'll buy you some time, in case you need more than today to recover." Recover? Recover from *what?* I'm fine- I just laughed.

"Kayla. I'm good. I was just laughing. *Honestly.* Please forget what I told you about Marcus and me. Everything's fine. I promise."

"Yeah, *right.* Anyway, I'm not taking no for an answer, so you might as well get going. You need a break Sweetie. You need to get out of here. I'll forward your calls to my phone, and I'll check your emails this afternoon. Everything will still be here when you return tomorrow."

Looking at Kayla, I'm so embarrassed. I can't stand to see her eyes on me because they are so full of pity. Ugh, I want to cry, but I won't. I don't cry. I will never cry in front of anyone. I don't do that, *ever.*

"Um...Okay. Please tell everyone I'll be back tomorrow."

"Sure. No problem. And Sweetie, don't worry about you and Marcus. You'll work it out. And don't worry about the dream either... *it happens.* I've dreamed about lots of people before. It's no big deal- it's flattering actually..." she says with a grin.

Blushing, I think I'm going to die. Right here, right now.

Standing, I grab my purse and head for the door, but before I can leave Kayla says, "Oh, and please tell Marcus that I'm not interested. I think you are more than enough woman for him. He is quite lucky to have you..." Turning, I leave my office, ignoring Kayla completely.

Sure. I'm *MORE* than enough woman for Marcus. With my *'big thighs and butt'*, I'm sure Marcus is just *drooling* to be with me. I'm sure he has dirty dreams about me. I'm sure he thinks about me constantly between the weeks-long break between love-making sessions.

==========

Returning home, I feel exhausted. Though my sleep was interrupted by Marcus in the night, I still slept for at least 6 hours. That's usually more than enough. So why am I so tired?

Walking to my bedroom, I remove my black dress suit, and climb on my bed in my bra and underwear. I never do this. This feels kind of illicit. I'm always dressed. If it wasn't for the mirror across from the shower, I would never see myself naked. I don't like naked. Naked feels dirty. Naked feels like *asking* to be hurt. I don't do half dressed, and I *certainly* DON'T DO NAKED...

==========

Waking from my nap, I realize it's after 7pm. I slept for over 7 hours? *What the hell?* Jumping from the bed, I listen for Marcus, but hear only silence. Exhaling, I run for my closet to pull on my 2 piece pajamas. Stripping off my bra and underwear... I'm suddenly alerted to movement in the room. Grabbing my pajama top, I try to cover myself, as I see Marcus standing in our room looking at my body.

"What do you want?" I ask a little too aggressively.

Taking his eyes off my breasts, Marcus replies, "Nothing. I was just coming to check on you. You didn't cook dinner, and the house was so quiet, I didn't know if you were home." When do I ever go out, especially on a week night? Where would I go?

"Sorry about dinner. I wasn't feeling well. Do you want me to make you something?"

"No. We had a late meeting, so we had sandwiches around 4:30. I'm good. What's wrong? You look terrible."

"Nothing," I exhale. I didn't even realize I had been holding my breath until then.

"Okay... Well, when you want to apologize for this morning, and talk about what you said to me, come find me. I'll be in my office, or in the spare room." Turning, Marcus leaves the room without a backward glance.

I am absolutely stunned again. Apologize? Apologize for *what?* Telling him sex isn't that great? Or that he kind of *assaulted* me while I slept? Or apologize for not wanting him to see my naked 'big thighs and butt'? The list is endless...

Quickly; I throw on my pajamas and run for the bathroom. Looking at my reflection... *EW!* I have mascara everywhere. I look terrible. No wonder Marcus asked me what was wrong even though he's mad at me.

See, he *is* a nice man. He cares for me. He *does* care, at least. Finally, I remove my smeared make-up, brush my teeth and go pee. I'm still so tired even after my 7 plus hour *nap.*

Crawling into bed, I exhale again. Why do I keep holding my breath? *That's* new. Laughing is new. Leaving the office is new. Talking back to my husband is new. Swearing *out loud* is new. What's going on with me? Am I *actually* crazy now, no longer *becoming* crazy?

Wednesday, May 25th

CHAPTER 3

When I wake up, Marcus is already gone. Somehow Marcus slipped into our bedroom and dressed in his walk-in closet without waking me, *thank god.* I can get up, dress and shower alone, in peace. I don't have to see his eyes of disapproval and disappointment. I'm free of his judgments, well, at least until this evening when he returns home.

Downstairs, I see his cereal bowl is in the sink and the coffee pot is half empty, which is somewhat comforting. At least he isn't acting strangely. He's just ignoring me, which I expect. I always expect to be ignored when someone is mad at me. I'm usually ignored regardless of what I've done. Being ignored is how I'm most comfortable actually, because when you're being ignored, no one *ever* makes eye contact with you.

===========

When I arrive at work, I'm nervous. I don't really want to see Kayla. I hated her seeing me freak out yesterday. I hate people seeing me act up. I like to be calm and controlled- *Not* like yesterday. Yesterday was just weird. I've never laughed like that before in my life. I think I lost 10 pounds laughing my ass off... *literally.* *Oh, no.* I feel a giggle bubbling up my throat.

"Hey, Sweetie," Kayla says, making me jump as she follows me toward my office. I push the giggle down deep. "How are you this morning? You look better. Did you and Marcus work it out last night?"

"Yes. We're good." I lie.

I hate lying. I absolutely *never* lie because it's just not worth the stress I feel after a lie, fearing whomever might find out the truth about me. But Kayla can be ruthless when she's on a mission, so it's better to lie to her, just this once.

Looking right in my eyes, Kayla smiles, "I'm sure you still need to talk to your Five Minute Man about *some* things, but I'm glad you guys are working it out." God, I *HATE* eye contact!

"Yes, we're working it out..." *with silence,* I mutter to myself. Ugh, different topic needed. "Did anything happen after I left yesterday?"

"Nope. I left your emails alone, because they had expense attachments, and your phone only rang a couple times. I told Heinrick's Receptionist to email over his expense reports pronto, and I think I scared her a little. *Oh well,* she'll learn. Big Daddy Shields called down to talk to you, but when I told him you had to leave for the rest of the day, he said it wasn't an emergency, and he would talk to you when you return."

Oh no! Mr. Shields knows I left before lunch. "Was he mad at me? Did he sound mad, Kayla?!" I ask desperately.

"No. I told you he was fine. He'll call you today." She's looking at me strangely again.

"What?" I ask defensively.

"Nothing. You just seem a little high-strung Sweetie. Are you sure you're okay? Do you need to spend more time away today?"

"No. I'm good." I almost yell at her... *almost.* Smiling to cover my intensity, "Kayla, thanks for your help yesterday, but I really need to start on these reports. The math alone is a killer. I'll see you later, okay?"

"No problem. I'll see you at lunch?"

"Ah, *no.* I have to run a few errands, but I'll talk to you later?" I smile.

"Alright, *later...* but Sweetie, if you want to talk I'm here, okay? I won't repeat a confidence. You can trust me, I promise."

As if I would trust anyone with my strange thinking patterns right now. As if I would trust anyone about anything, anyway.

"Thank you Kayla, but I'm fine. *Honestly...*" Obviously convinced, Kayla smiles and leaves my office.

Sincerely, I love having Kayla in my corner, even if I don't totally trust or confide in her. Kayla is awesome. I wish I was as tough as Kayla.

============

Turning on my computer, I check my emails. Yes! Another expense report completed. Only two calls to make today. Oh, no, not two... Kayla dealt with Heinrick. Hopefully I get his report today. That leaves only the Craig/Zinfandel expense report to figure out.

Checking my inbox, I see an email from Mr. Zinfandel dated yesterday afternoon. Opening the email, I'm so embarrassed, I blush like he's actually here in front of me. Who would have ever thought laughter could cause such stupidity in the workplace?

From: Z. Zinfandel
Subject: Laughter
Tuesday, May, 23
2:10pm

Dear Ms. Sugar, Honey, Sweetie, Babe,
How are you this afternoon?
After such an interesting name and introduction, I find myself wondering
 if you're doing well.
Sincerely,
Mr. Zinfandel (or just 'Z' for you *lushes* in Chicago.)

And there's another yesterday.

From: Z. Zinfandel
Subject: Breathing
Tuesday, May 24
4:45pm

Dear Ms. Sugar...
I do hope your afternoon was better than your morning.
Please tell me you're breathing easier.
Z

And another email this morning. *What the hell?*

From: Z. Zinfandel
Subject: Laughter and Breathing
Wednesday, May 25th
8:02am

Dear Ms. Honey,
I do hope you put my mind at ease and respond to me this morning.
I found myself thinking of you frequently last night.
Are you okay?
Z

Oh my god... Its 9:15 and already there's another email.

From: Z. Zinfandel
Subject: Still waiting...
Wednesday, May 25
9:01am

Dear Ms. Sweetie,
If you do not reply in the next 15 minutes, I will be forced to call you.
Please reply to me.
Z

Jeez... What the hell is his problem? I laughed. Is he going to call Mr. Shields and report me for *laughing* yesterday?

When the phone suddenly rings, I jump in my chair. Oh, no. Is it him? *Shit.* Do I answer? What the *hell* do I do? Grabbing for the phone, I inhale deeply and say...
"Good morn..." but I'm cut off.
"Well... if it isn't Ms. Sugar, Honey, Sweetie, Babe. How are you this

morning?" *God,* his voice is lovely. I just pause for a moment to absorb his voice into my body.

"Good morning, Mr. Zinfandel. I'm fine thank you. I was going to reply to your emails in just a minute or two." I try to sound casual but his voice is so distracting.

"Were you? Well, that's good to hear. I don't like to be left waiting... *Ms?* Never mind. I'll just add to the list, shall I? How about *Sweetheart?* Yes. I like the sound of that. You seem like you would be a genuine *sweetheart* to me."

My head is spinning. What the hell is he talking about? How would he know if I'm a *sweetheart?*

"Um... that would be *MRS.* Sweetheart then."

"Happily?"

"That's none of your business MR. Zinfandel," I respond, clearly offended by his bold question.

"*NOT* happily, I take it. You see, if you were happy you would have automatically replied, 'Yes. Very happily', like most everyone does when they describe a good relationship. You, however, told me off. This means, of course, that you don't want to talk about your unhappy marriage." Argh...

Slam. I hang up the phone. I hung up the phone?! *WHAT DID I JUST DO??* I just slammed the phone down on the New York Accounts Manager; the man who could have me fired with one phone call to Mr. Shields.

I think I'm going to throw up and it's only 9:21 in the morning. Trying to breathe through the nausea, I hear his voice...

"*Breathe with me... Come on... Breathe...*" and suddenly the weight lifts off my chest.

Glancing at my computer, I have 2 new emails. I hope they're not from him. Yes! One is Mr. Heinrick's expense report... And one is from Mr. Zinfandel of the New York office, timed one minute ago. *Shit.*

From: Z. Zinfandel
Subject: Phone slamming
Wednesday, May 25
9:25am

Dear **MRS.** Sweetheart,
That was very rude. But I will forgive you *this time* because you were not, in fact, told that I find the slamming of a phone in one's ear, to be quite rude. Please keep it in mind in the future, however.
I will call you again later to discuss the expenses Mr. Craig accumulated, and where exactly we should proceed from here.
Yours,
Z

"Yours, Z"?? WHAT THE HELL? He gave me a 'rudeness' warning? He wants me to *remember* the warning in the future? This is too messed up.

Maybe I'll show Kayla, and ask her what I should do. What would *she* do? Oh, Kayla would probably have him apologizing to *her* for not liking *her* rudeness. Kayla can turn any man any *way* she wants- I've seen her. She would probably love this, this... *what?* Maybe I'll tell her later? Maybe, I shouldn't? Maybe...? *No.* Nothing. I'll just ignore it, and hope I don't act *rude* again to Mr. Zinfandel so he won't tell Mr. Shields about my poor behavior.

==========

By 12:15, I'm starving. Checking my emails before heading for lunch, I see a new one from Mr. Zinfandel.

From: Z. Zinfandel
Subject: Checking up on you...
Wednesday, May 25
12:02pm

Dear Sweetheart,
I trust your day is better now than it was at 9:15 this morning?
I looked up your photo in the company directory, and I must say I am
   quite pleased. You are very attractive.
Your lips are gorgeous- they look like they were made for kissing.
But your eyes are simply *alluring*. I find myself looking at your eyes often.
Do you know what your eyes could do to a man?
Z

Wow! How inappropriate of him. My *eyes?* Yes, *I* know they're very pretty, but no one else really does. No one else sees me as *alluring*. No one really sees me at all.

After deleting the message, I grab my purse and run out the door. Once in my car, I have to think of an errand. I don't want to lie to Kayla, so if I actually *do* something, then I never *actually* lied to her. I'll go to the mall nearby. And buy... what? More black suits? More black skirts? More black heels? What do I need to buy?

Once in the mall, I am surrounded by teenagers. I guess it's lunchtime at the high school around the corner. God, they're so *loud.* Was I ever loud? No. I've never been loud, screamed, laughed, or been silly in my life. *Jeez,* I sound so boring, even to myself.

Entering a very posh shoe store, I'm instantly attracted to a pair of killer

cut-out 4 1/2 inch stilettos. Not entirely appropriate for work, but if I pair them down with black slacks; they might not look too slutty.

However, if I paired them with a skirt, I would look like I was walking the streets. Yeah, but how much could I really earn as a prostitute? My husband takes only five minutes to finish. Maybe a 'John' would take 15 minutes before *he* got off... What *is* the going rate per minute for putting out? I guess it depends on what I would have to do... *Ew.* Gross.

Totally unaware of my purchase, I'm suddenly standing at the store exit with my new shoes and the receipt in my hand. Well, I guess $125.00 isn't *too much* to pay for slutty stilettos I'll probably never wear.... Unless, of course, I do take up street-walking as a second income to pay for said slutty stilettos. Giggle. Ooops. What am I *doing* here?

Walking back to my car, I toss my new shoes in the backseat and pause. What do I do now? I still have 25 minutes to kill. So turning on my car, I fill it with a nice stream of cool air conditioning while I kill time. Leaning my head back, I close my eyes and relax.

Kayla will never know I'm stalling. I'll show her my shoes and pretend I had to look for a gift for my mother's birthday, which *is* actually in three and a half weeks... so not *really* a lie.

Wow. I better actually start looking for the perfect gift. God knows, I wouldn't dare to disappoint my mother... Marcus would be horrified.

==========

Waking with a jolt, I look at the clock and its 4:25. *OH, MY GOD!* I've been gone for 4 hours and asleep for over 3 hours *in my car! Why?!* What the hell is wrong with me?!

Snapping off the air, I try to recover from my drowsiness. What the hell do I say at work? Where the hell is my cell phone? *Christ,* did anybody call me from work? Upending my purse on the passenger seat, I have 2 missed calls and 2 text messages. *Shit.*

First message:
  "Hi, Sweetie. Where are you? Its 2:00 and you've been gone for over an hour and a half. Is everything okay?"

What do I say to Kayla?

Second message:
  "Hi. Me, again. Its 3:30. I'm not sure where you are, but I checked the company appointments schedule, plus your personal schedule on your computer and you have no appointments this afternoon... Are you alright?!"

Kayla sounds a bit pissed.

<u>First text: 2:43</u>
"call me. shields lookn for u. told him ur at a meetn. K."

<u>Second text: 4:12</u>
"where r u? Call me ASAP. I stalled shields. U O me. It's 4:13. WTF?"

Shit! Kayla sounds *really* pissed now.

Dialing Kayla's number as I speed out of the parking lot, I don't know what to say. One lie a day is too much for me. I hate lying. And I *really* hate lying to Kayla. Plus, I think she knows when I'm lying anyway. It's not like I have a poker-face or anything.

When she answers I just start spilling. "Hi Kayla. Sorry. I'm fine. Would you believe me if I said I fell asleep in the car? Honestly. I was sound asleep... "

"Is everything okay?" She laughs.

"Yeah... No. I mean, yes. I didn't even know I was tired. Thanks for covering for me."

"Ah, are you coming back to work?" She sounds totally confused.

"Yes. I'll be back in 5 minutes. Do you have any ideas what I can say to Mr. Shields? I'm totally desperate for a cover story."

"Um... What about the Marriot?"

"Oh, that's a good one! I'll say I was at the Marriott scheduling the Buyers luncheon. Thanks so much Kayla."

"No problem, Sweetie."

"*Really*, thank you for covering for me. See you in a few minutes."

==========

Running into the building, I pass Kayla's office, poke my head in the door, smile, mouth 'thanks', and head for my office. Passing the Receptionist Claire, I smile but she looks at me kind of shocked or something. *What?* Why is she looking at me like *that?* Shit! Am I in trouble with Shields?

Stopping, I smile at Claire again and tell her, "I didn't realize my cell was off. I was at the Marriott all afternoon preparing the Buyers luncheon. Did I miss anything important this afternoon?"

Still just staring at me, I wait. When Claire opens her mouth to speak, Kayla suddenly grabs me by the arm instead and starts pulling me toward my office. *What the hell?*

Once we're in my closed office, I pull my arm away. "What?! Why are you pushing me like that? I said I was sorry on the phone. I thought we were fine. You laughed at me when I said I fell asleep." Feeling so insecure suddenly, I whisper, "Are you mad at me Kayla?" But she just stares at me, looking kind of stunned herself.

"What is it?!" I yell at her.

Taking my hand again, Kayla murmurs, "keep your head down", as she leads me out of my office.

In the bathroom, I again pull away from her. "What? What's the matter? *Are* you mad at me?"

God, I hate being touched. I hate someone gripping my arms. I hate... *touch.*

Turning me toward the mirror, I gasp. *What the hell happened to me?* Stunned myself, I whisper, "Wow. I didn't realize..."

I am absolutely hideous. My mascara lies in streaks down my entire face. My nose is beet-red. My eyes are so swollen, they look half closed. My lips are fat and cracked, with one spot actually bleeding. I look like an assault victim. I have no color in my face at all. I look so pale, I'm actually almost bluish-grey. I'm *so* gross, that it's kind of funny actually. Ooops, I feel a giggle bubble up again. Huh. Maybe it's the same giggle I suppressed this morning.

"Wow," I breathe, and start laughing.

Kayla looks at me so sadly, that I'm instantly defensive. But before I can speak, she asks, "What happened, Sweetie? Should we go to the police first, or to the hospital? I'll take you, and no one will know, I promise..." The hospital? Why would we go to the Police? What is she saying? "...Sweetie, were you raped? Or...or just *assaulted?*" She begs. *Raped?* God, I hate that word!

Shaking suddenly, I can't breathe. Gasping for breath, I lean over the sink and try hard to breathe. Gagging, my stomach coils itself into a solid knot, but I've eaten nothing today to throw up. My legs start to buckle, so I gracefully drop to my knees, cover my face, shake violently, and try desperately to breathe.

"Breathe. I can hear you panicking. Breathe slowly. Come on, just breathe slowly for me..."

Eventually, my breathing slows and my chest starts loosening. My hands are totally numb, but no longer shaking. Looking up, I see tears in Kayla's eyes. OH! Please don't cry. *Please,* Kayla. If you cry, I know I'm done. *Please...*

Trying to stand, Kayla gently takes my hands and helps. Suddenly, I want my shoes off. Bending again, I slip off my heels and just kind of melt into the cool tiles of the bathroom floor.

I love this feeling. I love being in sexy heels all day with aching feet, then finally dropping my heels at my front door, to bathe my aching feet into the cool marble tiles of my home.

Looking back up, I'm almost shocked at how tall Kayla is suddenly. Stepping back a foot, I breathe, "I'm okay, but I need to go home. Honestly, nothing happened, Kayla. I really was just asleep in my car. I don't know why I look like this, but I swear I was asleep in my car. That's all. *Honestly.*"

I can tell she doesn't believe me at all. She thinks I'm a liar, and today I actually *am* a liar. I've lied twice in one day. *Wouldn't my family be so proud?*

36

Turning away from her face of pity, or maybe even shock, I don't really know which, I open the washroom door and walk smack into Mr. Shields. When he grabs my arms to steady me, I just can't stand it suddenly!

Jerking out of his grip, I scream, "Let me go!"

Mr. Shields is shocked into silence.

Looking at me, he stammers, "I, I wasn't going to hurt you, Sugar. I was just trying to help." I think I'm going to die of embarrassment, any second now.

"Sorry, Sir. I'm just not feeling well. I'm leaving now, but I'll see you tomorrow. Thank you. Sorry..." and racing to my office, I snatch my purse and run for the exit with my heels still in my shaking hands.

In my car again, my whole body begins shaking once more. Starting the car, I close my eyes and count to ten. Turning to pull on my seatbelt, I see Kayla standing beside my car window as I jump with a little scream.

Lowering the window a little, "Kayla. I'm fine. I'm going straight home. It's been a weird week, that's all... Okay?"

"Can I drive you home? I'd like to. You aren't fine, and if something happens to you, I'll feel really guilty for letting you drive. Okay, Sweetie?"

As Kayla tries to open my door, I suddenly yell at her. "No. It's not okay. I'm fine. *Fuck!* I'm fine! Just leave me alone!" And wrenching the gear shift, I start to drive off with her frightened, totally horror-struck face burned into my memory.

Driving a little erratically, I wonder what I just did. Kayla will hate me now. She'll be so mad at me. She'll ignore me every day at work. She'll talk about me behind my back. She'll tell everyone what a bitch I am. She'll hate me.

When I finally return home, I grab my purse and head up the few stairs to the foyer. I can't even remember driving home. I did drive, I'm pretty sure, but I just can't remember the drive at all. That's bad, I think.

Once inside, my feet are greeted by the cold marble tile. I love this. I look forward to these tiles. If I could lie down on them, I would. Huh. *Why can't I?* It's my house. So dropping my heels, purse and keys, I slink down to the cold marble and finally exhale.

==========

Marcus wakes me when he enters. The house is all dark because I didn't remember to put any lights on, so he narrowly avoids stepping on me.

"What the hell? Did you fall, or something?" He asks confused.

"Um, no. The floor just felt nice and cold, that's all." Ooops, I sound kind of deranged. And suddenly, I'm engulfed in light while my eyes burn and I turn my face into the tile.

"What the hell happened to you? You look awful." Marcus demands.

"Nothing. Stressful day. I'm just going to go to bed."

And lifting myself from the floor, I notice Marcus doesn't help me. Of course not, he's still mad at me. He's still going to ignore me for a while, I have to remember that.

Upstairs, I change into my pajamas and head for the bathroom. Gross. I have to once again *scrub* off my nasty make-up before I go to bed, which kills my eyes, cheeks and lips, but what can I do? Dirty a pillow case? Heaven forbid.

Entering my bedroom, I wish I had my purse and cell phone with me in case Kayla calls. God, I don't want her telling Marcus I flipped out again today. He would be so ashamed of my behavior.

Curling into bed, I see the time is 8:02pm Wow. I guess I lied on the marble floor for a few hours. Strange, it didn't feel that long.

On my side, I can't help but think of today. What *was* that? If I wasn't me, I would think I was some girl craving attention; A drama-queen, a *loser*. Maybe like someone who needs to act out in order to get attention.

Why did I act like that today? My lies were disgusting. My behavior was disgusting. My freak-out was disgusting. *I'm disgusting.*

==========

Waking to Marcus lurching over me, I look at the clock and see its 9:49. That's it? It feels much later.

"Were you raped today?" He asks me point-blank. *Flinch.*

"No." God, I *HATE* that word.

"I didn't think so. I told Kayla she was wrong, but she was so adamant about you getting to the hospital. As *if...*" and as Marcus shakes his head, he leaves my bedroom without a backwards glance*, again.*

As if? What the hell does *that* mean? As if someone would rape me? As if I'm *un-rapeable*?

I'm not ugly. I'm not fat. I have gorgeous lips and *alluring* eyes... As *if.*

God, I am *so* tired.

Thursday, May, 26th

CHAPTER 4

In the morning, Marcus enters my bedroom to get dressed. He's just glaring at me for a minute before entering his closet.

"You didn't make dinner again last night. Should I start eating out every night after work?" He asks blandly.

"No. I'll cook tonight. I was just not well last night, if you remember."

Shaking his head, he enters his walk-in closet and huffs. "Did you pick up my dry-cleaning yesterday?"

Is he for real? *Seriously?* I was sick. Did he forget he almost walked into me on the floor?

"No, Marcus. As you may remember, I was unwell yesterday... you know, when you found me on the floor. So, no, I didn't pick up your dry-cleaning. I forgot. I'll try to get it after work tonight."

Ignoring me completely he continues, "Oh, Kayla called. You don't have to go into work today or tomorrow. A nice little vacation, huh? Anyway, your boss has worked it out so your emails are forwarded to your iPhone. He says 'rest up'. What does *that* mean? All you've *been* doing is sleeping and resting," he glares at me.

I'm supposed to stay home? Who will do my work? Who will prepare the expense reports? Who will organize the check run for Monday? WHO?! I'm going to throw-up, I think.

"Sorry Marcus. I'll be fine today, and I'll cook you a nice meal. What time will you be home?" I ask gently, fighting the nausea.

Maybe he's not mad at me anymore?

"I don't know. Don't wait up though. If you don't want to cook dinner, don't worry about it. I'll just grab something later." He huffs again.

Okay, so he's still mad at me, *AND* he's passive-aggressive... *Awesome!*

"It's fine Marcus. I want to cook. I'll see you later." Rising to give him his kiss on the cheek which he likes, Marcus turns to me, shakes his head, and scowls like I'm hideous.

Wow. I'm stopped cold. His look is so, like, mean or something. Where is nice Marcus? What have I done? *Shit.*

After checking over my face in the bathroom, I'm relieved that my eyes are less swollen, but my lips are still cracked, bleeding and sore. What the hell *happened* yesterday?

==========

Downstairs, I grab some coffee and my purse and head to my sunroom. Dumping my purse, I grab my iPhone and count 19 emails. 4 texts. 8 missed calls.

Scrolling through the missed calls, I see 5 from Kayla, 1 from my mother, and 2 are from the 212 area code... *New York? Really?* He wouldn't call, *would he?* I'll get back to those...

All 4 texts are from Kayla. *Jeez...* She tenacious isn't she?

Over to email:
- An amendment from Mr. Close on his expense report. *Of course.*
- Another attachment from Heinrick. *It Figures.*
- Mr. Berber finally submitted his... Yes! Now I have everyone's, but Mr. Craig/Mr. Zinfandel's. I can start calculating probable's.
- 6 emails from Kayla. Jeez, is she tenacious, or *psychotic?*
- 2 from Mr. Shields. *Shit.*
- 1 from the Marriot. *Good.*
- 1 from the Detroit office. *What now?*
- And 6 from Mr. Zinfandel. *6? Holy shit!*

Okay, onto Mr. Zinfandel. I feel a nervous knot in my stomach, but I'm a little excited too. I wonder if he's going to bully me like he did earlier yesterday.

From: Z. Zinfandel
Subject: Expense Report
Wednesday, May, 25
2:12pm

Hello Sweetheart,
I still haven't heard from you regarding Mr. Craig's expenses.
Are you ignoring me?
Z

From: Z. Zinfandel
Subject: Expense Report... AGAIN
Wednesday, May, 25
2:49pm

Sweetheart,
You really need to reply to me. I thought I made myself perfectly clear this morning. If I contact you, you are to respond in a timely manner.
Z
P.S. I can't stop looking at your company profile pictures. You really are quite beautiful. Do you ever wear your hair down?

From: Z. Zinfandel
Subject: Where are you?
Wednesday, May, 25
4:03pm

Sweetheart,
I finally had no option but to call your Receptionist, and she kindly
  informed me that no one seems to know where you are.
Though I do not approve of her lack of discretion, I'm glad she told me.
Are you alright?
Please contact me soon so I no longer worry.
Here's my private number 212) 521-7511
Z

From: Z. Zinfandel
Subject: ARE YOU OKAY?!
Wednesday, May, 25
6:09pm

Dammit! Are you okay?!
Sweetheart, please call me soon.
Again, though I am not impressed with the lack of discretion in your office,
  Sam Shields has informed me that there was some kind of incident with
  you this afternoon.
What happened? Sam said you looked much abused, but wouldn't
  elaborate.
Shall I fly to Chicago to check on you myself?
Call or email me soon.
212) 521-7511
Z

From: Z. Zinfandel
Subject: **ARE YOU OKAY??!!**
Wednesday, May, 25
10:13pm

Sweetheart,
I have spoken with your friend Kayla, and she is very concerned.
Apparently, you looked like a rape victim this afternoon.
Is that the case? Please tell me.
I would like to help you.

Kayla also informed me that your 'charming' husband doesn't think it's
 true, nor does he care to 'get into it with you'.
Kayla has stated that she may yet drive to your home, and punch your
 husband on his ass for being such 'A Fuckin Prick!' as she called him.
I find myself of the mindset to do the same.

Please let me know how you are.
Please let me help you.
I have a flight scheduled tomorrow morning for Chicago.
I should be landing around 8:30am.
I sincerely hope you are well.
Yours, Z

Oh. My. God!! What the hell? Why is he coming here? He can't come
here. He can't! I've spoken to this man twice on the phone. What the
hell is he *doing?*

From: Z. Zinfandel
Subject: What's going on?
Thursday, May, 26
8:52am

Sweetheart,
I have just landed and I'm on my way to your office.
I am displeased to find you still have not contacted me.
Why is that?
Once I arrive, I'll try to track you down further.
I hope you are well, but your silence seems to confirm otherwise.
Yours,
Z
212) 521-7511

'Displeased'? I was *sleeping*. It's not my fault I didn't respond sooner.
God, he sounds like my father... *Ugh.*
 Looking at the word displeased, my mind starts reeling. I *hate* that
word. I hate many words. Isn't that strange? I actually hate a word
because of what it means to me.

Oh my god. The whole office is talking about me. What the hell do I do
now? I can't go back to work. I'm going to have to quit. I can't work with
people who think I'm a drama-queen, or like an idiot who looks all
screwed up in the middle of the afternoon. What if they think I was
attacked or something? What if they think I was an assault victim? I told
them I wasn't, but will they actually believe me? Oh, this is just great!

Now I'm the office idiot. I may as well return. What's the worst that can happen? Everyone ignore me? Yeah, like I'm not used to being ignored.

Sipping my coffee, I rise for another, but suddenly my cell starts ringing. What do I do? 212 area code. *Shit.* Grabbing for it, I answer.

"Good morning, this is... " but once again I'm cut off.

"Well, if it isn't the little lost one. I've been trying to reach you since yesterday. Did you receive any of my messages?"

"Um. Yes. But only 5 minutes ago! I fell asleep without my phone around, and I wasn't in the office to answer your emails or phone calls yesterday afternoon. I'm very sorry Mr. Zinfandel," I sigh. *God,* I spent my entire life apologizing to everyone.

"That's quite alright. I understand. You did leave me quite worried however... Are you okay? Can I help you in any way? And please, call me Z."

"No, thank you. I'm fine. Nothing happened yesterday. Nothing at all. I fell asleep in my car, that's it. I lied to my Receptionist about an appointment because I didn't want anyone to know I merely fell asleep in my car over lunch..."

I am so embarrassed by my confession; I'm surprised he can't feel the heat of my blush through the phone.

"Fell asleep? Please don't lie to me Sweetheart. I will NOT be lied to!" Mr. Zinfandel barks through the phone.

"I- I'm not lying. *Honestly.* I don't know why I looked like a raaa- ah, an *assault* victim when I woke up in my car, but that's the truth. I told Kayla, and now you the truth. I don't lie Mr. Zinfandel, though I did lie twice yesterday... I..."

"Z!" He demands.

"Okay... **Z.** I was not attacked yesterday, but I'm very tired and I have tons of work to catch up on because this week has been kind of bizarre for me. So, if you wouldn't mind, can I please go now, and get back to my work?" I ask timidly.

"Yes. I'll let you go. I'll be speaking to Sam and your friend Kayla today however, so I suggest you answer my calls and reply to my emails. Understood?" He asks.

"Okay, Mr... Z, I mean. I'll be at home all day *working.*"

Hanging up, I immediately call Kayla.

"Where are you? Are you at home?" She asks.

"Yes, I'm at home. Everything's fine. I'm really embarrassed about yesterday, but I swear *nothing happened.* Nothing! I honestly fell asleep in my car after I bought a pair of shoes at the mall. Kayla, I know it sounds weird, but it's the truth. I promise." My voice has started to quiver.

Could this be any more embarrassing? First Mr. Zinfandel, now Kayla. Oh, they're going to meet today. *Great.*

Before she can reply, I beg, "Kayla, Mr. Zinfandel is in Chicago this morning and he's going to see you soon at the office. Could you please assure him that I'm fine? Please? I don't think I can handle any more

embarrassment this week. I'm not sure why he came here, but he's really quite pushy, and I feel pretty uncomfortable talking to him. Would you mind buffering a little? Please...?"

"Yeah, I could tell Z was a little intense last night, when he brow beat Claire into giving up my home number. He seems pretty... *intrigued* by you. It's weird, it's like he has known you forever. Didn't you just talk over the phone for the first time on Tuesday, when I, ah, *intervened?*"

"Yes. I've only spoken to him 3 or 4 times. 3, I think, on the phone. Plus a couple emails. He's kind of... *intense*, Kayla. But, please don't tell him I said that... It's very unprofessional of me." Could I make this any worse? What the *hell* is wrong with me?

"No problem, Sweetie. I won't say anything. Uh, how are you though? *Seriously?* I mean, I believe you weren't attacked, because you say you weren't, but you still haven't explained what happened."

What the hell do I say? Kayla will know if I lie. What did happen? I have no idea.

"This will sound strange, but I have absolutely *NO* idea. I was shopping, then in my car, then asleep, and then rushing to get back to work. It must have been a bad dream or something. I don't know. I know I sound crazy, Kayla, or like I'm looking for attention, but I'm not. I just honestly don't know what happened."

"Okay. Well, I'm glad you weren't attacked yesterday because I've got to be honest... you looked really bad. But still, maybe you should go to a doctor or talk to a Shrink or something. I swear Sweetie... I have never seen anyone look worse than you did yesterday, and..."

Cutting her off, I can't stand to listen anymore. "I know, Kayla. I'm really sorry. I hope you aren't mad at me for snapping at you... I'm really sorry."

"Fuck! Don't apologize. Just don't do it again. You scared the shit out of me yesterday, that's all." Don't apologize? Yeah, o-*kay*. Then who would I be? I would be *no one.*

"Sweetie. Are you still there?"

"Yes. I'm here. I'll be working all day from home, so just call my cell if I should know anything. And thank you, Kayla. You've been a real nice person to me..." I mumble, embarrassed.

"A nice person, huh? Sweetie, I'm your *friend*, okay? If you need to talk today, call or email me. I really should go though. I have to give Big Daddy Shields the Buyers reports in about 20 minutes. Get some work done, but don't push yourself too hard. Okay?"

"Yes, alright. Thank you again Kayla."

Hanging up, I feel kind of freaked out again. A 'friend'? Kayla thinks she's my *friend*. I would love to have a 'friend' like Kayla. She is beautiful, and strong, and confident, and awesome, and *tall*. Actually, I don't want a friend like Kayla... I want to *BE* Kayla.

==========

Shortly after noon, I finish with 4 expense report summaries. When my stomach growls, I realize I haven't eaten in close to two days. Wow. That's bad... though maybe good for my *'big thighs and butt'*.

After some tomato soup and crackers, I'm ready to finish a few more summary reports. Checking my iPhone for any messages I see an email from Mr. Zinfandel.

Ugh. I really don't want to do this anymore. I mean, he's a nice man for showing me concern, but really, what's the point of his concern?

From: Z. Zinfandel
Subject: Yesterday?
Thursday, May 26
12:25pm

Sweetheart,
It appears you have caused quite a stir around your office.
   (Oh, god. No! My stomach suddenly cramps. I'm going to throw-up the soup.)
Gossip has it that you were attacked yesterday afternoon, you told everyone 'nothing happened' and I've learned everyone who saw you believes otherwise. I do hope you didn't lie to me, Sweetheart.
Where is your husband? Is he with you today? Is he caring for your needs?
   (Ah, Marcus? Why would he be with me at home? Why would I want him here with me at home? Why would I want him, period? Ooops. That was bad. He's a very nice man and he loves me.)
I have made all the appropriate introductions, and I had the pleasure of an early lunch with your friend Kayla. She is quite a brazen, yet charming young woman.
   (I bet she is! I hate Kayla. No. I don't. Kinda? God, I really am awful sometimes.)
I'm pleased you two are friends. Having someone like Kayla in your corner is good for keeping all the sharks away from you.
So, is it true that I make you 'uncomfortable' with my concern for your well-being?
   (I hate Kayla. She is such a bitch. I knew I couldn't trust her! I can't trust anyone!)
I'm sorry to hear that. It appears you are going to have to learn to become comfortable with my concern. I won't have it any other way.
I would like you to know that I am disappointed in you, however. I expected at the very least an email by now, telling me how you're doing today. But, I still have not heard.
Please note that I DO expect a reply from this email, very soon.
I sincerely hope you are well.
Yours,
Z

What the hell is that? A *threat?* What's he going to do if I don't reply? Come over here? What can he *really* do?

Sitting for a few minutes, I contemplate my response.

Reply
Subject: Yesterday?
Thursday, May 26
12:58pm

Mr. Zinfandel,
I DO appreciate your concern. However, there is no concern needed.
I am fine, as I have told you, Kayla, and everyone else who has asked.
 (No one else has asked, not even Marcus.)
I have worked steadily this morning, and I have made up most of the
 ground I lost in the last 2 days.
Please understand this has been a very strange week for me, and not at
 all the norm. I do not live with this kind of drama in my life, at all, ever.
I am a very competent employee, and I look forward to proving to you that
 your concern, though thoughtful, is highly misplaced.
Enjoy your stay in Chicago.
With kindest regards...

Sweetheart? Ahhh, *NO.* Not a chance. I am **not** his sweetheart. I am no one's sweetheart. I am no one's... *anything.* I just kind of... *am.*

Before I have even pulled up the latest spread-sheet, there's a reply.

From: Z. Zinfandel
Subject: Today
Thursday, May 26
1:14pm

Sweetheart,
I must insist that you call me Z.
Where is your husband? I didn't read a reply to my question regarding
 him.
Yours, with much concern,
Z

What the hell do I say now? He said I must always reply.

> Reply
> Subject: Today
> Thursday, May 26
> 1:18pm
>
> Z,
> My husband is at work, where I prefer him.
> I'm fine, but I really must finish my reports.
> I do hope you enjoy Chicago while you visit.

Oh my! He types fast.

> From: Z. Zinfandel
> Subject: Today
> Thursday, May 26
> 1:22pm
>
> Sweetheart,
> With much respect; I don't give a fuck about Chicago.
> Why are you alone? Why don't you want your husband with you?
> Answer me. *Now.*
> Z

His email reads quite aggressive, and I'm starting to shake a little. Is he mad at me?

> Reply
> Subject: Today
> Thursday, May 26
> 1:32pm
>
> Mr. Zinfandel,
> I'm not sure why you're mad at me, but I do apologize if I have offended
>   you in some way.
> I don't require my husband here today. We are very independent people,
>   and he is very busy with his own career. I would feel terrible if I kept him
>   from his work, when I really don't need anything from him here.
>
> Regards.

Okay. This is getting ridiculous. Why won't he stop emailing me? I have work to do, and he doesn't seem to care at all. *Dammit.*

From: Z. Zinfandel
Subject: CALL ME Z!
Thursday, May 26
1:43pm

Sweetheart,
If you call me 'Mr. Zinfandel' one more time, I **WILL** be very angry with you, and I'm not playing a game.
Every time you don't want to answer a question honestly, you retreat, and I become Mr. Zinfandel once again. Please stop retreating.
I expect *honest* answers from you, whether you are comfortable with me or not.
What is your address? I'm going to come over so we can speak face to face.
Z

Reading his newest email, I am absolutely stunned. *Oh. My. God!* He is NOT coming here. No way. I can't have a strange man in my home, whether it is to talk or not. What does he think I am... a *slut?* I am a respectable, married woman. I am NOT a Slut.

Reply
Subject: CALL ME Z!
Thursday, May 26
2:02 pm

Z,
I do apologize for my rudeness, but you are not welcome in my home.
I don't know what kind of woman you think I am, but you have the wrong idea. I am a respectable *MARRIED* woman, who does not have strange men show up at her home. Why would you even want to? We're strangers to each other.
You are my senior, and as such, it is highly inappropriate for you to even suggest such a thing as coming to my home.
Please refrain from emailing me again, unless of course, it is work related.
I must get back to my reports.
Thank you.

There. Sent. Finished. What the hell *WAS* that? My cell phone suddenly rings. *Shit.* Its Z's 212 cell number. What do I do? Ignore it? I'll ignore his call, and hopefully he'll get the message. When it stops ringing I finally breathe.

Shit! There's already another email.

From: Z. Zinfandel
Subject: ANSWER YOUR PHONE!
Thursday, May 26
2:18pm

Sweetheart,
Pick up the phone. Now!
I am starting to get furious with you.
Pick it up now!
Z

Suddenly, I'm scared to death. I don't even know this man. Why is he *doing* this? What's happening? Did I do this? I think I was fairly professionally detached. What did I do wrong? WHAT DO I *DO?'*

When my phone starts ringing again, I jump. Grabbing it, I answer on the second ring, "Hello..."
"Why are you trying so hard to push away my concern?"
"I'm sorry Z, but I don't know what I've done wrong to upset you. I've answered all your questions. I've been perfectly polite and professional."
Cutting me off, he almost snarls into the phone, "Yes. You have been perfectly polite and professional, and even respectable. Aren't you a little *tired* of it?"
"I'm sorry, I don't understand."
"Why don't you try speaking a sentence which does not contain the phrase 'I'm sorry' for starters? We'll work from there."
"I'm sor... *What?* What do you want Mr... *ah,* Z?" Jeez... I suddenly acquired a stutter.
"You're doing very well deflecting, but I am much better at attaining the answers I require. You are very adept at answering most questions with an emotionless quip. You are truly exhausting and frustrating. Do you ever just give an honest answer? Do you *feel* anything at all?" Pause. What the hell? Do I *FEEL* anything at all? Of course I feel. What the hell is he talking about?
"Yes, I *feel.* Do I seem so heartless to you?" I whisper.
"Stop deflecting! Do you *feel,* Sweetheart?"
"I'm not deflecting. I don't know what you mean. I'm sorry, but I'm really confused here. Could you please just tell me what's wrong with me, so I can get back to my reports," I ask desperately.
And there's another pause. A long pause actually. My heart starts beating very hard and my hands have started shaking again. Maybe I

should say something. What is he waiting for?

"I'm sor..."

Interrupting me, he shouts, "Do not apologize! I can't stand to hear another apology fall from your mouth."

All I want to say is 'I'm sorry' for saying 'I'm sorry'. I'm such an idiot. He's totally thrown me off balance. I feel less controlled. I feel out of control. *I feel...*

Out of nowhere, I can't breathe. Gasping for breath, I clutch the phone in my hand, and grab my chest with the other. Panicking, I want to go. I need to hang up...

"Jesus *Christ!* Don't you dare hang up, love. Come on. Stay with me right here. Breathe slowly, so I can hear you. Come on Sweetheart, breathe with me. Listen to my breaths and follow along. Breathe..."

Slowly, I dig myself out. Slowly, my breathing returns. Slowly, I feel my arms and legs tingling again. I have to go. I need to get away from him. I need my senses back.

"I need to hang up, Z. I need to lie down... okay?" I whisper, but there's just silence. "Please... Z. I need to hang up. I can't take anymore of this right now."

Exhaling loudly, "Alright, Sweetheart. I want you to lie down right now. I'll give you an hour and a half, and then I'm calling you again. I strongly suggest you sleep with your phone beside you so you'll pick up when I call. Am I clear?"

"Um... yes. I'll talk to you later. I really am sorry for all this drama. I'm not usually like this," I whisper.

"It's going to be okay, love. I'll talk to you soon. Lie down now. I insist."

After hanging up, I stumble to the small love seat in my sunroom. Pulling a throw blanket over my shoulders, I feel absolutely exhausted. With my phone in my hand, I close my eyes and...

I'm done.

===========

Abruptly, I wake to the sound of my phone ringing. Jumping, I answer quickly.

"H-hello...?" I'm completely disoriented.

"Hello, Sweetheart. Did you sleep well?"

Leaning over toward the end-table I see its 5:01pm. "Um... yes. Why did you let me sleep so long?" I ask.

"Say my name, Sweetheart. Say Z. I need to hear my name from your lips when you just wake sounding all sleepy and hoarse. You make me think of waking up *with* you..." he practically growls in my ear.

Holy shit! What the hell do I say to that?

"Ah, Z... I have to go. I shouldn't have slept so long, and I really need to get some work done. Otherwise, I'll be up all night working on these reports. Um, thank you for waking me..."

"It was my pleasure. I love the sound of your voice right now. Picturing

your gorgeous lips, and your alluring eyes and hearing your voice all sleep-sexy, makes me wish you would meet me at my hotel this evening." *WHAT?!*

"Ah... I'm, um... married. And I don't know you! And I don't do that! I'm sure you could find someone else in Chicago who would join you. Maybe give Kayla a call..." Did I just say that? Oh my god, I just made Kayla sound like a slut. *Shit.*

Chuckling, Z says, "Tempting as that may be, I would still prefer YOU join me this evening. Though Kayla is delightful, I'm not in the mood to fight for dominance in the bedroom; that's not really my thing. I would much prefer you, soft in my arms."

Soft? There it is. He thinks I'm heavy, and therefore 'soft'. NOT like perfect 'tight' Kayla. God, I wish I wasn't me some days, I really do.

"Sweetheart? Where did you go? I can almost *feel* your retreat. Why don't you think about meeting me later." As *IF!*

"No. I will NOT meet you later. I'm too *soft*. Not your type at all. You really should give Kayla a call though. She's all tight and *delightful,*" I sneer.

"Why are you speaking to me with that tone? I never implied..."

"What tone? *THIS tone?!* Please, Mr. Zinfandel, leave me alone. I'm done. I really can't talk to you anymore. Okay? I'm really sorry, but..."

"DO NOT HANG UP ON ME!"

"Sorry. Bye. Have fun with *whomever* you see tonight..."

I've done it. I hung up on him. Please don't call me again. Please don't call... *Shit!* My phone starts ringing. My phone even sounds louder when its Z calling to yell at me. Ignore it. IGNORE IT!

Five minutes later, my phone stops ringing and I'm totally stressed out. What the hell is going on in my life? I can't stand all this drama. Who does he think he is, anyway? He can't tell me what to do. Yeah, but everyone else tells me what to do, why can't he? *Dammit.*

============

Grabbing a glass of ice water, and making a turkey sandwich, I suddenly realize I haven't made a 'proper' dinner for Marcus. *Dammit.* What looks elaborate, but is quick and easy? What looks good, but can be prepared in half an hour? What can I make? I can think of nothing. Oh! I have lasagna in the freezer but I'll have to thaw it in the microwave first which will make it gross, but what else can I do?

Throwing the lasagna in the microwave to defrost, I feel all stressed again. It's like the potential for soggy lasagna will determine if I have a panic-attack or something. Why does a lasagna have this much influence over my life? Why am I giving a lasagna this much power over me? *Christ!* I *AM* crazy!

Twenty minutes later, the nearly defrosted lasagna is in the oven for an hour and a half. That brings me to 7:30. Marcus should be arriving home

around 7:30, and it'll look like I planned his dinner properly, at exactly the proper time.

BUT WHAT ABOUT THE STUFF?! *Argh...*

Grabbing a package of ground beef from the freezer, I cut up as many small pieces as I can before dumping it down the garberator and leave the empty package face up in the trash can. From the fridge I pull out and also empty 2 jars of my homemade sauce down the sink, and rinse and line up the jars beside the sink to dry. Brick of Mozzarella Cheese? *Um.* Grabbing it from the cheese drawer, I hide it behind the vegetables in the crisper drawer. Ricotta? Hidden behind the pickles. Spices? He'll never know. Does Marcus even know where I keep all the spices and seasonings? I doubt it. Noodles? Opening a box of lasagna noodles, I smash them into smaller pieces, hide them in a brown lunch bag, and push them low in the garbage with the empty ground beef package back on top. Crushing the box of lasagna, I make sure it's on the top of the recycling bin in the pantry.

There! *Ha!* Marcus will never know I didn't make it today. God, my hands are shaking. I was in such a rush to prepare my *already prepared* lasagna; I hadn't noticed that I've been holding my breath for hours it seems. Marcus will never know though, so I'm safe from disappointing anyone tonight.

Trying to calm my nerves, I head back to my desk in the sunroom. There are 6 new emails:
- 1 email from Mr. Wallace in Washington, with an amendment.
- 1 email from Mr. King in Sarasota.
- 2 emails from Kayla.
- 2 from Mr. Zinfandel timed in the last 45 minutes.

I don't want to read them, I really don't. I can't handle any more of this... *SHIT!* I have to. Opening the first email...

From: Z. Zinfandel
Subject: I'm disappointed
Thursday, May 26
5:19pm

I am very disappointed in you, Sweetheart.
That was very rude.
I thought I made myself perfectly clear. I will not tolerate rudeness.
Do not hang up on me. <u>Speak</u> to me.
If I frighten you, or you feel uncomfortable, please say so.
I *want* to know what you're thinking.
I would really like to know what you're *feeling,* as well.

I will give you a little time to gather your thoughts.
I am very aware of your incessant need to feel in control of yourself, but

try to understand that it is NOT my goal to undermine your need for control.
Please do not push away my concern and affections...
  You will only hurt yourself further.
Yours patiently,
Z

His *concern and affections?* He doesn't even know me! *I* don't even know me anymore. Oh, but at least I've *disappointed* him. One whole day without someone's disappointment might have actually given me a false sense of security or something. Thank god! I'm back on track today.

From: Z. Zinfandel
Subject: It's a date
Thursday, May 26
6:00pm

Sweetheart,
I do hope that you've settled down some.
I'm going to call you this evening at 10:00pm sharp.
I suggest you have your phone with you and find a private location.
I will be speaking to you rather bluntly, so I *strongly* suggest you find some privacy.
Please do not think it would be wise to ignore my call; I have ways of forcing your attention, even if you do not *desire* my attention.
I look forward to speaking with you this evening.
Yours,
Z

10:00? **10:00?** Marcus will be here. It's not like I could go anywhere else. I never go out through the week. What am I going to do? What will I do? This is INSANITY! I'm married. I have a husband who'll be home while I'm talking to another man? *Who does that?* Not me. I'm not answering. What can he actually do? It's not like he'll show up at my home. Does he even know where I live? Ahh... *probably.* Oh *god.* I have to email him back.

Reply
Subject: It's a date
Thursday, May 26
6:34pm

Z,
Please don't call me. My husband will be home by 10:00 and I have
   nowhere to talk in private.
I am *feeling* very stressed out by you and your demands.
Please, leave me alone.
I have to finish work, and I can't with all these emotional distractions.
I'm begging you to stop harassing me.
I can't handle much more.
Please...

There. I sounded a little pathetic but maybe that'll work. I can't do
anything else but beg. Hopefully he'll take pity on me, and leave me
alone.

===========

Returning to my spreadsheets, I once again begin calculating expenses.
This is the easy part; it's mindless. Number crunching is easy. I've
already researched all the approvals, and categorized the approved and
unapproved expenses for each Accounts Manager. Now I just need to
formulate grand totals. I may even have this completed by mid afternoon
tomorrow, in which case I could email off the summary reports to Mr.
Shields before Monday. Maybe if I'm early, I won't look so incompetent
this week.
   At 7:35, the lasagna is out of the oven. Running to my bedroom I have a
quick rinse-off shower and finally get dressed. Black capris and black
cami top with cardigan. There, I feel much better. Returning to the
sunroom, I work a little more while I wait for Marcus to come home. I
feel like I actually accomplished something today.

   By 9:30, I'm scared. Marcus isn't home. I have no additional emails
from Z, but I'm scared to death he's going to call me anyway. Where the
hell is Marcus? Why hasn't he called to say he'd be late? Marcus always
calls if he isn't going to be home by 7:30, except on Mondays.
   Walking to the kitchen, I look at the dried out, hours old lasagna I spent
all day *slaving* over. Huh. I feel a giggle bubble up at the thought. I
haven't had one of those for a while. Trying to suppress my laughter, I
call Marcus from the kitchen phone.
   "Hi. What can I do for you?" He quips.

"Ah, hi honey... When are you coming home? I told you I would prepare a proper dinner for you this evening."

"Oh. You've been so *tired* lately, I assumed you had forgotten to cook again," he sneers.

Wow. He really is pissed at me. Maybe I should just apologize for questioning his sexual ability. Maybe I should just tell him it's my fault.

"Marcus, I'm sorry I haven't been well. I'm not sure what's going on, but I'm calling the doctor tomorrow..."

"Look, I'm very busy here. I'm not sure when I'll be home, so don't wait up, okay?"

Holy shit! Marcus hung up on me. Marcus doesn't know when he'll be home? Marcus doesn't even care about the doctors? He *always* cares about stuff like that. He wants his wife to be healthy and drama-free. *Wake up!* Marcus doesn't care about me anymore.

At 9:58, I check my emails again, but there's nothing. Good. Maybe Z decided to back off. Maybe my begging worked. Maybe he called someone else. Maybe, Kayla? Maybe he became bored with me...

When my phone suddenly rings, I jump once more. Will I ever learn to handle a phone ringing again?

"Hello?"

"Hi Sweetheart. Do you have privacy?"

"Um, yes. My husband isn't home from work yet."

"*Pardon?* He didn't stay with you all day, and he isn't even home before 10:00? Please tell me he at least called every hour to check up on you?" Do I lie? Will he know if I lie over the phone? Probably.

"Um... No, he didn't. I assured him this morning that I was fine though, and he trusts me, so he didn't really have to call me today." God that sounded so pathetic.

"To quote the charming Ms. Kayla, 'your husband is a fucking prick'!"

"No, he's not! We're just not like that. If I say I'm fine, he trusts that I'm fine. There was no need for drama or concern today, because I told him I was FINE. Marcus is a good man, and he's nice, and he loves me."

"Well, I am delighted to hear that. I'm pleased that your ignorant, selfish, jack-ass of a husband is *good and nice.* I'm sure that's exactly what you want in a spouse."

"You don't know me! *God,* Z. Why do you keep talking to me, like we know each other? We don't. Marcus is EXACTLY the kind of man I want. He is calm and stable and he loves me. He'll never cheat on me. And he's good to me..."

But even as a say it, I don't really believe it. Marcus isn't actually *good* to me, he just kind of acknowledges me, has sex with me once a month, and that's really about it... *Huh.*

"Are you through, Sweetheart? Have you convinced yourself yet, that your husband is the kind of man you actually want?" No, *not really.*

"There is no convincing needed. I married him, and he is wonderful. We have a nice life. We have a lovely home, and beautiful furniture to furnish our lovely home."

Furniture? Am I actually stressing Marcus' marital merits to a stranger with *FURNITURE?*

Z laughs, "Did you just try to defend your husband's lack of thought and concern for you, with *furniture?*" Yes. *Yes, I did.*

"N-no. I was just saying that we have a nice home together because Marcus likes nice things."

"Marcus likes nice things? And what do you like, Sweetheart?" Um...

"I like nice things too. We have a nice life together because he and I usually agree on everything." Ah, except before, during, and after sex. There we *really* do not see eye to eye, I giggle to myself.

"Why are you laughing? Is it because you are finally seeing the absurdity of your statements?" Nope. It's because I'm thinking about sex with Marcus.

"No. I'm just thinking about something Kayla told me, um, yesterday." Another lie? *Shit.*

"*Really?* And what did Kayla tell you that was so funny?" Pause. I can't think of a single thing. I have a complete blank where cognitive reasoning used to be. And the pause just gets longer...

"Um... It's private. Just between girls..." That's believable, *right?*

"Interesting. I think you're lying to me. Kayla informed me today, that though she tries very hard to be your friend, you're very emotionally detached from her and everyone else she has ever seen you speak to. So I find it *intriguing* that you and Kayla would suddenly share something *just between girls.*"

What the hell? Why would she say that? Why would she talk about me like that? I'm not emotionally detached. I *attach*. I hate Kayla right now. And I hate Z for talking about me with her. I don't know what to say anymore. I want to hang up and go to sleep.

"That's n-not true. I am emotionally attached to people; I just don't feel the need to tell everyone everything about myself." God, I hate this. In a near whimper, "I have to go now. Thank you for calling... Ah, enjoy your stay in Chicago." I am so polite, *always*. I. Am. So. PATHETIC. *ALWAYS.*

"We're not finished with this conversation yet. Do not hang up. I would like to talk to you about what you're feeling right now. Your mood changed rather drastically. Listen, Sweetheart, I didn't mean to sadden you."

"Oh, I'm not sad. I'm fine. But I really must go. Good night."

"*Sweetheart...*" It sounds like a threat, but I just don't know what to say anymore.

"What do you want me to say? Please tell me. Tell me what is a proper response, and I'll say it, and then we can hang up. What am I supposed to say, Z?" I think I'm getting to that shaky place again. I'm not breathing very well.

"Why don't you tell me what you're feeling right now? You sound slightly distraught."

Slightly? I feel awful inside. My hands are officially shaking, and my chest is getting tighter, and now my head throbs.

"I'm not dis-traught. I, I'm fine." *Shit.* I can't breathe properly. *WHY DOES THIS KEEP HAPPENING TO ME??*

"Breathe, Sweetheart. I don't want this for you. Please try to relax. Breathe with me. Right now!"

Within seconds I'm almost hysterical. Everything hurts. I'm just so confused. Why does this keep happening?

"Please try to stop thinking. I want you to concentrate on breathing with me. *Slowly...* There you go. Slowly, catch your breath. I want you to lie down right there."

I can't even protest. I don't want to protest his instructions. Lying down, I close my eyes and listen to his voice.

God, his voice is so beautiful. His soothing voice makes everything slow down. My body is slowly returning to me. I have the tingles from head to toe. I can still hear him murmuring in the background, but I'm concentrating on relaxing my body now. I am so tired suddenly, I just want to stay here on the floor.

"Sweetheart, are you there? You didn't fall asleep on me, did you?"

I gasp a small laugh. "No. I'm here, but I'm really tired now. Can I please hang up? I want to sleep..." I whisper.

"Yes, love. Hang up and go directly to bed. I'll call you tomorrow. Sleep well."

I know I should be worried. I know Marcus might hear me on the phone, but I really want to hear Z's voice again. I love his melodic voice. I know Z might call when Marcus is still here in the morning... but I just don't care right now.

==========

"For Christ's Sake! *Again,* with the floor? What are you doing on the kitchen floor?"

"Um... What time is it?" I ask groggily.

"11:55, Why? Are you going to give me hell for *working* late?"

Well, I'm certainly not groggy enough to miss the implication of 'working'. And when have I ever given him hell? Never. I *never* say a word about anything. I don't say a word to any*one* about any*thing*. And if I do ever speak my mind, everyone is mad at me. Like Marcus is- right now.

"There's a very dry *homemade* lasagna in the fridge, if you're hungry. I'm going to bed. Good night Marcus." There! Do you like *my* implication, Marcus? Actually, he probably didn't even notice.

Trying to steady my legs, I nearly run from the kitchen to my room. I can't stand this. I hate being disliked by anyone, and with Marcus it always feels worse. Maybe it feels worse because he's *supposed* to love me. Or maybe it's worse because I have to live in silence with him when he's mad at me. *Whatever.* When it's Marcus, it feels worse than even silence from my parents.

In my bathroom, I brush my teeth quickly, and change my capris for pajama bottoms, but keep wearing my black cami. Finally, nine minutes later, I crawl into my bed.

Thank god today is over. I hope tomorrow is better. Anything has got to be better than the last two days. Hopefully, I'll even feel better tomorrow. Hopefully tomorrow I'll actually *feel...*

Sarah Ann Walker

Friday, May, 27th

CHAPTER 5

Waking to the sounds of Marcus in his closet, I look at the clock. 8:40? Wow. He's really late.

"Are you okay?" I ask gently.

"No. The stupid alarm clock in the spare room doesn't work. Why didn't you tell me?"

"I didn't know. Didn't you use it yesterday morning?"

He grunts, "Yes, so? Are you saying I broke it?"

"No. I just think it's strange that it worked yesterday, but not this morning. Did you remember to set it?"

"Of course I did. *I'm* not an idiot." Wow. What does *that* mean? Marcus thinks *I'm* an idiot? *Since when?*

"Do you love me?" Where the hell did that come from? Please don't answer. *Please...*

"Why? Does it matter?" *What!?*

"Of course it matters. Do. You. Love. Me. Marcus?"

Shut up! Stop speaking! You do NOT want an honest answer to this question. You do NOT want to hear this.

"Yes, I love you. But I hate when you act like this. *I'm* the good guy here. Everyone thinks so. Even your parents like me better than they like you. But you act like I'm *NOT* a good guy and I don't like it. Please stop acting this way. It really doesn't become you. I didn't marry some drama-queen; I chose to marry YOU, okay?"

Okay. That was sooo not touching, thoughtful, or filled with concern. Z would have said something like... *Shit.* Don't go there!

"Did you pick-up my dry cleaning yesterday on your *day off?*" *Day off?* It was a sick day.

"Not yet. I was unwell yesterday, so I just worked in the sunroom all day, remember? I'll try to get it today. Sorry..."

"Okay. Could you *try* hard?" *Try hard?* That's all I DO. All day. Every day. I try so hard. God, I'm so sick of *trying.*

"Okay Marcus... I'll try *real hard* to pick-up your dry-cleaning." Was my sarcasm obvious?

"Why are you being so sarcastic? Never mind, I don't want to know. I'm leaving for work." Yup. My sarcasm was obvious.

==========

Finally alone, I reach for my phone and there's an email from Z. I kinda want him to stop emailing me, because he stresses me out. I really do want him to stop, but then again, I really hope he doesn't stop. Z stresses

58

me out *and* he calms me right down. What the hell am I supposed to do with that? I really am all over the map here.

Here we go… *Shit.*

> From: Z. Zinfandel
> Subject: Panic
> Friday, May 27
> 7:53am
>
> Good morning Sweetheart,
> I do hope you are well.
> You gave me another little scare last night.
> Do you practice yoga? If not, maybe you should.
> Yoga helps with panic-attacks due to all the breathing exercises.
> Yoga also increases flexibility, which is *very* beneficial for everyone.
>
> I'll give you a call around 10:00am.
> Until then, stop thinking!
> Z

Is he teasing me? Is that a sexual joke? Does he even joke? He seems way too intense for joking. Stop thinking? How the hell does one accomplish that? I mean *really*, how the *hell* do I stop thinking when I have work to do?
 After reading Z's email, I send an email to Mr. Shields explaining that I should have the expense summary reports to him this afternoon, instead of Monday morning. I hope he's impressed when they arrive early. Maybe he won't think I'm such an incompetent drama-queen.
 Maybe I should try to schedule a meeting with him Monday morning to explain my actions this week. But what would I say?
 "Ah, nothing happened on Wednesday, but I've been freaking out anyway? My husband doesn't really love me? I'm kind of lost and panicky right now, but don't know why? Oh. And I can't stop holding my breath, losing my breath, or forgetting to breathe altogether."
 Yeah. That would *definitely* reestablish my reputation as competent within the company.

==========

10:01… He's late, and then I jump. Why does the phone keep *doing* that to me?
 "Good morning, this is…"
 "I know who you are Sweetheart. How are you this morning? Better, I hope?" *God…* His voice is just stunning to listen to.

"I'm well, thank you. I wanted to apologize for last night. I'm not sure what came over me, but I can assure you it won't happen again."

"Uh huh. You're apologizing again, and making assurances you may not be able to keep."

"Oh... I, I'm sorry." *Shit!* Why do I keep saying that?

Laughing, "Apparently, there are some habits you find very hard to break. Have you always apologized endlessly? Almost on demand?" Yes. *Yes, I have.*

"When the situation requires it... Yes. What's wrong with being polite?" I snap at him.

"Nothing at all. Politeness is required in almost any industry and social setting. However, endless self-recrimination is not. Why do you feel the need to always apologize?"

"I DON'T feel the *need*," I almost whine. "But if I've done or said something requiring an apology, I give it. Why is that a problem? I don't understand."

"Oh, I have no problem with a polite apology when it is required. What I have a problem with is an intelligent woman who constantly vilifies her actions, therefore *creating* an opportunity, for said intelligent woman to apologize for a supposed offense. Do you see the difference?" Ah, not really. What the *hell* is he talking about?

"I don't do that. Last night, I acted out, so I apologized. I'm embarrassed that you had to stay on the phone with me while I acted all dramatic, therefore, I apologized. That's it. I'm not *creating* anything." There. *Ha!*

"*Acting out? Dramatic?* Listen, love... You. Had. A. Panic-Attack. You could not control it, and it certainly does not require an apology. And I did not *have to* stay on the phone with you, I *wanted* to."

"Well, then, thank you."

After another long, seemingly uncomfortable silence, Z breathes, "I would like you to meet me today for lunch. Or I could stop by your home? I'm sure your *nice* husband won't be there to care for you... So I could be over by 12:30." Gulp. *NO!*

"Ah, no. Thank you. I MUST finish my reports and email them to Mr. Shields by early afternoon. I really don't have the time to meet you for lunch... But, I do appreciate the invite." That was good- firm intentions, yet polite refusal. Yay me!

"Still not comfortable with me? After all the time we have spent via email and phone conversation? Again, I suggest Sweetheart, that you become comfortable, because before I leave for New York we WILL meet face to face."

Gulp, again, and more silence. I don't want to meet him. Yes. I do... And more silence until...

"When was the last time you experienced pleasure?" *WHAT?!* What the hell is he talking about? Is he actually waiting for my response?

"Um... That's really none of your business."

"*That* long? *Oh, Sweetheart...* that's sad."

"What? No. It hasn't been long. I'm not sad. What are you *talking* about?!" Shit. I'm getting louder. Come on... calm down.

"I didn't say YOU were sad, though that seems fairly obvious. I said

60

THAT is sad. I would like to imagine you feeling pleasure, but I find it quite difficult." Ha!

"You and me both..." I snort. *Shit!* That was out loud?! Oh. My. *God.* "I'm just kidding. *Honestly.* My, ah, *pleasure* is none of your concern."

"Oh, but I find it is my concern. I would like to see you experiencing pleasure. I like to imagine those beautiful lips of yours swollen by kisses, and those gorgeous eyes of yours, bright with pleasure, pupils dilated with lashes lowered."

That was the sexiest thing anyone has EVER said to me, but I have to stop him, *right?*

"Z, these comments are very inappropriate, and I'm very uncomfortable with this conversation." That sounded somewhat truthful.

"Yes. I am rather inappropriate. And yes, I can see how my words would make you uncomfortable. However, I don't believe I'm going to stop. Therefore, I suggest once again, that you *get* comfortable..." How do I do that?

"I find myself thinking about you frequently. From the moment I heard your low, reserved, slightly raspy voice, to your laughter... including your slightly *hysterical* laughter... I have wanted to hear your voice, while you succumb to pleasure."

OH MY GOD! **THAT** is the sexiest thing anyone has ever said to me!

"Please stop. I really DON'T want to discuss this with you. I'm not *that* girl, okay? Go find someone else to try to seduce. I've never been a whore and I'm not going to start being a whore now."

Did I just say that? That sounded so judgmental and prudish. *Christ,* maybe Marcus is right- I AM a prude.

"A whore? I would never classify you as a whore." Good. *Why not?* I can be *whorish* if I want to.

"Well, before you start panicking, I'm going to hang up now. But, Sweetheart, I would like you to think about *sexual* pleasure, and how it applies to you. Think of it as a homework assignment. I'm going to call you back at 3pm sharp, and I WILL be asking you questions." *Questions?* Like what? What the hell do I know about *sexual* pleasure?

"Um... That's not really appropriate... "

"I'm well aware of this inappropriate conversation, but I stand by it. Finish your reports for Shields quickly, and prepare yourself, love. I look forward to asking you questions, and I *really* look forward to hearing your responses. Until later..."

He hung up? He hung up like *that?* My *pleasure?* My responses? What do I say? What is he going to ask me? God, will he want to know about Marcus and me? Will he ask about Marcus... *pleasing* me? What do I say?

Homework?! Thank god my college Professors didn't require this kind of homework assignment, I would have dropped out. Dammit! He's going to know that *I* know absolutely NOTHING about pleasure.

==========

By 1:45, my mind can't focus on my reports. I have just two left, but I'm drawing a blank. The numbers won't balance. I can't find my error. I try to concentrate, but I'm always distracted with thoughts of *pleasure.* Nothing is balanced. Jesus, *I'm* not balanced anymore.

By 2:30, I have finished one more report summary. It finally balanced and the Detroit office is secured. Mr. Shields has only to approve it. The last one however, is proving to be quite difficult. I have gone over it, again and again. I have all the names and each expense memorized, and everything is right there in front of me. It's all there, but it won't balance. I'm actually more frustrated than upset.

I could email over to Shields every other summary, and explain that the 9th is on its way, but I don't want to look incompetent. Shields asked me to be thorough each month of this next quarter, so Shields would think I'm a total flake if I send over every summary, but one. *Shit.* I have got to do this. Start again.

By 2:56, I'm really nervous. I haven't thought about my 'homework assignment' in a long time. Actually, I am so far from thinking of pleasure that I'm cold and detached. What *IS* pleasure? Pleasure, at the moment, would be balancing this summary. That's about all the *pleasure* I can contemplate right now.

By 3:01 my phone rings. *Dammit.* I'm not in the mood for this.

"Hi, Z. This really isn't the best time right now. I'm desperate to finish my last expense report summary, and I still need a little more time... Okay?"

"Absolutely. Call me when you are finished. Until then..."

He hung up? Just like that? Nothing more? No demands? No hostility? No, nothing? Is he mad at me? He must be. Z doesn't like being *disappointed.* Z doesn't like me to tell him no. Z probably doesn't like *me*, anymore.

==========

Finish the report. Okay. Focus. Where is the balance? What is out of line? List the groups and subgroups. Make two lists. Compare and contrast. Look at them. Focus. Where is the problem? *What* is the problem? It has to be the incidentals. It has to be!

Okay. Focus. Two lists. Look closely. Match. Match. Match. *OH MY GOD!* The Marriott! The bloody Marriott! No wonder I forgot... I haven't been to receive the receipts. I just lied and *said* I was there on Wednesday. I had to pre-pay the conference room last week, but I didn't have to *expense* the luncheon, yet. I am SUCH an idiot. Maybe Marcus was right and I *am* an idiot.

It's 3:52 and I'm done! The summaries are emailed to Shields, with a 'thank you' reply from him in return. I can breathe! I've done it. Even with the strangest week of my life, I still managed to do my job well, A DAY *EARLY*. I didn't fail. I didn't disappoint my boss. I didn't disappoint anyone today.

I notice another email in my Inbox after Shields reply. It's Kayla. Where has she been all day?

From: K. Mueller
Subject: Happy Friday!
Friday, May 27
3:56pm

Hi Sweetie,
I hope you had a good day. I'm getting ready to duck out early. Shields has been upstairs all afternoon.
Anyway, I just thought I would say hi, since you haven't responded to any of my messages. I figure you wanted to lay low a little. Plus, Z told me last night, that you had suffered another "set back" and he thought it best if I let you come to me when you're ready, so I agreed not to call you again.

I can't wait to see you on Monday.
Have a great week-end!
Kayla
P.S. Wish me luck with this week-end's Hot New Screw! Ha Ha!

She talked to Z last night? Were they on the phone? Did he call her? Did she meet him at his hotel? Did he meet her at her apartment? *Oh. My. God.* He DID actually hook-up with Kayla. I am such an ass! I told him to. I told him she was essentially a 'sure thing'. I told him… *And he did.*
Well, at least now I don't have to call him back. Why would I? He can go screw Kayla and ask HER about *her* pleasure. Though I'm pretty confident Kayla has any man, AND her own pleasure all figured out. She is such a whore! I knew I couldn't trust her. I knew it! *Dammit.* I sound like an insanely jealous *Psycho!*
Jumping in the shower, I'm still mad. *Why?* Mr. Zinfandel is a creep, nothing more. So he talked to me? So he seemed interested in me? So? It's not like I was ever going to actually see him. I will NEVER actually see him. When does he return to New York? Probably this evening. Why stay in Chicago? Oh… maybe for Kayla. Maybe Mr. Zinfandel is her 'Hot New Screw' this week-end? Yeah, probably. Kayla is hot, and *not soft*, and intelligent, and attractive, and most likely EXCELLENT in bed. Any man would *do* her. Why not Mr. Zinfandel? Well, have her. I'm terrible in bed, anyway.

=========

By 5:00, I've calmed down. What is there really to be angry about anyway? I'm nothing to him, but an interesting… *What?* Loser?

Incompetent, immature, panic-attack having, emotionally detached...
Psycho? Yes, that about sums it up. Five days ago, I was calm, reserved
and incapable of seeking attention... Now it looks like that's ALL I do. I
am so embarrassed with myself for being such an embarrassment... *poor
Marcus.* No wonder he can't stand to even talk to me.

Munching on a cucumber chicken salad, I decide to call Marcus. Where is
he? It's almost 7:00. He always comes home by 6:00 on Fridays. Oh,
yes, he's still mad at me. How very *passive-aggressive* of him.

Dialing, I wait and wait. Wow, I was kicked into voicemail? That's
strange. Marcus always, *ALWAYS* answers, especially if it's me. Wow.
NOT this time... I guess because it *IS* me.

==========

When my phone rings minutes later I answer.
"Marcus?"
"Luckily, no. How are you this evening, Sweetheart?" *Jerk.* Hang up.
HANG UP!
"I won't talk to you anymore, and you can't make me. You have no right
to force me to. Go tell Mr. Shields if you want. I don't care. But I will sue
you for sexual harassment, and with my *prudish* reputation and with
copies of all your emails and voicemails; you surely won't be able to turn
it around against me. Leave. Me. Alone. I'm done Mr. Zinfandel! Go play
with Kayla!"

Wow! That felt good! Slamming the phone down makes me feel
powerful. Who knew yelling loudly at someone was really quite
soothing? I feel a giant weight off my chest. That was awesome! *I'm*
awesome!
When my phone rings immediately, I decide I'm not doing this back and
forth crap anymore. After shutting my phone off to ignore the incessant
ringing, I'm proud of myself. I hear nothing but silence. There is nothing
torturing me. There is no sound to make me jump or panic. There is
nothing but complete silence, well, *except in my head*, but whatever.

==========

Changing into yoga pants, sneakers and a jacket, I decide to go for a
walk. It's cool enough to be refreshing, without being cold. I need air. I
don't think I've ever spent 2 solid days in my home before. I work all
week, and go out on week-ends, and I've only had 4 sick days ever, but
they were spent in the hospital, so they don't count.
Am I ever truly comfortable anywhere? Huh. I don't think so. I'm not
even remotely comfortable in my parent's home where I grew up. Isn't
that strange? Why can't I get comfortable?
I love my home. I tell everyone I love my home, but I hate being in it.

I do love the sunroom however. If there was one room that was truly mine, it would be the sunroom. Marcus rarely enters *MY* sunroom. He hates the love seat and chair I chose and bought. He complained for two solid weeks about them, and he ignored me for another two weeks after they arrived. He hates the sunroom furniture, refuses to even entertain or talk to me if I'm in it, therefore, it's *my* room. I love the sunroom. In the sunroom... I am totally alone.

==========

40 minutes later, I'm rounding back to my house, but I feel very unsettled. I can *feel* something is wrong. I can feel *something*. Picking up my pace, I practically run past the last few homes until I'm in my driveway. Exhaling, I walk up the driveway with my keys tight in my hand as a defensive weapon. Now that I'm steps from the front door, I can look over my shoulder safely. I still feel it. Searching, there's nothing and I see no one. I see nothing, but I definitely *feel* something.

Slamming the door closed, I lock it and set the alarm and just wait. What am I waiting for? I have no idea, but I feel like I have to wait for this *thing* to pass.

Removing my socks and sneakers, I let my toes suck up the cold marble of the foyer. I love this feeling. I love the cold marble, working the knots out of my toes and feet. I love the contrast of cold feet and warm body.

Once upstairs, I grab my phone and check for messages from Marcus, but there's no message. There are 3 from Mr. Zinfandel however. Deleting his messages feels good. I need to go back to my proper, staid existence. I need to stop thinking about him because he is nothing to me, and never will be. I have Marcus. Where *IS* Marcus anyway?

After a quick rinse-off shower, I'm dressed in my 2-piece pajamas and back in the sunroom, and everything is exactly as I left it. It looks a little messy actually. So straightening all my spare papers, spreadsheets and files, everything goes back in my briefcase where it belongs.

The desk is tidied of pens, ruler, and coffee cup. My laptop is closed down. The throw blanket is placed neatly over the arm of my love seat. The pillows are fluffed. The coffee table is cleared. Mugs are returned to the dishwasher. The clock is in its proper place in the corner. Its 8:35, and I settle in with my dirty book in my proper, tidy sunroom.

==========

Waking. I'm startled by a sound. What is that? Standing, I'm instantly on alert. Who is it? "Marcus?" I call out, but there's no reply. "Hello?"

I hear loud noises and a bang. Oh, I think those are keys dropping at the door. Walking toward the foyer I call out again nervously, "Marcus?"

"Yes, honey. Who else would it be?" He slurs. Has he been drinking?

Walking toward him, I'm shocked. Marcus rarely drinks, and certainly not enough to slur his words.

"Marcus. Are you alright?"

"Yup. I'm fine. How are you? You look better. Did you have another *relaxing* day at home?" He grins.

"I worked all day, actually. And it was not relaxing in the least. Where were you?"

"I went for a drink with Stephen and Kyle after work. Why? Are you gonna give me hell?"

"Um, no. How did you get home?"

"I drove. *And yes...* I know I probably would have been arrested if the police caught me, but they didn't catch me... so good for me," he smiles.

"Why didn't you call me to pick you up? Or call a taxi? Why would you drive like this?" I am just stunned. *Marcus?* Drunk *driving?* What the *hell?*

"Well, I didn't want to *bother* my wife. You see, my wife has been very distant, and *dramatic* lately. And though I love her, I can't stand her when she acts like this. So, I chose not to disturb my *wife* when she's *relaxing* at home after *I* worked all day."

"Marcus. I'm right here. Why don't you just say whatever you want to say? Please stop all this passive-aggressive shit, and just say what you want." There! AND I said shit out loud, which I never do... I say shit in my head... **A LOT.** But NEVER out loud. Marcus must be horrified.

"Well, *Honey...* I think I just did. Don't try to out-smart me, you won't win. I'm much smarter than you, any day of the week."

Wow. *Really?* I seem to remember my GPA was much higher than his, AND my college was ranked higher, but whatever...

"Okay. I won't try to *out-smart* you, honey. Have a good night. I'm going to bed."

Turning to walk away, Marcus grabs my wrist hard, and spinning me toward him he tries to kiss me. *What the hell?* Marcus doesn't kiss. 'It's *gross'*, he says. I wonder if it's gross with everyone... or just with me? Actually, I don't want to know.

Trying to pull my arm from him I can't help my raised voice as I bark, "Marcus, leave me alone. I'm going to bed, ALONE." Christ! 'Leave me alone' seems to be my theme tonight.

Suddenly, his hands are pushing at my pants and he's trying to pull them off me. "Stop! Now, Marcus!" I scream.

"I don't want to. I'm going to *show* you how good I am in bed. *You're* the problem you know, *honey*. Not me. You're the one who isn't any good at sex. I've had lots of sex, and NO ONE complains about me. You're the ONLY one complaining." Lots of sex, huh? Sex with the TWO women before me... I'm *so* sure.

Thrusting his fingers down my pants in between my legs, his nails scratch my lower stomach. SLAP!! I actually slapped Marcus! *Jesus!* I think he's as shocked as I am. Grabbing his cheek, he just stares at me cold and kind of scary looking. Oh, I don't like this look.

Backing up a step, "Leave me alone! I swear to god, Marcus, if you touch me one more time, I'll leave you. I'll be gone and YOU can explain to everyone that I left you because you tried to take me against my will...

AGAIN!"

"What the FUCK are you talking about?! I've never taken you *AGAINST YOUR WILL!!* You're fucking crazy!! Women *love* fucking me! You're the only one with a problem. I'll say it again, *honey*... You're The Problem. Not me!!" *What?* What the *hell* is he talking about? "Your fucking parents warned me about you! They told me you *might* be some trouble. They said you act up and get all strange every once in a while, but I thought you were gonna be fine. I thought I could help you. I thought being with me was a good thing for someone like you!" *Someone like me?* Like *what?*

"You've barely acted up in 6 years, until this week. Not since we were first married, except for that one time two years ago. I called your parents by the way, and they told me to IGNORE you! Even they don't want to deal with you! No one wants to deal with you. Your *friend* Kayla? She feels bad for you, that's all. After she and I had sex, she wanted to be your friend, Out Of Guilt... Not because she actually *LIKED* you!"

Oh. My. God. Kayla slept with Marcus? When? Where was I? *When?* I can't breathe. Suddenly gasping for breath, I stumble away from Marcus.

"Honey? Oh, for fuck's sake! Stop being so melo-dramatic!"

"G-good night, Marcus..." *CHRIST!* I'm always so polite. I'm going to throw-up, but I can't even catch my breath to vomit.

"Shit, honey, I'm sorry. Get some rest... You'll feel better tomorrow."

I can't stand it anymore. I can't be here anymore.

"Honey? Look, we'll talk in the morning, okay? Honey?"

I can't think anymore. I can't see anymore. I can't breathe anymore. I can't *be* anymore...

My knees collapse on the stairs, and I can feel Marcus watching me. Using my arms to pull at the spindles, I try to get to my room. It takes hours but I can't move any faster. I can't feel my arms or legs, and my chest is so tight; I think I'm having a heart-attack.

Please... get me to my room. Get me out of here. I am going to die before I make it to my room...

Closing my eyes, I gasp. My breath is coming in little infrequent puffs of air. There is not enough air. My door is so close. If I could just crawl a few more steps, I'd make it to my room. *Please...*

And slowly I make it. Closing the door behind me, I turn and lock it. Leaning against the door, I try to breathe. I just need a little breath in, and a little breath out, but there's not nearly enough air. I have a kind of tunnel vision and my body is shaking uncontrollably. Everything is turning numb. Where is all the *AIR?!* WHY IS THIS *HAPPENING* TO ME?

Please... Opening my eyes, I see my bed. Oh god, I need my bed. I just need to lie down for a minute then I'll be fine. Crawling, my stomach cramps, and my legs give out, so I begin dragging myself across the floor to my bed. Just a little more and then I can stop. I can stop *everything*...

CHAPTER 6

No, I can't stop. I *WON'T* stop. I won't let Marcus kill me here. Reaching for my phone I dial and thankfully...

"...please... h-help meeee..." I wheeze.

"Jesus *Christ!* Breathe Sweetheart. Listen to my voice. Listen to me now. Come on. I want you to listen to me. I want you to breathe in and out slowly. Sweetheart, are you there?"

"I can't... it hurts..." I whisper.

"I know it hurts. Come on, love. Breathe with me. Take gentle breaths in and out, nice and slow. Breathe. That's good, but you can do better... Breathe, Sweetheart. Where are you?"

Gasping, "floor... bed... room..." God, I am so tired, even speaking quietly is exhausting.

"Breathe, Sweetheart! Stop this, RIGHT NOW!! Focus on my voice. Focus on me. I'm giving you my breath. Can you feel it? My breath is slowly filling your lungs. Can you feel my breath? Sweetheart? I asked if you can feel my breath."

"Yes... I can... It's...easi-er."

"Focus on my voice. I'm rubbing your back and neck. Can you feel me? I'm slowly breathing for you. Do you feel my breath in your lungs? Sweetheart? Can you feel me?"

"Yes... Thank y-you. I'm bet...ter." I gasp.

Marcus is suddenly pounding on my door. No! Not now! Not Marcus. I can't deal with him anymore. I can't deal with any of this because I'm just trying to *breathe* right now. *Oh god.* Wheeze.

"Is that your husband?"

"Yes. He w-wants in... He can't..." Gasp.

"Ignore him and stay with me. Breathe, love. It's almost over. You're coming back now, I can hear it. Listen to *MY* voice! Not his..."

There's even more pounding and yelling from Marcus. Ugh. Why won't he leave me alone?

"Is he trying to help you or hurt you?" Z demands.

"Hurt..." I moan.

"Ignore him. Just stay with me, and breathe. Come on... in and out, slower. Come on, nice and slow..."

My head is pounding in tune with Marcus' hammering on the door now, and my arms and hands are all tingly, but my vision is better.

"What is he saying? Why is he trying to hurt you?"

"Drunk. Not n-nice Marcus..." I whisper.

"Okay. I'm going to keep talking to you, but I'm on my way over." *What?* No!

"No. My door is locked... He was mean w-with words... He won't hit me... He'll just *take* me." *Shit.* Did I just say that? Based on Z's growl... yes I did. "It's okay. I- I'm the problem again... it's always me. I'm always the problem. It's always me, because I, I'm always the problem..."

"Sweetheart, breathe slower. You're getting upset again. I want you to stop talking about him and focus on me. Come on, I want you to breathe slowly. It's almost passed." Has it? Yes it has. I can almost pull in a full breath.

Marcus has stopped banging and yelling too. *Thank god.* I can't even look at him right now. Go away Marcus, *forever...*

"Thank you. I'm so s-sorry about this. I didn't know who else... Your v-voice helps... I can hear it and I breath... *better,*" I whisper.

"I'm glad you called. Don't be sorry. If my voice helps you, than I'm very pleased. Breathe, Sweetheart. Don't get worked up again. You're doing very well."

"Thank you. I'm very tired now. I need to sleep...."

"NO! Stay on the phone with me a little longer. Just so I know you're really okay. Stay with me... for now."

"Okay... for now. I'm almost better. My chest doesn't hurt that much anymore."

Then I realize, my heart actually hurts, not my lungs or chest any longer. I think I actually feel broken-hearted. *Weird.* I didn't think I would feel anything for Marcus.

==========

After a long silence between Z and I, while my breathing becomes almost completely normal, I just can't hold my tongue. I have to know, and Z doesn't strike me as the type of person who cares about direct questions.

"Why did you sleep with Kayla? Was she really good in bed? I bet she was."

"Um, I wouldn't know, Sweetheart. I've never had sex with Kayla," he states calmly.

"Yeah, right. Please d-don't lie to me. It's none of my business anyway. Actually, never mind. I don't want to know. I've heard enough about Kayla's sex life this evening."

"I did **not** have sex with Kayla, nor do I plan to. Why do you think I have?"

"Um, she said last night you both talked about me... And I assumed it was in your hotel room, or in her apartment, or..." *in the backseat of a rental car, or behind a dumpster, or...*

"Did Kayla say we had sex? If so, it's not true. I do not lie, love. And I certainly don't lie about sexual relations. I don't discuss them period."

"Oh. Sorry." Big exhale. YES! They DIDN'T have sex! Why am I so *relieved?*

"Why do you sound so relieved? You just had a very long, slow exhale."

"It's nothing. It's none of my business..."

"Yes. You've already said that, and yet you're relieved. Why would it bother you if I had sex with Kayla?" He demands.

Christ! This is a long silence. Fine!

"It doesn't bother me. Just forget it, alright?"

"I don't think so. You're sounding a tad jealous, Sweetheart. If you *are* jealous, I'm delighted. Your jealousy means, you feel *something...* Maybe even towards me?" Nope. No, I don't. LIAR! I *totally* feel something.

"Look. I've had a very long, intense day that just keeps getting worse. I thank you for h-helping me, but I really want to lie down now, okay? I'm very sorry to have called you. I'm quite embarrassed, actually."

"I don't give a fuck about your apologies, your thank you, or your embarrassment... though very polite as usual. I want you to tell me what happened this evening. Now."

Shit. What do I say? The truth? Ah, *no.* The truth will sound pathetic. *I'll* sound pathetic. What do I do? Do I protect my privacy? Do I protect Marcus? No. Screw Marcus!

"Well, I thought you screwed Kayla because I told you, essentially, that she was *easy* which bothered me at the time, now however, I've found out it shouldn't have bothered me at all. So I didn't want to talk to you anymore, especially about my *pleasure* when you most certainly experienced pleasure with Kayla."

"I didn't experience Kayla's pleasure or her anything else, for that matter."

"But I didn't *KNOW* that! I thought you were a total pig for talking to me the way you did while screwing Kayla at the same time as you *flirted* with me."

"Flirted?"

"Yes, *flirted*, or whatever the hell it is you're doing with me. Whatever! Anyway, I felt bad for portraying my *friend* as easy, which incidentally, I just found out Kayla really, *REALLY* is... kind of a moral-less, home-wrecking WHORE, actually..." Big inhale.

"Go on, Sweetheart. Let it all out. This is the most you've ever spoken."

"I think I will, thank you *sir...*" I sneer. "Anyway, I decided you were a jerk and I would never speak to you again. So, I went for a walk, felt all creepy, like someone was watching me, or like something was wrong... I don't know what..."

"I *was* watching you. I wanted to make sure you were okay after you abruptly told me to leave you alone." Oh. Ha! I'm NOT crazy!

"*What?!*"

"Later. Continue please." *Later?*

"Anyway, I went back home... which *apparently* you know already, had a shower, tidied my sunroom, must have dozed off and woke to my husband stumbling through the door."

Wow. I'm so calm. No panic-attack in sight. Maybe anger is the key. Maybe I should get angry more often.

"Go on, Sweetheart..." Yeah. Ok. I will!

"So, my calm, nice, stable, boring, tax accountant husband is not only drunk, which is a first, but he drove home drunk too, which is a shock. Then Marcus attempted to have sex with me but when I said no and had to fight him off, he proceeded to tell me *I'm the problem.* The *many* women he sleeps with enjoy his company, and no one complains about his sexual habits but me." Of course I'm the problem. "Even *KAYLA*

enjoyed Marcus' company, when they had sex. When? I don't know. But apparently, Kayla is only my *friend* Out. Of. Guilt. OH! *And* she thinks I'm pathetic. So, as you can see, once again, *I'm the problem*. I'm *always* the problem. It's always *my* fault... even my parents agree with Marcus' assessment, who incidentally, he called this week..." Why is this *HAPPENING*? What did I do wrong?

"And...?" Z asks.

"And? And, **WHAT?!** Marcus said my parents told him 'I'm a problem', I go through these fits of 'acting up' and that I should be ignored. I'm always ignored. Why would that be any different THIS week?! FUCK!" Gasp. Ooops. I said the f-word out loud.

"It's okay, love... I've heard the f-word before, even said it once or twice. Continue please."

"That's it, *OKAY?!* My husband only has sex with me, maybe, once a month, and it's awful and usually painful, but thank god it only lasts about 5 minutes... But everyone else *enjoys* it; so again, the problem is mine, not his. My husband cheats on me. My *friend* Kayla fucked my husband, and doesn't really like me, but rather pities me. My parents are cold, unfeeling, assholes who tell people I'm a terrible, attention-seeking *problem,* who should be ignored. And, as usual, EVERYTHING IS MY FAULT. It's ALWAYS *my* fault..." Exhale.

"Well... You certainly have had a rather shitty week." *WHAT?!* Pause.

Laughter bursts from my chest. I heave with rolls of laughter. I try to catch my breath but I'm laughing too hard. A shitty week? *A. Shitty. Week?* Try a shitty *LIFE!* Dammit, I can't stop. I feel lightheaded and giddy. This is good. I don't cry, ever... So laughter is good.

"Easy, Sweetheart. I want you to slow down. You're getting a little hysterical, and I want you to calm down again. I'm here. Listen to my voice, and breathe slowly."

"I'm f-fine, honestly. Laughing is better than..."

"Laughter is good when something is funny. This is *not* funny. Today, *for you*, is *NOT* funny. I want you to stop now."

This feels good though. Still giggling, I slow it down a little, as Z continues to murmur soothing words in my ear.

==========

Marcus is back, pounding on my bedroom door, yelling to let him in.

"FUCK *OFF,* Marcus!! Leave me alone!! Leave. Me. ALONE!!" Ooops. Another swear.

Listening, I try to hear his actual words... "Doctor... My parents... Talking to myself... Crazy... Getting help... Ambulance..." What the *HELL?*

Charging for the door with my phone still in hand, I rip it open and scream in his face. "What did you say?! What did you just say Marcus?!"

Watching him shaking, Marcus stumbles backward, like I'm going to hit him or something. I might hit him. Actually, I kinda *want* to hit him.

Taking another deep breath, I ask calmly, "What did you do, Marcus?"

"Ah... I called your parents, and they said I should call an ambulance, to get you some help at the hospital. Um, they're very concerned about you and so am I, Honey. You're not acting normal."

"What? Did you call the ambulance yet?" Be calm. Breathe.

"Ah, they suggested I tell you first, to see if you would calm down." A *threat?* I see.

"Well, I'm glad you told me first. As you can see, I'm fine right now. I was not talking to myself, but was on the phone- See..." and holding the phone up to his face, he flinches back again, quickly. "I'm fine, but I would ask that you leave me alone RIGHT NOW. I've had a terrible night, what with my cheating, drunk-ass husband destroying my life, and all. So please leave. And if you call a doctor, or the hospital, or my parents again, I will hurt you Marcus. I SWEAR TO GOD, I will knock you on your ass before I leave this house forever."

"Honey... I..." Ha! Marcus looks like *he's* going to have a panic-attack, which is *too funny.*

"Do not speak Marcus. If you need to talk to someone, go call Kayla. I'm sure she is more than willing to deal with you. Leave me alone. Now!"

"Ah... I still think we should call someone about your behavior..."

"My behavior? Yes, my *behavior* is a little troubling at the moment, isn't it? Well, don't worry- Not that you ever worry about me, but I'll be fine. Marcus, I *strongly* suggest however that you get out of my face right now. I'm not kidding you. I'm going to hurt you if I have to look at you a moment longer."

And slamming the door, I turn and run for my bathroom. I have to grab stuff. Grab enough stuff. Grab lots of stuff. Damn, my head is spinning, but this is kind of exhilarating, too.

Where's my luggage? In my walk-in closet. Yanking out my luggage, *thank god.* Running back into my bathroom, all my toiletries are thrown in a travel bag. Running, I head for the walk-in closet again for clothes. What kind of clothes? Anything. Which shoes? Many. All my black shoes are thrown in the suitcase.

I have to change. Grabbing black slacks, and a light cami/cardigan combo, in black, *of course*, I'm clothed properly. Which shoes? I need heels. I *NEED* to feel better, more secure in my heels. Got them. These are sexy, high, yet amazingly comfortable. I need comfort right now.

I'm frantic to be quick. What will Marcus do? *Shit.* Have my parents already called an ambulance? Fuck! I HATE that threat. *SINCE WHEN?* When have I heard that threat before? Huh, good question.

Looking around, everything I need from my room is packed. Dammit, the sunroom. One more stop needed for my laptop, keys and phone. *Shit.* THE PHONE!

"Are you still there?" I panic.

"Yes. I'm here. What are you doing?" *Running for my life.*

"I'm leaving for... I don't know how long. I'll call you later, okay?"

"*Sweetheart...* I'm very serious. I expect a phone call soon. Do you understand me?"

"Yes. Okay. I'll call you back soon. I just have to hurry and get out of here. I think he's trying to get me taken away. I... I think my parents are going to take me away. I'll call when I'm out of here." I nearly lose it.

"Promise me. Promise right now, Sweetheart. Promise that you will call me very soon."

"I promise I'll call you soon. But I have to go. I have to hurry. Don't call me though. I don't want him to hear my phone ring," I whisper.

"Okay. But call *SOON*," he demands, as he hangs up.

Throwing the phone in my travel bag, I wheel my luggage to the door. Inhaling, I unlock the door and... silence. Marcus isn't behind the door waiting to attack me. Good. Exhaling slowly, I open the door and listen. He's murmuring something down the hall. Maybe he did call Kayla. Good. Have each other. I hate you both. I knew I should have never trusted her, or Marcus for that matter. I can't trust anyone. I was right!

I have to get down the stairs. *Stairs?* Dammit! Please wheels... please don't bang on the stairs. Lifting, I make my way down to my sunroom. Laptop. Purse. Keys. Money? Ha! My funny 'for a rainy day fund' jar. Marcus thought it was stupid. 'Why wouldn't you just buy what you wanted, whenever you wanted?' FOR **TODAY**, *ASSHOLE!* My rainy day jar is going to save me. God, I hope I make it out of here.

Heading for the front door, I hear nothing. Marcus doesn't know I'm leaving. Thank God, I don't have to see him, and I don't have to hear him again. There will be no more drama this evening. There will be nothing. There is just me, alone, without Marcus or my parents.

Banging my luggage down the front walkway, I'm almost there. Come on. Yes! Opening the back passenger door, I lift and shove my luggage inside. Done. Running around the car, I'm in. When my door is closed and locked, I finally exhale. I made it. Inhale. There is nothing they can do now. Exhale. I'm free from them tonight. Inhale.

Pulling out of my driveway, I look back, but there's still no Marcus. Good. I can't see him in any window, and he's not standing in the front doorway. Marcus didn't even notice me leave. Marcus doesn't notice me ever, and tonight it worked for me! Exhale.

CHAPTER 7

Where am I going? The Marriott? No way! The Hilton? Ahh, *no.* I should probably try to save as much of my 'fund' as possible. I'll just use my ATM card once, right now, in case Marcus looks for me tomorrow, though I'm sure he won't. Actually he might. Will he? NO. *Maybe?*

Rounding Sheridan Road, I see a 7Eleven. Pulling into the parking lot a little too aggressively, I actually get a dirty look from a man holding a little girl's hand. Ah, how cute- *Daddy and his little girl.* Did my father ever hold my hand when I was little? I can't remember but I don't think so. Why are they out at this time of night?

Running into the store, I spot the ATM. What's the code? I'm drawing a blank. Oh, yeah, Marcus' birthday. *Of course.* Why not *my* birthday? I know, because Marcus told me to use his. '$500.00 maximum limit at this machine'? What happens if I get the money and put my card in again? Will that work? I'll try. No. *Dammit.* I need more money.

My iPhone starts ringing. Did he realize I left? Please no... Yup, it's Marcus. I'm not answering. No way. Why don't they have an ignore button? Actually, I'm sure there's an App or something for that. There's an App for everything, so there *has* to be an *'ignore husband'* App.

Across the street is a mom and pop store. How does it stay in business with the big 7Eleven across the street? Who cares? ATM? Yes. $400.00 daily maximum. What IS this? Even the ATMs are against me tonight.

A few blocks away there's a gas station with another store attached. I should fill up before Marcus cancels my credit cards. $56.00 dollars in gas? *Jeez...* I didn't even notice I was on empty.

In the store, I run for the ATM. $500.00 daily machine maximum, but it's a different bank. How many banks are there in the Chicago area? *Whatever.* I'm up $1,400 plus my *rainy day* $450. Just a few more stops and I should be good.

==========

Across this street, there's another store with an ATM. Ha! 'Exceeds daily limit'. *Shit!* The same bank as the mom and pop store. Oh well. Maybe I should get some food.

Argh... My phone is ringing again. Marcus? No- my parents. *Jesus...* My *parents?* I am NOT answering that one. The endless ringing is so annoying. Okay. Vibrate. There! Now I can ignore the ringing and experience a little vibrating pleasure... Ha! *Gross.*

Shopping I grab; Chips x 2. Chocolate bar x 6... (For my sanity, of course!) Is there a cart around here? Yes! Found one. Water x 12. Whole wheat bread. Chocolate chip Muffins-a 6 pack. Some gum. A big bottle of Pepsi. Oh, licorice! I haven't had that in years. Yogurt... EW, why? Ice-cream... Yum. Oh, no freezer in the car. Damn. Okay, at least one ice-cream sandwich for the drive. Yum, again. What else? Go by

aisle.

I grab some turkey slices, followed by mustard and a few apples to balance out the chocolate bars. Jar of salsa. Jar of nacho Cheese. Bag of tortilla chips. Apple jacks cereal. A small carton of milk. Cheese slices for my turkey. Ummm, I think that's it. Oh, a bottle of cheap Zinfandel. Why not?

At the counter I start unloading my stuff. The cashier is obviously looking at me like I'm crazy. What do I say? Think.

"Our kitchen flooded so badly, we lost all our food. So my husband and I have to eat in the car..."

What The *FUCK* was *that*?? *'Eat in the car?!'* I sound totally INSANE!! And kind of manic, actually. Calm down. Don't cause a scene. No response from the cashier... Good. Scan. Scan. Scan. There's an angry guy behind me huffing and shifting back and forth on his feet.

"Ah, sorry," I mutter to him. Why is he looking at me strangely? *Honestly?* Can't a woman buy up a damn store? What's HIS problem?

"That'll be $69.26, please." *69?* Like the sexual position Marcus wanted to try one time only... 69? *Seriously?* Giggle.

"No problem. I'll pay debit."

Vibrate. I jump. *Honest to god...* Even *vibrate* makes me jump. What's up with that? Who are you...? Ah, Marcus. Nope. We're *still* not talking, honey. *Jeez...* Leave me alone.

In the car, I'm trying to remember a bank branch nearby. Oh, Main street, *naturally.* Okay, I'll just make one more stop, than I'm done.

Finding the branch on Main Street is easy, and I can't believe it actually has a drive-thru machine. Thank god! I was scared to get out of my car tonight. I'm feeling a little creeped-out or something. $500.00 max. again. Okay $1,900, plus $450, plus a full tank of gas, plus enough food to service a nuclear take down. Where do I go now?

Suddenly my phone vibrates. Jump! I have *got* to stop DOING that! It's Marcus, again. Still no, *honey.* GAG. I'm not giving in. I'm not answering, listening, or swallowing, everything he says is wrong with me. Not tonight. I just can't do it. I'm awesome right now. I'm strong and determined. I'm back in control. I'm not letting Marcus weaken me.

Ignoring my phone, I drive a little more downtown. Maybe I should drive to Evanston. I know there are decent hotels on the way; hotels less like the Marriott, but still better than a motel. I've passed them every time Marcus makes me visit my parents in Lake Forest.

Pulling up to a Super8 downtown, I finally exhale. Inside, a perfectly delightful hotel manager informs me that I cannot pay in cash without a credit card. What? *Why?* IT'S CASH! That makes no sense. Sadly, I'm then versed on hotel policy, starting with credit card security, and ending with *secured* credit cards. What do I do? I can't use my credit card. Marcus will find me.

Okay. Think. *Think!* I have no one to ask. I have no one to call. I *knew* it was going to come down to this. *I KNEW IT!*

Dialing, I am absolutely mortified.

"Sweetheart, where are you?!"

"Ah, that's the problem. I'm where I need to be tonight, but they won't

take just cash. I have lots of money Z, *in cash.* I'm NOT asking you for money. I swear! But, ah, could you please call the hotel and give them your credit card information- JUST for security purposes, *I swear!* I'm not using your credit card, and I'm not going to trash the room, but..."

"Which hotel?"

"The Super 8 on Sheridan Road."

"Give me 10 minutes, and they'll escort you to your room. Do you have any luggage?" Luggage? Giggle. Yes. I have luggage, but the real problem is all the food I just bought. I can't help another little laugh.

"Stop, Sweetheart. You're doing very well. In 10 minutes, I want you to bring your luggage into the foyer and wait to be escorted to your room. Okay?"

"Yes. Okay. Thank you. But PLEASE don't pay for my room, or anything. I WANT to do this on my own. If I wasn't afraid of Marcus and my parents tracking my credit cards, I would have used my own, and never asked you for a thing... I just didn't know what else to do. I have no one else *to* call." Ooops... That sounded bad. "Ah, what I mean is..."

"Don't worry. It's fine. I know you're struggling right now, so I'll excuse the occasional *poor choice of words* on your part." He actually sounds like he's smiling at me. Is he?

"Thank you... I'll call you back soon," I whisper.

My room is very nice. It's much nicer than I expected, and much nicer than I had hoped for. There's even a small mini-fridge under the counter with a freezer. Damn. I could've bought the ice cream. Oh well- my big thighs and butt will thank me later. Stop! Not now. Torture yourself later.

Walking back to my car, a nice, male attendant soon follows and offers to help me with my purchases. Did Z tell them to help me? Probably. What took us one trip with 8 bags, would have taken me at least 2 or 3 trips. Thank you nice attendant man. Thank you, Z.

==========

Finally, I'm here. After putting my groceries aside in the fridge and on the counter as best as I can, I pull my luggage to the dressers and unpack all my clothes and shoes. All I have is black. Lots and lots of black.

In the bathroom, I finally see my face. What is *WITH* this mascara? *Shit!* I look like a raccoon. This is so embarrassing. No wonder the store clerk, the impatient man in line behind me and the hotel staff thought I was demented. I look weird.

I'm wearing a beautiful Movado watch and Vera Wang heels. I have a stunning 1 carat diamond pendant and matching earrings. I also have a large 2 carat diamond solitaire ring on my hand, but I look like a crazy person, recently released on her week-end pass from the asylum.

Once my toiletries are lined up neatly, I scrub my face, brush my teeth... And exhale again. Why do I always hold my breath? I don't think I ever did that before. Why now?

Entering the room again, I know I should call Z. Taking a big breath while dialing, I mentally prepare for his intensity, as I crawl into the bed.

"Hello, Sweetheart. All settled in?"

"Yes. Thank you again. I promise I'm not going to use your credit card. I have enough money to stay for weeks, if I need it." Huh. Do they offer weekly discounts? I should ask.

"I wouldn't care if you did."

"But I would. I don't want to take anything from you. I don't expect anything, I promise. I just needed…"

"I know what you need, love, and I am more than happy to provide it." *What?* Gulp. Why does he sound so *seductive* all of a sudden? It's his tone, I think.

"Um. I really should go now 'cause it's after 3am. It's been a very, very long day for me, and I'm exhausted. I'm very sorry I kept you awake this late."

"Would you like some company? I'm only offering to *be* there, nothing more." Yes! *Yes, I would.*

"No… but thank you. I hope I'm not offending you, but I really need to just sleep now. I am beyond exhausted, stressed out, and feeling a little weak from all this," I sigh.

"*Weak?* Yes, I could see how *weakness* would stress you out. No worries. Please call me when you wake though. I would like to know how you are after a good night's rest."

"Okay. I'll call you. Thank you again, Z, for ah… being, *ah…* there for me." God that sounded pathetic, even to me.

"You're very welcome, Sweetheart. I'm glad I could, ah… be, *ah…* there for you." God, he has a lovely voice, and he's smiling at me. I can actually hear his smile in his voice.

Smiling myself, I whisper, "Good night, Z."

"Sweet dreams, Sweetheart."

Saturday, May 28th

CHAPTER 8

At 9:47, I finally wake up. I've only slept 6 hours, but I feel fairly rested. What now? Start small and just eat breakfast. Oh, I bought muffins last night. Good. I haven't had a muffin in forever. Marcus always said 'muffins are for fat woman who don't care that they are eating *empty calories* and gluing it to their asses'. Yeah, well... *This* woman is eating a chocolate chip muffin, maybe even two.

I'm stalling. By 10:09, I'm officially bored. What do I do now? Normally, on Saturday mornings, Marcus and I have a nice breakfast, and drive to the Market Place 4 blocks away from our home. We HAVE TO buy fruit and vegetables from the Market Place because Marcus believes strongly in buying produce from local sources, to aid the local economy AND because local fruits and vegetables are macrobiotic, therefore better for you.

I have heard this same lecture almost every Saturday, for 6 years of marriage, and it never changes... except of course, during the winter months. During the winter, it's perfectly acceptable to buy fruit and vegetables in the massive grocery store around the corner from our house, where it's nice and warm. God, he is SUCH an ass!

By 10:30, I'm still stalling. I wish I remembered my filthy, pornographic novel. Oh, no! Marcus might find it if he enters my sunroom. How embarrassing! Would he tell my parents about it? Oh, probably. Just another example he can use to show the world that I am the problem, not dear, sweet, secure, stable, reliable, innocent... Marcus. *Gag.*

Maybe I can go to a bookstore today. I'll just visit the Erotica section and I'll pay in cash so no one knows what I've purchased. Where is a bookstore around here? Probably in a perfectly obvious strip-mall nearby. I won't walk downtown, I'll drive instead, just in case. Good.

And stalling some more...

============

By 11:25 my bed is made and I'm showered. My hair is dried and styled in a nice chignon. My clothes are perfectly acceptable, and black. My make-up is done. I look totally together, and sane. Stop stalling. *OK!*

Dialing Z, I'm holding my breath again... That I know I'm holding my breath doesn't actually *stop me* from holding my breath though.

"Good morning, Sweetheart. Did you sleep well?"

"Yes. It's very nice here. I wanted to thank you again for helping me last night. I..."

Cutting me off, Z says, "How about you say 'thank you' once more and

say 'I'm sorry Z' twice." Ummm... *What?*

"I beg your pardon?"

"You heard me. I want you to say 'thank you, Z' and 'I'm sorry Z, very sorry' right now. Say it." What the HELL is he talking about?

"I don't understand..."

"I *WANT* you to say 'Thank you, Z' and 'I'm sorry, Z... very sorry'!"

"Okay. Thank you and I'm sorry, very sorry." Why am I doing this?

"Ooops. You forgot the 'Z'." *What?*

"I'm sorry, but I don't know what you want." This is getting kind of annoying.

"You're an intelligent woman, love. Repeat these words. 'Thank you, Z' and then 'I'm sorry, Z, I'm very sorry'. It's really not that difficult, Sweetheart. Please try again." What does he think I am? A *moron?*

"Why are you speaking to me like I'm an idiot?"

"Say it!" He yells at me. *WHAT THE HELL?!*

"*Fine!* THANK YOU, Z. Thank you, thank you, thank you. Good, enough?!"

"And? Continue please..."

"I. AM. SORRY, Z. SO FUCKING SORRY!! Please FORGIVE me!! I don't know what you want, but there!! I'M SO SORRY, YOU *ASSHOLE!!* Ooops. You didn't DEMAND that, but I threw it in any way! Good enough NOW?" Ha! *Asshole!* TAKE THAT!

"Yes. Thank you. That was perfect. Though, I could have done without the *asshole,* the rest was lovely."

Is he insane? *Shit.* I can't hold back my laughter.

"Ah... That's better. Now, please don't get hysterical on me, but a little laughter is acceptable..." he chuckles in return.

"You're crazy, Z. Why did you want me to say that? I really AM sorry for all this. It's very embarrassing for me. And I really AM grateful to you for aiding me last night. There is nothing wrong with that," I breathe as a little giggle carries over.

"No. There is nothing wrong with that. However, I want you to just relax so you can simply talk to me with honesty. Therefore, I thought it best to get all your obsessive gratitude, embarrassment and apologies out of the way. Now, I would like to have a conversation with you without either of the following... 'I'm sorry' and/or 'thank you'. Do you think you could please try to avoid those two statements?" *Doubtful.*

"Um... I can try. But it's hard. I was *bred* to speak a certain way, and I always have..."

"I understand about your *breeding*... but please try. For me?"

Sighing, "Yes. I'll try."

"Well, now that all *that's* out of the way, AND you've called me an asshole... I would like to ask you a few questions." *Ugh.*

"Okay," I whisper.

"Oh, Sweetheart... don't sound so frightened. This is going to be fun." Again, I can *hear* his smile.

"I'm guessing this will *only* be fun for you... but I'll try." Here we go. This is going to be awful, I just know it.

"Okay. For starters, what do you want to do about your marriage and your *husband?*" He sneers.

"Um... I don't know. I haven't had any time to think about him yet. I know I don't really want to go back, but I'm not sure if it's that easy for me."

"It IS that easy. Just make a decision, and change your life to fit your decision."

"Nothing's that easy, Z. We have a home together. We have joint bills, and joint money invested. We have joint everything. He holds the title to my car, though I paid for it. He is the major buyer on our home, though my pay checks pay the mortgage equally. Financially, I am completely eclipsed by him. So, it's NOT that easy." This is bad. I am so *screwed*. "Ah, I didn't even realize it until now, but I'm pretty screwed actually, at least *financially* by Marcus." *Shit.*

"Finances can be manipulated, altered, or changed. Money and financial issues are probably the easiest hurdle."

"Marcus is a tax accountant. He knows money. He knows all the 'loop-holes'. I think he even drafted a few such loop-holes. So, financially, I really *am* in quite a bit of trouble. Going up against Marcus will be very difficult. Plus..." Shit.

"Plus, what?"

"Um... Marcus is very close to my parents... actually, he's more like their child than I am. So, it'll be even harder to change things because Marcus invests much of their money. They're very wealthy, and Marcus has made them even wealthier. He uses their money, invests, buys and sells, and splits profits without taxing himself, or indirectly *me*... I guess. I know he uses small 'dummy' companies within a lower tax bracket. I'm assuming it's kind of illegal, or right on the fringe at least, but my parents and Marcus all have an agreement and I think he could easily change that if I leave him. Or he could at least *threaten* to, which would force my parents to force me to behave. And he is the Executor of their will, not me, so he can take whatever he wants and ruin me." Oh. This is so much worse than I thought.

"So, again... I'm hearing *financial* issues. If I told you my dearest friend, whom, incidentally, I trust with my life, was a senior corporate Rep for the I.R.S., what would you say?" Gulp.

"Ah... I'd say I'm sorry I told you any of this."

Barking a laugh, Z responds, "I love your quick, witty responses. No worries, Sweetheart, I would never divulge a confidence, unless you ask me to..." *Which I never will.* "...Which you never will, I'm assuming." *Jeez...* He's good.

"Probably not. I like to do things on my own."

"Yes. I am well aware of your rather obsessive independence." Oh, good. *Obsessive?*

"I'm not obsessive about it. I just find it easier to do things for myself, rather than be disappointed when..."

"Disappointed when you are let down, and/or betrayed? Am I right?"

"You know you're right. Please... *please* don't play games with me," I beg. I don't like this at all.

"Oh, Sweetheart... I'm not playing games with you. I'm listening to what you do and don't say and repeating it back to you. I want you to hear all I hear. I want you to see all I see. Remember, I'm just learning you, but

you have known yourself always. Therefore, I am a fresh perspective to all you know, say, and feel. Do you understand what I'm trying to give to you?"

"I know when you give back to me my own words; I don't like to hear them. I sound pathetic. I sound like a loser. I never thought I was a loser, until all of this and I hate it. I hate the way you see me. I'm embarrassed that I'm essentially, completely transparent. I don't like this game, anymore." I feel so sad suddenly.

"You sound very sad right now. That's not my intention. I would like to help strengthen you for a potentially difficult upcoming fight. You may or may not leave your husband for good, but you need to strengthen yourself to make some changes. I don't want you in a situation where you ever feel this trapped again. I would like that for you, *Ms. Independent.* Can you see the contradiction?" *Christ!* Even Z thinks I'm an idiot.

"Yes, I see it! This wasn't my intention, you know! It just *happened,* okay?! Marcus and my parents are very strict, very *strong* people. They think they always know what's best for me, so they push their decisions on me. If it had been just one or the other, I could have fought. I bought the love seat and chair!" Not that he knows what the hell *that* means. "But it's not one or the other- It's always THEM, *together.* If he says, they agree. If they say, he agrees. I'm the only one who ever has a problem with their decisions. It's just easier to give in every time, because as they always say, *I. Am. The. Problem,* not them."

What am I doing here? What am I going to do? *I'm going to give in.* I always give in. I have no other choice *but* to give in.

"You are not going to give in this time. Your husband emotionally and somewhat physically abused you. You don't have to give in this time, and quite frankly, I will be very disappointed if you do. He cheated on you, by his own words, 'with many women', so you have grounds to fight. You can have anything you want, if you choose to fight."

If I *choose?* I'll never win the fight. There is nothing I can say to Z to make him understand. There is nothing I can give but my silence.

"Ah... I'm starting to hear the refusal to fight. I can sense your retreat. Listen to me; I'm not trying to force you to do anything, as they force you to do. I'm just giving you options, that's all. A different perspective, if you will. Maybe a better perspective than what you've always known. You can *do*, or *have* anything you want, starting today. Today, you can map out your whole life. You can do anything..."

"I CAN'T do *anything!* I NEVER can! That's the point, Z. You don't know me, and you DON'T know my life. It's NOT easy. It's NOT filled with options and opportunity. This life of mine is completely *constructed* and static. It is me who has upended my life. If I hadn't felt *weird* and kind of messed up this week, I wouldn't have told Marcus sex was 'not good', I wouldn't have been home working, looking horribly incompetent for my boss, and Marcus wouldn't have been drunk and aggressive. I wouldn't know about the cheating. I wouldn't fear my employment stability. I would be at home, right now, unloading the local, macro-biotic fruit and vegetables Marcus insists I buy..."

There. That was a mouthful, but I don't actually feel better though like I thought I would.

"Yes. I don't know you well, and I certainly don't know the intricacies of your life, but I know a tragic situation when I see it. And I want to help."

"No, you DON'T! *Jesus!* Can't you just leave me alone?! Stop talking for five minutes. I just need to think, okay? This is *MY* life, and I don't want you *interfering* with it. I don't want YOU to have an opinion. I don't want you..." Shit. Breathe. Calm down.

"There. That was better. You calmed a rising panic-attack. Good girl. I AM going to help you. I decided to help you when I first heard your voice on Tuesday. I know you enough, and I know what you need. So you can either work with me, or fight me. It won't matter either way, because I will still help you. But if you fight me, you'll just end up more exhausted and battle weary. But it is your choice."

My choice? When have I ever had a choice? "It's not my choice. You just told me you were going to help regardless... So again, I have NO choice. Can you see how absurd your statement is?"

"No. I said you have a choice, not *ALL* the choices. I'm helping you regardless of what you choose. Whether you accept my help or not, is not going to change anything. But you can *choose* to accept my help. Think about it. I will give you two hours, and then I'm calling you back and we'll talk." Two hours? What the hell will I figure out in two hours?

"Um... I need more time to..."

"No, two hours is what I'm offering. I'm going to call you back, and we're going to talk. *Really* talk. You will accept my help, or not, but you WILL give me your decision in two hours."

"Z... I can't think anymore..."

"That's the point. I'm here now, to think *for*, or *with* you- *Your* choice. Two hours, love. I'm calling you back at 2:15. Please have your answer ready." *Shit!*

==========

At 2:10, I realize I want Z's help. I actually want it. And knowing I want his help gives me a sense of peace I have rarely, if ever, felt before. Knowing I will have such a straight-forward man in my corner makes me feel a kind of relief, an actual sense of calm. I'm content and excited, so when the phone rings, I'm ready. I don't jump or gasp. I answer calmly.

"Hi."

"Hello, Sweetheart. How are you feeling?"

"Good. I'm good. I, ah, have decided to accept your help. Um, please help me." There! I jumped off the cliff.

"I would love to help you, and I'm honored that you are *willing* to let me. I would have helped anyway, but I'm glad I don't have to fight you as well." Again, there's a smile in his voice.

"Thank you. But I still don't quite know what I want. I need a few days to clear my head a little. Is that okay?"

"Absolutely. Do you love your husband?" Ah... Yes? No? Um...

"Yes, I love him... I *married* him. But it's just not, you know, like passionate love or anything. Marcus is more like a room-mate." A *gross* room-mate.

"A *room-mate*? Well, that *WOULD* be disappointing. Did he disappoint you sexually as well?"

"*Oh god yes...* " SHIT! That was out loud again. Argh! THINK BEFORE YOU SPEAK!

"*Really...?* Well, that's very sad to hear. Did he ever please you sexually? Or has it merely faded over time? Incidentally, how long have you been married?"

"We've been married 6 years, and no, he's never *pleased...* me." Gulp. I don't like that word much either.

"6 years? You would have been a baby when you married. Why would your parents allow you to marry so early?" They wanted rid of me?

"Um... 23 isn't a baby, and Marcus was 29, my age now, so it was balanced out, I think." Was it? Was it *ever* balanced between is? No, I don't think it was.

"Does this conversation make you uncomfortable?"

"Very much so. I don't talk about stuff like this. I'm not that kind of woman. I don't *do* this. My life and especially my marriage are, or *should be* private," I whine.

"Yes, they should be private, and I do appreciate your discretion. However, I am trying to understand your marriage for *your* benefit, therefore, I'm going to ask many private questions. Are you ready, Sweetheart?" *God, no!* I HATE this.

"Um, no. I'm not ready. I really don't know what to say. I don't know..."

"Why don't you just answer my questions, then. Honestly."

"I'll try..." I whisper.

"Okay. In general, would you call your marital relations making-love, having sex, or just fucking?" *Christ!* I don't know. It's not like I was an *active participant*.

"Um... I, I don't know. I, ah, don't really think about it. I mean..." *Shit*. What *do* I mean?

"You don't think about it afterward? Or *during?*"

"Both, I guess. It's not really something I participate in..." Oh, that sounds bad.

"What does *THAT* mean?" He asks so aggressively, that I feel suddenly threatened *and* embarrassed.

"It just means that Marcus just kind of did it to me, and I just waited for it to be over."

"I see."

"Um, I guess I'm not very good at sex. Marcus always told me I was frigid, but I'm not. I mean, I've, you know..." God, I can feel how red my face is.

"You've masturbated." *Oh. My. GOD!* Kill me RIGHT NOW!

"Not really. I mean the shower-head...." ***Seriously?!*** "I'm not good at sex, okay? So the sex with Marcus wasn't very good. I know it's my fault, but I just couldn't really get any better. So, that's it. I guess when we had sex and it wasn't very good, it was because *I'm* not very good!" Well, THAT was painful to admit.

"How often did you and your husband have sex?"

"Maybe once every 3 or 4 weeks, like once a month, maybe."

"Even during the honeymoon period?"

"Yes. Why is this relevant? Honestly? I mean who cares how often Marcus had sex with me, or whether I was any good at it, or if I even liked it, or if it hurt? These questions have nothing to do with where I'm at now." Deep breath. Come on, exhale slowly.

"It *HURT* you? *Every time?*" His voice is lower. Why is *that* the word he picked up on?

"Um, not really..."

"*Sweetheart,* honesty please..." he growls at me.

"Fine! Yes, it hurt *every* time. I hate sex. I've only had sex with Marcus and I hate it. I dread it. I felt nothing but relief when it was over and nothing but relief knowing that I didn't have to do it again for 3 to 4 weeks when it was over. Okay?" Breathe. Come on. Deep breath.

"Deep breath, love. I don't want you agitated right now." *Seriously?!*

"Then stop asking me these questions! This is hard, okay? I've never, *ever* talked about sex before, well once I slipped and told my *friend* Kayla something, but she just laughed." *WHAT A BITCH!* "She knew the whole time..." I whisper. *Shit.* "...She knew Marcus was a Five Minute Man, and she laughed at my description. *Oh my god*, may- maybe Marcus wasn't a Five Minute Man with her... Maybe it's just with m-me. Oh my god, this is so, so embarrassing..." Gasp. I can't breathe!

"Sweetheart! Stop this now. Breathe deeply, right now. I want you to stop thinking about Kayla, and the *what ifs*... We're talking about YOU only. Not what she did to you. Not what Marcus said about you. Nothing else, just *you*. Breathe, love. It's just you and me here and nothing, absolutely NOTHING you say to me goes any further, nor will I judge you for anything you tell me. Please, Sweetheart. Please breathe, and trust me enough to talk to me."

God, his voice is so beautiful and soothing. I could listen to him always, he is so calming. I should be worried about any kind of attachment to him under the circumstances, but I don't want to think about it right now. I *want* to be soothed by him.

"I'm going to have to k-keep your voice on retainer for all these p-panic-attacks."

Laughing, Z replies, "No retainer required. I'm here for free... though usually my services are not cheap. For *you* however, I'm willing to work pro bono."

"Thanks. Pro bono sounds good... for now. But depending on how good your s-services are, I just may pay you in the future." Wow. That sounded kind of *sexual*. Ooops.

"That sounded a little risqué, love. Am I bringing out the temptress in you?"

"Sadly, no. I have no inner temptress. I never have."

"Well, I'd like to challenge that statement. But no worries, *that* challenge is for another day, I assure you." Not today, but *another day?* Awesome! No! *Not* awesome! Shit!

"Um, Z? Can I please let you go now? I'm feeling a little tired and I would like to go buy a book and just relax a little."

"Of course. You don't need to give me any excuses, or explanations. Please, just speak freely to me. I understand you have a lot to think about, and you need time to do it."

"Thank you. I'm so afraid of being rude to you. I don't want you to be mad at me..." Ugh. That was absolutely pathetic sounding.

"I'm not going to be mad at you for needing time to yourself. And I'm not that easily upset in general, so just relax." *Really?* That'd be new for me in my world.

"Thank you. Can I call you later, maybe in a few hours?" *Please...*

"Of course. But if you don't call me in a few hours, I WILL be very upset."

"Okay. Bye, Z."

"Enjoy your book hunting, Sweetheart. Please be well."

That sounded so... so *nice*, but in a good way- not in a Marcus sickeningly *fake* way. Z sounds like he truly wants me to *be well*.

What the hell am I doing? I feel like I can actually trust Z. But that would be insane. No one can be trusted. My own father told me that, time and time again. Yet, here I am... starting to trust a stranger. I really am a stupid woman.

==========

When I return from the bookstore, its 5:05. The selection of 'Erotica' books was seriously lacking, but then again, I now have a taste for the *really* raunchy novels of my favorite dirty author. Her books, however, I can only buy on Amazon. I don't think typical bookstores *could* even carry her nasty novels. Smiling, I can just picture asking Marcus to pick one up for me. Ha! He would die of embarrassment. Too funny.

My dinner consists of tortilla Chips with nacho cheese, one chocolate bar, a glass of Pepsi, and licorice for dessert. My parents would be so proud. Marcus would have a stroke. Oh well, what they can't see, won't hurt them. Curling up in bed and propping the pillows, I crack the spine of my new dirty novel...

Okay, so it's been an hour and I'm bored to tears. I barely even remember what I've read. This isn't so much filthy as just kind of *slightly* dirty. *Boring!* My favorite author did me in. She set the bar too high for filth. So closing my eyes, I decide to rest for a minute, and I'm done...

==========

Waking to my phone ringing, I panic. I haven't heard from Marcus or my parents all day, and somehow that doesn't sit well. Their lack of interference seems really bad. Oh no. What are they planning? What are they *waiting* for?! What are they going to do to me?!

Panicking, I look and it's Z. Grabbing my phone I almost scream at him,

"I'm in trouble, I think!"

"Why? What's happened? Where are you?!"

"I'm still here. I just woke up, but there's something wrong... I can *feel* it. I'm not crazy Z, I'm not! It's just I KNOW something's wrong."

"Breathe Sweetheart, and tell me what's been going on." Breathe. Gasp? No!

"I fell asleep. What time is it anyway?"

"11:45. I waited to call you. I wanted you to call me, but I just couldn't wait any longer. What has you nearly in a panic?" Wow. I've been asleep for that many hours?

"Nothing's happened. *Nothing at all. THAT'S* the problem. I haven't heard from Marcus, or from my parents. Can't you see? That means they're preparing something bad, something *big*."

God, I'm so screwed. Z can't help me with this. He can't. It's going to be too big. I have to tell him to get out now.

"You can't help me! Honestly, I'm not trying to sound all dramatic, but I know them! They're planning to get me. They *always* get me. Whatever they're planning to do is too big for me to fight... It's too big for *you* to fight. You don't even know me. You shouldn't get involved in this. This is going to be... very, *very* bad for me, Z."

"I think you mistake me for someone who breaks easily, love. I'm not that weak, nor do I cave to others' demands. Don't worry about me, at all. Worry only about yourself."

"But I DO worry about you. Z, they're very rich. They have sooo much money, and influence, and *friends*. You can't possibly help me. They'll find a way to hurt you too if they think you *are* or *have been* helping me. And I really don't want that. I don't want you hurt because of me. I'm sorry, but I have to go. Thank you, sincerely." Breathe, Dammit!

"DO NOT HANG UP ON ME! I won't stand for it. If you hang up now, I'll just be at your door in minutes. Listen to me closely. I am not afraid, nor can they hurt me."

"Yes, they can. And they will. They always get what they want. *Always*. I'm going to be punished for daring to embarrass my family by leaving Marcus. They're going to find something to use against me, to force me to g-give in. I can *FEEL* it. I *know* it, Z!" Shit! Where is all the air?

"Listen to me. They cannot hurt me. I too have money..." I snort at his words. "...I have *a lot* of money, and influence, and 'friends', as you call them. They CAN NOT hurt me! Do you know who I am? Have you never researched me?"

"Um, no. Why would I? That's rude." *Seriously?* Who researches people?

"*Rude?* Ha! That's very naive, love. Everyone researches everybody else. Everyone wants to find the 'thing' which gives them an advantage over someone else."

Shocked, I ask, "Did you research me?"

"Of course I did. You were intriguing to me from the moment we spoke. I heard the reserve in your voice, and the manic attempt to hold control. I heard you lose it, and I had to know who you were." *Really?* Well, this is a surprise. No one ever wants to know me.

"What... What kind of research did you do on me? I think I'm very

uncomfortable suddenly. I feel like you have something on me. Do you? Can you hurt me?" I'm going to freak out any second here. I can't trust anyone!

"No, I have nothing to hurt you with. That wasn't my intention. I wanted to know you, not what you may or may not have done. I was only looking for a clue into the mind of this strange, intriguing, slightly erratic, attractive woman, with the beautiful lips and the alluring eyes..." Well, *that* sounded nice. "... And I would NEVER hurt you. I told you that in the beginning, and I keep my word... *ALWAYS*. Knowing I researched your background changes nothing."

"It does for me. We're not on even footing. You have an advantage over me. I have nothing but a funny last name. That's all. It's really quite unsettling, and unfair."

"You can ask me anything, and I will always tell you the truth, barring any issues of confidentiality, or discretion and the sort. Ask me anything, Sweetheart. I don't hide, and I don't cower. There is nothing that can hurt me."

"God, I wish I was as confident as you."

"You will be. By the time I'm through with you, you will exude confidence, and power. No one will ever again force their will upon you... Well... *except for me*, of course." Again, I hear his smile-voice. I love hearing it. It's sexy and charming. *HE* seems sexy and charming.

"I'm still a little unsettled by all this. You have your research over my head, and Marcus and my parents have my past and future over my head. What do I have? Nothing."

"You have me. I'm still here, and I'll help you. Even if you decide to return to your faithless, prick of a husband, *by your own free will*, I will still help you balance out the financial power in your marriage. But I WILL state this; I do hope that is *not* the case."

"Why? Why do you care if I return to Marcus? I need to know. I don't understand anything at the moment, and I *really* don't understand why you want to help me; it just doesn't make sense to me, Z."

There's another long pause. Wow. Did Z just dramatically exhale? Did he learn that trick from me? Ha!

"Well, love... To be completely honest, I know my answer will probably terrify you, but I'll tell you anyway. Basically, I think very fondly of you, though admittedly I don't know you very well...*yet*. I feel a *connection* to you and I enjoy it. I can't explain it, and at this point in time I don't really care to try to explain or analyze too closely why that is, but I cannot help but think of you as *mine*- mine to care for, and mine to help." Long exhale. *What?!* Why does that seem kind of dangerous, and nice... and *sexy?*

"What the hell does *that* mean? I'm nobody's. No one wants me to be theirs, and you shouldn't either." God, he really IS insane. *I knew it!*

"I told you, Sweetheart... I can't really explain it and at this point in time I don't want to. You will just have to accept it. I'm here, I'm going nowhere, and I plan to help you, because I need to... because I *want* to."

After his statement, I can't think of anything to say. This is so strange to me. No one needs me. I am empty and alone. No one thinks I'm worth knowing, or helping, or caring for, if they even think of me at all.

I don't know what to say to any of this. I know I should be grateful. I know I should be happy, but I just feel, well, *numb* actually. And more silence...

"When did you last have an orgasm, Sweetheart?" Wow! Topic change. *Christ!* My head is spinning.
"*Pardon?!*"
"You heard me. When did you last have an orgasm?"
"Um...a while ago." Jeez, my red face must be burning through the phone.
"With your husband? By yourself? With a toy? Or the shower-head...? I believe you mentioned."
"Um, the shower head." Ugh. This is SO embarrassing.
"When was the last time you gave yourself an orgasm without the shower-head?"
"Never. I can't. It doesn't work." I don't work, *down there.*
"Can you say the words, 'pussy', 'cock', or even 'orgasm'?" No. *No I can't.*
"I don't want to. They're gross words. They're very *ugly* to me."
"So 'vagina' and 'penis' are okay?" *Flinch.*
"No. Not really. I don't like those words either. *Why?* Ah, this is really..."
"Okay. How do you ask for your pleasure?"
"Um, I-*I don't.* I don't talk about this stuff."
"Okay. I want you to think of your vagina, as your 'pussy' from now on. Pussy sounds much less clinical, and much more sexy, don't you think? Tonight, after we hang up, I would like you to touch your *pussy.*" *Flinch*
"Can you do that for me? You don't have to get-off, just touch yourself while thinking *'I'm touching my pussy'.* Can you do that? It's simple enough, just a little touch on, or even *in* your pussy. If you do get-off, great. If not, don't focus or obsess about it. An orgasm isn't the point of the exercise. I just want you to think about your pussy tonight. Okay?" *HOLY SHIT!* I can't! I just... **CAN'T!**
"Ah, o-*kay.* But why?" Did I just agree to this? *What the hell?*
"I'll explain tomorrow. Tonight, just think about your pussy. I know *I'll* be thinking about it..." *Oh. My. GOD!* Did he just *say* that?! "... And yes. I just said that. Sleep well, love. I'll call you in the morning."

==========

HOLY SHIT! Did that just happen? This is insanity. This is crazy! An *EXERCISE?* My god, he is the strangest, most dominant man I've ever met.
Why does he talk to me like that? No one talks to me like that. I'm 'virgin-sacrifice girl', not 'dirty-girl'. No one says bad words like that to me. Touch myself while thinking of it as a *p-pussy?* That's just so gross. It's a gross word. I can't think it. I can't say it. I'm *not* that girl. I don't ever think about my body *down there* at all, if I can help it.

God, I remember when I met the shower-head by accident after a
particularly aggressive thrusting from Marcus a few years ago... Oh *god,*
it hurt. I remember I asked him to slow down. I remember lying there
tense, gritting my teeth. I actually started counting in my head during
the sex. I counted seconds until I hit five minutes, hoping it was almost
over. It figured, *that* night Marcus went for almost 10 full minutes. It
was brutal. When he was finally done, he kissed my forehead and said,
'That was awesome, honey'. Uh huh. *Right.* But like an idiot, I just smiled
at him.

I remember the shock of the pain when I stood up to use the bathroom.
It was excruciating- much worse than usual. Stumbling to the bathroom, I
dropped the sheet to get in the shower, and there was blood on the
sheet. I was shocked. Blood... *again?* What was I? A *VIRGIN?* I
remember laughing at the absurdity of bleeding again, and realizing I
definitely needed lubricant in the bedroom from that night on.

In the shower, I remember I turned the shower-head to the light pulsing
mist to clean away Marcus from my body. It hurt like hell, but there was
another feeling as well. I remember pausing and just holding my breath.

Strangely, the small pulsing of the water felt *good.* Eventually, I sat
on the edge of the shower and just let the streaming pulse stay right
where it was on me, *down there.*

I remember, it felt good, if not a little intense. But I waited. I remember
holding my breath, and forcing myself to stay right where I was. Even
when my legs started shaking, and my hips began moving on their own, I
waited... And then there was another little feeling. It was like when I'm
about the sneeze... a kind of *hiccupped* breath, and then a little exhale
from inside my body down there. It was nice, and slightly exciting. My
body even relaxed a little afterward.

So... my *pussy.* Yuck. But at least I'm not stuttering the word anymore.
Why is it called that anyway? I know many people say it. I've heard both
men AND women say it. It just sounds so derogatory. Then again,
vagina sounds clinical and foreign. I'm not really comfortable thinking
about my body like this at all, no matter what I call the parts.

Well, *that* little exercise was useless. I'm tired. It's after 2:00am. I
should be thinking about important things, like Marcus and my parents,
and what exactly they're going to do to me- NOT about my ... *whatever.*
I'm not doing it, so I don't have to say it. Suppressing a little laugh, I'm
done. I need sleep. I am so tired...

Sunday, May, 29th

CHAPTER 9

Waking to the bright sun, my face feels almost sunburned. It's only 8:23, but I feel fairly rested. Maybe, I'll go buy a proper breakfast in the hotel. I wonder if they'll take cash in the dining-room, or if they only accept credit cards again?

Hopping in the shower, which does NOT have a shower head, I try to think about my body again, *down there*. Z wanted me to think about, touch myself, and to get familiar with the word. But I'm not in the mood. I don't think I've ever *been* 'in the mood'. I don't even know what *that* particular mood feels like. I never touch myself, it just seems silly somehow, or dirty, but not in a good way. Not in a Kayla, *dirty-girl* kind of way. Ugh! Screw her! I'm not thinking about *HER* anymore.

I love reading my horrifically graphic, raunchy novels, but even then, when the women touch themselves, I read about it with a kind of detachment. I don't get it. Touching myself does nothing for me. I've inserted a tampon and felt more inside, then when I have purposely decided to touch myself during the *what?* Two or three occasions... *ever*. Nope. I'm not doing it. What can Z really do anyway? It's not like he can force my hands down there. He'll just have to get over it.

Shaving my legs and armpits feels good. It's been a few days, oh actually, it's been since Thursday night for my legs, but Friday morning for my armpits. Gross. No wonder my underarms felt all stubbly. Thank god, I threw pretty much everything I own in way of toiletries into my luggage.

Grabbing a bottle of my vanilla-jasmine scented body scrub, I vigorously scrub my arms, thighs, chest and feet. My feet have a tendency to get all dry and scaly, probably from all the heels I torture my feet with. There, all done. My body feels smooth again. No little bumps or nasty dry skin, only scented smoothness.

Out of the shower, I moisturize my whole body with my favorite vanilla-jasmine scented lotion. It's kind of thick, so it always seems to really get into my skin, and it holds the moisture for a while. I love the feeling of touching my legs hours after shaving and moisturizing, and they still feel heavily moisturized and soft.

Drying my hair takes forever. My hair is down now to my lower back, but it's lovely, well kept, and perfectly straight. I love my long hair, but no one really sees it down but me... and Marcus, I guess. I always wear it up at work. I don't want to look like a bimbo or too young and stupid, or unprofessional by having it hang down my back. I've always wanted to be taken seriously and professionally at work, and that would have been a little difficult if I was walking around with a ponytail bouncing around my head in the office.

God, my mother has always *HATED* my long hair. She insisted until I was married that I must keep it short, in a 'sharp' style, 'that reflected my

breeding'. After the first year of marriage, she finally gave up making little comments about 'letting myself go', or 'ruining my appearance' with 'such *dreadful* hair'.

Marcus would laugh along with my mother, and tease me about my growing hair. He would joke with her, saying, eventually I would stop being so stubborn and immature. My mother would always smile at Marcus and say, "I hope you're right, dear." And I would just sit there, *IN THE ROOM,* while they bantered back and forth, talking about me while ignoring me completely.

Applying my make-up is easy. I only have two things to work on; my lips and eyes. I wear no other face make-up, concealers, or blushers. Easily, I apply a pale pink lipstick which brings out my pouty full lips shape and size. And second, the only *real* effort I ever put into my make-up is on my eyes. I apply long sweeps of dark blue shadow in the crease, light brown shadow on the lids, and a silver shimmer along my lashes. Finishing with dark mascara, my eyes look so large and blue, it's quite lovely... maybe even *alluring.* I love my eyes. My eyes scream 'look at me' without being the kind of girl who screams, *LOOK AT ME!!*

Dressing is easy this morning. I put on a black cami with a pushup shelf, no bra required and a black blouse over the cami for modesty. And rounding out the look is a simple black skirt. There, I'm done.

See, an entirely monochromatic wardrobe is easy. No matching colors. No question of shoes. No question of jewelry matching. A couple simple pieces of jewelry, and a pair of black heels, Jimmy Choo's this morning, and I look totally complete and 'polished', as my mother would say.

===========

Heading for the dining-room, I feel okay. I don't look crazy or stressed out. I don't have raccoon eyes and I'm breathing fine. I hope they accept cash. I'll ask... Yes! They do. After perusing the extensive breakfast menu, I order a cheese omelet with bacon on the side; and I decide to call Z while I wait for my food to arrive.

"Good morning, Sweetheart. Did you rest well?" His voice is so lovely. I smile.

"Yes, I did. Thank you. And you?"

"I slept quite well, however, I did have some things on my mind that were both intriguing and erotic at once." *Really?*

"Oh, I see." This is kind of sexy.

"Yes. I had quite a few intensely erotic dreams as well. I woke up almost panting... Would you like to hear about them?" *ABSOLUTELY!*

"Um, no. I'm in the hotel dining-room, waiting for my breakfast to arrive. It seems a little inappropriate to hear about... such things."

"Why? The other diners will never know, unless of course, you put me on speaker phone." Suddenly laughing, I'm a little less stressed out by this conversation. "Shall I tell you about the absolutely delightful, yet shockingly sinful little strawberry-blonde I dreamed about...?" God, yes! *Sinful? Me?*

"Um, I think I'll have to pass. I don't want every diner here to see just how red and embarrassed *this* particular strawberry-blonde can get."
Tell me anyway! *Please!*

"Why do you insist on being so reserved, love? I know you want me to tell you about my dreams. I can hear it in your voice. Ask me to tell you. Ask me, and I'll tell you all about the delicious things I did with the stunning strawberry-blonde of my dreams." Again, I can hear the smile in his voice.

"I don't want to know such things. You have me mistaken for some other girl." *Liar!*

"Hmmm, I thought I told you about my dislike of lying. Do I need to teach you a lesson?" *A lesson?* What they hell does *that* mean?

"Um, no... No lesson required. I'm not lying. I really don't want you to tell me about your dreams..." I whisper. God, I hope no one can hear me.

"Sweetheart, since you insist on lying to both of us, I'm going to have to show you my dreams." Show me? Yes! SHOW ME?! *WHAT?!* No!

"And how are you going to do that?"

"At my hotel, of course."

"Ah, I don't think so. I'm not coming to your hotel."

"Yours, then?"

"NO!!" *Shit!* The table beside me is looking at me. Please, don't get crazy. *Please...*

"Okay. You won't come to me, and you won't let me come to you. Why don't we choose neutral territory?" No. Way.

"Um, Z? That's not a good idea. I'm sure I'm not the kind of woman who you usually... um... *have.*"

"My usual kind of woman? Yes, I believe you're right. However, my *usual* kind of woman doesn't intrigue me half as much as you do. Therefore, I would like to find out why it is I'm absolutely captivated by you." *Captivated?* Holy shit!

"Look, Z. My breakfast has arrived, and I need to eat and calm down a little. I don't know how to handle someone like you."

"Handle someone like me? Who would that be? A man who desires you?"

"Yes! That's exactly who. I don't even really believe you. I still think you're playing a game with me, okay?! Just stop doing this."

"I don't think so. I'm not going to stop, and you ARE going to trust me."

"That's highly doubtful. I don't trust anyone, *ever.* Do you remember what's happened to me in the last few days, Z? My *husband?* My *friend?* I tried to trust them, and look what they did."

"I am neither of those people, and I have never lied to you, or betrayed you. I will not betray you, love. You need to trust me."

"Well, I DON'T. Please, just leave me alone. Please, Z. I don't want to do this anymore. It will never work between us. *I* don't work, okay?!"

"Oh, we'll work. I know we will. I'm going to make you stop all this reserve, and I'm going to help you *feel.* You may not know what I can do to make you feel, but *I* know what I can do. Trust me."

"Z, I'm not able to do what I *think* you're asking me to do, okay?"

"No. It is NOT okay. Pick a place to meet." *What?*

"I'm sorry...?"

"Pick a place to meet. Now. Pick another hotel, or a cheap motel, or a public park, if you're into that sort of exhibitionism. I don't really care where you choose. But, Pick. A. Place. Now!" I don't know. Where? Think. *Ugh,* I CAN'T!

"Umm..."

"Now! Sweetheart. Pick a location."

"Um, there is a cheap motel, just outside Evanston on I-92..." I sneer at him.

"Name?"

"'Good Times Motel', I think. I used to laugh at it, when I drove past to visit my parents." I'm rambling now. Good times? *Good times?* Not for me!

"It's now 10:40. I'll meet you there at 12:30 this afternoon. Do not disappoint me, Sweetheart. I know we can have something *special* between us. I expect you to be there at 12:30 sharp. Are we clear?"

"You sound like a real jerk right now, you know?! What happened to you not *allowing* anyone to bully me anymore? YOU'RE bullying me!" I yell, to my embarrassment. *Shit.* Everyone can hear me. I should leave the dining-room.

"12:30 sharp. Oh, and did you think about your pussy last night, while touching yourself?" Gulp. *Oh. My. God.* Silence... "Did you?" Don't answer him! Don't tell him the truth!

"Um, I thought about it, *a little...* But I, ah, didn't *touch* myself..." I whisper again.

"Well, that's a little disappointing, but no worries, I plan to show you what a man can and *should* do with a stunning woman such as yourself. I'll see you at 12:30, love."

===========

*OH MY **GOD!!*** What have I done? I can't meet him at a motel. I just can't. I'm not like that! I've never even been in a motel before... *in my life!* Holy *SHIT!* In less than 2 hours, I'm supposed to meet Z, a stranger, in a cheap motel?

Rising, I leave the table quickly. I had one bite of the omelet, one piece of bacon, and that's it. I don't think I even had a sip of coffee. What do I do now? What do I DO...? Pay for breakfast first. Panic, second.

After a painful conversation with my waiter, I'm free. 'No, there was nothing wrong with my breakfast. No, I would not like anything else, as a substitute. No, you do not have to comp the meal.' CHRIST! He really was annoyingly polite. Leave me *ALONE!* $11.00 later, plus tip, I'm finally free and back in my room. What do I do now? *Run?* Yes. I'll run from Marcus, and my parents, and now from Z. This is too much. My head is spinning. I'm about to panic again. Breathe. Come on, breathe deep.

"Breathe, love. Listen to my voice. I am pushing my breath into your lungs... Can you feel me in your body?"

93

NO! I don't want to feel him *IN MY BODY!!* Sit down! And just breathe for *Christ's Sake!*

===========

Slowly, I return to my senses. Looking at the clock, its 12:02. Shit. How long was I just sitting there *breathing?* What do I do? Just do it! Meet him. I can always leave... *Can't I?*

What if he hurts me, or forces me to stay against my will? What if he is huge, and mean-looking? What will I do? *Shit!* I hate being this scared. I hate feeling like this. Why am I so insecure and frightened all the time? That's it! I'm always afraid. Why is that? Why am I *ALWAYS frightened...?*

Walk to your car. Now. Just do it. Maybe Z won't be big. Maybe he won't be mean-looking. Maybe he won't force you to stay against your will. Maybe he won't hurt you. Just do it. Now. *Okay.* SHIT!

CHAPTER 10

What am I doing here? I wanted this. I wanted a… a *what?* What is, Z? I have to get out of the car but I'm too frightened and paranoid, and even slightly aroused actually, but my fear is strongest and too overwhelming. I just can't relax, or even exhale, or even *move.*

What if Z is disappointed in me, *physically?* I'm still dressed as before; in my black cami and blouse, black knee-high skirt and black heels. I pulled my hair down and my make-up is light. But I find my demeanor is almost hard or something, from the fear.

Meeting Z for the first time in person, in this cheesy motel, feels so *cheap* to me. I know he and I have spoke and emailed frequently, but I don't *know* him. I really don't know what he's *actually* like. He always sounds so strong and secure, and like forceful and dominant or something.

What the hell am I doing here?! Oh, god… *HELP ME!*

==========

Knocking on the door, Z's already inside, and I'm 20 minutes late. Opening the door to me, Z steps aside smiling, as I walk into the room. I think he knows I'm uncomfortable and frightened. I think he knows I can't breathe. Closing the door, he turns back to me and smiles once more. I still haven't exhaled. I'm shaking and wretchedly embarrassed. I hate this and I think he knows it.

Dammit, he's beautiful. He's tall, and fit, and darkly tanned, and strong looking. He is ideal. He has that 'tall, dark, and handsome' female fantasy-thing going for him. Women must *love* him. God, how disappointed is he in *my* looks? This is awful.

"You look beautiful, Sweetheart. You're much more attractive in person than by photo."

"Thank you," I whisper. Can I even inhale fully?

Walking a step toward me, Z slowly bends and removes my heels. Without my heels, I drop to my pitiful 5'3, and he suddenly has such a height advantage over me that I can't help but retreat a step. I hate this feeling. I hate feeling overwhelmed and over-*heighted.*

Bending to me, Z kisses me softly, and so gently. He kisses me, opening my mouth with his tongue as he slowly dips into my mouth. He doesn't thrust into me awkwardly, but rather impales me slowly with his tongue. Kissing my lips, he gently bites and tugs on my lower lip. He pulls away and looks at me again and suddenly I exhale for the first time.

Wrapping his fist in my hair, he pulls me back to his mouth as I brace myself to be taken hard. But again, he licks, kisses and bites my mouth in slow dragging pulls, and finally I feel something; other than bone-numbing fear. He keeps watching me… and I think he knows I'm relaxing slightly.

Taking my hand, Z walks us to the bed and leads me to sit on the edge. Instantly, the fear returns. I feel cold, and I'm completely stressed out. My body is tasking itself. Oh, god! I HATE this! Here comes the thrusting...

Z kneels on the floor in front of me, looks at my face, smiles, and says, "Breathe. I want you to breathe with me. Look at me, Sweetheart. Look! Just breathe." And slowly staring at his handsome face, I breathe slowly for him.

Placing his hands on my thighs, I flinch. But Z just moves his hands back and forth slowly, calmly. He stays away from touching me *there* and I breathe slower once again. Z watches my reaction, smiles and nods when I'm steady.

Lifting his hands to the buttons on my blouse, again I flinch, but this time my hands clamp around his wrists. Stopping, Z smiles, "You're beautiful, love. I love your body. I love your breasts and hips, and your delicious ass. I love a woman who is curvy. I want YOUR curvy body. I want *you*."

Not convinced, like most women, I find fault all over my body, and I can barely breathe again. Angry with all my drama and insecurity, I give up. Dropping my hands, exhaling hard, I turn my head and mumble, "Fine. Just do it." But Z doesn't move. *Christ!* I am SUCH a loser.

After forever, I can't stand the stillness and silence and turn to look at him. Grasping my hair tightly, Z finally kisses me hard. Eating at my mouth, I'm overwhelmed and frightened, but suddenly kind of aroused too. Z takes my hand and places it on his erection. Jolted, I try to pull away, but he keeps our mouths together and my hand in place against him.

Eventually, Z releases my hair and mouth and once again begins undoing my blouse buttons. Sliding my blouse off my shoulders, he looks at my tight black cami. Knowing my breasts are pushed up and open for him, he kisses the top of my breasts and slides his tongue in my cleavage. I can't feel this. I'm numb. But he stops again.

Looking at me, he smiles and says, "We'll keep this on then?" I exhale hard. I just can't be completely uncovered, and somehow he knew it.

Suddenly, Z tugs at the bodice of my cami, and my breasts push up and out. Taking a nipple into his mouth, his hand holds my other nipple. Sucking and nipping one, tugging and pinching the other, he works me. I stop breathing. I'm stuck. My hands grip the comforter, but there is nothing, I *feel* nothing, and I think he knows it. *How humiliating.*

Inching his hands down my sides, Z slowly lifts my skirt. I can't even move. There is only my silence and my stillness suffocating in the room. Raising my skirt to my hips, Z takes an appreciative look at my black lace panties and rises on his knees again to give me another slow, seductive kiss.

Wow. I *feel* this kiss. Finally my hands move. Releasing the comforter, my arms circle his neck, pulling him toward me as I kiss him. I WANT to kiss him. I kiss him hard; *my* kiss, NOT his.

Pulling away, Z shakes his head but smiles. "Not this time, love; this time *I* kiss you. *I'm* giving to you. But when you're ready I'll let you take what you want and need from me."

I am so stunned and embarrassed, and I feel so rejected, I try to pull away but his hands grab my wrists and pull them behind my back. He watches my face like he knows I'm about to retreat. Holding me in place, Z pushes himself fully between my legs and rubs himself against me. Creating friction with our clothing, I feel physically uncomfortable. My body isn't ready, and I'm dry and uneasy.

Z seems to feel my retreat. I'm here, but I'm far, far away from him. Moving slightly, I suddenly feel a sash around my wrists. Flinching, I try to pull my hands away while Z grins. I'm going to hit a full panic any second now.

"Please don't! I don't like this, Z. Please, *I'm scared...*" I whisper.

"Do you believe I'll hurt you? *Honestly?* Look at your fear. Are you frightened because I *could* hurt you, or because you think I *will* hurt you? Tell me, love. Are you only frightened because your physical control is gone?" Z asks and waits.

I can't face him. The shaking has increased and I'm so close to panic. I hate all this drama, and I think he knows it.

"Stop, Sweetheart. Breathe. Look at me. I will not hurt you. I *could* not hurt you. I want to give you pleasure *only*. Look at me!"

Turning my face toward him, I try to calm myself. God, he's so lovely. He has beautiful brown eyes, and a gentle smile, and he is not out of control. He is even and calm, and I see no malice or anger on his face.

I'm starting to feel embarrassed again. *Dammit.* I'm behaving like a frightened child. Embarrassed, I smile slightly and whisper, "I'm sorry." Z smiles back and nods. I think he knows I'm trying.

Sitting back on his heels, Z looks at my face while sliding his hands back up my thighs. His eyes on my eyes reassure me. Slipping his fingers under the lace, he touches me there and I know I'm dry. This is so embarrassing.

"Well, what should we do about this?" He questions with a grin. Slowly his hands move behind my butt as he eases the lace down. "Lift, love." And as I lift, Z pulls my panties from my body. And then, he's looking at me, *down there.* Shit. What does he see?

Turning away, I focus on the window covering. It's such an ugly curtain. It's so dark and old, but at least it keeps the room in near darkness. I'm slowly slinking away. I'm almost gone. I feel *nothing...* And suddenly my world ERUPTS! Z is pinching my nipples hard, staring directly at my eyes.

"Stay With ME. Stay right here. Don't look away. Look at me. Watch *me.*"

Once again, I can barely breathe. Trying to fight the near-panic, I breathe deep and stare back at his eyes as he watches me. Eventually he nods his head again... He seems to know when I'm back with him.

"You smell like vanilla, Sweetheart. I bet you taste like vanilla too. Shall I give you a little taste...?"

Knowing I'm blushing, I shake my head no and I'm punished with another little pinch, this time on my body *down there.* Shit! I jump on the bed as my legs start shaking.

Smiling, Z leans forward, still looking up at my eyes, while extending his tongue as he licks me slowly down *there.* I'm shocked, embarrassed, and strangely, *slightly* aroused. Rising quickly, Z gives me a kiss, as if in reassurance.

Stunned, I watch as Z dips back down between my thighs. Once there, Z pulls my body further off the edge of the bed and begins doing all kinds of things to my body at once.

I'm lost. I can actually *feel* something inside. There is a flutter. There is *something...* I FEEL this while Z continues to lick and suck at me. I can even hear it, and I feel embarrassed by the noise. Looking up, Z's eyes touch mine, and though I want to retreat, I hold his gaze. Nodding once more, Z continues.

Lifting my legs, my thighs are placed on his shoulders. Oh no! I want this to stop. I feel so alone. I can't place this feeling. I feel like I'm outside myself, though feeling everything he's doing to me at the same time. Z notices my emotional retreat.

"Look. At. Me." He demands loudly as I jump at the force of his words. "Watch *ME*," he says, as slowly he impales me with a finger.

Again, I jump on the mattress, but he's staring at me, so intensely, I can't look away.

"Watch my fingers. Watch me please you. Watch *me*, Sweetheart." And sliding his finger in and out of me, his thumb starts a heavy rotation on my clitoris. *THIS* I feel. *Oh, god...*

With his eyes on my face, and his fingers working me, and the sounds in the quiet room, and the scent of my arousal, the embarrassment is so strong; I'm shaking with the desire to escape. But I can *feel*. There is an internal tugging beginning. Two fingers are now working inside me, and as they turn and reach within me, I am jolted with sensation. *Oh god...*

Z's watching me so closely and my reactions are obvious. My legs are shaking. My stomach is starting to contract. My hips are bucking slightly against his hand. I feel a low-level hum beginning.

Suddenly, Z bends again and his mouth joins his fingers. His tongue is relentless. The humming is getting louder inside me, and my body is reacting to the hum. I want this suddenly. I want to be *this girl*. I WANT to feel this... *Or do I?*

Shit! My brain starts spinning. My head is pounding. All my thoughts and vulnerabilities surface. My panic starts. The coldness settles inside me, and I can't shut it off. No! Not now! *Please....* But everything starts receding anyway. *Dammit.*

Frantically looking at Z, he has raised his head, but his hand is still working me. I can't stand the look in his eyes. I'm so embarrassed. I want to just die here. I want to leave. I want to retreat. I want to thank him for trying but run away quickly.

In a moment of complete insanity, I know I have to finish this. I'm desperate. I need to be away from this.

Deciding my fate; I arch my hips, pant and moan loudly, and let out a back-breaking scream. And then the room is bathed in complete silence.

Opening my eyes a minute later, I look at Z and his face is hard. Shit. Shit. *SHIT!!*

Suddenly, he withdraws from me, and as I jump, he growls, "Is that your best, love? If you're going to *fake it*, please put forth a little more effort than *that*. My ego can only take so much..."

With no words, I'm watching in horror, as Z rises from his knees and turns from me for the bathroom. He's left me. I AM SUCH A LOSER!

Once alone, I feel like I'm dying. Pulling and tugging at my wrists, I finally get my hands free of the sash. Shaking, I stand fast, grab my blouse and throw my panties into my purse.   Quickly, I run for the door.

Jerking my blouse buttons closed, I'm just reaching the door when suddenly **STOP!** echoes through the room. Jumping, I turn to see Z leaning against the bathroom door.

"I'm sorry. I'm just going to go. Thank you..." Z stalks across the room and grabs my arms hard, while just glaring down at me.

The silence in the room is oppressive. I need to leave. I can't stay here anymore. This is done.

Watching my face, Z doesn't speak; he's just standing here silently in my face. Staring at me, I can't tell if I'm in trouble, or if he's just too disgusted with me to speak.

Through the weight of this oppressive silence, I finally just SNAP!

"*WHAT?!* Why are you just *STARING* at me?? I told you it wouldn't work!! I TOLD YOU!! But you were so sure we could have something *special*..." I sneer. "I want to leave, okay? Just let me go, Z. Please!"

I'm about to lose it. I know it, and he knows it. I don't do this. I don't lose it in public, at least I didn't before this week.

Shit! One more, "*please*..." I beg.

Total. Silence.

==========

"Are you through Sweetheart? Is there anything else you want to scream or would you like to talk to me about what happened, why you closed down?" He asks so seriously, I feel like a child being scolded. I hate this, and he knows it.

"No. I'm fine. Thank you, but I really would like to go now. I want to get out of here, okay?" But Z just stares at me.

Finally, he says, "No, it is NOT okay. But I'm going to give you what you *need*, not necessarily what you want. Do you understand me? Do you understand the difference?"

"No. I don't know what you mean..."

My breath is erratic. My chest is tight. My hands shake, and my head aches. I feel sick. I can't do this. I want to cry. I don't want to do this anymore, and I think he knows it.

Suddenly, grasping my chin with a rough hand and pushing his body against mine into the door, he growls in my face, "Cry, sweetheart. I want to see you cry. Let this out. Be. With. Me, and let me be here *with you*. Right now, *CRY.*"

Stunned, I try to pull away. I try to push his body away from my own. I try to rip my jaw free of his hold, but he won't let me. *What the hell?*

Panic starts to build. I feel it coming. I feel the fear I knew earlier. I knew this would happen. I knew he would hurt me.

"Let me go!" I scream in his face, as I push his body once again. Z pushes

against me even harder, so I'm trapped against the door. *Fuck!*

"No! Look at me. Look. At. Me..." he breathes in my face. "Do you think I'm going to hurt you now? Do you? *Answer me!*" He yells.

But there is nothing but silence. I can't even respond. There are no words. I have nothing. I knew this would be bad. I knew this wouldn't work. I knew *I* wouldn't work. *I knew it...*

Moving his fist to my hair, Z quickly kisses me; a hard, painful, bruising kiss. Again, I am stunned. Pushing his knees into my thighs, I am held hard against the door.

Moving his left hand, he pushes down my blouse, wrenching buttons open as he grabs my nipple. Screaming into his mouth, he pinches and plucks my nipple, rolling it in his fingers.

My hands push against him. I try to fight him, and I punch him in the chest, hard. Grunting; Z stops kissing me long enough to smile wickedly at me. ***Oh my god...***

So quickly I'm shocked, Z spins us further into the room and onto the bed. Pinning me beneath him, he straddles my hips as I continue to fight with my hands. Catching my wrists easily, Z grabs the sash he used earlier from the bed with his teeth and begins to tie my left wrist. Pulling me up by my hair, he forces the sash behind my back and begins to tie my other hand. My arms are trapped at my sides as he pushes me back to the bed.

Screaming loudly, I dig my heels into the mattress and try to buck him off me. Clamping his hand hard on my jaw once more, Z leans in and says calmly, "If you scream again, and it is *NOT* from pleasure, I will gag you." Once again, I am just *shocked* into silence. "You need this. I want to be the man who provides this to you. You *need* this, love. You need... *ME.*"

I can only pant and stare at his eyes. What have I done? What will *he* do? *Oh god.*

A full panic-attack sets in. So hard and fast, I am desperate for air. I'm gasping and struggling. Nearly overcome with blindness, I'm suddenly lifted into his arms.

"Breathe with me. Come on. Listen to my breath. Come on, Sweetheart, just listen to my voice and breathe with me... " he murmurs as I fade away...

Slowly, the room comes back. Slowly, I match his breathing. Slowly, I breathe for him. Even as time passes, I don't move. I do nothing. I just want to lay here and die here... *alone.*

"You really have to stop doing that, Sweetheart. I don't like to see you so pale and shaken. I'll tell you again... I WILL NOT HURT YOU. Can you hear me? Do you understand me?" I nod slowly, but can't speak.

Z gently lays me back down on the bed. Adjusting my arms, so my hands remain tied and restrained by my sides, he lays down beside me. I'm still trapped, but with him beside me, not straddling me, I feel less fearful. I'm still horribly intimidated, but less frightened.

With the panic-attack over, I feel exhausted, and raw. Every sense is acute and on the surface. I'm struggling with my equilibrium. I'm struggling with my control. I'm struggling to maintain my life. *I'm struggling...*

"Cry, sweetheart…" Z whispers, tracing my features with gentle fingertips.

I am so lost, I feel like I'm losing my mind. This wasn't supposed to be like this. We barely know each other, but we're friends, *kind of*. Z has kept in touch with me this week. He has kept me somewhat grounded. We built up to this moment. This should have been easy, after all the teasing, and all the honesty. Z should have had a good time without all this heaviness.

"I don't want to cry…" I whisper.

"I know, but as I told you before… I'm going to give you what you *need*, not always what you want. Cry, sweetheart. Wipe this all away…" he whispers in return.

With my control gone, I just… *snap.*

I've lost it. I've lost everything. I don't even feel me. I can't feel. I am *lost.*

Sudden, great, wretched sobs rack my body as my stomach turns. Fighting nausea, fighting this crippling weight, I lurch to my side as Z tucks me into his chest. Rubbing my back, while murmuring soothing words into my ear, I sob.

There is no consciousness. There is no pleasure. There is only unbearable *pain.*

Sobbing… minutes pass, hours, days and months. My sobbing slows and I finally breathe. There is nothing left. There is just *nothing…*

===========

Becoming aware, I feel only confusion. Jumping, I try to sit up, but Z still holds me tightly in his arms, while he gently wipes my face with a tissue.

With a grin, he whispers, "Welcome back. How do you feel, love?"

But I can't seem to find my voice. Maybe it's gone. Maybe I *HAVE* lost my mind. Maybe, *I'M* gone.

"No, love. No more thinking today- just feeling. That's all you have to do. That's all I want for you. *Feel* Sweetheart, nothing more. Can you do that?" But before I can answer, Z takes my lips once again, but this kiss is different. This kiss crosses between urgency and sweetness. This kiss consumes me.

My arms start to pull at the restraint. I want to feel him. I want to hold him closer. I *need* to touch him.

"*Please…*" I beg while pulling at my arms trapped by my side, but he shakes his head no with another grin.

Leaning in to kiss me once more, Z fully unbuttons my blouse and pushes it wide again. Kissing my lips, his hands tuck back under my tight cami and lift my breasts up and out. Moving slowly, his hands trail down my stomach, further, further, until he reaches the hem of my skirt. Lifting it slowly, I can feel my nakedness.

Pulling away, Z watches my eyes as he works his mouth down to my

breasts. Latching onto a nipple, I jump, and my body arches closer to him.

Z continues to watch me, as his hand slides through the folds of my vagina. Gently, he touches me. Gently, he suckles me. And I hear, to my shock, a moan escape my lips. Z's eyes crinkle as he watches me.

Again, I moan. *WOW!* I *FEEL* this. I can feel his touch. I *WANT* to feel his touch. What do I do now?

"Don't think," he states. And closing my eyes, I try to feel... "Do you trust me, Sweetheart?" I hear him, but I can't answer. Oh god, I don't want to ruin this feeling with honesty. I can't answer him. "Okay. Do you trust me not to hurt you?"

"Physically?" I ask, as he laughs.

"Always the pessimist... yes, *physically*. Do you trust me with your body? Do you trust me with your pleasure?"

I can only answer, "I, I *think* so."

Z chuckles at my reply, but it's like a switch has been thrown. Z slides down the bed between my thighs once again. *Oh, god...* I want to panic. I want to kick him away. I want to stop, but I tighten my stomach muscles, and say nothing.

Shaking his head, Z murmurs, "Nice try, love. Lie still and try to relax. I know what *I'm* doing, even if you don't." *What?!* What an Asshole, and as if he read my mind, Z laughs and bites my upper thigh lightly in punishment. And then, I'm done.

Stroking my vagina with his tongue, I am engulfed in the pleasure. *This is amazing.* His tongue is incredible. His fingers enter me slowly and I actually begin to writhe on the bed trying to get closer. I can't believe what's happening to me. A moan escapes my mouth. Panting, I'm overcome with the pleasure fluttering inside me. I want him deeper. I want more. *I want...*

As time fades, the tension inside me is building and my muscles are straining. As Z moves my legs up and out, I know I should be so embarrassed, but I can't feel embarrassment right now, I just feel him, all of him. I feel his tongue and his fingers. I feel his breath on me. When he blows on my clitoris my body jumps at the sensation. He impales me quickly with two fingers and my back arches. He licks me all over, and a moan bursts from me. *Oh. My. GOD!*

Suddenly, I feel it. I know this feeling. I've had it with the shower-head before. But not like this; this is different. I've had this feeling... *kind of.* I know this tightening inside. I know this heart pounding. I know this need clawing in me as Z increases the pressure with his tongue.

"Ahhhh... *Z?* Ummm... What do I do?"

There is urgency now. My body feels suspended and chaotic. *"Z?"* Ignoring me, he just seems to work me harder. My body is tighter, and everything hurts with the building tension inside.

"Z...? Please, help me. *Ummm, help...*" I moan and close my eyes again. I feel it all. This is brutal. This is awful. This is pain and tension. This twisting of my insides is agony...

Suddenly, Z whispers, "Let go, love..." *and I do.*

Climaxing; everything explodes forth from me with a scream. My body arches and my legs coil up on themselves. My heart is racing. My hands

are strained and grasping the bed. My neck is corded and tight. My mind goes from madness to calm.

There is nothing here. There is nothing left. I am nothing. Floating away...

I am gone.

==========

Waking in Z's arms, I realize I'm not alone and I feel an unexpected *happiness.* Z is kissing my brow, and my hands are against his chest. When were the restraints removed? How long have I been unaware?

"How are you feeling?" He asks with a grin. But I can't even answer, I'm still too mindless and limp, as I just stare at him in a trance.

Time continues to pass. I don't know what to do now. What do I say to him? Do I thank him? What's next? Shit. I don't know what to do.

"Always thinking... *relax,* Sweetheart. We don't need to talk about this right now. We have time. We have forever to work you out." With another grin, he rubs his cheek against my hair, and exhales.

"Um... What about you? Ah, do you want to have sex now? It's fine. We can if you want to..." God, I'm going to die of embarrassment again.

Z leans over my body and looks into my eyes. "No. I'm in no need right now. There is always next time, and hopefully you'll be able to relax easier next time we're together." *NO?!* "Oh, look at your face... always so sensitive and insecure. Of course, I *want* you- very badly in fact. But I would rather have you when you *want* to have me, not when you feel *obligated* to have me." Smiling, Z bends and kisses me so tenderly, I feel confused and relieved. I feel suspended between what I have known, and what I now know.

"I should go then," I whisper, trying to look away from his intense stare.

Holding me in place, he whispers in return, "This isn't done, Sweetheart. I'm going to teach you and you'll learn many pleasures. I will guide you, because you are mine to teach."

"No, Z. I am *mine.* But I WILL try to see you again, and I WILL try to relax if we see each other again."

"We'll see each other again, Sweetheart... *soon.* Trust me."

Rising from the bed, I close my blouse and straighten my skirt. My panties are still in my purse and I'm glad I don't have to suffer the embarrassment of looking for them.

Walking to the door, I turn to Z as he gracefully lifts from the bed. Stalking toward me, Z smiles, and suddenly drops to the floor to replace my heels.

"I think you were running away without these babies last time," he says with a smirk.

Standing, Z takes my face in his hands and kisses me so gently, my *heart* feels it. I don't know what I feel, but sadness is buried deep in this moment. I like this feeling; it's kind of hopeful... or something *close* to hopeful, anyway.

Pulling away from the kiss, Z smiles at me once again. "Drive safe, love. I *will* see you soon, and I will call you sooner... because you are *mine,* whether you believe it or not."

And before I can argue his statement, he quickly opens and pushes me out the door, laughing.

CHAPTER 11

OH MY GOD! What just happened?! Whatever it was, it was AWESOME! Well, the second part was awesome, the first part was... *intense.* But that was the best *non-sex* sex I've ever experienced. Running for my car, I jump in giggling. That was *AMAZING!!*

Almost back at the hotel, I realize I'm still driving with a ridiculous grin on my face. *Jeez...* other drivers seeing me must think I'm crazy. I don't care! That was great, and Z was amazing. I should call him. So dialing and smiling, I wait out the second ring.

"Hello, Sweetheart. How are you since I last saw you 15 minutes ago?" I can hear his smile-voice and I *love* it.

"I'm good. I, ah, just wanted to say thank you. I had a *really* nice time with you this afternoon." Oh! What if he didn't? Damn, my mood plummets. "Um, I don't expect anything, I just wanted to say thank you..." I'm so pathetic.

"Sweetheart, relax. I, too, had a very good time once you relaxed a little. See? Isn't *relaxation* good for you?" Yes!

"Ah, yes. I'm glad I *relaxed* too."

"I'm glad you had an orgasm as well, though it did take a little coercion from me. Did you enjoy yourself?"

"Um... yes." I'm blushing scarlet.

"Did you enjoy meeting with me? I'm sure you're not used to the kind of sexuality I possess."

"Um... yes." Do I have any other words? "Should I call you later, or something, or just... um, never mind. I should go..." Christ! I'm such a pathetic loser!!

"Stop thinking, love. This is the awkward part, always. Everyone struggles with the 'what ifs' and the 'what now's'. I'm not going anywhere, even when I return to New York. So breathe, Sweetheart. We'll work this out. I'm going to pick you up in a few hours for dinner. Say 5:00?" Yes!

"Okay." Breathe. He's not going anywhere yet.

"One more thing, Sweetheart..." Here we go. What? What's wrong with me? "... I *WAS* right. Your eyes are absolutely beautiful when bright with pleasure, pupils dilated and lashes lowered. While glazed over with orgasm, your eyes are simply stunning." *They are?* YES!

"Oh, ah...thank you..." What do I say to that?

"I'll pick you up at your hotel at 5:00. So, you have 2 hours to stress yourself out, over-thinking, and over-analyzing, while dying of embarrassment. *Okay?*"

Laughing, I mutter, "Yeah, okay. I'm sure I *will* be. I'll see you at 5:00."

==========

Arriving at my hotel, I expect to see Marcus and my parents waiting for me in the hotel lobby. Have they somehow found me? Nope. I'm alone, but I won't be in 2 hours. *Yes!* But as I make my way to my room, I'm nervous again. Could they have talked the staff into opening the doors for them? Likely not, but still, maybe? No. The room is booked by a Mr. Zinfandel. Let's hope... Ha! I'm alone. No Marcus. No mother and father. No one. Just me, alone, waiting just under 2 hours for Z.

I wonder where we're going? What should I wear? Should I dress up? Probably. Z doesn't strike me as the McDonalds type. What will I wear? My black, of course, but *what* should I wear? Black slacks and blouse? A black skirt and blouse? A black dress? Yes. I'll wear my beautiful knee high black backless cocktail dress. This is so exciting!

I want to hop in the shower again to clean my body... *for Z?* I don't know. This is so strange. I have never felt this excited, even when Marcus and I began dating. Maybe because Marcus didn't 'woo' me, or even date me really. He knew my father, was introduced to me, and we began seeing each other mostly in the presence of my parents at all their friend's parties, banquets, the Country Club, and at various fund raisers.

When my phone rings I look nervously, but am thrilled to see its Z.
"Hello?"
"Hi, Sweetheart. I have a question, and I would like a thorough and honest answer." Oh, shit. I *hate* Z's questions.
"Okay..." Here we go.
"How did Marcus propose marriage to you?" Jesus *Christ!* How did he know I was just thinking about this?
"Um, honestly?"
"Yes. All of it. The truth please." Why does he always say that? I don't lie, *not really.*
"Well, Marcus didn't really propose to me. Isn't that strange? One day over brunch in January at my parent's home, my mother began asking Marcus how many people he needed to invite to the wedding. Marcus pondered the question, while I looked back and forth at them confused because I didn't know whose wedding they were talking about. Was Marcus getting married? I remember thinking I should be sad over this, shouldn't I?" I exhale into the phone.
"Continue, please."
"Ah, then my mother announced that her *tentative* list held 525 people. Marcus looked at my father, not at me, and the two of them dramatically rolled their eyes, with my father saying to him, 'Welcome to the family son, be prepared for *THIS* tornado' as he smiled at my mother tenderly. Tsking, my mother threw her table linen at him, and all three burst out laughing." Oh, good times... *As if!* "At that point, I realized they were talking about *my* wedding."
Quietly, Z asks, "And how did that make you feel?"
"Um, I remember the feeling I had of complete and total detachment. I was looking at the three of them wondering, '*am I even in the room? Do any of you even see me?*' Marcus then leaned over to me, *finally*, but

instead of proposing, he asked, 'I have at least 100 people, what about you, honey?' and I just sat there staring at him. My mother piped up, 'Oh, her people *are* my people, so our number stands around 525'. And that was it. Nothing more was said to me... Oh, that's not true. Marcus and my mother did ask if the 12th of May 'worked for me?' I think I just nodded. I don't really remember speaking."

God, that sounds terrible to me. I really *am* nameless and faceless to my parents and Marcus.

"Please don't retreat, Sweetheart... though I can imagine it's difficult at the moment. I don't want you saddened. I was asking because I'm trying to set up my own loop-holes should you choose to end your marriage, which again I'll confess... I *sincerely* hope you do."

"Oh, I'm not sure what I'm doing anymore..." I whisper.

"Please, Sweetheart. I would like you to forget these questions, if you can, just for tonight. I'm picking you up in a little over an hour, and I can't stand to hear the sadness in your voice."

"I'm fine, Marcus. Don't worry about me."

"You are NOT fine, love. And I am *NOT* Marcus." Oh. *What?*

"I'm sorry? What did you say?" Shit. I feel so confused now.

"I'm on my way over now. I'll be there in twenty minutes, okay?"

"Okay... WAIT! No! I'm fine. *Really*, I'm okay. I'll see you at 5:00, okay?"

"Are you sure? I don't like hearing you this way. You sound... *lost*."

"I'll see you at 5:00, Z. No sooner, okay?" There that sounded less *'lost'*.

"Okay. 5:00 it is. Please relax, Sweetheart. I'll see you soon."

==========

I should move. I *know* I should move, but it's too hard. This bed is very comfortable and warm... but after forever, I finally rise and head for the shower. In the bathroom, I disrobe and look in the mirror. There I am... *naked.* Ick.

If I *could* be objective *which I can't*, I would admit that I'm probably not as bad as I think I am. From my neck up, I'm reasonably attractive. My hair is pretty, my lips are full and pouty, and my eyes are beautiful. But from the neck down, I'm... *what?* Voluptuous? Curvy? *Shapely?* How about, I'm *not skinny,* and I'm short.

My breasts are average, if not a little big. My stomach is flat-ish, but not at all toned. My waist is average, but my hips are too big for my height. And my butt really is too big for my body. It's... *what?* A *booty?* A *J-Lo?* Ha! I wish. No, my butt is just big, jiggly and seriously *un*toned. THIS leads to my thighs, which are pretty much the same as my butt. Marcus was right; I do have a big butt and thighs. At least my calves are good though. Strangely, they look muscular and toned. Thank you, high heels! So, when I wear a black knee high skirt with my calves showing, it's actually kind of deceiving for the rest of my legs.

Ugh. I HATE being naked.

I hear my phone ringing in the bedroom. Nope, I'm not answering. If it's Z, he'll understand. And if it's Marcus or my parents, they can piss off! I'm tired of them.

Once in the shower, with my hair piled high on my head, I quickly scrape a razor over my still smooth legs and armpits. Coating my body in my vanilla-jasmine body wash, I relax a little more. I love this scent. It's kind of flirty vanilla, and sensual jasmine. I always feel better after I apply the body wash and then follow it with the moisturizing lotion. Why am I obsessing about a vanilla-jasmine scent? There are many more important things to obsess over- like Marcus, or my parents... *or Z.*

Z is going to turn away from me soon, I know it. He is too intelligent a man, not to. What the hell would he be attracted to? I'm loopy this week. I'm going through... *what? A separation? A mental break? A fit of rebellion?* Panic-attacks and melo-drama do *NOT* make for an attractive woman.

Christ! Maybe I *should* just have sex with him. At least then I would know what it's like to have *that* kind of sex, before he moves on. And I'm sure he would be enough of a gentleman to wait a few days afterward, before lecturing me on the difficulties of seeing me right now. We would both know he meant not so much 'right now' as more of a 'never again'. Well, *I* would know. I *always* know. But at least Z would probably word his absence as I generic, blameless 'life just got in the way' kind of thing. At least I hope he would. I don't think I could handle any more blatant rejection in my life right now.

Then again, maybe we'll have sex and it will be terrible. Actually it *WILL* be terrible *naturally*, and I'll die of embarrassment, and he'll be wretchedly disappointed in the sex AND in me, and *then* he'll move on. So, essentially I'll still be rejected but then I'll have another example of my sexual incompetence to further destroy me. Marcus *and* Z... two men I will have disappointed sexually. God, I think I'm going to throw up.

Okay... problem solved. I can't do it. I really shouldn't be feeling anything for him anyway. I'm still married, whether I like it or not. I'm still *not* skinny whether I like it or not. And I'm still *just me*, whether I like it or not.

I have nothing to offer him. I have nothing to give him. I am nothing. There is nothing he would want from me. I am SUCH a loser.

God, I am so tired...

CHAPTER 12

Looking, I see Z has entered the bathroom with another man. *What the hell?* Is this going to be a ménage scenario? I know I'm *definitely* NOT ready for *THAT.* Ha! I start laughing. *Me* in a ménage? Two men to disappoint *AT ONCE?* How embarrassing.

Turning, Z says something to the man, and the man nods, looks at me once more, and leaves the bathroom. What the *hell?* Am I *that* gross? God, I'm so cold.

Slowly, Z walks toward me, with his hands outstretched. Closer to me, Z kneels on the floor beside the tub, while resting his forearms on the edge.

He is so handsome. I would love to look at him forever, and though that's not an option... a girl can dream. The thought of staring at him forever has actually warmed me a little.

"Hi, Sweetheart, how are you?"

Smiling at him, I reach my hands out to touch his handsome face. "I'm good. You're early though."

"Yes. I couldn't wait to see you. Would you like to get out of here now? You're a little cold, and I don't want you sick." That is SO sweet.

"You're so kind, Z... it's weird. Ooops that sounded rude. Sorry."

"No worries. I can see how a man being kind to you, *would* seem weird.... Can I get you a towel?"

"You're very handsome, Z. You must hear that all the time, huh?"

"Thank you, Sweetheart. But you're the only one I like to hear that from."

"Uh huh. I bet all the women you know are *totally* in love with you. I wish I could be, but I can't. Ooops, that was rude, too. I'm really sorry Z. I'm just going to stop speaking, okay?" God, I'm so mean, and rude, and bad. "I'm sorry I'm so bad, Z. I try, I really do. I HATE being bad, but I have all this stuff that wants to come out, and I can't really stop it, and it's bad. And *I'm* bad."

Z stands to leave. Oh god he's leaving me already!

"I'm sorry! Please don't go!! I promise I won't say anything else. We can have sex... if you want!" God, I'm such a whore- such a *desperate* whore!

Walking back toward me with a smile, Z holds a towel out motioning for me to get in it. Okay. I *am* kind of cold. He hasn't said anything about my offer. Maybe, he really doesn't want to have sex with me. I thought all men wanted sex, with anyone, anytime.

Standing, I suddenly see myself in the mirror. SHIT! I'm *NAKED!* Jumping back, I smash the middle of my spine into the metal shampoo shelf in the shower. *CHRIST!* It hurts! My entire back screams in red-hot agony, as my knees buckle.

OH MY GOD! The pain is shocking. I vaguely hear Z swearing and staggering to pick me up, but I really can't hear him over the pain ringing in my ears. I've never realized before that pain can make a sound in your ears. That's actually kind of cool.

Inside the shower stall, Z wraps me up tight in a huge towel, and it feels

so good, I can't help but lean into his arms. He's so warm, and so nice and kind. And he's *so* handsome. Why isn't he with anyone? *Oh.* Maybe he is. *Dammit.*

"Are you married, engaged, or otherwise committed to someone?" There. I think I covered everything. *Holy shit!* My back is killing me.

"No, Sweetheart, I don't cheat. It's not my style to cheat," Z says, as we enter the bedroom.

"*Really?* I thought all men cheated with anyone, at any time? Whenever and wherever with whomever?"

"I don't know about other men, but that is certainly not true of me." Huh. That's reassuring.

Oh, but I'm a cheater now. Dammit. I let him do stuff to me today. Shit. I'm a whore.

"I'm sorry I let you do that *stuff* today, to a *married* woman. I didn't mean to be bad." I feel like crying.

Z sits me on the bed, and makes his way behind me. Lowering my towel slightly, I feel him touching my spine. Flinching, I try to be still, I really do, but I can't help moving. The pain is excruciating. I hear sounds coming from my mouth, like whimpers.

"I'm sorry..." I whisper between pain-filled breaths.

"For *what?!*" He asks, sounding almost offended.

"Well, for many things, but especially for moving right now, when you're doing whatever you're doing to my back, but I can't help it. My back hurts very, very badly. And I'm sorry also for talking about sex, for, um... being a *whore.* I'm sorry for that. You don't have to say anything, I know how you feel, and I don't blame you. I just really don't want to hear you tell me no, okay? I much prefer your silence on the subject, um, it's easier for me to handle." I wish I was dead- right now. This is awful. At least my back is toward him so I can't see the pity on his face.

I feel Z take a large inhale, and as he exhales, I feel his body shaking slightly.

"Sweetheart, you're going to have a very bad, very large bruise on your spine, and I'm trying to access whether there is any nerve damage, so of course it's going to hurt you. Actually, I'm really, *really* glad it hurts. The alternative would be horrendous for us both. I can't stand the thought of you physically hurt." There's another deep inhale and loud exhale for Z. This isn't going to be good, I can feel it. "As for your second apology, I have to fight myself not to have sex with you at such an inappropriate time. You are not well, Sweetheart. I'm not sure if you're even aware of your surroundings at the moment, but if you were fully here with me, I would have already had sex with you, if you would have allowed me the pleasure," And another deep exhale. "But you are NOT fully here, and it would be *grossly* inappropriate for me to be with you at such a time. That's why I'm silent. Not because I don't want you and NOT because I think you are a *whore.*" Oh. That's good then.

"I don't understand. I'm here with you, right now. I don't know what you mean."

"Sweetheart, its 6:15. I'm assuming you didn't enter the shower at 5:00, or even minutes before, therefore, again I'm assuming you must have

been sitting in that shower for at least 2 hours..." *What?!*

"Um, I think I jumped in the shower around 4:15ish. Wow. That *was* 2 hours ago. Weird. It didn't feel that long."

"No. I can't imagine it did."

Z and I seem to have another long pause, with nothing but silence in the room. I don't know what to say, and I don't know how to explain my shower incident. Everything just feels a little confused and distant to me.

"How do you feel, Sweetheart?"

"Good, why?"

"Well, you're a little dazed, horribly water logged, and you have hurt your spine, quite painfully."

"I'm fine, Z. Honestly. I'm not sure why I sat on the shower floor for so long though. I barely remember it. I do remember my vanilla-jasmine body wash though."

Oh, I have to put the matching lotion on, or it won't work! I have to have both! "Oh, no! Where's my lotion? I *need* it, Z. I have to put it on after the shower, or it's not right. Do you know where it is?! Can you help me find it?! Please!" This is so upsetting. I have to have the lotion, to finish.

"Hold on, love. I'll get it for you."

"Thank you. You're very nice, Z," I breathe through my relief

Returning from the bathroom, Z holds up my lotion. Yes! That's it, I nod. "May I put it on you? I would love to." *He would?* What guy likes that?

"Marcus would never do that..." I whisper.

"*Ahhh*... but I'm not Marcus."

"Oh, okay." Shit. Breathe. I'm holding my breath again.

"Breath, Sweetheart. I'm not going to hurt you, or touch you inappropriately, I promise." Well, that's good... *and* disappointing.

"Okay. Thank you."

Sliding back on the bed behind me, Z tugs gently at my towel to lower it on my back. Gripping the folded panel tightly in the hand at my breasts, I try to relax. When the cold lotion hits my shoulders, I jump and giggle a little. Turning to look at him, Z smiles a cheeky little grin.

"You did than on purpose."

He's smirking. "Yes I did. Now relax please. I've already made my promise to you."

"I'll try," I whisper as I turn away from his grin.

Z's hands are incredible. He uses just enough pressure on my shoulders and neck to be firm, but not painful. This is heaven. I've always wanted a massage, but it felt kind of dirty to me. Plus, Marcus would have thought it was obscene and even somewhat self-involved of me.

"Stop thinking and just enjoy. Would you like to lie down so I can do your back while you're lying on the bed?" Yes. *Yes, I would.*

"Um, okay..." and turning I can't help the huge flinch and groan, as my spine feels like it has been broken *and* set on fire from the inside.

"Relax, love. Breathe through the pain for me." Oh, his voice is so calming, it nearly takes away my pain.

Once on my stomach, I feel Z tug the towel down even lower. Suddenly, grasping for the back of the towel, I'm afraid my butt is showing.

Gasping, the pain from my quick movement to my spine is absolutely stunning, but Z just waits until I calm down. He hasn't lowered my towel too far, and I probably should have trusted that he wouldn't do that to me. God, I'm such a jerk. He has been very honest with me, and has yet to break a promise. Why can't I trust him? Why can't I just relax?

"Stop thinking, love," he growls.

"Sorry... I'm trying. I really am. But I have all these thoughts in my head, all over the place, and I can't seem to make them stop."

"Try inhaling and thinking the word 'in', while on each exhale you think the word 'out'. It's a modified version of the Relaxation Response by Herbert Benson and it's very helpful. Every time your mind wanders, force it back to the two words 'in' and 'out', until it becomes automatic with your breathing."

"Okay..."

Inhale, 'in' and exhale 'out'. I wonder if I'm doing this right. It seems way to easy, maybe I should practice for a while. *Shit.* Okay. Try again. Inhale 'in', exhale 'out'... 'In', 'out'. 'In', 'out'... Hey I'm doing pretty well. *SHIT.* Stop thinking! God, I'm terrible at this.

"Sweetheart, you're still thinking. Please keep trying. It takes a while to calm your mind. There is no right or wrong way, so stop thinking you're doing it wrong. Just breathe, and repeat the two words in your head."

Z's hands are magic. I can feel him kneading my arms, down to my palms, and back up to my shoulders. Everything feels good. I am surrounded by vanilla-jasmine and the scent is so soothing, I'm in heaven. He is careful to avoid the middle of my back, but he works the sides of my back, and my shoulder blades in long sweeping motions.

Making his way down the bed, I flinch again when I feel his hands on my thighs. I know his hands are under the towel a little, so my body isn't *actually* showing, but I hate it. I don't want him to know what my heavy thighs feel like- *Not* that he doesn't already. *Oh, god.* He's put my thighs on his shoulders before... *Shit!* Today. That was *today?*

Getting back to breathing 'in' and 'out' I'm relaxing slightly. When Z moves down to my calves, I'm much better. My calves are much better. This, I can handle.

Once he touches my feet, I moan; an actual moan. How embarrassing. I hear his chuckle, but I don't bother looking. I'm sure I'm beet-red with my moaning blush. Damn, this is awesome. I never knew a foot massage could feel like this. I'm going to have one everyday... if Marcus lets me.

"Turn over, Sweetheart." *WHAT?!* I can't!

"Um... But..."

"You're still covered, and I did promise not to touch you inappropriately, remember?"

"Yes. I'm sorry. I've just never had a massage before, so I didn't know you did the front as well..."

"*Never?* Not even by your husband?"

"Um, no. I don't really like to be touched, and Marcus doesn't really like to touch me, so it kind of worked out well." Laugh. Oh, I couldn't help that one, as I gently turn over onto my back.

"I'm pleased to hear that. Your husband doesn't know what he's

missing. Your skin is so soft; it's a delight to touch. And I'm honored that you're allowing *me* to touch you."

There is nothing to say to that. He likes the feel of my skin? Well, I like the feel of his hands on my skin. So that kind of worked out well, too.

Rising on the bed, he once again begins rubbing, massaging and moisturizing my shoulders, neck, and the top of my chest. Inhaling the vanilla-jasmine makes me smile to myself. This is so nice.

"Why are you smiling?" Z grins at me.

"Well, because I love this scent all around me, and because you like touching my skin, and my skin likes to be touched by you. So it's the opposite of Marcus. And it's really nice..."

"That IS nice. I'm glad I'm the opposite of your husband. And yes, I very much like touching your skin, *everywhere*." He says with another smirk. Oh. Blush. *Dammit.* Look away! "Please don't look away from me. I love your eyes, and I love them on me."

"I'm embarrassed..."

"Why? Because a man desires you?"

"Do you? Um, desire me?" Major blush. Shut up!

"Very much so. And I look forward to showing you another time. But right now, I just want to touch you and make you smile, as you've been."

"Okay," I sigh.

Z moves down the bed to my legs. Why does the front of my thighs seem worse than the backs? My whole body goes rigid. *Ugh.* He could see me *down there* if he looks. I hate this.

"I'm not looking at your pussy, love..." *Flinch.* "...Please relax."

"Okay. It's just, I feel..."

"Vulnerable? Exposed? *Nearly* naked?"

"Yes, that about covers it. I don't really do naked ever. I don't like it, so..."

"You feel horribly uncomfortable that I may see your body naked?"

"Yes." I'm blushing again, I know it. "Yes. Marcus said I had big thighs and a big butt, so I just kind of stayed clothed... *always*." God, this is so embarrassing.

"Marcus is an ass. You are lovely. You're all soft, and voluptuous. Your breasts fill my hands perfectly, and your hips and ass were made for holding. I want you to believe me when I say there is nothing wrong with your body, AT ALL. As a matter of fact, I'm desperately fighting the urge, right now, to slide my hands under your towel. I'm dying to touch you. I *need* to touch you..." Oh! *Well...* if he's *dying...* "...I want to see your body. I want to feel your breasts fill my hands. I want to taste you again. I've been dying for another taste..." *HOLY SHIT!* "...But for now, I will try to massage away some of your tension." Oh... okay. Good. *Dammit.*

Down my thighs and calves, Z never touches me inappropriately. EVER. It's kind of annoying, actually. *NOT* that I want to be touched, but *jeez... Just a little?*

When he gets to my feet again, I'm in heaven. I feel his touch everywhere. My whole body seems to react to his rub, knead, and touch. This is *awesome.*

"Can I keep you on retainer for *this*?" I ask with a grin.

Laughing at me, "No. Foot massages are on the house. As is my voice for you. Now, be quiet and enjoy it while it lasts..."

"Okay..." And quieting, I feel all soft and floaty. I *love* this...

==========

"What happened earlier, Sweetheart? When I found you in the shower?"

"When you found me in the shower...?" What is he talking about?

"Yes. Do you remember when I found you?"

"I wasn't in the shower..." *Was I? Oh. My. God.* I was!

Jumping up, I cover myself better and yell, "I forgot! I forgot you saw me naked! Oh my god. I'm so sorry! Oh! Who was the other guy?" Looking around frantically, it's like I expect the other man to be in the closet or something. Shit! I can't breathe.

"Stop! Take a deep breath right now. Don't do this. *Please...*" He sounds like he actually cares.

"I-I'm sorry. I'm try-ing to breathe." My breathing calms slightly at his request.

"What happened? You seemed *well* earlier, I'd say even happy. You seemed to have calmed down some from all your upset this week. You seemed okay with our time together. But when I found you, you were so... *lost*. What was it? I need you to tell me. What were you thinking about? Did I push you too hard?"

"Who was the other man?" I'm desperate. How many people have seen me naked?

"Stop deflecting. He was no one- just the hotel manager. He helped me into the room, when I said there may be a problem, and that I had forgotten my key-card. He is irrelevant. But the *why* of your upset and confusion is not. Please, trust me enough to tell me. What were you thinking about?"

Do I tell him the truth? What the hell do I say? I can't even think clearly about all the reasons. What do I confess to this lovely man? Dammit, the silence is dragging but Z is just patiently waiting for me to speak.

"I was thinking about many things actually. I was thinking about my engagement and marriage. I was thinking about all the disappointments in my life. I was thinking about all the times *I* was a disappointment in my life. I was thinking about how I will disappoint you, and when and how you will walk away from me... Not that I blame you! I'm not trying to guilt you or anything. You want the truth, and that's it, basically...

"...I don't know why I stopped functioning, and I don't know why I flipped out in the shower. I don't know why I can't remember any of that time either. I'm so sorry I ever got you involved in any of this stuff. I'm not right anymore. I'm not good. I'm not really in control anymore. But I used to be, I used to be really good. I was controlled and well-bred. Um, now though, I'm just a woman who sits on a shower floor for hours, and let's strange men see her naked."

Christ! I may as well finish. "I'm not good, Z. And you really, *really* should leave quickly. Actually, I WANT you to leave. Please. I'm very

tired, and I would like to sleep now. Could you please just go? If you want, I'll call you later, or tomorrow or sometime. Please... Please just leave now. I'm really tired and embarrassed and I just want to sleep for a while. *Please?*" *Jeez...* That was a mouthful, but I still feel terrible inside.

"No. I'm not leaving, and you're not resting. I think that's part of the problem. Every time you start to think about your life, you close down and sleep. I want you awake. I want you to talk to me about all your 'stuff' as you call it. I told you I'm not leaving, and I meant it. You can fight me if you would like, but the end result will still be the same- I'm not leaving, Sweetheart."

"Are you STUPID or something?!" *What?!* Did I just say that? How rude! "I'm sorry."

"No, I'm not stupid, and that was fairly rude. But I think I'll forgive you again, for momentary fits of rudeness under the circumstances." Is he smiling at me? *Smiling?* "What would you like to eat? I doubt we're going out for dinner, so I'll just order in."

Food? As if I could eat right now. I'm all weird and kind of confused still and my head is spinning and my back is killing me, and...

"I'm not really hungry. I'm tired, Z. Please..."

"Either you choose, or I do. What would you like for dinner? Something conservative, like a nice pasta? Something greasy, like a yummy cheeseburger? Or something healthy and *boring,* I might add, like a tragic salad? Personally, I'm opting for the greasy cheeseburger, with fries." *Seriously?* A greasy cheeseburger? Z so doesn't look like the greasy cheeseburger type.

"Okay. A cheeseburger, with fries." Damn. Now he knows why I have a big butt and thighs.

After calling in our order, Z asks, "Would you like to get dressed? I could slip into the washroom to give you some privacy."

"Yes, please. I hate feeling like this." Exposed! Almost naked! Slutty! "No problem."

And turning, Z leaves me to scramble for the dresser drawers. Ow! My back *kills* when I move. Pulling out black yoga pants and a black cami, with, *naturally*, a little black cardigan to cover up my butt, I finally relax... *a little.*

Pulling on my clothes, the pain in my back is still shocking. I am actually SHOCKED by the intensity of the physical pain.

"Are you dressed?" He asks through the door.

"Yes. You can come out now." And as Z exits the washroom he takes in my outfit from head to toe with a grin.

"Very cute, Sweetheart. You look very petite without your heels. And I love your hair piled on top of your head like that. Your hair just begs to be wrapped around a fist. You're quite the little sex-kitten, aren't you?"

"*What?* No. Of course not! I don't do sex, and I'm certainly not the sex-kitten type." There!

"We'll see..." he murmurs.

===========

Waiting for the food, I decide to check my messages. Turning from Z, I'm shocked to see 14 missed calls. Wow. My parents-ick, Marcus-prick, Kayla-bitch, and Z. Wow. Z called 6 times between 5 and 6 o'clock. *Jeez...* Obsess much?

"There are many calls from me there. I became a little frantic when you wouldn't answer your door, but I could see your car was still in the lot." That's nice *and* strange.

"I'm sorry, I didn't hear the phone."

"No worries. Everything worked out fine. I'm glad I found you when I did though. Otherwise, you may have eventually drowned in the shower."

I think he's joking, until I look over and I'm absolutely stunned by his expression. Z looks so sad, and kind of lost himself.

"I really am sorry. I wasn't trying to hurt myself or anything. I would have answered, but I didn't know my phone was ringing."

This is awful. I feel like such a loser right now. And Z looks like I frightened him or something. What an ass I am.

"I hope you weren't trying to hurt yourself, *or anything.* But honestly, Sweetheart, if you ever find yourself feeling like you DO want to hurt yourself, please... *please* promise me you'll call me so I can help you. I don't like this feeling, and I really don't like the thought of anything bad happening to you. Promise me, okay?"

"I'm not like that, Z. I don't do drama like that."

"Promise me! I want you to promise that you will call me if you ever feel confused, or like you want to hurt yourself, or like you just want to sleep for a long time. Say it. Promise me!" He looks awful *and* mad at me.

"I promise. Please don't be mad at me. I didn't mean to do anything wrong. I'm really sorry." Whispering my words, my throat chokes up, and I feel like crying.

He's like this super sexy, *nice* man, and I've upset and frightened him. I feel really bad about it, though I didn't do it on purpose.

"Come here, Sweetheart." And when I can't move for my sadness, Z demands, "Now. Come here, now." *Wow.* Dominant much?

Slowly walking to him, Z pulls me onto his lap, and hugs me. He actually *hugs* me. I don't think I've ever been hugged like this in my life. Actually, I don't think I've ever *been* hugged in my life. This is so soothing I barely even feel my back right now. Z smells wonderful, and he's so warm. Actually, I'm overcome with his feeling of... *warmth.* I want to soak up his warmth, and I want to cry.

"Cry, love. Cry for your sadness, and cry for the fear I felt today. Please, just cry, so you can free us *both* of all this sadness today."

Oh *god,* I never had a chance. Snuggling closer, I just let go. My tears fall, and my breath hitches, and my heart hurts. I feel good in Z's arms but my heart is still aching. Why is that?

He is so nice and kind to me. Yet, I can't trust his motives at all. What *are* his motives? What's he going to gain from all this? I can't stop my tears. I don't understand any of this.

Still sobbing, I finally tell him in a whisper, "I don't trust you. I'm s-sorry, but I don't know what your motive is. What is it? Please, Z. Please, tell me your motivation for being here, so I can understand what's happening. I can't handle any more surprises. I can't handle any more

p-pain. And I can't stand anymore weakness. Please, tell me what you want from me. Why are you here? Why are you doing this to me?"

I sound so pathetic that I should be embarrassed by my words, but I just can't feel embarrassment right now. I feel only sadness and confusion in Z's arms.

"*Oh, Sweetheart...* You won't believe me anyway. You won't trust me even if I tell you I have no ulterior motives but to help you. So, I'll just try to show you. That's all I can do. You won't believe me if I tell you, so I'll show you over time." And after his words we continue to hug in silence.

When there's a knock on the door minutes later, Z gently lifts me off his lap, wiping my tears away with his thumbs as he sits me on the bed.

Walking to the door, he opens it, speaks quietly, and pulls our dinner into the room. Turning and smiling at me, "Here we go...greasy cheeseburgers and fries. This meal can cheer anyone up- even you. Come on, let's eat."

"Okay," I grin.

Fifteen minutes later, I'm totally embarrassed that I've nearly eaten all my food, but Z keeps insisting I finish it and it's just so good, I can't stop.

It's exactly what I need. We even talk a little about work. Z does a great impression of Mr. Sam Shields, '*of the Texas Shields'*. Laughing, I finally finish all of my food. God, I'm full, and really tired.

==========

Looking over at the little bedside clock, its 8:34 and way too early to be this tired. Yet, I am absolutely drained. I wish Z would leave... Not because I don't want his company, but because I just want to curl up in bed and sleep for hours, *alone.*

"I see how tired you've become, and I won't prevent you from sleeping, but there are two things I must tell you first." Oh shit, here it is.

Bracing myself, I wrap my arms around my ribs, but Z pulls my arms away from my body and tugs me over to the bed again. Sitting beside me, he looks like he's struggling to speak.

"Go ahead and just say it. It's okay, Z. You've been very kind to me."

"I'm not going anywhere, Sweetheart- I've told you that countless times. I'm just looking for proper phrasing so you don't go all '*panic-attack*' on me." *What?!* And then he grins at me. *Seriously?* He's grinning after a statement like that?

"Okay- like a band-aid. First, I'm not leaving you tonight. That doesn't mean I expect sex or anything else from you... It just means I'm not leaving here, whether I sleep on the floor, the couch, or beside you in bed. Second, you have the next week off work. Wait!"

"*WHAT?!*" I scream. "What does that mean? What did you do?!" Christ, I feel frantic or something!

"I spoke with Shields, told him you had some personal time needed, *which you do,* and for which you actually have an abundance of, and he

117

agreed to a week's vacation."

"How could you *DO THIS* TO ME?! I don't want to stay here! I want to go to work! I *NEED* to go to work! If I lose my job because I'm all drama-queen, I'll have nothing... *NOTHING!*"

Oh. My. God. He DID screw me! Well, *not literally*, but close enough! *SHIT!*

"Sweetheart, you need this week off to figure out what you're going to do, and since you so efficiently submitted your reports on Friday afternoon, there's no reason for you to be there tomorrow. It's the perfect week to have off."

"But I can't! Shit, Z. Why would you do this to me? *HOW* could you do this? Shields hates people taking their vacation time. He doesn't actually *say* it, but he lets us *know it.* He's going to be so mad at me. He's probably already looking for my replacement. OH MY GOD! What have you done to me?!"

I can't breathe again. Shit, this is brutal. Why would Z do this? He doesn't know what I need. I didn't want any time off. I already had last week and that was enough. I've already planned my morning tomorrow. I'll be fine. I'LL BE FINE! *SHIT!*

"Breathe slowly. Come on, Sweetheart..."

"I'm not your S-SWEETHEART! I'm your NOTH-ING! You're s-screwing me over, just like them. Is this f-fun for you? Why? *WHY?!*" Shit. Breathe. My vision is getting weird again.

"Stay calm. Right now. Stop doing this to yourself. I hate it! Stop it, NOW!" He roars in my face while gripping my upper arms.

I am so shocked and scared of him suddenly, that I try to lunge away from him. Grabbing my arms harder, Z easily pulls me back, until I'm half across his body, and half kneeling on the floor. Closing his knees around my waist tightly, Z holds my hands against his thighs.

The pain in my back is excruciating. What the hell is he *doing?* Is he going to spank me or something? I don't know what to do right now.

"STOP THIS NOW! I will NOT tell you again. You DO NOT run from me. I'm helping you, though you are too stubborn to see it. You are being self-destructive in your insecurity and fear of others' assistance. I will not allow it anymore. You *AGREED* to let me help you, and that's what I intend to do. Stop this *NOW!*" And I do. My struggling ceases as I glare at him.

"You had this year *and* last year's time earned, 4 weeks in total. I merely pointed out to Shields that if the company is audited, which it probably will be due to the new Phoenix Acquisition, he'll have trouble on his hands. You're not the only one I mentioned. And I can guarantee you many other employees will be forced to take vacation days in the coming weeks..." Deep breath for both of us.

"I did not hurt you *or* your employment. You are just as secure in your employment as you always were, except now you have a little time to figure out what you're going to do in your personal life. You *need* this time. Can you imagine yourself arriving to work in the morning to face Kayla? Can you imagine facing all the strange eyes and questions of

your co-workers after what happened last Wednesday? I can't. You are amazing, but you're still struggling right now... today even, and adding to that pressure was going to be too much, I believe. Therefore, I intervened. This is a good thing for you. You don't have to face anyone, or you can *choose* to face everyone. Do you see what I did for you?"

I force myself to take deep, calm breaths. I'm still shaking with my initial rage, but my adrenaline is fading. *Christ!* I'm all over the place. I'm tranced-out, crying, hungry, tired, and angry, all in the span of an hour. This is too much. Maybe, Z is right. It's all too much. I really can't handle much more. Shit. He's just like Marcus and my parents. Everyone knows best. He was right, and I was wrong. *Oh, the story of my life...*

"You're right, and I'm wrong. That really does seem to be my theme song. I'm sorry I acted childishly Z. I was just taken by surprise. You're absolutely right. I'll just stay here and, and *think*. Thank you for intervening and making the decision for me. I really appreciate what you've done." I can hear the defeat in my own voice, and it's a sound I'm quite familiar with.

"Please, Sweetheart. I wasn't hurting you. I was *helping* you. You really do need this time to yourself."

"Yes, I know. Thank you again. I'm just going to go to bed, because I'm pretty tired, but I would appreciate it if you left now. I'm fine, I really am, but I would like to be alone now. Okay?"

"No. I told you I was staying the night and I meant it. You can ignore me, talk to me, or try to beat the shit out of me, but regardless, I'm staying with you tonight." *God,* he's such an Asshole!

"Fine! You won! Jesus! Go celebrate your victory or something!"

"Nope. I'm staying right here tonight."

"May I use the washroom and brush my teeth alone, or do you have to follow me?!" I'm angry again? God, calm down. I'm like a full out, up and down, back and forth Psycho.

"No, I won't follow you. Use the washroom. Brush your teeth. But don't be long. After 10 minutes I'll break the door down, Sweetheart. Don't push me," he snarls the warning.

"You know, you're being a real *asshole* right now. You ruin *MY* life and then punish *me* for it. I don't understand you at all. At least I understand Marcus..."

Ouch! Z grabs my face in his hand, so suddenly- I'm shocked into silence again.

"Don't EVER compare me to your husband. You're right! I am *NOTHING* like him. And don't make the mistake of thinking I ever will be. Now go use the washroom," he growls while pushing me away from him.

Shit. Z looks really angry. I don't like this Z. *THIS* Z is *scary as hell.*

==========

After my bathroom break, Z walks past me to the washroom himself. Slamming the door behind him, I'm pretty nervous suddenly. I really, *really* don't like Angry Z. Ugh. I want to get into the bed. Now! So removing my cardigan quickly, I slip under the covers. I forgot the lights, but *who cares!* Maybe he's not ready to sleep yet anyway- not that I feel very tired anymore. *Oh well,* I can fake it; it's not my first time faking with Z.

When Z exits the bathroom, he moves to the other side of the bed, turns on the lamp, walks to the door, locks it, and shuts off the main light. Walking back to the bed, he crawls into the bed, in his pants *only* (Nice chest, by the way!) *Oh. My. God.* He said the floor, or the, ah, couch. What is he *doing* in the bed?

"Relax, Sweetheart. I told you I'm not going to take you this evening. I would just like to be near your body, when I feel so annoyed with you right now." *What?!* Annoyed with *ME?*

"Uh huh. Good night, Z. Incidentally, I don't want to be near *YOUR* body when *I'm* so annoyed with you right now. Not that I have a choice in the matter." Ha! There! *Mr. Choice!*

"You could *choose* to leave the bed, Sweetheart... not that I wouldn't follow wherever you end up, but you *do* have a choice."

He sounds so pleased with himself. What an ass! Well, I'm not going to respond. Nope. Let him have the last word. I don't care. Let him think he's won. Let him think he's more annoyed than I am. I'm daughter to the *Beaumonts* for Christ's sake! I know silence, and I know how to feel victorious even in someone's silence.

"*Asshole...*" I murmur. Oops. *Whatever*

"Clever, love. You said that already today. Sweet dreams." Dammit. I can hear his smile-voice, though I refuse to look at him. What an *ASSHOLE!*

Refusing to see what Z's doing, I try hard to fall asleep. I try very, very hard. This is brutal. The clock is in slow-motion.

Suddenly, I hate time. I usually love time. I've always loved time. Time is how I relate to all events. 'This only took 9 minutes.' '*That* was only 6 minutes.' 'Oh, *THAT* was an hour.' Even Marcus is the 5-8 minute man, depending on how hard he thrusts inside me. Ew. Groan. Don't go there.

Actually, I feel very close to sleep now. Please, keep falling, stop thinking of Marcus, and stop thinking of everything else. I'm very sleepy now, and almost gone.

Good night, Z...

CHAPTER 13

When I wake in the night, I realize I'm half on Z, half on my side. He is so warm that I don't want to move, but it's just not right to stay here. Huffing lightly, I try to turn from him, but Z grabs me and holds me against him.

"Stay, Sweetheart. After the day we've had, I like the comfort of your body against me." Wow. That sounded so... so *sweet,* or something.

Not wanting to open my eyes, I ask, "Aren't you sleeping?"

"No. Actually, I'm reading a rather enjoyable, filthy novel. Would you like to hear an excerpt?" *What?!* Shit!

Gasping, I open my eyes as I struggle to see in the blinding light. Shit! He has my book. *Oh, the horror!* Marcus would be appalled. Is Z disgusted with me, too?

"Relax, love. You're not in trouble, though I am curious why you can read such things, but you are unwilling or *unable* to discuss them with me."

"Um... It was in the room when I got here. It's not mine. I didn't even look at it. Is it a bible? What *is* it?"

Pathetic, lying, loser! There is no way he believes me. Turning my head, I bury my face into the pillow as he laughs at me.

"Are you *lying* to me, Sweetheart? Come on... *tell me.*" Dammit!

"Ah... *of course* it's my book, and no I don't know why I buy them, or why I can't talk about them, or why I even *like* them. But I do, okay? I. Like. Dirty. Books." I mumble into the pillow.

"*Really?* I wouldn't call this a dirty book, so much as a shockingly filthy, pornographic novel... much worse than just *dirty.*" And there's his smile-voice.

Turning my head from side to side, I mutter, "Actually, that IS just a dirty book, some of the other novels I've bought from Amazon *ARE* shockingly filthy, pornography..." Ha! I can be brazen, *see?* "...And I love them, though don't ask me why."

Why am I not shriveling up and dying at the moment? Why am I teasing with Z about this? I should be horrified and mortified. I should at the very least be extremely embarrassed. I'm not supposed to buy these kinds of novels, never mind actually enjoy them. Someone like me, or rather the daughter of people like my parents, married to a man like Marcus should never buy, or even entertain novels like these.

"Well, I'm delighted you like these novels. This book gives me much inspiration. As a man, I like to believe I am well-versed with the female body and all its passionate wants and needs; this book however, has taught me that my arrogance may be a little overblown. I've actually learned a few things which *I can't wait to try.*" Wow. That sounds scary but really, *really* sexy too. "So tell me. Why do you like these books? And be honest." Ahhh...

"I don't know- *honestly.* I honestly don't know why I like reading them. They're gross, and graphic, and usually I'm appalled by the women and the men, but then I'm kind of excited by them a little, as well. I'm not

comfortable with most of the stuff in those books, and I can't DO any of the stuff in those books, but I don't know if that's because I'm a prude, or because I'm just not very comfortable with *anything* sexual, including myself. Does that make sense?"

"Yes. It makes perfect sense. Do you know what I take from this reading material, and from your endearing little confession?"

"No. But please be gentle with me... I've had a shitty week." I smile, using Z's own words against him.

Laughing, "Oh, I'll be gentle, Sweetheart." Wow. *That* sounded sooo suggestive. "Here is what I have so far, and please feel free to correct me if I'm wrong."

"I will..." Ha! I hope I can handle this.

"You have never had *good* sex; therefore, it's unknown to you. You read these filthy novels about strong women who actually *want* sex, and they want it *filthy* and sexy. And they actually ask for what they want... *You*, however, could never do that. Whether because you are afraid to ask for what you want, or because you don't know *how* to ask for what you want, or maybe because you're married to a *sexually inept asshole*, who you can't ask, I'm not sure of which. Therefore, though much of this content is graphically over the top, even for me, someone who does enjoy good, dirty, sometimes filthy sex, you enjoy reading about what *those kind of women* do want and do ask for. You are so hung up on being well-bred and proper that you can't even imagine yourself being like *those kind of women.* How close am I? *Honestly?*"

"I don't know. I mean, I guess you're right. I've never really thought about it in depth before. I just thought reading these novels because they ARE so illicit, *was* the 'dirty little secret'."

"I see. Well, what do you like about them?"

"I really couldn't tell you."

"Would you like to be in a relationship with a man that was as graphic and as sexually charged as the heroines in these novels are?"

"I seriously doubt it. No, I don't think so. Most of the sex stuff actually scares me. I don't like feeling sexually overwhelmed and I KNOW *that* kind of sex would overwhelm me. I think I just like knowing those women, and yes I'm aware that they are fiction... but I like knowing that those women who want sexual stuff like that, just take it or make it happen. I like knowing that they actually enjoy it. It's like I feel good for them that they're happy being like that."

"*Like that?*"

"Dirty. Slutty. Whorey. I don't know. I'm not really judging them, because they are just characters in novels. But I know in the real world I could never be like that without judging myself."

"I see. So, in a perfect world, *sexually speaking*, would you want to be dirty, slutty and whorey like in these novels?"

"I don't think so. I think I would be too uncomfortable- too insecure. I would be too afraid of sexual *failure* to ever enjoy myself enough to not fail in that type of scenario."

"I would love to prove you wrong. I think you could be *exactly* like those women, if you wanted to be. Do you remember earlier today? Do you remember what you felt? What you experienced once you dropped your

guard and relaxed a little?" Oh, no. Blush.

"Um, yes... I remember." Oh shit. This is going in a bad direction now.

"Do you think you failed at any point during our time together?"

"Yes. I mean, you didn't... you know. And I was a mess in the beginning. And I was awkward and unattractive...." Shut up! Stop speaking! *WHY* does this man make me speak and confess?

"Well, as I explained to you earlier, I didn't get-off because I was happy with where we were at. I wanted you to be comfortable with me, and I didn't think hopping on, and thrusting inside you, was where you were at, or where you would be most comfortable with me...

"....And yes, you were a mess and awkward in the beginning which is to be expected. You weren't comfortable with me yet, and you certainly aren't comfortable with your own sexuality. It takes time to build both those elements, and it takes trust. As for being unattractive- You couldn't be more wrong. Just watching you struggle to overcome all your sexual hang-ups and burdens, to overcome them enough to experience even a little pleasure, was *very* attractive to me. And physically, you were *gorgeous*. I loved watching you experience pleasure with me, and I cannot wait to experience it with you again... Now, are you convinced?" Um... This is so awkward, but kind of good, too. What do I say now?

Suddenly taking my hand, Z places it on his erection. As I try to pull my hand away, he holds it firmly against him. "*Now*, are you convinced?"

"Oh, okay. I believe you." Give me my hand back! NO DON'T! *ARGH...*

"Don't be frightened, Sweetheart. I would never push you too hard, or force you past your limits. Do you trust me to know the difference?"

"No, not really. Most people don't even acknowledge, never-mind respect that I have limits."

"Well, *I'm* not most people, and I will. Now, I would like you in my arms so I can kiss you. Move up my body, and let me kiss you."

Do I move? How do I move? I'll be too heavy on him. But Z doesn't wait for me to decide. Pulling me up by my hips, he slides my body up and over him, resting me between his legs. God, I can feel his erection against my body. Am I too heavy on him? Am I crushing it?

"Stop thinking. You feel perfect against my body. Now, kiss me."

Leaning into Z's mouth, I kiss him tentatively. He is barely moving, but he feels so warm against me. Kissing is nice. I haven't really kissed in many years, since I was maybe a late teen, and with only one boy. Marcus thinks kissing is '*gross and unnecessary*'. Marcus only gives quick lip brushes on my forehead most times.

Z's lips are softer than I remembered, and his chin and cheeks are a little more course. Stubble, I guess. It's not totally unpleasant. Marcus never had stubble. *Ever.* He was so anal about shaving. He took shaving kits with him everywhere. It was... **Oh *Shit!*** I flinch. Z's staring at me and we're no longer kissing.

"Are you back, Sweetheart? You know, I can recognize your emotional and mental retreats now. I know when I've lost you. Is kissing me really so boring?" Ha! This time I can see his smile-voice. He's teasing me. *Oh, yeah...?*

"Well, it's not MY fault your kisses are so boring." Ha! I can tease, too.

"Really...?" He asks with a grin. And suddenly he twists us and I'm under him. His body is right between my legs, holding me down. Before I even have time to panic, he's kissing me... *really* kissing me. Ravaging my mouth, I barely move my lips because I don't know how to keep up with him... And then I am. My lips start battling with his until I'm nearly breathless. When his tongue slides into my mouth, I hear myself moan.

Z is awesome! Z's lips are awesome. *This* is awesome. I can barely breathe, but not from panic. This time I am breathless from... *a kiss.*

Pulling away, Z smirks and asks, "Are you alright, Sweetheart? You're looking and sounding a little out of breath." Uh huh. But I feel a giggle surfacing, and it keeps pulling at me until I burst out laughing.

"Yes. Yes, I'm fine. That was, however, my first kiss in over ten years. So, I may have to work-out a little. I wouldn't want you to confuse a panic-attack, with my pleasure." Oh no! Did I just say pleasure? *Pleasure?* I'm blushing furiously, trying to turn my head from him, but Z holds my face still in his hands, watching me.

"It's okay to say the word pleasure. I like to hear *that* particular word coming from your mouth. It's a turn on, actually." Oh.

"Um... It sounds kind of dirty or something. I don't really like it," I blush.

"That's okay. I'm hoping you will get very comfortable with the word pleasure, maybe even enjoy it. Shall I continue kissing you?" Hell, yeah!

"If you want to..."

"Oh, I want to," he growls.

Taking my lips once again, Z moves one hand slowly down my chest to my breast. Cupping me gently, I feel his thumb moving back and forth over my nipple below my cami. It's not entirely unpleasant. Z doesn't just grab me hard, *squeezing* over and over like Marcus does. Actually, Z doesn't really do anything like Marcus does.

"Marcus usually hurts me right there. He just grabs and squeezes my breasts until I'm bruised... sometimes..." Shut up! What the *HELL* are you doing?

"Marcus is a fucking prick. Breasts are meant to be fondled a little, cupped and held gently. Nipples are meant to experience pleasure. They seek attention and beg for pleasure. Can you feel my thumb? Does it feel good?"

"Um, yes, kind of. I don't think I'm very sensitive there."

"Really? Let's see..." How? OH!

Lowering his head, he takes my nipple into his mouth. Z's mouth is warm and soft on my nipple. His tongue flicks at it, and when he starts sucking, I actually jump.

Oh, I *feel* that. *That* feels very good. I can feel a tugging in my stomach or my uterus or *somewhere* inside me- I don't know where. It feels weird because it's *all over* my body somehow too.

"Feel good?" He murmurs around my nipple.

"Yes..." Was that me? I sounded all breathless and *moany.*

Moving his mouth to my other nipple, Z does the same tongue flicking, sucking thing. With his thumb he continues moving back and forth over my other sensitive nipple. Working both at the same time, I feel all excited, or *turned on,* I guess. *Weird.*

"Good?" He asks while continue to flick and suck.

"Yes."

"Shall I continue a little further then?"

"Yes, *please...*" Again with the voice.

Slowly, Z moves down my body, as he lifts my cami up over my breasts to my neck. I think he's being cautious, kind of non-threatening. I appreciate the gesture.

Placing little kisses, ah, and little biting nips on my stomach, Z continues his path down my body. Again, this feels good. I'm not freaking out. I'm a little detached though, trying to understand what he's doing, and how he's doing it, and...

"Stop thinking. Lie back. Close your eyes, and *feel.* I'm just going to remove your pants, very slowly so I don't hurt your spine." Now, I'm uncomfortable. My whole body freezes in place. *My pants?* NO!

"Um, I don't want you to see me *down there.* I think I'm kind of ugly. I have some m-marks..." Shut up! Shut the hell up!

"I've seen you naked before, Sweetheart. You were beautiful. A natural strawberry-blonde... *very rare* I'll have you know." Is he teasing me?

"Well, we were in the dark before, and this time there is too much light. And last time you were under my skirt, and this time you will see everything...." God, I sound so whiney.

"Would you like the light turned off?"

"Yes!" Thank god!

"Okay. But I want you to know, it's only for you- *Not* for me. I love your body, and I look forward to seeing all of it... when you're comfortable."

Leaning past me, Z turns off the bedside lamp, and then kneels between my legs. Slowly pulling my yoga pants down my body, he seems so serious and intense; it's kind of funny actually. *God,* he's just pulling my pants off. Marcus always ripped them down, quickly. Actually, Marcus did *everything* quickly.

Reaching for my cami, Z pulls it up and over my head slowly as well. My back hurt a little that time. Shit. I'm totally naked. I know it's almost completely dark, but now I see that the bedside clock is giving a slight red glow to the room. I can still see him, which means, he can still see me. Maybe I should turn the clock around. I HATE this.

"Stop, Sweetheart. I can barely see your body, and though you're freaking out a little, I wish I *could* see your body clearly. You are so beautiful, and it bothers me very much that your husband never took the time to appreciate you or your body. You have soft curves, and gorgeous skin... all smooth and pale, and creamy. I love it. I wish you would love it as well." *Very unlikely.* "I'm just going to touch you a little, okay?"

"Okay..." I breathe.

Z slowly trails his fingers around my vagina. *Ew,* still a gross word. He's very slow and gentle, and it doesn't feel gross when he touches me. He doesn't thrust his fingers inside me, but rather, trails around the entrance, opening me up, touching me everywhere. When his fingers move to the bottom of my opening, I know exactly when he feels the

scar tissue. Jumping, I try to close my legs.

"What happened here?"

"Ummm..." What do I say?

"Sweetheart, why are you scarred here? I felt it earlier but I didn't want to ask you then. Tell me."

"Marcus, ah, hurt me a little... *By a mistake!*"

"By a mistake? *Really?*" No, *not really.*

"Um, he kind of entered me quickly, and I wasn't ready, and I was kind of torn..." Shit! Did Z just growl again? "*... a little* down there..." I finish quietly.

"How many times did that happen?"

"Just a couple. I mean sometimes I was bleeding, but I only had stitches a couple times..."

"*STITCHES?!*" Shit.

Z is all angry and intense. I don't like hearing his clipped voice. Is he mad at me? As I try to pull my legs back together, Z's hands and thighs hold them firmly open. I'm going to die of embarrassment soon. Please, just let me close my legs and get dressed.

"I'm sorry. It's nothing. Please don't be mad at me," I beg.

"It's nothing? *Nothing?* It's very much something. What a FUCKING asshole! When did he do this to you? You're fucking stitched from your pussy to your anus." *Flinch.* "He did more than tear you *slightly!* WHEN?!"

"Ah, I don't know. The first few times he had sex with me, but then he didn't like it with me, so he only did it every 3 or 4 weeks. But then I wasn't ready again, so it really hurt, and sometimes I bled... *just a little!* It wasn't bad. He wasn't being *mean* or anything. Marcus just likes sex kind of quick and hard." This is brutal. I HATE talking about this.

"*Quick and hard?* CHRIST! When did *THIS* happen to you?" I can feel his fingers sliding over the large scar.

"A few years ago. Marcus was really excited, that's all. He just really wanted to do it and I wasn't ready. Ah, I told him, but he was too excited, so he just kind of pushed into me quickly, and I knew he was a little too hard. I was fine though. He didn't take too long, so I just waited for him to finish." This is *MORTIFYING!*

Z is visibly shaking when he asks "Did he take care of you? Did he take you to the hospital? What the fuck did *he* do?"

"No! God, no! I waited until he fell asleep, and then I went myself. I didn't want him with me. That would have been so embarrassing. I just went, and was stitched up, and sent home with some pain medication. It was fine. *Really.* Can we please stop talking about this? *Please?*"

"Did he know? Did He Know What He **DID** To You?"

"Yes, I mean, there was a lot of blood, but he doesn't really like dealing with that kind of stuff, so I just took care of it. Its fine, Z. Please stop."

I try grabbing for my clothes because I feel so horrendous suddenly. I think I'm going to die here. Right now. This is awful, but Z holds my hands against my pants and doesn't let me dress.

"When was the last time he made you bleed?" Shit... this week.

"A few days ago," I confess.

"*Really?* Does it still hurt when you have sex with him?" God, he

sounds so mad.

"Yes. But it's my fault. I wasn't really ready. I'm never really... ah... ready *down there*. So when he decides to do it to me, I just try to grab some lubricant quickly. I don't really feel anything, I just kind of wait for him to finish."

"When he decides? And when do *YOU* decide?" Ah, never?

"I'm his wife, Z. It's fine. I'm supposed to have sex with him. It's not like he's a stranger or anything. It's fine. I don't even really feel anything anymore. I bleed sometimes but I barely feel it! Could you just stop now? Please? This isn't what I wanted, and I'm kind of tired now, so could you just stop this? Please."

"No. I want to understand what's happened to you."

"Nothing happened to me! Please! Just stop it!"

"Much has happened to you. Your body has been ravaged by your husband, and you are NOT fine. This is fucking brutal, and I'm so fucking angry right now, I could kill him."

"Please, let's just have sex, okay. If you still want to. I mean, I know I'm kind of gross down there, but it still works. You could do it. It's okay. Do you want to? *Please...*" Oh. My. God. I'm begging him to have sex with me. What a *LOSER!*

"*Sweetheart...*"

"This is so embarrassing. Just do it. Do *whatever*. Please! I can't take it anymore! I want you to just do it to me! God Z, *please!*" I know I sound hysterical, but I can't help it.

"Are you ready, love? Is your body ready for sex?"

"Yes. I'm fine. Just do it to me."

"You're fine? You want me to just do it to you? *Now?*"

"Yes. Now! Please stop being like this. I hate it. I *want* to be good for you, *okay?* Just have sex with me now. *Please!*" Pause.

"No. It is NOT okay. And I am NOT going to *DO* anything to you."

I finally beg someone for sex, and he says no. SHIT! I SNAP!

Throwing myself from the bed, I land on my knees, forgetting about my back until the agony rips through me. OH MY *GOD!* A quick gasp and a scream while reaching for my own spine, I am absolutely STUNNED by the pain. As I scream, Z joins me on the floor, while I struggle to breathe.

Wrapping his arms around me gently, he yells, "What is it?!"

"My BACK...my body... I'm in **AGONY!!**"

"Okay, Sweetheart. Push your weight forward into my arms, and I'll help you stand." *Oh GOD!* "That's it. Slow and easy. There. Let me just get you back into the bed."

Placing me gently on the bed, Z rolls over my body, and tucks me into his side. God, he is so warm. I love his warmth. Z starts pulling the blanket up and over my naked body, and it's then that I realize I'm shivering. Ow. Shivering *really* hurts my back.

"It's just shock, Sweetheart. The shivering will pass soon enough. I'm going to get you a drink of water. Don't move. Do you want anything for the pain?"

"No. I just want to sleep, Z."

When he returns, tilting the glass to my lips, I realize how thirsty I am. I can't stop taking great pulls and gulps of water, but Z takes the glass from me too quickly. *Dammit.*

"I'm so tired, Z. I'm very, very tired. Can I just go to sleep now? Please?"

"Yes. Go to sleep, love. I'll be here with you tonight. Rest easy."

Tonight. Not always or forever, but *tonight.* At least there are no false promises or lying claims for more than just this. Turning slowly to my other side, I see the clock reads 4:12am. Wow. Well, at least Z will be here this morning too.

"Good night, Z. I'm glad you're here *tonight.*" Did he hear my inflection?

"Yes, I'm glad I was here *tonight* as well. Sleep, Sweetheart." I guess he heard it.

Snuggling closer to me, Z wraps his arm around my hip, and tucks the blanket tighter under my chin. I am so warm. I feel calm, and safe. The pain is receding from an agony to just a continuous ache even as I settle in for sleep. I am so tired suddenly.

Good night, Z

Monday, May 30th

CHAPTER 14

When I wake from my dreamless sleep, I feel almost *happy*. Z is lying beside me, and he is so warm and snuggly, I don't want to move. God, I can't help but stare at his face. He is so handsome, even with his eyes closed. He has awesome cheekbones and full lips. He's like a male-model or something. What the *hell* is he doing here?

Its 8:22am, so rising slowly, I grab my clothes and head for the bathroom. Once there; I pee, brush my nasty teeth, and start the shower. Showering seems like a good idea. Hopefully this one will be quick.

Washing my body with my vanilla-jasmine body wash, fills me with even more happiness. I love this scent. There is nothing dirty about it. There is nothing to make me gag.

Looking out the *very* transparent shower curtain, I notice Z leaning against the sink. *Argh!* Scrambling to cover up my body, I almost scream, "What are you doing here?"

"Just watching. I wanted to make sure you were okay."

"I'm f-fine. Do you have to look at me though?"

"Yes. I love to look at your body. Does it really bother you that much?" He asks with a grin.

"Well, *yes*. I don't really like naked, Z."

"May I join you, if I promise to keep my eyes closed? *Pretty please...?*" Oh, how adorable.

"Um, okay. If you promise to keep your eyes closed." Am I smiling?

Watching Z remove his pants is... *sexy*. That's it; it's totally SEXY. Turning from me, he begins brushing his teeth in the sink. Holy shit! Look at his butt. It's perfect. It's just so, so, *yummy* or something. I don't know. But wow! I can't stop staring at it.

"Do you like my ass, Sweetheart? You're smiling..." *What?* Shit! He's watching me through the mirror watching him through the curtain. *Dammit.*

"Um, yes. You have a nice body." There. Semi-detached.

"Thank you, so do you." Uh huh.

Z turns and walks toward the shower, well actually, more like he slowly stalks toward the shower. Opening the curtain, he brushes against my back with his chest. *This* is sexy, I think. Is he actually going to keep his eyes closed?

"Your back looks terrible, Sweetheart. I hate to see that bruise." I guess not.

"You're supposed to have your eyes closed."

Z leans forward, against my back again and whispers, "I know, but I don't want to. Is that okay with you?" NO! Yes? *Shit.*

"I guess so..." *Idiot.*

"Step forward a little, and I'll wash your back for you. I'm very disappointed that you already cleansed your front... but your backside is

quite nice as well." My back *side?* Or my *backside? Which one?!*

Moving forward a step, Z reaches around my waist and grabs my body wash. Sudsing up my bath scrunchie, Z begins to wash me very gently. I still feel my back burning, but I know he's being extra careful.

"Exhale, love. I'm just going to move down your back a little." To my *backside?*

"Ummm..." but then he's washing me, and it feels so good. It's like his massage, *almost.*

Suddenly dropping to his knees, Z continues down my thighs, all the way to my feet. Oh, this is good. Shit, did I just moan out loud?

"Moaning? I like that sound from you." Yup. I did.

"Ah... would you like me to wash you now?"

"With this delightful vanilla-jasmine scent? I don't know... it's not very *manly.*"

"I'm sure your delicate male ego can handle it," I grin over my shoulder.

"Okay. But go easy on me..." Yeah right.

I want to touch him so badly right now. Wow. Did I just think that? Taking the scrunchie and body wash from him; I work up a good lather. Okay, in theory, this was easy, but now I have to turn toward him. I have to look at his naked body. I have to touch his naked body. Why did I offer to do this? What the *HELL* was I thinking?

"Turn around, Sweetheart. I'm just standing here. I won't touch you at all." Not at all?

"I'm fine."

Holy shit... It's big. *Oh god.* What did I do? WHAT *DO* I DO? I don't know what to do. Touch him. Cleanse him. How? I can't breathe.

Moving slowly, Z lifts my chin and whispers, "Breathe, Sweetheart. It's just my body, and I'm not going to touch you. *You* however, can touch me however you want. Okay?"

"Sorry... You're just big, like *everywhere,* and kind of scary like this. And you have so much body, and I'm not sure where to touch and... how tall are you anyway?" *Christ!* I'm babbling again.

Smiling, Z says, "I'm 6'3. Not too tall, not too short. Does my height bother you?"

"Yes. Ah, I mean... *well,* yes. You're a whole foot taller than me. So yes, your height *intimidates* me a little. Well, a lot, actually. God, I can't stop babbling."

"I think it's endearing. Just relax. Wash me or don't. I'm not going to move, I promise." And then he closes his eyes and exhales.

Okay. Touch him. You have a scrunchie. It's not like your hands are touching him. Just do it!

Slowly, my arm lifts, and I feel myself circling Z's shoulders and neck. This isn't so bad. He's not moving, just like he promised. Moving down his chest, I'm shocked by the sheer size of him. He's not largely muscular, but he's got that whole lean and toned thing going for him. He feels nice. His chest is very nice. I actually like the feel of his chest muscles. Wow. He seems strong like this.

Moving down to his stomach, I find I'm stunned by his erection. It's just so *there.* I can't stop staring at it. It's bigger than Marcus', so it'll hurt more, and it's a bit darker than Marcus' as well. Suddenly, I want to

touch it. I'm just so curious what it feels like.

"Can I touch you, *there?*" What. The. *HELL?* Did I just ask that?

"*Please...*" Holy shit. His voice sounds so sexy right now.

"I don't really know how."

"Touch however you want; I doubt you'll hurt me." He says with a grin. So, grabbing his erection, Z abruptly steps back a foot, and groans.

"Ah, maybe you *will* hurt me. A little softer, Sweetheart. I *AM* attached to it." Oh. Ooops.

I burst out laughing. *Oh my GOD!* I'm laughing and still holding it in my hands.

"I'm sorry..." but I'm still kind of laughing and still *holding it.* LET GO!

"A Sadist, huh? I never would have thought it of you." More laughter.

"No, of course not. I just didn't know how hard to touch it. Marcus uses his as a brutal weapon, so I thought I had to touch you hard, too..." Still laughing, I notice Z is very still and his face looks all tight or something.

"What? I'm sorry! I didn't mean to hurt you. I knew I shouldn't have touched you, I knew I would be bad at it..."

Get out of the shower! Turning from him, I try to leave the shower, but Z grabs me by the shoulders and pulls me close to his chest, essentially folding his erection up my back.

"You did nothing wrong. Nothing at all. I'm not mad at you. I just hate knowing what your sexual experience is like. I wish I could erase all that for you. To be honest, I fucking hate your husband." Oh.

"Ah, Z, can we please not go there again? I really shouldn't have said anything, and I really don't want to talk about it again. Okay? Please?" There is total silence, but for the water falling around us.

"Will you let me kiss you?" He finally asks.

"Yes, please."

Turning me back toward him, Z bends down, a lot actually, and kisses me gently. His lips are so soft, and his breath is still minty, and I love this feeling. Being here actually feels good. Before I'm even aware of it, I've risen on my tip-toes and with arms wrapped around his shoulders, I'm pulling him to my mouth harder. I love, love, *LOVE* this! Kissing Z is the best *anything* I've ever had.

"Can we get out of here?" He breathes into my mouth.

"Yes, please."

After reaching behind me, to turn the taps off, the silence is suddenly very loud in my ears, and I really want clothes, but I try very hard to control any panic from surfacing. I'm doing quite well in fact.

Stepping out of the shower, Z kisses me again, and grabs for a towel to wrap me in. Covering his hips in a towel, Z takes my hand and leads me back to the bedroom.

Oh, my, *god. Is this it?* I hope so. Please don't do anything wrong. Please don't say anything wrong. Please, please, *please...*

Z stops beside the bed, and kisses me again. This kiss is fantastic as well. Oh, I could just eat his lips. I want to devour him. Huh. That's new, I don't feel like cringing with Z.

"Come lie down with me. I want you in my arms for a little while. I need to talk to you."

Moving onto the bed, lying in Z's opened arms, I ask timidly, "What is it?"

"Sweetheart, I am NOT your husband. If you don't want something, or you don't like something, you MUST tell me. I won't be angry, and I will stop *immediately*. Do you understand me?"

"Yes, but..." Shut your mouth! Just lie down and keep quiet!

"But what?"

"Nothing. I just want to be good for you. That's all." *Please* let me be good at this.

"Between *us*, there is *only* good. You are wonderful to me, and I hope to give you something wonderful in return."

Don't cry. DO NOT CRY. Oh, no. I can't hold them in. Blink! Blink FASTER!! *Dammit!* I can't blink fast enough and the tears are sliding down my temples.

"Sweetheart?" God, Z sounds so concerned. It's really a nice sound, one I am totally unfamiliar with.

"There's nothing wrong. Your words are just really, *really* nice, that's all. You make me kind of happy, or something. No one asks about me. And no one is ever concerned for me, so it's just nice, and strange for me, and, well, quite frankly, a little overwhelming at times to hear you sound like you're concerned about anything to do with me. That's all, I promise."

"Well, just so you know, I plan to make you *very* happy..." *What?* Oh.

Z takes my lips again. Moving me under him, he lies between my legs still wrapped in our towels. His kisses have a drugging effect. I don't really know what he's doing; it just seems okay when he's doing it. Feeling my towel pulled from my body is okay. I'm not panicking and I'm not too nervous.

When his mouth leaves mine for a nipple, I suddenly grab his head and force him closer. Wow, *that* was aggressive, and I *liked* it. Oh, apparently Z did as well by the sound of his groan.

Moving his hand down my stomach, he once again touches me *there*. There is no thrusting or impaling, just a light touching that actually feels kind of good. I like this.

Opening me up a little with his fingers, Z slips one inside. Oh, that feels good too. I like this so far. Oh, he's moving again, kissing his way down my body. I like these little nips and kisses. They're sexy but not painful. I want to do that to his body too. I bet he likes it.

When his mouth kisses me down there, I jump... *and* moan. That feels so good. I like his mouth on me there. My hands reach out and grab his head again. Pulling him in closer to my body, my hips seem to move on their own. I like this *very* much.

Time seems to fade while he's kissing and licking me there. I don't know if I've spoken or screamed. I can't hear or see. I don't know how long Z has been pleasuring me. I just feel this, *everywhere*.

When I'm at *that* point, when my legs are shaking, and I'm gasping for breath, Z suddenly works me harder with his mouth and hands; and I explode!

Screaming and shaking, my whole world seems to just expand and then retract. And then... there is nothing. I am mindless and limp with the release.

That was AWESOME! Even better than yesterday. Better than my shower head, better than anything I've ever felt before. It was just INCREDIBLE!

"I'd like to be inside you Sweetheart when you cum again. Is that okay?"

"Um, yes... of course." *Dammit.* Here's the end.

"Sweetheart, stay with me. It's just you and me here. I'll be very slow and gentle, I promise."

"I know you'll try, but you're very big, bigger than *him* and he hurts me, and you'll hurt me, and I'm going to be bad at this..."

"I'm NOT him, and you *are* good, AND you're ready to be entered ... I made sure you were. But I'll still be slow and gentle."

"Okay. Whatever you want." Please be good at this for Z.

"I have to grab a condom. Don't move, and don't think." Ha! When don't I think?

Reaching to the side of the bed, Z pulls at his slacks and I hear him tear open a condom wrapper. Here we go. This is it. *Shit.* I'm scared, but a little excited too. Z seems different though. He seems like he might like a woman to enjoy this. He seems like he might *WANT* a woman to enjoy this. He seems like...

"Sweetheart? Is this too much? Please tell me the truth."

"No. I'm fine. I want to do this with you. I'm just nervous that I won't be very good, that's all. I think you'll be very good, and I don't really want to be bad for you."

"Well, then. Let's do this together, and then we'll both be good at it. Okay?" With tears pooling in my eyes for his kind words, I can only nod.

"Oh, love... you're breaking my heart. I can't stand to see your beautiful eyes cry. Just kiss me for now."

And I do. Kissing Z is soothing and though tears fall from the corners of my eyes, I'm not sad. I don't feel any sadness.

I feel Z's lips on mine, and his hand between my legs, and his fingers entering me gently. I feel myself rocking against his hand, and my legs parting further for him. I feel his slow movement back between my legs, and his fingers still working me down there.

I am surrounded by him, but amazingly, not *overwhelmed* by him. When he shifts slightly with his body at my opening I merely kiss him stronger. Z doesn't thrust into me, but rather uses a gentle rocking motion at my entrance. I feel a little tugging, but no actual pain. He is doing as he promised- he's slow and gentle.

When he finally breaches my body, we both seem to exhale into each other's mouth. Giggling a little, I whisper, "Thank you..." as he smiles at me and kisses me again.

Z rocks gently, slowly. He never really seems to speed up. I'm nervous that it isn't enough for him, but he seems to be enjoying himself.

"You're wonderful. So tight and soft inside. I could be with you for hours, if you'd let me..." *Hours?*

"Is it enough for you? Can I do anything better?"

"Just touch me and kiss me. That's all I need." Oh, I can do both those things.

Bracing himself on his forearms beside my ribs, Z leans down and begins working my nipple with his mouth. *Ahhhh* that feels so good. He is doing that flicking sucking thing, and I feel it deep inside again.

Moaning, my hips seem to move a little more. I'm almost moving against him. Oh, that feels better. I move against his slow movements. *Annnnd* I move some more.

Moving a little faster against him, Z increases his movement as well. He never pulls out of me completely, so he never has to enter me again. Maybe that's the secret. Maybe that's what Marcus does differently. Maybe that's why Marcus' sex is so painful.

"How do you feel, Sweetheart? Are you okay? Comfortable?"

"Oh, yes. I feel good, I'm very okay, and I'm *more* than comfortable," I say with a grin.

"*Really?* Shall we try a little deeper now?" *Deeper?*

"Okay..."

Z kisses me once again, but I feel his left arm slide down and around my body. Lifting my butt slightly, he impales me just as slow, but definitely deeper. Oh. That feels good. I think I'm moaning again.

"You like that. Shall we try some more movement?"

"Please..."

And this time when he lifts me and pushes in deep, Z does a kind of rotate thing against my pelvis.

"*Ohhh...*" Yup. That was out loud. Blush. "Please do that again..." And he does.

"Lift your legs, love. Wrap them around my waist."

"*Ahhhh*, that feels good. Oh. Z, that's feels very good. I *like* that."

"Do you want to cum soon?" Gulp. Huh? "Because I can get you there if you want... or we can just do this forever. I'm happy either way."

"How do I do that? Tell me." Damn, I sound aggressive.

"It's more about how I touch you, to bring you to orgasm. Would you like me to?"

"*Yessss...*" Oh! My raspy voice again. *Cool.*

"You please me very much, Sweetheart. You are simply breathtaking."

Smiling... actually, I think I'm beaming, I tease, "Thank you Mr. Zinfandel, you're not too bad yourself."

Bursting out laughing, Z kisses me hard. Oh, I love this kiss. There's a bit of urgency to it, without the brutality. It's sexy. His tongue strokes my mouth, but he doesn't impale and gag me with it. He makes me *want* to kiss him.

Suddenly, I almost buck him off me. **WHAT DID HE JUST DO?!** *Oh, god...* That felt really, *REALLY* good. Holding my breath, I try to stay still. I try, but it's too intense.

"Breathe, Sweetheart. Does that feel good when I touch you like that?"

"*Yessss...*" Holy shit! He did it again. *Ahhhh...*

"Come on, love. Move with me. Feel the pleasure. You're so close. I can feel you gripping me inside you. I'm not going to last much longer with you doing that." He's smiling at me.

"I'm sorry... I, *oh god* Z! Ahhhh..."

Suddenly, I'm frantic to hold him tightly to me. I'm almost crawling into him. Grabbing his shoulders, I'm pulling myself up his body. My hands are pulling at his skin. My head is deep in his chest. This is so intense, I can barely stand it.

"Sweetheart, let go. Just feel. Feel me inside and outside you. *Feel* me."

Shaking, my body seems to pull up tight. When Z touches me again with wet fingers down there, my whole body hardens. My breath stops. My arms and legs lock in place. My mind stops, and suddenly, everything just SNAPS!

Screaming, my head is thrown backward, and my limbs go rigid, then limp. I am frozen and paralyzed. I am *mindless.*

"Hold on, Sweetheart." And pushing into my limp body a couple more times, Z finally releases his hold, groans, and falls on top of my paralyzed body.

Suddenly turning us, I find myself lying on Z's chest. His breathing is rapid, and his pulse is pounding, much like mine. He is sweat covered and sticky, kind of like me. He is still shaking and panting, *just* like me. We were together, and I was *good.*

Bursting into tears on his chest, I whisper, "Thank you... I didn't know. I've n-never known. You are wonderful, and so good to me." And jumping up to his mouth, I kiss him in between repeated thank you's.

Crying, I'm dripping tears all over his face and neck. Ew, gross. "Sorry for the tears..."

"Not a problem, Sweetheart. Incidentally, you were wonderful, exciting, and very, *very* sexy. For all your worries, you are quite good at the whole sex-thing." Is he grinning?

"*Really?*" God, I sound like an insecure loser, but I can't help but ask.

"Yes, *really.* I feel like I *made love* with you today and I couldn't be happier. Did I hurt you at all?"

"No! That's the best part. You were good, and you didn't need to hurt me."

"Nobody *needs* to hurt you when making love. But are you sure? You were very tight, and though I did my best to prepare you, we did have sex for quite a while." We did? What time is it anyway? Oh, 10:38. He went over an hour! *An hour?!*

"Wow. You, ah, can do that for a long time. An hour... um, good for you," I blush.

Barking a laugh, Z smiles and says, "Actually, I lasted over an hour, but I could have gone much longer, if some little sex-kitten hadn't had a particularly stunning orgasm around me. That pretty much did me in."

"Oh. Well... sorry then," I giggle.

Pulling me closer, Z holds my head in one hand, and places the other on my butt, massaging it gently. This feels so nice. I'm really, quite happy here. I wonder how long the happiness will last. When will he go? How long do I have until he leaves me for New York or until he leaves forever, really?

"Stop thinking, Sweetheart. This is the time for post-coital bliss, not life-changing decisions. We have time to figure this out. *YOU* have time to figure out all that you want, *later.*"

"What do we do now? I'm not sure how this works. You're my first One Night Stand." I grin.

"*One night stand?* Says who? I plan on feeding you, bathing you, and then introducing you to some of my *other* sexual talents. And after that, I'm going to feed you again, bathe you again, and maybe try for a third this afternoon..."

"That's just this afternoon? Wow. I think I'm going to need lots of carbs today."

"Yes, you will. And then we'll talk about tonight... *later.* Okay? No obsessing right now. Just be with me. Can you do that? *Please?*"

"I'll try." And then we just seem to snuggle into each other.

"Um, can you feed me soon though? I'm starving, especially after *that* particular work-out."

"Absolutely. Did you want to eat in, or would you like to go out with me this fine, fine, Monday?" Um. Gulp.

"I'm afraid of my parents, or Marcus finding me. I haven't listened to their voicemails, so I don't know how much trouble I'm in, or how bad it's going to be. Would you mind if we just stayed in for now? Please?"

"Alright, *for now.* But I'm not going to hide, and *you're* definitely not hiding anymore."

"Yes, okay. After today, I won't hide. Thank you for letting me hide today though."

"Oh, and I'll be listening to all those voice mails with you. Understood?"

"Yes, Mr. Zinfandel."

"It sounds *very* sexy when you say my name like that." *Really?*

CHAPTER 15

After begging like a child for Z to close his eyes, I manage to get out of the bed with the sheet covering me *everywhere* and head to the bathroom while he calls in our lunch order.

Usually, the first pee after sex stings, but not today. Today, my body is slightly tender, like I've been well loved, but I'm not actually sore at all. There is no bleeding, and I don't have the heavy feeling on my chest of being hurt, which usually accompanies me after sex with Marcus. This is so wonderful, and I feel so good.

Exiting the bathroom, I see Z on the phone, so I head for the closet. Getting dressed is difficult. What kind of day are we going to have? Slacks and light sweater should do. I can always dress these up or down, or just take them off as needed. Oh, I hope *that's* needed. Wow, I'm so *dirty* now. I didn't think I had it in me, but apparently there's a little dirty girl in me somewhere. *Cool.*

While heading back for the bathroom to change, Z motions with his hand for me to come to him. Walking over, he takes my hand and kisses the inside of my palm. Stunned at such an act of tenderness, I just freeze... *That* was the single most romantic thing anyone has EVER done to me. I'm stuck in a trance. I'm simply stunned.

Z is talking to Tamara from the office apparently, but he smiles up at my expression. Mouthing, 'What's wrong?' I can only shake my head, smile, kiss him lightly on the lips and walk toward the bathroom in my sheet.

Putting on my bra and panties, I pause. What am I doing? What am I going to do? What does Z want from me? When is he going back to New York? When is he leaving Chicago? When is he leaving... *me?*

Suddenly, I'm overcome with sadness. I'm almost blindsided by the weight on my chest. Z is going to leave, and I'm going to have to go back, and I HATE the thought of going back.

Running for the toilet, I gag and wretch. Ow. This hurts my empty stomach, and absolutely *tortures* my spine. Annnnd there's another gag.

"What is it? What happened?" I jump at the intensity of his voice.
"N-nothing. I'm fine. Please leave me alone for a minute." Jeez... some privacy?
"I don't think so. What happened?"
"Nothing happened. *Honestly.* I'm just tired."
"Bullshit, Sweetheart. I know you well enough to know when you're deflecting. What were you thinking about that made you this sick? Are you okay with what we did?" DEFLECT!!
"Can I *please* have some privacy?" And there's another gag for emphasis. *Great.*
"What happened? Tell me, NOW!"
"No. I don't want to. Okay?! Just leave me alone for a minute. Go back and work or something. I just need to get it together, in PRIVATE."
"This isn't going to work..." *What?!* Already?

"I told you it wouldn't work. When are you leaving?" I ask on a moan.

"What? Oh, that's not what I meant. I only meant you pushing me away wasn't going to work. I'm here, and you're going to have to start trusting me, and you had better start communicating with me. So start now. What the hell happened to set you back?"

Staring at Z, I refuse to budge. I'm not talking. He can't force me to speak, so I'll just wait him out. Except, Z seems to be thinking the same thing as me. *Shit.* Crossing his arms over his chest, he leans against the sink, crosses his ankles, and just smirks at me.

Rising from the floor, I walk over to the sink, excuse myself, and begin scrubbing my hands with soap. Afterward, brushing my teeth, I stare at Z's naked back through the mirror, while he maintains his static position against the sink. *Jerk.*

When there's a knock on the door, I turn to him, but he doesn't move a muscle.

"Um, that's probably lunch." *Duh.*

"I don't give a fuck about the food. Talk." Wow, he's *really* stubborn.

"No. There's nothing to talk about. I was nauseous, that's all. It happens. Please stop this."

"Not until you tell me what you were thinking about." *Christ!* This is annoying.

Moving from the sink, I grab my sweater and slacks and head for the main room. Surprised, I actually had that whole conversation in just my bra and panties, hunched over a toilet no less, *on the floor.* It looks like I've lost all my breeding now. My parents will be so thrilled.

Z grabs my arms just after I pull on my sweater. "*What?!* God! Just leave me alone, okay? I'm fine." Wrenching my arms from his grip, I pull on my slacks while he glares at me. Ripping the door open, I startle the poor man behind the door. Smiling, I apologize, accept the food, throw it on the table, and storm back toward the bathroom. Where else can I go? But again Z stops me.

Snarling right in my face, "What happened? I want to know. NOW!"

"Fine! I was thinking about you and I this morning and how wonderful I felt, and then I was thinking about the life I have to go back to, and it made me throw-up. Okay? Stop bullying me! If I had wanted to talk to you, I would've, but I didn't and still you got your way. *THAT* seems to be the story of my life. So, thank you for that. You fit right in-demanding and taking from me like they all do, whenever *you* want, whether *I* want it or not!" And slamming the bathroom door closed, I lock it. There!

"Open the door, Sweetheart. Open it now or I'll break it down, and don't think I won't, because I absolutely will. So, I guess the hotel will be glad they used *my* credit card as your security deposit then, won't they?" What? Is he making a joke? I think so. I think I heard his smile-voice.

"Now, Sweetheart. I want to talk to you, now. If I must, I'll count to three, but be warned, I won't be held accountable for what I do to you if I have to break down the damn door. Open it, now!" He sounds *really* angry now. Is he going to hit me? How will he punish me?

Opening the door slowly, I peek my head out tentatively and ask, "Are you going to hit me?" God, I sound like such a child.

Z staggers back a step looking at me in... *what? Shock?* "Hit you? *Hit you?* Jesus *Christ!* No! I'm not going to hit you. Why would you ask me that?" He looks so offended, I feel bad.

"Well, you said you were warning me, and that you wouldn't be 'held accountable for what you'd do', so I was nervous you were going to hit me, or, or punish me hard, or slap me or something."

In the complete silence that follows, Z is just staring at me like I'm insane, or like he's thinking of what to say, or like I'm *INSANE.*

An eternity later, Z finally walks 2 steps closer to me and takes me in his arms. "I'm sorry if I gave you the impression I would hit or *punish* you. I would NEVER hit you. *EVER.* I was more joking than anything else. I was thinking about picking you up fully clothed and throwing you in a cold shower until you spoke to me... I was never thinking about hitting you. Sweetheart, where did that come from? Who hits you? Does he hit you, too?" He looks so sad again.

"No. Not really... "

"He does, or he doesn't. Which is it?"

"Um, Marcus slapped me across the face a few times when I was being stupid or something, or acting out, but not too often. I just kind of *wait* for it though all the time, just in case."

Z takes another large breath, and as he exhales, he nearly moans, "I will never hit you. *Ever.* Please trust *that,* even if you don't fully trust me yet." He looks so sincere; I can't help but believe him.

"Okay. I'm sorry Z. I just got scared when I wasn't doing what you wanted me to do."

"Fuck, Sweetheart. Please, don't be afraid of me, *ever.* That freaks *me* out." He says with another huffing exhale.

"I'm really sorry, Z. I didn't mean to upset you. Please don't be mad at me."

"I'm not mad- it's fine. You didn't know, and now you know. I. Will. Never. Hit. You... No matter what you do, or *don't* do...."

"Okay. Sorry... "

And after another long silence, Z takes my hand and tugs me over to the little table, pulls out the chair, and says 'sit'.

Removing our lunch from the bags and packages, Z looks around for the little hotel room glasses and pours our drinks from the cans. He is too quiet, but he smiles at me frequently, as if to reassure me that he's not mad at me.

"After we eat, I'd like to listen to all your voicemails, and then we'll discuss tonight, and the next few days, alright?"

"Okay, but you really don't have to listen with me. I can handle it by myself."

"Actually, I want to. Plus, I'll have a better idea of where your *husband...*" sneer "...and your *loving* parents..." another sneer "...are headed with you, and this separation."

"I'm sure they've just threatened to cut me out of their will or something similar to that. Maybe even given me the '*You're a Disgrace*' lecture, followed by the '*After All We've Done For You*' lecture, topped off with the '*You Are Such A Disappointment*' grand finale. Really, it's all very standard stuff," I say with a little giggle.

Grinning, he asks, "Heard that often, have you?"

"Often enough to not have to listen anymore. I can quote the lectures *verbatim*, if you'd like?"

"No, thanks. I'd much prefer to hear the live version, if you don't mind. Why spoil the fun with your imitation, though I'm sure it would be wonderful." Now, he's laughing.

"No problem, Z. I'm sure it will be entertaining for you." I laugh in return.

==========

Sitting down on the bed with our backs against the headboard, we begin. At first I'm a little distracted by my sore back, but Z is listening so intently, it seems rude not to pay close attention as well. Z is even holding my hand.

The first few calls Friday night, well, actually early Saturday morning, are fairly standard from both Marcus and my parents. 'Where are you? Are you okay? What's going on?' To the slightly more aggressive voicemails later Sunday afternoon 'What have you done? How could you do this? How could you do this to me? How could you do this to Marcus? How could you do this to us?' Blah blah.

Z and I listen with a sort of comfortable silence. Still holding my hand throughout, he seems relieved that there wasn't any overt threats... *yet*. I want to warn him that they're coming.

"That's only Sunday, Z. They still have today to speak with lawyers, doctors, each other, and anyone else they think could influence me into being good," I sigh.

"I understand, and I'm waiting for it. Let's listen to Kayla's, okay?" Gulp.

"I'm sure it will be colorful, at least." *Whore!*

"Yes, Kayla does have a way with words doesn't she?" And turning his head to me, Z gives me a tender kiss on the lips.

Preparing for Kayla's voicemail proves challenging for me, but Z grabs my hand tighter as we begin to listen.

"Sweetie... I. Am. So. *Sorry*. That fucking prick told me what he said to you. I am so FUCKING SORRY! I DID sleep with Marcus, ONCE. That's all- **One time**. I didn't know he was your husband, I swear I didn't. He never told me at the time. He told me Saturday morning that he conveniently forgot to tell you *that* part Friday night. *Dickhead!* It was after that Buyers luncheon in Tampa 5 years ago, right after you started at the company. I met Marcus. He told me he was alone, and *available*. He said he had to make a call and would be right back, and we left together. He had NO wedding ring on, and he didn't tell me he was married, never mind to the new quiet girl I *worked* with!! Fucking Asshole!"

I can't help but laugh at her language...

"... I HAD NO IDEA! After he left that night, I thought I'd never see him again. And, and then the next morning, there you were... *together.* Both of you having breakfast before we all flew out for Chicago. You even introduced us. Marcus was perfectly polite and calm, and *I* left to go throw-up. I felt like such a fucking whore... Anyway, Marcus called me two days later, and I screamed bloody murder at him. I was mortified and horrified at what had happened. I insisted he never, EVER call me..."

Oh, the call ended. Okay... Next voicemail. I find myself grinning, which is weird.

"FUCK! I hate fucking voicemail. Anyway, I told that *ASSHOLE* to never call me again. I threatened to tell you, but Marcus gave me this long speech about you being *too weak* to handle something like that, that it would *destroy you,* etc. So I decided not to tell you. I didn't want to hurt you, and I didn't even really know you then. You were like this tiny, *what?* 24 year old girl? You just seemed too quiet or something. I knew your *Fuck-Head* husband was an asshole, but I didn't know how you would handle finding out, so I didn't tell you. I'm sorry. You were always so polite, and quiet, and nice to everyone. And as far as I knew, you never trashed me behind my back like the other office bitches did, so I decided to be your friend. I wanted to protect you from all the shit in the office, and I think I did. I know you don't want to hear this, but honestly Sweetie, I did protect you, and I did do it because I care for you; though maybe not at first. At first, I *was* only acting out of guilt, but then I saw how sad you actually were, sometimes looking, really, like *lost* or something, and I just kind of fell into *wanting* to protect you, or something, or..."

Another disconnection. I'm not really grinning anymore.

"*FUCK!* I really hate this. I sound all manic over here, because, well, I AM! Sweetie, I really, *really* am sorry. I would never have fucked that *PIG,* if I had known he was your husband, and I never would have hurt you intentionally. I think of you as a friend, and I hope you can forgive me someday. And if you need anything from me, I'll do it. *ANYTHING.* I'll even testify in a divorce hearing that he cheated with me, if you want. I don't care how I look, I just want to help you, to, ah, make this right or something. Oh, and I'm sorry to drop this on you now, but there were others, too. *Fuck-Head* told me about a few... I would testify to that as well, if you want...though I know it's hearsay, believe me, I would convince the judge to hear me out... Look, I'll shut up now, but, I. Am. Very. Sorry. Please call me if you need a friend, but I won't call you again. I'll just wait for you, if or when you're ready to talk, scream, or punch me. You can you know? You can punch me right in the face. I won't even hit back, I promise. I'm sorry Sweetie. Please forgive me. Um... bye."

Wow. Punch her in the face? Giggle. *Holy shit.* Laugh. That is so messed up. But it might be a little fun. I've never punched someone in the face before.

"How do you punch someone in the face, Z?" And more laughter. I

can't hold it in anymore.

"It's quite simple really. Were you thinking of taking Kayla up on her offer?" Ah, the smile-voice.

"Maybe." *And...* more laughter. This is too funny.

"Well, I have to admit *I* believe her. Do you?" He asks me through my laughter.

"Yes. I don't really see Kayla as the home-wrecker type, just the easy type. And she really does sound upset, doesn't she?"

"Yes, Sweetheart, she really does. I'm sorry about all of this for you of course, but I'm sorry for her too. I spoke to her the night she *thought* you were attacked, and she was absolutely frantic to help you, but Marcus kept blocking her attempts. I believed she was your friend then, and I still do. Do you want to talk to her?"

"No. Well, not yet anyway. I'm a little too shaken right now, to switch back into thinking of her as my friend again. But maybe in a while. I don't know."

In the silence that follows, I can't help thinking about 'manic' Kayla. God, Kayla sounded really upset and angry about all this. I do actually believe her story. I could see it happening. Actually, if I remember correctly, Marcus did leave me for a few hours when we were in Tampa. He said something about 'talking taxes' with someone. *Taxes?* Yeah, right. What an asshole!

"Sweetheart? Do you want to listen to the rest? Or do you need to stop for awhile?"

"No. I'm good. What can Marcus really say at this point?" Lots actually. Gulp.

"Darling, where are you? This is your mother speaking." *No shit.* "I'm not sure what you think to accomplish from such behavior but it's embarrassing and highly unnecessary. Marcus feels terrible. He told your father and I about his little infidelity, and I have to say, he sounds very apologetic about it. I think you are acting *grossly* inappropriate, and I would like you to stop it now. You're lucky to even *have* someone like Marcus in your life. I know he could find *much* better than you- why don't you think about *THAT* before throwing your life away. I expect a phone call soon. Your father is very disappointed in your behavior."

Wow. She cuts deep, doesn't she?

"Well, your mother certainly is *charming*." Again, I burst out laughing, as Z pulls me tightly into his arms.

"Charming, huh? I always thought she was kind of a bitch, myself." More laughter.

"How the hell did someone as delightful as you come from someone like *that?*" I. Don't. Know.

"You're so warm, Z. I'm a little cold right now, and you feel very nice to snuggle up to."

"Sweetheart? Are you feeling *unwell* right now? You sound a little detached and sad."

"I'm okay. I just wanted to tell you that," I whisper while snuggling in closer to Z.

"What are you thinking about right now?"

"Nothing much. But I'm really tired. Do you mind if I have a little nap? I've had a busy morning and afternoon. Is that okay, Z?"

"You don't have to ask my permission to do anything, love. Yes, nap if you need it. I'll just use your laptop for work while you sleep. We can finish listening when you wake up."

"Thank you. I really am very tired."

Sliding down the bed, I pull the covers over my body and try to relax. The clock only reads 1:12, but it feels like midnight. I am so tired.

Closing my eyes, I hear my mother, *of course*. Why couldn't I hear Kayla calling Marcus a 'fucking asshole' or a 'fuckhead'? No, I have to fixate on my mother's voice of disgust and disappointment.

I have to stop thinking. 'In' and 'out'... *In and out.* It's working this time, and I feel my muscles relaxing, and my mind slowing. I'm almost there...

==========

When I wake up, its 5:30 exactly. Z is lying against my back, kissing my cheek and temple. Wow. That feels good. I have never had someone kiss me awake before. I didn't know how decadent, and romantic it was.

"Good afternoon, Sweetheart. Did you sleep well? From the sounds of your snoring I would assume so." *What?!*

"Are you teasing me? Because if I actually snore, we can just tack that onto the list of 'All Things Wrong With Me'."

"I'm teasing. You were out like a *quiet* light." Oh, thank god.

Minutes later, Z breathes in my ear, "I have to ask you something, and I need you to be calm. I need you to *stay* calm." *Shit.* Here we go.

"Yes?" Be gentle, please be gentle...

"I have to leave for New York this evening, the red-eye actually, and I would like you to come with me."

"*What?!*" Jumping up to face him... OUCH! My back still hurts. *FLINCH.*

"Take it easy, Sweetheart. I just want you to stay with me. You don't have to do anything if you don't want to, or you can do anything that you want to. I'd just feel much better if you were with me this week, but there are no strings, if you don't want there to be."

"Um... I can't. I can't go to New York."

"Why can't you? You'll just be thinking here, probably in this very hotel room, or you can think in New York, in my apartment." Oh, I want that.

"It wouldn't be right."

"Says who? And you don't have to tell anyone, or you can tell everyone. I don't care one way or the other." There's another long silence while I reason my arguments.

"Why though? You don't even know me. I don't want to be a burden in your home. What if you have something to do, you'll feel obligated to take me, or worse, to just stay home. I don't want anything from you, Z.

143

You've been very, um, nice to me, but it was in Chicago."

"What does geography have to do with it?" What, indeed? *Shit.*

"Well, in Chicago, you're like, *helping* someone. In New York, you'll be *taking care of* someone- *Me.* I don't really like that. I'm fine here. I'll work this out. Maybe by tomorrow I'll have it all worked out." Yeah, right. What the *hell* am I going to do?

"No offense, Sweetheart... But that's bullshit. You'll just give in tomorrow, if you do anything at all."

"No, I won't. I still have to figure out what I want, and I won't be able to do that in your apartment in New York. That will just confuse things. You are very nice to me, and I don't want to start mistaking your niceness for more than it is."

"*More than it is?* What if I told you I was feeling more than *niceness* toward you?"

"Um, I would say that you just pity me or feel bad for me or something..."

"*Really?* So you don't know your own feelings on anything at the moment, but you know mine?"

"No, I don't have a clue what you're feeling, but I don't want to at the moment. If I start thinking you're *more than nice* it will twist me into doing something I might not have otherwise done. Does that make sense?"

"Yes, it makes sense. But I still want you to come to New York with me tonight. I have a spare room, if you want it, or you can share my bed, *with* me. I don't want you alone anymore. I told you I was going to help you, and I still am. It'll just be easier for me to help if you ARE with me in New York. We can fly back by Thursday evening, if you like. I have a meeting Thursday afternoon, and then I'm free again for a few days. You could even help me figure out what the fuck Craig was doing with his expenses..." He's grinning? "... I would very much like you with me in New York. Please come. You could just spend the days relaxing, or thinking, or obsessing, or sight-seeing, or reading... Oh! I have a Kindle at home, so you can instantly buy all your filthy novels from Amazon. Sound, good?" Yes. God, this all sounds too good.

"The raunchiest novels I can buy?" What am I *doing?!*

"I look forward to it. I need to enhance my skills in the bedroom a little, I think."

"No. You. Don't. *Okay,* I'll go to New York. But NO STRINGS, for both of us. I don't want you feeling like you have to take care of me. I'll die of embarrassment if you look at me like I'm all pathetic and needy."

"I won't look at you as if you're pathetic, but I do hope to see you looking at least a little *needy...*" Oh my god, he just wiggled his eyebrows at me. He's flirting with me. This is awesome!!

"I'm only agreeing because of your Kindle."

"Fair enough." Z pulls me into a hug and a deep kiss.

Wow. I could get used to this. Don't! You are still VERY married. Don't get attached! Don't be stupid! This is just a nice man who is helping you. That's all. He is a sexy as hell, unattached, beautiful, sexually amazing man, just *helping* you... nothing more.

"Please stay with me. I feel your retreat again. I promise you, you dictate what we DO, or DO NOT DO in New York. You're safe with me. I won't hurt you. I *couldn't* hurt you. Do you trust me? Even a little, at this point?"

"Ah, a little. I'm sorry, but this is just so new and strange for me. Kind of whirl-wind like. I'm just trying to keep up with my life at the moment."

"I do understand. I know how all this is for you right now and I'm not trying to add to your stresses; I just want to be there when you need help with them, that's all, I promise." *My god.* This is the greatest man I have ever known.

"Okay. Um, what time do we leave? I have to check out of here."

"I suggest we leave this hotel room no later than 9:00, so I can pack up my hotel room quickly. We should be at the airport before 10:45. Our flight is at 11:30."

"You already booked me on your flight?" *Seriously?* "Am I really so *easy?*" Ah, yes. Where Z is concerned it appears I'm really, *really* easy.

"Of course I booked a flight for you. I knew I could convince you with my charm and argumentative skills..."

"*Really?* Well, I'll have you know, you almost lost. Your argumentative skills only got you so far. It wasn't quite the adorable eyebrow wiggle or *needy* suggestion that did me in, but rather it was the Kindle that convinced me to go."

Hugging me to him, Z replies, "Well, whatever convinced you, I still win."

==========

After we've eaten dinner in the dining room, Z asks if I need help packing when we return to my room. Looking at all the food, he actually laughs and suggests we stop by a homeless shelter. Ha! Smart-Ass! Wondering where the muffins are, I finally see them in the trash.

"Not a fan of muffins?" *Shit.* Is he like Marcus?

"Muffins are fine. I just dropped them on the floor. Why? Would you like me to buy you more?"

"No. Marcus wouldn't let me have them, because they are for fat women, so I was worried you felt the same... *Sorry.*"

"I'm not Marcus, Sweetheart, and I could give a shit what you do or don't like to eat. Just relax." Wow.

"Do you need help packing your clothes?"

"No, thank you. I can manage. Actually, I'll need to buy more in New York, but that should be fun. I haven't shopped in New York in a few years."

"Do you have enough money?"

"Of course." Gulp.

"Sweetheart... *Do you?*"

"Yes, but I would like to hit a few ATM's before we leave tonight. That way I have extra money, AND Marcus won't know I'm in New York."

"Whatever you want to do... but I have plenty of money, and..."

"No! I'm not taking a dime from you! *Please*, Z. I need a little pride,

okay? I have money, I just have to access it before we leave Chicago."

"No problem. We'll stop at an ATM on the way to the airport. Breathe, love."

Kissing his lips quickly, I mutter a thank you, as I turn to begin packing my clothes. Z's using my laptop again while I pack. He just looks so relaxed on the bed, and so handsome. His relaxation actually makes me relax some.

If he was freaked out, or regretting his suggestion that I go to New York with him, he'd look stressed, right? Actually, Z seems like the type who would just speak up and tell me if he'd changed his mind. Okay, that directness is comforting too. Maybe I won't always have to worry or wonder if I'm doing something wrong. Maybe I won't have to question his feelings and motivations all the time.

Z seems like he'll just tell me anything he feels like telling me, whenever he feels like it. I won't have to second guess, and I won't have to search him for clues. Yes, this is good. I can relax a little. Z will tell me things, and then I won't panic at the unknown.

After all 6 pair of heels, and my one pair of sneakers are packed, I start on the dresser drawers. I have lots of black bras and underwear, a few black camis, a couple black t-shirts, 2 pair of black yoga pants, and 2 pair of black 2-piece pajamas. In the closet, I pull out my couple black sweaters, my 5 pair of black slacks, 4 black skirts, a few black blouses, and my sexy little backless cocktail dress in black, *naturally.*

"Do you ever wear any color, besides black?" I jump as his voice suddenly surrounds me.

"No! *WHY?!*" And here it is, I've been waiting.

"I was just curious. You look very good in black…"

"But…?" Christ my voice is high. Breathe, *Dammit.*

"Why are you so tense right now?"

"I'm not. It's nothing."

"But…?" He asks and waits patiently, *again.*

Exhaling, "Okay, fine. Marcus used to criticize my black, but then he also said he understood why I liked black, because of my 'big thighs and butt'. I just feel a little defensive about my clothing. Well, my clothing *color.* Sorry, I'm fine now."

"Marcus is an asshole. I love your clothing… *though,* I do think with your pale skin and gorgeous blue eyes, you would look stunning in a little red."

"*RED?!* ARE YOU KIDDING ME?! Red is for **DIRTY SLUTS!!**" *What?*

"*Pardon?* Says who? Where did *that* come from?"

"*Um,* I mean… um… actually, I don't know what I mean. I'm sorry. I don't know where that came from. Ah, please just forget I said that." Gasp. Z is walking toward me.

"Sweetheart, you're starting to panic again. Breathe slowly for me. Come on. That's better. Breathe. What just happened?"

"I, I don't know. I'm so embarrassed. I don't know why I yelled that at you. I'm really sorry for yelling."

"I don't care about you yelling at me… But who told you red was for *dirty sluts?*"

"I have no idea. I must have read it, or heard it somewhere. Please just forget it. I have to finish packing now; it's almost 9:00." Turning from Z, I run for the bathroom to pack up my toiletries.

What The FUCK Was *That?* I've never thought that before in my life. Why now? What the hell? Forget it. Just pack quickly. The sooner I'm packed, the sooner I can get out of all this tension in the room.

Okay, placing my carry-on by the shower, I grab my Shampoo, Conditioner, vanilla-jasmine body scrub, vanilla-jasmine body wash, vanilla-jasmine pump soap, vanilla-jasmine lotion, lotion, lotion, and another lotion. 4 vanilla-jasmine body lotions? Okay. I don't remember that when I left my house, but who cares? At least I won't run out.

Packing, I grab my make-up bag, blow dryer, and curling iron... *Why?* I've never used a curling iron, but I always think I will, so I bring it with me everywhere I go- It's really quite stupid actually. Continuing, I have my razors, tooth brush, toothpaste, vanilla deodorant, and 4 more vanilla-jasmine body lotions on the counter. Oh my god, there's another one beside the bed.

Panicking, I look and there's *7 more bottles* under the sink... 16 bottles of vanilla-jasmine body lotion? *16?* Have I completely lost my mind? Why did I think I needed 16 bottles of lotion? Was I planning on leaving Marcus for 6-7 years? Why do I even *own* 16 of the exact same vanilla-jasmine body lotion? What the hell is going on? Obsess, much? Jesus *CHRIST!*

Did someone plant them here to drive me crazy? Did Z? When a knock sounds on the bathroom door, I'm still stunned. Sitting on the floor, with my back against the tub, I realize I'm surrounded by 15 lotion bottles, because *sadly* I couldn't get the 16th bottle from the bedside table, *without looking crazy.* Yeah, because the 16th bottle would have done it... Holy *shit!*

"Sweetheart... I'm coming in. What are you doing...? Wow! That's a lot of lotion."

"Uh huh..." I can't help my small giggle. NO! Be normal! "I was just thinking about opening my own supply store." Oops... bigger giggle.

Kneeling beside me, Z asks, "What's going on? Are you feeling alright?" And now my small giggle turns to a laugh.

"No. Not really. Did you put these here?" More laughter. Ooops. Keep it together.

"No. Why would I?"

"To make me feel crazy? I don't know. Why ARE you still here, at all?!" And back to a giggle. Shit.

"I'm here because I WANT to be, and I DON'T want you to feel crazy, whether you believe me or not." That makes sense. Why would he want me crazy? Crazy chicks can't be all that fun, well, except to themselves, I suppose.

"Okay. I'm just going to leave these here then. I'll grab the one in the bedroom, and then I'm ready to go. Is that *okay* with *YOU* if I leave these here?" Come on psycho... Answer me!

"Yes, it's fine. Do you believe me?" Not At All.

"Of course, Z. If you say you didn't than it's the truth, right?" Come on... lie to my face again. I dare you!

147

"Yes. It IS the truth. Are you trying to pick a fight because you've changed your mind about going to New York with me?" *What?*

"No! I want to go! I just don't know why you bought all these bottles of lotion! I don't know why you want me to feel crazy! I want to go to New York. Please, *please Z*, I'm sorry. I won't bring it up again. *Please,* don't be mad at me anymore!" Gulp. Breathe.

"I'm not mad at you, and I still want you to come with me. But I didn't buy all this lotion, and it offends me that you think I would, or that I would lie to you about it. I really want you to believe me. Do you?" Nope.

"Of course I do! Let's go! I'm ready." Hurry up, before he changes his mind. I don't want him to change his mind. I want to see his apartment. I want to be in New York. God, I *really* want to be away from Chicago and my parents and Marcus. Chicago sucks for me right now.

Grabbing Z's head, I kiss him hard and deep. I want him to still want me. Pushing myself on his body, I try to straddle his thighs, but he stops me. Dammit! Fighting a little harder, I start rubbing myself on his crotch. Moaning, I try for more of a kiss, but he has stopped moving completely. His lips are motionless beneath my own. How embarrassing.

"Um, what's wrong? Don't you want me anymore?" I whisper.

"Of course I want you, but not on the bathroom floor, not when we're leaving in less than 5 minutes, and NOT when you're scared." *What?*

"I'm not scared of you right now." Not at *this* moment, but sometimes.

"You're frightened that I'm mad at you, so you're trying to *please* me, in any way you can. I don't want that, nor do I need it. I want you only when *you* want to be with me- NOT when you are desperate to make me happy." Fine!

"Okay. Never-mind. I'll be out in a minute. I just want to use the bathroom before we go."

"2 minutes, Sweetheart."

"No problem." *Asshole.*

After going pee, I throw all the vanilla-jasmine bottles into the garbage, except for 4... *just in case.* Everything is ready. My make-up is fine... No raccoon eyes. My hair is in another semi-perfect chignon. My clothes are neat and clean. Nobody would think there's anything wrong with me. I look okay. Everything is going to *BE* okay. So, I'll just pretend *I'm* okay.

==========

Z drives my car over to the Marriott, *of course*, to be left there for the rest of the week. After we enter, he escorts me to the ATM in the bar, and also to the second ATM in the gift shop. I withdraw $1000.00 total.

I'm still good. Marcus can't find me. No one saw me here, or at the Super8. I'm okay for now. No one can find me. Ha!

While Z packs his room up, I stay quiet counting my money in my head smiling at him frequently. Maybe *too* frequently? Maybe I should stop smiling for a bit. Maybe all my smiling is making me look crazy or

something. I don't want him to change his mind. I *CAN'T* have him change his mind. I know, I'll just smile if he smiles at me first, that way I'm not smiling all the time. Yeah. I'll use Z's smiles as the basis for my own smiles. Good plan.

My old hotel charged me 4 nights at $120 after taxes, so I'm down $480. I had $1,900 when I arrived. And I just ATM'd another thousand. So, I'm still actually up to $2,420, plus my $425 'Rainy Day Fund'. I spent $10 rainy day dollars on my dirty book, and $15 on the breakfast I didn't eat. I like this. I'm not down anything. It's like the week-end and today didn't count. Oh, except for the Z-sex part... *That* part counted for sure.

After Z packs quickly, placing his carry-on and luggage by the door, he sits down and looks at me closely. Oh, no. Now what? I've been totally unsmiling and *un*crazy for the past ten minutes at least, I think.

"Are you feeling well, Sweetheart?"

"Yes. Why? Don't I *seem* well to you?"

"No. Not really. You *seem* to be struggling with something, but unable to talk to me about it. Am I correct?" *Totally.*

"No. Not at all. I really am fine. *Honestly*, Z. I would tell you if something was wrong. But there's nothing. Can we just go now? *Please?*"

"Can you promise to talk to me before you panic, or before something becomes too much for you? I realize you still don't trust me, but I don't think I've hurt or betrayed you yet... *Have I?* Do you feel as though I have hurt you in some way?"

"No. You're wonderful, Z. I'm so sorry I'm bad, I promise I'll be very good in New York."

Christ! I'm crying again. Why did he make me cry on Sunday? Before Sunday I never cried. I didn't even know I was capable of crying. Now I cry endlessly. Not only is it annoying, but I'm super ugly when I cry. No one with this pale skin color is attractive when they cry. I know it and now Z knows it. I have GOT to stop crying all the time.

"You're not bad, and I know you'll be good. But are you *happy?*" Not really.

"Of course I am. Why? Aren't you?"

"I'm fine, Sweetheart. I'm just concerned with you. You're crying again."

"Well, that's your fault. You made me cry on Sunday, and now I don't know how to stop," I say with my best smile.

"Cry whenever you want to, but if you could talk to me about what's bothering you at the time, I would really like that. It would be helpful if I knew *why* you were crying. Maybe I could even help you." *Doubtful.*

"I really am fine. Can we please go?"

"Yes, let's go." Thank *god!*

==========

Everything is moving smoothly. Z looks happy again and I feel the same. No better, no worse. We have boarded the plane, first class, *of*

course. Is the company paying for my ticket as well, or is Z paying? I should ask.

Z orders a scotch, and I shake my head no for a drink, then change my mind and order a glass of Zinfandel, *naturally.*

We're quiet on the plane, but Z seems okay with the quiet. He's even holding my hand which feels very nice. Marcus never holds my hand. Hand-holding is *'antiquated, and unnecessary'* Marcus told me. Well, I guess Z finds it *'current and necessary'.* Ha!

It's weird. I'm starting to think of Z and I as a couple- like married or *together* or something, but actually happy. Thank god it's a short flight to New York, so I don't get all loopy with thoughts of Z and I. I have to remember that this is just a vacation. There is no love or even a relationship in my future with Z. He hasn't offered anything like that, and I seriously doubt someone like Z would want a relationship with someone like me.

Z even told me that the taxi ride into Manhattan will probably feel longer than the flight, and he was right. I don't care though, I just want to get there.

Z is always a gentleman. He opens doors, helps me to and from, and lifts or moves things when needed. He is usually polite, and even when he's a little aggressive or overbearing, once the initial fear fades, I always find him charming. He speaks to everyone with a kind of polite authority, a dominance that seems a little out of place in my *other* life. But he makes me smile when I'm with him, and he makes me proud to be with him.

When we pull up to his apartment, I'm very excited, almost bouncing in my seat. Looking around in the dark, I'm stunned by the building. Holy *SHIT!* This is beyond exclusive. This is beyond even *celebrity* exclusive. What the hell? Z lives here? I don't understand.

"Ah, *nice apartment.*"

"Thanks. But I hear your sarcasm. Don't judge me, I inherited the place and only finally moved into it last year, because I was a little rebellious in my youth." He's grinning again.

"Inherited it from whom? A Vanderbilt? A Rockefeller? Or maybe *a Kennedy?*"

"Pretty much. Now, watch your step." *Seriously?! Which ONE?!*

Once we are greeted by the doorman and the head of security, we finally ascend in the elevator and arrive at his place. Not quite the penthouse, thank god, but still, the second from top floor. Who owns the top floor? *Bill Gates? The Crown Prince of Dubai?*

Opening the door, Z steps in and turns on many lights. Oh! It's lovely. The whole area looks warm and inviting. There are beiges and creams and even red-browns, everywhere. I love this room. It's not gaudy, or gold washed, there are no gilded mirrors, antique chairs or Greco-Roman statues. It's just a very nice and comfy, living room. I love it.

"This room is *beautiful.* It's not tacky or gaudy at all. I LOVE it!" I think I'm stunned.

Laughing again, "Did you think I was the type to live in a tacky, gaudy apartment?"

"Oh... Oh, god no! Sorry. I just had a visual of huge statues, and gold frames everywhere. This is much better, it's stunning really."

"Thank you. I chose the colors for this room, but not the furniture-though I have no complaints."

Standing in the doorway like an idiot, my brain finally wakes up and I ask, "May I go in?"

"Of course. Please Sweetheart, make yourself as comfortable as you can be. Would you like a quick tour?" God, yes!

"Please."

Taking my hand again to begin the tour, I'm thrilled. I love this! I love this apartment! I love Z holding my hand! I love everything here in New York.

"Okay. To your left is the kitchen, dining room and atrium, but we'll see that in the morning. To the right, follow me, are the bedrooms, library and bathrooms."

It's so nice. I would love to live here forever. *As if!*

"This is the library. It's a little pretentious, but I just couldn't change anything in it. It felt like it had a kind of history all its own that I didn't want to mess with." I see what he means.

"There's the main bathroom. It's fairly generic. This is the first spare room, also fairly boring. This second spare room is where most guests stay because it's larger and it has an ensuite bathroom."

"Wow. It's huge, yet still warm and comfortable. I like that it's the same color scheme as the main room." Am I staying in here? He hasn't stop wheeling the luggage, so maybe not.

"And here's the master bedroom..." *Oh. My. GOD!*

"*This* is very, very big, and beautiful, and wow, kind of sexy." Shit. That was out loud!

"Yes, most women like it. I love the furniture, but I'm not overly fond of the color. It's an acquired taste I think, at least for a man."

Most women? Well, *shit...* that statement kinda hurt my chest a little. But what? Did I really think Z was a virgin before he met me? Get a grip. Pull it together.

"It's red and burgundy and black. These are stunning colors, Z. And yes, I could see a manly man such as yourself having to get used to it. I love the furniture too. Wow. The mahogany furniture is antique, no? And just beautiful."

"Yes. The bedside tables are reproduction pieces, Kittinger, to be exact. But the rest of the furniture are original pieces; a few bought overseas, and some are very old, bought for the apartment in the late 1800's. Again, I love the furniture, but the colors are a little too *boudoir* for my liking." It's so SEXY! Am I staying in here??

"Where would you like me to put your things?" Here! Right, here!

"Um, wherever you want." There! You decide!

"Where would you be most comfortable?" Shit. Right HERE! "You're the guest. Where would you like to sleep?" In your bed. HERE! Dammit!

"The guest room next door will be fine." I want to stay here! With you!

"Okay. Are you tired? You must be. Would you like anything before bed?" **YOU!**

"No. I'll just settle in and go to sleep. What time do you have to leave in

the morning?" Please say you don't have to leave me. Please!

"We can have breakfast together, then I'll set you up with my Kindle. I have to leave by 10:30, but I should be back around 3:00. Is that okay?" No. I want you here with me, ALL day.

"Yes. Thank you." I hate this. I feel all abandoned or something.

When Z takes me back to the bigger spare room, he again asks if I need anything, and after I decline, he kisses me gently on the lips. It's a nice kiss, if not very bland. *Dammit.* He was much more flirty and sexy with me in Chicago. I guess 'what happens in Chicago, *stays* in Chicago'. Maybe I was just that- a *'Chicago-thing'* and now that he's on his home turf, he no longer wants me. Or maybe because he's already had me, he no longer wants me. Or maybe I was so bad earlier he no longer wants me. Or...

"Stop. What is it? Please tell me what you're thinking." No way.

"Nothing. I'm just tired. Good night, Z, and thank you for everything. You've been very kind to me." God, I feel so sad suddenly I just need to be alone.

"If you want or need anything at all, just come get me, or yell for me, or even knock on the wall... Okay?" He states grinning.

"Okay. Good night, Z." No kiss. *Dammit.*

Closing the door behind me, I head for the bathroom, remove my make-up, brush my teeth and use the toilet. I'm all done.

Opening my luggage, I pull out my pajamas, and don't even bother putting my clothes away right now. Who cares about wrinkles when I feel all sad and lonely inside? I just want to crawl into bed, and sleep away all this sad, heavy feeling.

Crawling in, the antique clock reads nearly 3am, and I feel exhausted. I can't even fight sleep and I don't want to. I need to sleep off all this sadness.

Closing my eyes, I feel the pull quickly. After a whispered good night to Z, I can feel myself sinking. I'm so tired.
I'm done...

Tuesday, May, 31st

CHAPTER 16

Slowly waking in a gentle wash of sunlight, I feel cold and groggy. It's 8:52 am, and I've slept long enough. Trying to get out of bed, proves challenging though. I simply don't want to. I just want to lay here for another 6 hours. I want the lethargy to fade, but I don't actually want to do anything about it. Get UP! *No!*

Quickly waking in a harsh glare of sunlight, I'm overheated and alert. It's 11:41am, and I have slept way too long. Hopping out of bed is easy. I simply have to. I don't want to lay here for another minute. The lethargy has faded, and I didn't have to do anything about it. Should I get moving? Yes!

As I walk out of my room toward the living room, I am amazed at the beauty of the apartment. All the big and little details I didn't see or notice last night, are simply gorgeous in the daylight.

Who owned this place before Z? Who DID he inherit it from? How old is it? How much is it worth? Downtown Manhattan, huge apartment, original *almost* everything... I would have to say at least 20-25 million, probably much more. It's just spectacular. Where's Z?

In the kitchen, I see a bowl on the table and beside it Apple Jacks and a note. Smiling, I grab for the note from Z.

Sweetheart,

I hope you slept well. I did check up on you through the night, and this morning, and you seemed well, and OUT COLD. Therefore, I didn't want to wake you before I left. As you can see, I too love Apple Jacks, so dig in. There are many other food supplies in the fridge and cupboards, so help yourself to whatever you would like. The coffee pot is also ready, just turn it on if you feel like some coffee.

My Kindle is ready for all your tantalizingly filthy novels. The account is up and ready, and the Kindle is in the library beside the window. I hope you're comfortable in there, but feel

free to change locations if you'd like.

I plan to return close to 3:00. If you need anything, or just want to talk, please call my cell. Even by Manhattan's standard of time and traffic, I can be back fairly quickly if you need me.

Make yourself at home, and enjoy your time off. Hopefully, you won't think yourself to death before I return.

Yours, Z

Okay. Good. He sounds the same. He's not freaked that I'm here, and he doesn't seem freaked by *me.* Maybe I should do something before he gets home so I'm not a bother. I could cook him dinner, or I could clean his house, or I could tidy up... Or I could *snoop* around? No! That would be very ungracious, and yet my feet start walking to his bedroom anyway.

Once inside the red and burgundy *boudoir*, I reach for his closet. Wow! On the left side of the walk-in, there are the requisite dark suits... many dark suits, but then there are hundreds of dress shirts, in *hundreds* of colors. On the right side, Z's *casual* clothing is hung in a crazy array of rainbow colors. There is so much color it's almost blinding. He doesn't discriminate at all. From canary yellows, to teals, red, and even a few pink golf-type shirts. As for my favorite black? Z has very little black anything, excluding, the 5 or so perfectly pressed tuxedos in the back of the closet.

I am stunned by all the color. I didn't know someone could live like this. Even Marcus who *did* wear color, only apparently wore *some* color... blues, greens and browns... *boy* colors.

Shit... Z is crazy for color. No wonder he asked about all my black. He must have gone into a near coma surrounded by all my black the last couple days. Maybe I should go buy something with a little color. Yes! That's what I'll do.

Returning to the kitchen, I think about eating a bowl of cereal quickly, but I'm too excited to eat. Running back to the spare room ensuite, I shower quickly. Washing my hair is required, but it is so time consuming to dry I decide to just twist it into a chignon wet. My hair is so heavy, that the twist won't really frizz my hair, but rather turn it to light waves when I pull it out this evening. It'll have to do.

Heading back to my luggage in the spare room, I dress quickly in black slacks and blouse, with a light black cardigan overtop. Quick make-up, quick hair twist into a chignon, quick everything, and I'm done. I'm going to do this.

What am I going to buy? Color in what? Pajamas? A blouse? A cardigan? Bra and panties? Oh, *god no.* I'm not going *there* today. I am definitely not ready for lingerie shopping, though it might be fun...? Ah *no,* lingerie shopping will NOT be fun. Christ, what average sized woman

wants to see herself well-lit in a change room filled with perfect bras and panties? Plus, I don't know if Z even wants me anymore now that we're in New York.

By the door, I see keys in a glass bowl, filled with crystals. Fitting a key into the keyhole... Yes! It works the front door. What else do I need? Grabbing my purse, cell phone, money, and the key, I'm good to go. Downstairs, the doorman whistles and... *Seriously?* ... in mere seconds a taxi pulls up.

Where am I going exactly? Um, Macy's on West 34th Street? It's a little generic, not super posh like the little shops in the Fashion District, but I think I'm more comfortable in a large store with lots of security, just in case. The taxi driver is nice and friendly, and very non-threatening, so Macy's it is.

Arriving at Macy's, I'm almost shocked at the sheer sizes of it. I've been here before, many times with my mother in fact, but I had forgotten just how large it is.

Where to begin? Staring at the floor plan I read; 3rd Floor: 'Women's Dress clothing' and 4th Floor: 'Women's Casual clothing'. And the 5th Floor: Yay! Shoes. Where the hell *DO* I begin? The 3rd floor and then make my way up to the 5th floor? That makes sense.

Um, sweaters... Not much selection. The summer line is in full swing. I see a few though, in various shades. One particular light cardigan jumps out at me. I'll try it. Walking over to the blouses, there are hundreds. I see blue and white stripes, very nautical. I hate sailing, another disappointment for my parents. Yuck! There are pinks and oranges, and even a crazy collage of color and shapes on one very loud blouse. Choosing one, I head for the pants.

Jeans...? Ah, *never.* Slacks...? There are so many choices again. Grabbing a sleek pair of slacks was easy. Pants just do or don't work. I actually prefer skirts, because I find my 'big butt and thighs' look much less obvious in skirts. Huh. I wonder if my aversion to jeans is based solely on the obvious *inability* to hide any extra weight within them.

Leaving the slacks, I head over to the dresses. Again, there are hundreds to choose from. I see sexy, slinky, elegant, youngish, and middle-aged styles. Where the hell do I fit in? I look younger than my age, but I'm older than I look. Do I go younger or older? Maybe both? Oh! I see a particularly sexy, low-cut, cleavage showing, short cocktail dress with a little bolero jacket for modesty. It's very nice. Actually, I think I love it.

I pick my size in everything, and then the duplicate piece of clothing in a size up. You never know... Macy's might have their own sizing gauge. I swear some department stores do this either to excite or depress their customers. Though, why they would want to depress us into *NOT* buying their clothing, when we try on a size higher than our usual, I'll never understand.

On the fourth floor, I am almost overwhelmed completely. Where do I even begin? There is just color, and clothing, and people, and stuff everywhere. This is insane and awesome too.

I don't remember it like this with my mother. Then again, I was usually just focusing on her words and moods and agreeing to whatever or

whomever she was talking negatively about at the time.

Choosing a couple cute t-shirts, and casual tops, plus 2 knee high skirts, I head for the fifth floor. Oh! This is a very cute hat. It has a large brim and even flowers and feathers. It's perfect for the beach, or for a wedding, or for *anything* in England. Oh! This is a much cuter hat. I have to have it! Jeez... my arms are getting tired, and my back is killing me. Why are there no shopping carts in here? Ha! Probably because women could use them as weapons if need be.

Yay! Now I'm onto the shoes. After the escalator drops me on the fifth floor, I just stop and take in the sight of the heels, and the smell of all the leather. Most women love shoes, but I *LOVE* them. I *need* them. High heels are the only things that keep me from being trampled. Shoes give me the height needed to survive. Like right now. If I wasn't wearing these particularly painful 4 1/2' heels, these women might simply step over me to get to all the incredible heels. Why the hell is everyone in New York so freakin' tall? *Survival of the fittest?* Probably.

Shit. There's a major sale today, so it seems everyone is grabbing, reaching and shuffling each other to get what they want. I see security in place, and I almost want to ask for assistance shopping. Oh, I can't help my giggle.

And then I see my shoes. I will knock any bitch on her ass to get them. These are them. I HAVE TO have them. I LOVE them. I'm done. These are high-heel heaven. They are beyond gorgeous. They are **MINE!** Just like that, these heels reached out and smacked me in the face. *Hello babies... mama's here.*

Walking to find the change rooms is somewhat challenging, but once there I eventually convince a Sales Associate on the fourth floor to take pity on me. She agrees and allows me to change in the slightly more secluded wheelchair accessible room after I promised to vacate immediately if the room is needed.

I don't really want catty women watching me, or judging me. The Sales Associate seems to understand my reservation, especially since I'm struggling with the huge bundle of clothing in my arms.

Just as I close the door, and finally exhale, my phone rings and its Z with perfect timing. Dumping all the clothes, and my fabulous pair of shoes on the large couch inside my awesome change room, I quickly answer.

"Hi. How's your day, dear?" That sounded so cute. I love asking Z that.

"Um, good. Where are you? I called the house, but you didn't answer. Are you okay?"

"Oh, yes. I'm completely okay. I'm shopping at Macy's on Broadway, and it's crazy here. I came on major shoe sale day, so the women are a little scary." Giggle.

"I can imagine. How long do you think you'll be?"

"Not long. I'm just trying on all the clothes now. Why? Do you miss me?" *Please,* miss me.

"Of course I do. I've found myself thinking of you non-stop today." *Really?* "Its 3:15 and I'm done for the day, so I thought I'd meet you there. Maybe we could have an early dinner?"

"SURE!" Ooops, tone it down. "Sure. I'm in the change rooms on the

156

fourth floor. I think I'm going to try to leave with the clothes on, if I like them."

"What? You're going to pay for them though, *right?*" *Duh.*

"Yes, of course Z. I just meant I would ask the Sales Associate to cut off the tags, so I could PAY FOR THEM, and wear them out. Women do that, you know?"

"No, I didn't. But that's good to know. I should be there in twenty minutes. Have fun."

"Okay. See you soon. I hope you like the clothes..." I whisper as I hang up.

==========

Hurrying, I'm frantic to be dressed and changed by the time Z arrives. Though my back is a constant agony, I could care less!

The slacks and one skirt are a giant NO! Ick. They are major weight adding clothing- as if I need that. A few of the tops are adorable and user friendly, for sure. I don't look extra heavy in them. The dress is stunning, and it fits well. I hate all the blouses but 2 of them. And the high heels are to die for. They are a stunning display of grace and height. I don't look short in them at all. I'm like an awesome Amazon woman or something. I love them!

Asking for help, I'm dressed and all the tags are removed and ready for purchase when I finally leave the change room. The Sales Associate is looking at me a little strangely, but I think she's just a little jealous because the awesome shoes look so good with my new outfit.

Leaving the change room area, I'm told that it's 'standard procedure' to be escorted by security to the check-out, when buying and wearing the clothes out of the store. That makes sense, because people steal stuff all the time.

While walking, I talk to the security guard who is escorting me to the check out. He offers to carry my old clothes and heels, my other new clothes, and the tags for the clothes I'm already wearing. He even lets me hold his hand as we walk to pay for my items. I'm so excited; I want to kiss him for being so nice. I can't wait to see Z.

When we get to the check-out room, another woman joins us. Reaching in my purse, I smile and hand over my American Express. This is awesome. I haven't done this in years. Sure, I buy clothes, but it's usually one item at a time, and one week or even one month at a time. I can't remember the last time I bought a bunch of clothes at once. Ooops, pay attention.

"I'm sorry?"

"Mam, would you like us to call anyone for you?" Why?

"No, thank you. Z is meeting me here. He's probably looking for me by the change rooms on the fourth floor. Um, Mr. Zinfandel." Little giggle. "Honestly, that's his name. Mr. Zinfandel. You could page him if you like. I don't know his first name though." Oh, that's bad. What the hell *IS* Z's first name? "Maybe it's 'glass of' or 'bottle of'... I really don't know,

but who has the last name *Zinfandel* anyway? Honestly, you could page him. Please, go ahead."

I'm feeling a little giddy but shaken suddenly. I haven't eaten since yesterday, and god knows shopping should be classified as an Olympic sport.

"Would you like us to page him?"

"Yes, please. I'm sure he's here already."

And then there is just silence. What the hell? Just do it already. "Jesus! Just page him! He'll be here in a minute."

Why is she so quiet? I can't handle anymore silence. Ugh, I HATE this bitch. Stop staring at me!

===========

However long later, there's a knock on the door. Jumping up quickly, I strike my best pose for Z. When he opens the door, he looks shocked, and then smiles at me. Oh, thank god. He likes my clothes, I think.

"Do you like my clothes? I'm buying them for you because you like color." Please, like them!

"You look beautiful, Sweetheart. Have you paid yet?"

"I gave my credit card... Have you rung it through yet?" The woman shakes her head, but my security guard smiles kindly at me. I really like my security guard. He's just so kind.

"You've been so nice to me, like Z is. Can I hug you? *Please?*" He looks at Z for a second then nods. Thank god. That would have been embarrassing if he'd said no.

Walking over to the security guard, I whisper, "What's your name?"

"Brian, Mam."

"That's such a nice name, for such a nice man. Thank you for not being mad at me Brian."

"My pleasure, Mam. What is your name, if I may?"

"Sweetheart."

And leaning in, I give him my very best hug. Wrapping my arms around him, I squeeze tightly and rest my cheek against his chest. He even squeezes me back.

"You are just so *good*, Brian. Do you have a wife?"

"Yes, Mam."

"Do you hug her like this?"

"Yes."

"Oh, Brian, she's so lucky. Would you tell her for me please? Would you tell her she's very lucky to have someone hold her like this? I've never had that before, Brian. No one's ever held me or loved me before, and it's really nice."

"Yes, Mam, I'll tell her." I can't let go of him.

"Please call me Sweetheart. It's better. You're so warm Brian, but I should go now. Can you charge my credit card now?"

"Yes, Sweetheart." Finally, I let him go.

"May I give you a little thank you kiss Brian? Nothing bad or dirty, I

158

promise."

"Absolutely, Sweetheart."

And then I kiss his lips gently. Just for a second. Nothing slutty or inappropriate- just a chaste little kiss. And I feel so happy, I think I'm going to cry a little, but luckily I blink and hold the tears in. Wow. That was close.

"Thank you, Brian." And turning from my nice Brian, I walk over to Z. "Are we ready to go?" I ask while taking his hand.

Nodding, Z hands over his credit card to the ugly woman, and smiles at me. I hear her. She says something weird, and then Z nods. How much of my 'rainy day fund' did I spend?

"What was the total please?" Z slightly shakes his head but...

"4,388.46," she says in return.

I see Z shaking his head at her again. I think he's being sneaky. Why? What's he doing?

"What? I'm sorry? How much did you say?" *Seriously?*

"Everything's fine, Sweetheart. We have to go though. I want to change quickly at home before dinner. Okay?" Oh. *Dammit.*

"But I'm already ready. I made sure I was good for you. You wanted to go for dinner from here, so I got dressed here for you. Let's just go to dinner, *please?*"

"I would really like to change first. I hope you understand. You look so beautiful, so I want to dress up too."

"What? *Why?* You look very nice, very professional... and *really* sexy, too." Did I just *purr* at him? *Cool.*

"Why, thank you. But I just really need to freshen up a little. Please understand."

"Sure. But can we hurry? I think these shoes are going to kill me soon. Oh! Do you like them? Please like them. They're FABULOUS!"

Winking at me... Oh, *how cute*, Z whispers, "Yes, I *love* them."

"Okay. Let's go then. Thank you again, Brian. You made me very happy today. And *you*- **YOU'RE FUCKING MEAN**!" I scream at the ugly woman.

Startled, she jumps, as Z tugs my hand to leave. Did he just apologize to her? I really, *really* hope not.

Once we leave Macy's, Z hails a taxi immediately. Once inside, he pulls me into his arms and gives me a tight hug. Oh, he feels so good. I love his warmth. Z is like so warm and clean or something. I don't know how to explain it.

Breathing into my hair, Z asks, "How are you Sweetheart?"

"I'm very good. I love your hugs, you know? I really hope you do like my clothes. They're special for you." I can't help my blush.

"I do, very much. You look stunning."

I see the taxi driver look at me in the rear view mirror when Z speaks. "Do you think I look nice, mister?" He looks at Z, then back to me, and then nods without a word.

"Wow. That feels so good, Z. No one ever notices me or thinks I'm good. I only like it when you're happy. Oh! *ARE* you happy?" Shit. What if he isn't?

"I'm very happy, Sweetheart. We're almost home, would you like to rest

while I quickly shower and change?"

"Oh, god no! I feel so excited. I can't wait to go out." I'm almost bouncing in his arms.

"Okay. I'll hurry then," he says into my ear with a light kiss on my temple.

When we arrive, Z walks me quickly into the building, and into the elevator wrapped tightly in his arms. I feel so happy here, it's going to be awful when I have to go back, I just know it.

"I'm going to be really sad when I have to go back."

"Who says you have to go back?"

"I'll have to. They'll make me," I whisper quietly.

"Well, let's not think about that now. Could you try to be happy for a little while?"

"I *AM* happy... That's what makes me so sad." Huh? "That made sense, right?"

"Yes, it made perfect sense. No worries."

When we enter the apartment, Z asks me if I have to use the washroom. What a strange, personal question. Ah, actually, I do have to pee again.

"Can I take you?" *WHAT?!*

"Um, why? I'm just going to go pee." Blush. Giggle.

"I won't look. I promise. I'll stay on the other side of the glass cubed partition."

"O-*kay...*" *Weird.*

Entering the bathroom, Z does this strange moving thing kind of around me, kind of leading me to the toilet. It's like we're dancing, kind of. I'm getting so embarrassed. Why is he acting this way?

"Why are you acting so strangely? I *have* peed before." I can't help another awkward little giggle.

"I know. Go ahead, Sweetheart. I'll be over here by the sink." Okay.

After peeing, I'm totally embarrassed, but at least Z had turned on the water, so he couldn't hear me. Walking toward him and the sink, he spins toward me and begins cleaning my hands with a cloth. Why?

Trying to reach around him, Z again gives me a nice hug. Uh oh. Something is definitely wrong. I can actually tell by his strange smile. It's not his usual beautiful easy smile, this one is... well, *strange.*

"What's wrong? You're acting very strangely. Please just tell me. If you don't like my clothes I can change."

"Nothing's wrong. I was just helping. Would you like to join me while I change?" Hell yeah!

"Okay... just a second. I want to check my..."

OH. MY. GOD!! What the *FUCK?!* I think I just heard Z say fuck too. At. The. Same. Time. Did he? Who fucking cares? I am stunned into silence, absolutely **STUNNED**! This is truly incredible! This is an out-of-body experience! This is crazy! This is shocking! This is so... so *FUNNY!*

Gasping on my laughter, it explodes from my chest and mouth. I can barely breathe for the laughter. I have never IN MY LIFE seen anything funnier! I'm going to die from laughing to death!!

Z begins trying to tug me away from the mirror. Fighting him, and the laughter, I almost fall over, on my FUCKING HEELS! As he grasps my arms steady, I'm almost hyperventilating with laughter.

"I'm o-okay. Honestly. I'm almost d-done laugh-ing."

"Sweetheart. *Please...*"

"No. I'm good. I'm just... *Shocked!* What d-did I *DO?!*" And a little more laughter escapes.

"It's okay, love. You..."

"It is **NOT** okay, but it **IS** very funny. *Oh. My. God! You poor thing!* You had to walk with me like this. Holy **SHIT!** You must have died of embarrassment!" And another giggle.

"I was fine. I was a little concerned about you though."

"Well, you are more man than most. How could you *stand* to be seen with me?" *Jeez...* more laughter. I just can't get a grip.

"I was fine." *Seriously?!*

"You were *fine?!* Well, then... *You*, Mr. Zinfandel, are as FUCKED UP, *as I look!*"

Howls of laughter follow my words. Will this laughter never end? Christ, I'm getting stomach cramps from the laughter. Finally Z smiles a little, while I continue to laugh.

Looking at me kindly, "Are you okay, Sweetheart? Are you *back* with me now?" God, yes!

"I'm here. But *holy shit!* What the *hell* did I do?"

Smiling again, Z says, "Um, I'm not really sure what look you were going for..."

"No kidding! Neither am I!"

All I can do is stare at myself in the mirror. There's nothing else *to* do. I don't even know how to proceed from here. I'm just kind of in shock or something. This is just too much to process.

"Can we please talk about this now? I'd really like to talk to you for a minute." No doubt!

"Um, sure, but can I have a few minutes to clean up and change? I look like a, a *freak* or something."

"It's not that bad, really..."

"Well then, you are either the kindest person on the planet, or you have *completely* lost your mind. I have never seen anything like this IN MY LIFE, and I hope I never do again. I'm fine, Z, *really.* I'll be out in a couple minutes, I promise."

Staring at me with obvious concern, Z almost begs, "I'd rather stay here with you. I'll turn away if you'd like."

"No. Please give me a few minutes. I really, *really* need to be alone. I'm fine, Z. No worries. I mean honestly, how much worse can I get?"

Nodding, Z doesn't look convinced, but at least he finally leaves me alone in the bathroom.

What the hell did I do? Actually, more importantly, how the hell do I explain away what I've done? Jesus *Christ!*

CHAPTER 17

Where do I start? My hair I think. Pulling the red beret from my hair proves challenging. Apparently, I stuck it to my head with my chignon bobby pins. Ouch. Once removed, half my hair falls down in strange ringlets, while the other half stays firmly in place on my scalp. It looks freakishly unkempt. Pulling the rest of the bobby pins out, I quickly re-twist my hair and secure it up against my head again, *NEATLY*.

My make-up is horrendous. Black mascara lies chunky, streaked and clumped all over my face. Christ, it's even in my eyebrows. Holy Shit, I look like some gothic freakin' nightmare. I'm like a Tim Burton character for Christ's sake! Was I crying again? *Apparently.*

My lips are dark, dark red. Where did I even get the lipstick? I've never owned red lipstick in my life. My mother always told me, 'red lips are for harlots'. Scrubbing my entire face with soap is my only option...*twice.* I may as well brush my teeth while I'm at it.

Next, I have to deal with the clothes. Honest to god, I've never seen such insanity in my life. I am wearing a huge red pull-over sweater, over a red cardigan, over a red blouse, over a red t-shirt... *FUCK!* All this clothing is even overtop of a slinky skin-tight red cocktail dress. How the hell can I bend my arms? I look like a 300 pound fucking *tomato!*

Removing the first 4 layers is easy enough, however the zipper on the dress proves to be a bit of a struggle. It really is quite a lovely dress, though... If worn properly. Maybe if the dress was paired with black heels, it might look classy, and sexy.

As it is with my nearly 6' strappy red stilettos, I look like a cheap whore... playing dress up... *in an asylum.* I wonder where the bolero jacket is? Without the jacket, the dress is much too low-cut, and my breasts look way too big to be stuffed into it. Plus, it's rather short. *Jesus Christ!* What was I *doing?*

Once I'm naked, with the dress finally removed, I hop in the shower. What else can I do? I need to seriously wash all *THAT* insanity off me. Z hasn't returned, and quite frankly, I'm frightened of his thoughts right now anyway.

I don't want any of this. I was supposed to just have a relaxing mini-vacation in New York. I wasn't supposed to go crazy at Macy's and spend... *Holy Shit!* Did I just spend over $4,000 dollars ON MY CREDIT CARD?! *SHIT!* Now Marcus will find me in New York. Oh no. This is bad.

Jumping from the shower, I plow right into Z, while naked. *Dammit.*
"Oh! Sorry. Um, how long have you been here?"
"Long enough. How are you feeling?" He asks while handing me a towel. Thank god!
"I really am okay, but I'm a little nervous about Marcus finding me now. I used my Amex."
"Actually, you didn't. I used *my* Amex, so don't worry about him."
What?!
"I'll pay you back. I swear! Why would you do that? Why would you

pay for my clothes?!"

"No worries, I have it covered. It's really not a problem."

"Well, it's a problem for me! I don't like you blowing money on me. I'm nothing to you, and you certainly shouldn't be spending over 4 thousand *dollars* on me! *Christ!* This is humiliating!"

"Come with me." And taking my hand, Z leads me into the bedroom.

Sitting on the edge of the bed, Z pulls me beside him. I'm still in the towel, but I'm feeling very *exposed* to him at the moment. Jeez, maybe it's the insanity I've just lived, or maybe the fact that I was a complete nut-job, that the poor man had to help. Whatever... I'm feeling kind of exposed and insecure right now. Actually, I want to get out of here now. This really is too much.

"Why are you humiliated?" *Seriously?*

"Would you like a list, preferably alphabetical?" That was snide. Oops.

"No. Just tell me what has you humiliated."

"Everything! All of it! The clothes! The money! Being here! Everything! I would like to go home tonight. I really, *really* need to go home."

"I don't give a *FUCK* about the clothes, or the money! I do, however, give a *fuck* about what's making you so fucking crazy! Could you please at least tell me that?! What happened at Macy's?" Oh, he's mad.

"I'm sorry Z. I didn't mean to make you angry."

"I'm not angry! FUCK!" And taking a deep breath, he continues... "I'm concerned about you! There's a huge difference. What. The. Fuck. Happened. Today?" This is bad.

"I'm so sorry. I'm just going to leave. Please forgive my behavior."

Standing, I nearly run for my *normal* clothes, but Z grabs me quickly. Essentially, he grabs me, turns me, and slams me into his body.

"What HAPPENED today?!!" He yells in my face.

"I don't know," I whisper without eye contact.

"What. Happened. Today?! Tell me! NOW!!"

"I DON'T KNOW, *OKAY?* I remember I wanted to make you happy. I remember you liked red. I remembered your sexy bedroom. I remembered all the color in your closet. I WANTED TO MAKE YOU HAPPY!! I'M SORRY I FAILED YOU!!" Gasp.

"You didn't *fail* me." Yeah, *right.*

"Look, I want to go back home now. *Really.* I have to leave, Z. TONIGHT!"

Turning from him I run for the spare room and start grabbing my clothes as he follows and watches me silently. Shimmying on a pair of underwear, I follow them with slacks. Turning my back to him, I put on my bra, as I drop the towel to the floor.

I feel sick with sadness. Tears are pouring down my face, and I can't stop them. Reaching for a black t-shirt, I put it on as well while Z still just watches me.

Continuing with my clothes, I basically throw them in my luggage, with no rhyme or reason. Who cares at this point? Walking back into the ensuite, I grab all my toiletries and throw them in my other luggage. I'm almost done.

163

This trip to New York was a nightmare. I can't stand all this drama anymore. I can't stand feeling like this anymore. I can't stand *me* anymore. It's too much, and I'm done now. This little 'mini-vacation' was a test, and I've failed it. I just can't seem to do anything right anymore.

"What do you want to do?" Z asks calmly.

"I'm just going to hail a taxi and return to the airport. It doesn't matter anymore if Marcus tracks my credit cards; I'll be going back anyway. Oh, and I *AM* paying you back for all the clothing from Macy's."

"I don't care about the clothing," he says so calmly, it's a little unnerving.

"Maybe not, but I do. And I am sending you the money as soon as I return to Chicago."

"Where are you going?"

"Home."

"I mean, where in Chicago?"

"My home."

"You're going back to your husband? Are you *fucking* insane?!"

"*Apparently.* Didn't my little Macy's adventure prove that?" I whisper on a breath.

"You are NOT going back to him. Stay in a hotel if you want and I'll pay for it. I don't care. But you are NOT going back to that fucking prick!"

Exhaling all the drama of the last hour, I finally just talk. What's the point hiding anymore? What's the point denying what will happen whether I want it or not? There is NO point.

"Actually, I am going back to Marcus. I know what to expect with him, and I know how to be ignored, chastised, criticized, and belittled with him."

"Are you implying *I* did any of those things to you?" Z asks sounding totally offended.

"No. Of course not. You have been *beyond* wonderful. You have been a blessing for me, but I'm through with all this. I'm just going to go home and face the consequences of my actions, and I'm going to try to move on."

"*The consequences of your actions?* What the fuck did you do, other than leave your cheating, control freak, abusive, asshole of a husband?"

Deep breath. "That's exactly what I did- I *left*. That's all it takes in my world. I'm really sorry Z, and I thank you for trying to help me, more than you'll ever know, but I'm done now. It's all over. I can't continue this way. And I don't want to. Please just say good bye, so I at least feel like you don't hate me." And here come more tears. I am so tired suddenly, I can barely move.

"I don't hate you, Sweetheart. I care for you, and I do feel bad for you, but I *want* to help you."

"I'm leaving Z, right now. Thank you for absolutely everything. You gave me hope, and some experience, and even some pleasure to remember, but I'm done. Just, um... Bye."

Walking away is brutal. I wish we had had sex again. Once just wasn't enough. I wish I hadn't freaked out in Macy's. I wish I could have been better for him. I wish so many things and I have such pain in my heart, it actually hurts to walk. Walking out the door is agony. Everything is

hurting and my chest is so tight, I'm again having a hard time breathing. Will I ever breathe normally again? God, I hope so.

Standing in the lobby, I'm just sobbing. Trying to look graceful and failing miserably, the apartment manager asks if I need a taxi. Nodding is the best I can do. And there's the pity again. *Christ!* I'm so sick of that look from people. I hate it!

Trying to get myself together, I straighten my still sore spine, wheel my luggage outside, and wait for the taxi to pull up. No more crying. It did nothing useful this week to cry. Crying isn't useful. My parents were right- *crying doesn't solve anything.*

Once the trunk is loaded, and the taxi begins to pull away, I sink back into my seat shaking. Looking one last time at Z's apartment, I suddenly see Z motioning stop with his hand to me. STOP! I scream, as the cab jerks to a stop a few feet after starting the trip.

Walking to me, Z bends toward the window, with his arms resting against it. God he is so handsome to look at, even now, like this. He is just so... *beautiful.*

"What can I do to convince you to stay? Tell me what you need from me. Tell me what you want, and I'll give it."

Oh! That was so lovely... just like a scene from a romantic movie. God, he always makes me cry with his words.

"It's not about you, I promise. You have done *everything* right. It's about me. I'm not right and I know it. *Please-* let me finish. I don't want to be a burden to you, or to anyone else, I never did. I thought if I tried hard enough, did enough, swallowed down enough misery, I would be *good* enough, but I know that's not the case any longer. I can't do any *more*, but I'm still not good enough... so I want to leave. It's not about you. You are truly amazing. I'm really very sorry about all this." Oh. My breath just left me on a *whoosh.*

Still leaning against the window, Z asks, "Please return with me? Just for tonight. I'll take you to the airport in the morning if you still want to leave. Just stay tonight."

"Why? Nothing about me will change in one night."

"Because I asked you to, and I haven't asked you for one single thing since knowing you, but now I am. Are you really going to decline my one request of you? Stay with me one more night." No? *Totally...* Yes.

"Okay. *Tonight.* Tomorrow morning it's a whole new world for me though. Promise me, just tonight."

"I promise, though I'm still going to try to change your mind in the morning," he says with a bright cheeky grin.

Throwing the taxi driver a $20, I hop out as Z collects my luggage again today. In the elevator, Z holds my hand, but neither of us speak. What can I really say at this point? Humiliation and desperation have left me wordless, and sadly I think Z feels the same way.

In the apartment, I move to the couch and sit, as Z wheels my luggage down the hall. God, I love it here. It doesn't feel foreign or strange; it's simply *relaxing.* I feel safe and kind of at home in Z's apartment. Strangely, I'm more at home here than in my own house in Chicago.

"Would you like anything to drink? I've ordered our dinner which

should arrive in 45 minutes or so. We could just have a drink, relax, maybe talk... *Or not*, judging by your face right now." Ooops. He can read my face now?

"My father always said I didn't have a poker face. I guess it's true."

"It's completely true. What would you like to drink?"

"Do you have any Zinfandel?" I ask with a grin.

"Of course. My own private label and everything."

"I'm sorry...?" I ask confused as he walks to the wine cooler behind the bar in the living room.

"Williams Estates... That's me." *What?!*

"It is? What does that mean?" I ask as he begins pouring me a glass.

"It means... My parents were Peter and Conchetta Williams, and I began making my own labels and wines at the ripe old age of 14... very successfully I might add," he grins.

Holy shit! I know his family.

"I've met your parents before. They were at my parent's home many times. They used to come to my mother's parties!"

"I don't doubt it. My parents only made the rounds within the greatest of the *American Elite*," he sneers.

"I'm sorry about their deaths... Are you okay?" I am absolutely stunned. I can't believe I know, well, *knew* Z's parents, Peter and Conchetta, known always as Connie.

Handing me a glass of Zinfandel- his own label apparently, Z sits beside me on the couch.

"Thank you for your condolences. We weren't particularly close, especially in my formative years. And they died a few years ago, so I'm fine."

God, I have to change the subject! I remember the Williams. My mother seemed genuinely taken with Connie, though she was *Italian,* as my mother said it. I think Connie only survived my mother's friends and the elite set they associated with in New York, Boston and Chicago because Connie was from a very old family of the Italian Upper Class herself. Therefore, though not *American* Elite, she was tolerated among them. *Christ!* My mother's crowd is so messed up. *Honestly.*

"Explain Zinfandel, please. You're a Williams called Zinfandel. I'm very confused." Z offers to refill my drink as I wait anxiously for his story.

"Okay. I had already made much of my own money by college; due to my *amazing* touch within my father's winery- too much money actually. I got into trouble here and there, typical rich-kid crap. So one night when I was twenty-one, I was drinking and driving a carload of my friends, and I was pulled over by the police, failed the roadside alcohol intoxication test, and was hauled to a police station in Manhattan. Once there, I announced I was Marvin Zinfandel, because I was drunk off my ass, on my own zinfandel at the time."

"You're *MARVIN WILLIAMS?* You don't look like a *Marvin.*"

"Tell me about it. Why do you think I go by Z?" Little giggle. *Marvin? Too funny.*

"Anyway, when I was released the next morning because my father pulled some strings, I decided to *become* Mr. Zinfandel. Strange, I know. My friends all thought it was *cool*, and so did I, at the time." He smirks,

shaking his head.

"Not anymore?" I smirk back.

"Ah, no. However, my changed name brought me a certain notoriety and an independence from my parents I wouldn't have otherwise had. So, I filled out the necessary paperwork, paid all the fees, hired a lawyer, and legally changed my name to Mr. Z Zinfandel. Again, my friends thought it was hilarious, and once my parents found out and lost it, I thought it was an even better idea...

"... Enraging my father was a sort of hobby of mine, at the time. He had always called me Mr. Zinfandel, because of my success within his winery, so it pissed him right off that I used his little nickname for me, and made it legal. My mother was more tolerant, and she loved me regardless, but she did try to intervene. Actually, she thought since I was changing my name anyway; why not change it to her maiden name... *Marvinelli,* my name-sake. But, *Marvin Marvinelli* didn't really work for me either."

SERIOUSLY?! When he smirks, I can't help but burst out laughing.

"No, that does s-sound a little odd," I say through my rolling laughter.

Grinning Z continues... "So many months later, much money later, and many fights with my father later, I officially became Mr. Zinfandel, a 21 year old independently wealthy, heir to the Williams Estate and the Williams Estate Wineries. It's quite a mouthful actually." Again, he grins at me, like he's both proud of his name, and mortified by it at the same time.

"That's fairly impressive, Mr. Z. Zinfandel. What did you do after the name change? In College?"

Actually, I vaguely remember this story, *kind of,* told by my judgmental mother years before. I think the Williams' must have kept it as quiet as possible.

"Afterward, I took control of the shares I had been given over the years in the Wineries, convinced my father to either let me be the CEO of my own labels, or I would sue him for monies owed, copyright infringements, and basically, for the theft and usage of my own blends, which I could prove were mine from my teen years. You see, my father had made the monumental mistake of telling many, *many* people at the time about my success within the winery. Therefore, all his boasting and bragging would come back to bite him in the ass, if he hadn't signed off as CEO. Strangely, though he was obviously quite pissed at me, he was also impressed, maybe even proud of my tenacity...

"... And that's it. I'm CEO still, but of the *entire* company, not just my own wineries within it. I own everything now that my parents have died, *and* I make an excellent Zinfandel. Wouldn't you agree?" Again, with the smirky grin.

"Yes, I would. It IS quite excellent."

I can't believe Z is the same Marvin Williams I had heard about in my youth. It's all a little too 'small-world' and kind of strange to me. Then again, my parents' influence and social circuit knows no bounds, so I've probably met most of the Upper Class in all parts of the Continental U.S. at some function or other.

"Why didn't I ever meet you before now, at some of the parties our parents attended?"

"Well, I'm 5 years older than you, and I rebelled early, refusing to attend all the *elite* parties my parents attended by the time I was 13 or 14, so really, you wouldn't have ever met me after you were maybe 8 or 9 years old." Oh. That makes sense.

"I bet I would have had a crush on you, even then..." Sipping my Zinfandel, I smile at him.

"Even *then*...? Does that mean you have a crush on me now?" Blush. *Shit.*

"No! No, I just meant, you were probably cute, and older, so naturally any of us younger girls would have had a crush on you."

Grinning, Z takes my hand and squeezes it lightly. "Relax Sweetheart. I was just teasing you. How are you feeling?"

"I'm good. But I have one glaringly obvious question."

"Which is?"

"Why the hell are you working as an Accounts Manager for Petri-Dunne?"

"Ah, yes. I'm working, as a favor for my friend Marty's father, Mr. Johnson Petri." *What?! Argh...* I'm choking on my drink now. *Awesome.* I even snorted a little. Yay me!

"Relax. It's nothing. I've done it before for Petri. He likes me; sadly, almost more than he likes his actual son. He brings me into his companies and offices, to clean out the messes... and Craig was a mess. So, he's out, I'm in *temporarily*, and my replacement for the New York office is being searched for as we speak. Incidentally, Shields isn't going to last long- just thought I would give you a heads up." He's grinning? *HE'S GRINNING? Why?!*

"Why is that funny? You know too much about me. You could tell Mr. Petri, and get me fired. Oh, god, you could humiliate me further in the company. Why are you grinning?"

"Your lack of trust no longer bothers me, it's almost *endearing*. I wouldn't do any of those things, and I think you know it. You *should* know it by now. But I think you're just so stuck on betrayal and trust issues that you wait for it at every turn. I am NOT going to fuck you over, Sweetheart. At least trust that, even if you can't entirely trust *ME*."

"I'm sorry but it's hard for me. I don't really trust anyone, ever."

"I know, and that's the only reason I'm not yelling, offended, or pissed at you over it."

With absolutely perfect timing, Z's front door buzzes. "Saved by the buzzer..." he grins again walking toward the door.

After putting everything on his dining room table, Z and I are quiet. Though it's not an *uncomfortable* silence as such, I know my last accusatory outburst has offended him some. I really should try to either trust him, or *pretend* to trust him better. Eventually, we thaw a little.

When the meal is over Z becomes relaxed enough with me again to tell me a few funny college pranks he participated in. God, I couldn't have done anything like he did. I spent my entire childhood and teen years scared to death of my parents and their disapproval. When I say as much, Z shakes his head. I can tell he's shocked and bothered by the way I was raised. Even I can finally see that it *is* a little bothersome, now that I'm slightly removed from the situation in Chicago.

==========

When we're finished tidying the dishes, and I am absolutely stuffed, my phone suddenly rings and I jump again. Well, to be fair, it's been a while. Should I? Shouldn't I? Why ruin a perfectly good meal. Z nods, and tells me to put it on speaker phone. Okay here we go...

"Hello, Marcus." I'm firm, steady, and I sound good.

"Hi Honey, where are you?"

"That's none of your business. What do you want?" Wow. I'm all *tough* with Z listening.

"Oh? I think it IS my business, and so do your parents. There's no reason to be so uncivilized. They're here with me. Would you like to speak with them?" No way! I'm not *that* tough. Gulp.

"No, thank you. What do you want Marcus?"

"I'll ask you again, honey. Where Are You?"

"And again, that's none of your business."

This back and forth is kind of fun actually. I can't help grinning. Marcus is silent for a minute. He's probably shaken from me challenging his authority. Good!

"Listen Honey, you've proved your point. I'm sorry about Kayla, *very sorry*, so why don't you come home, and we'll discuss it. Your parents would really like to see you as well."

"I'm not coming home right now- maybe never. I'm not entirely sure what I'm going to do. So, why don't you just wait for me to contact you?"

"Oh, I don't think so. Come home, *NOW*. I know you withdrew money, and I know you were at the Marriott, but you're not there now. I had your car returned home. Where are you? Just tell me, and I'll come and get you, and we'll work this all out."

"There's nothing to work out, Marcus. I'm furious with you, and your cheating, and a list of many, many other things. I'll return *if* and *when* I'm ready." There! That was firm.

Marcus is silent again. Quietly, I hear a muffling in the background, and low voices. *Shit!* My parents *are* actually there with him. Great! My resolve starts wavering slightly. Z suddenly takes my hand and squeezes it. Looking at me pointedly, he mouths, 'Relax. Be strong.' Okay. I'll try, I nod.

"Honey, your mother would like to speak with you." *Cringe*

"No. I'm not really in the mood for my mother's threats and accusations Marcus. Why don't you just deal with her?" There's another pause, and more silence.

"Your mother would like you to know she has spoken with Dr. Simmons..." *Who?* "...You remember Dr. Simmons, don't you? Well, he has kindly agreed to see you, to help you sort through all your issues. Would you like that?"

Z mouths *who*, and I shrug my shoulders.

"Sort through *my* issues? My issues are rather easily *sorted*, Marcus. My husband is a cheating asshole who spends his days either ignoring me or berating and chastising me based on his current mood... So no, I wouldn't like to see a doctor about *my* issues."

169

I swear I heard my mother gasp in the middle of that speech. *Asshole?* Yup... that's enough to set her off.

"Darling... That's ENOUGH!" *Flinch.* Z squeezes my hand once more. "You will stop behaving like a child this instant. Poor Marcus has been frantic to find you, and your father and I have been quite concerned as well. I want you to come home. You have played your little game long enough, and I expect you home in the next hour. Do you understand me?"

"I'm not going to be there in the next hour, mother. And please stop speaking to me like I'm a child..."

"THEN STOP BEHAVING AS SUCH! Poor Marcus has had to field questions..."

"Poor Marcus? *POOR MARCUS?!* Are you *insane* mother? *Poor Marcus* has been sleeping around a lot, *mother,* and though that may be acceptable in your life as a *slight infidelity,* it's not acceptable in MINE!"

And here's another long silence. I have to remind myself to breathe. I know Z is watching me with concern. Is my mother counting to ten as well?

"Darling, I will not continue to speak with you this way. You are being highly irrational and I will intervene if I must. You have one hour, or I take matters into my own hands." *How?*

Gulping, I ask, "How will you *intervene,* mother? What can you do? *Force me* to live with a cheating, abusive husband, against my will?! What can you *really* do?"

"Don't push this. You won't like the consequences. I guarantee it."

"I can't be there in an hour. And even if I could, I *WOULDN'T* be there in an hour. You can't do anything to me, anymore. Goodbye, mother. And goodbye Marcus."

"Dr. Simmons has the legal right now to forcibly confine and/or commit you *Darling.* I've had the paperwork drawn up. Marcus and I have signed and approved it all. This is over, and out of your hands. Return now and we'll talk about any *choices* you may have left." And then the phone slams down. *Huh.* I guess I got that particular talent from my mother. Giggle. *No!*

Catching my breath... What the *fuck* was that? Holy shit! *Forcibly confined? Committed?* Jesus, I'm shaking. I can't even think at the moment. Everything in my head is all confused and kind of fuzzy or something. What does that mean?

"What does she mean, Z?" I whisper. I can barely breathe at this point.

"Who is Dr. Simmons, Sweetheart?" Z asks me in return.

"I don't know. I have *NO* idea. What is she talking about? Can she do that to me?" Gasp.

"Breathe, love. Come on. Breathe slowly with me. Breathe with me..." *Oh my god.*

"What is my mother going to do Z? What does that *MEAN?* I don't understand. Papers drawn up? Marcus' and her consent? For *WHAT?!*"

After an eternity, Z pulls away from me. Oh! I hadn't realized he was hugging me, that's so nice of him. Pulling away, Z looks so concerned but I don't know if it's *for* me, or because of what might *happen* to me.

"I'm going to make a quick call. My very good friend is a psychiatrist in New York. He is *very* professional and *very* discreet. I'm just going to ask him a few questions. Okay?"

All I have in me is a nod. Everything else is cold and just kind of blank. I don't know that I can even walk at the moment.

==========

When Z returns, minutes later, he looks a little tense. What now? Christ, if he now wants me out of here, I'm in trouble. I don't even know if I can function, let alone leave for Chicago. Please don't make me leave. *Please don't leave me alone.*

"Okay, this is what I have so far. Simmons is a very well known, much respected psychiatrist out of Chicago. I say that because on paper he is above reproach. He has never been accused or reprimanded for breach of any ethics laws. He's never even had a formal complaint. There is absolutely nothing against him, anywhere…

"…However, my friend has heard, and it is widely known within the psychiatric community that Simmons practices a little controversially, and these practices are *loosely* regulated. He has a major 'god complex' and he practices within the upper crust of society only, because he's one of them. And he specializes in unruly teens, teens with alcohol or drug dependencies and the like. Basically, any teen who has, or *could* embarrass their very wealthy, established parents are sent to Dr. Simmons… to *cure*."

"But why me? I'm 29 years old! I've never seen him before. I don't know who he is. Why would he agree to my mother's demands to have me…" deep breath "forcibly confined and/or committed against my will? It doesn't make any sense Z! Because I left my cheating husband, this well-known psychiatrist is willing to break the law? It's not like I'm a minor. He would have to prove to a Judge that I'm unfit, or like, mentally incapacitated or something, right?"

"My friend Mack is curious as well. I gave him a slight overview of events, and he was shocked that your mother thinks any of this is necessary or even easily possible. Mack would like to talk to you, to understand your take on things. He's willing to work with me to help you, if you let him."

"Why would he want to? I'm clearly more trouble than I'm worth, especially if he has to go up against someone as well known and respected as this Simmons is. Why would he want to?"

"First; because I asked him to get involved. And second; because Mack is a good man. I've known him a long time, and I trust him with my life. But more importantly, I trust him with *your* life."

God… I need to think, but I just can't think anymore. The fear is making me mindless. What do I do? I have to return. I have no choice.

"Why are you doing this?" I whisper.

"Because I care about you, and I want you to have a little peace in your life. I want you to experience life for yourself. It's not like you've ever

really lived for yourself. And I want that for you. I want you to make choices, because *you* choose them, not because you are *forced* to choose them."

I just can't think anymore. There is nothing working in my brain. Everything seems strangely distorted or something.

"Would you please meet with Mack? He's a great guy, and I'll be here if you need me to be, or I'll give you privacy if you need it. I promise this is a good thing."

"Um... okay. When?"

"He said he can meet us here tomorrow evening for dinner. That way, when you and he meet it will be in a friendly, casual environment. I explained you have major issues with trust, and he seems to think you would do well on familiar ground. Does that sound okay? You can always change your mind tomorrow. There's no pressure, Sweetheart."

"Okay, tomorrow for dinner. But don't think you've fooled me. I know you were going to cook something up to have me stay here tomorrow anyway."

"Yes, I was. And this worked out perfectly." Finally, he's smiling again and much less tense.

After a long pause in conversation, while my brain still spins, Z sits back down beside me. Taking my hand he asks, "How are you? *Honestly.*"

"I'm a little shell-shocked, I think. I hate my mother's voice- I always have. So, even now when she speaks to me, I cringe. Good or bad, I can't stand speaking to her, *ever.* I always thought I was lucky that Marcus and my mother got along so well, because they usually spoke and arranged things and events... and I just sat back and let him because it was easier than me having to deal with her."

"Your mother sounds like a classic, wealthy, well-bred, superficial Bitch. I can see why you hate the sound of her voice. To tell you the truth, it gave me the willies as well." The *willies?*

As I burst out laughing, Z pulls me into his lap for a very tight, very warm hug. I love this. I *need* this.

"Are you tired, Sweetheart? You've had another horrendous day. Would you like to have a rest, or maybe a long bath? I have an *amazing* Jacuzzi tub." Did he just wiggle his eyebrows again? Oh, yup, he did.

"Um, that sounds good. Will you join me?"

I can't believe I just asked that, but I don't really seem to care anymore. My life is spiraling out of control, and I want to spend time with this man, just a little longer.

"Absolutely." And lifting me from his lap, Z takes my hand and leads me to his master suite.

============

Once in Z's tub, I'm in heaven. Covered in millions of bubbles, I'm naked, but fully covered so I can relax completely. The tub is deep and large and I have lots of space, while wishing I didn't have sooo much

space. Z is leaning naked, against the tub wall opposite me. Our feet are tangled with each other. I know my legs are slightly prickly, and I dread him touching them by mistake, yet I also want him to touch me, *not* by mistake. *Christ.* I really am nuts.

"What are you thinking about?" No *way.*

"Nothing."

"Sweetheart, tell me please. I can see you thinking over there."

"I'm not. I'm just enjoying your tub, which IS amazing, as you said it would be."

"No. There's more. Are you thinking about your asshole husband, or your atrocious mother?"

"Of course- both. Also, about my life, this tub, Macy's, your home... pretty much everything. My brain doesn't ever really stop. It never stops. It's exhausting actually."

"Come over here."   Okay!

Moving across, I lean against Z's side on the Jacuzzi seat.

"Sit on your butt on the bottom of the tub between my legs. It's okay, you won't drown. I promise I can swim."

Moving, I sit on the bottom and the water rises to just below my chin when Z asks, "May I massage your shoulders, love?"

"Yes, please."

Why does he always ask before touching me? That's so nice of him. I wish everyone asked permission before touching me.

As Z starts massaging my shoulders and neck, I feel boneless. I want him to touch me all over suddenly. I find myself moving closer to his body, I want to be surrounded by him. I need to be surrounded by him. Oh my *GOD!* DON'T ask it. DON'T DO IT! **DON'T!!**

"Um...Z?" and before he can answer, I whisper, "...will you have sex with me? Ah... *now?*"

"Give me your hand," he growls.

And that's it. I asked, and we are stepping out of the Jacuzzi. I can't believe it worked. I can't believe he's going to have sex with me again! This is so exciting, I'm shaking with anticipation.

CHAPTER 18

After toweling me off rather quickly with an infectious little grin, Z takes my hand and leads me out of his bathroom.

"Where, Sweetheart?" *Where?* What does *THAT* mean? "Which bedroom would you like to go to?" Oh, *thank god...*

"Here... if that's okay?"

"Absolutely." And holding my hand firmly, we cross the room to Z's huge, sexy, red and burgundy bed.

Bending his head, Z kisses me deeply. It feels like forever since we've kissed, and I've missed it. Moaning, I reach around his neck and pull him even harder to my mouth.

Bending me backward with one hand, Z uses his other to pull back the bedding. This is so sexy. I've never had sex like this before. I've never really been a part of the step by step motions of *getting* to the sex. Sex just kind of happened to me, except with Z.

Tugging my towel off, Z continues kissing me as he lifts me by my waist onto the bed. On my knees facing him, Z and I are the same height. I don't feel overwhelmed or frightened at all. I *want* to do this. I *want* to be a part of this.

So, tugging Z's towel off, I reach for his penis and start rubbing at it. I'm not actually sure what to do, but I figure a back and forth stroke is standard, and going by Z's moan, I assume I'm doing it right.

"You're touch is amazing Sweetheart. I love you holding me in your hand..."

"What else can I do? What would make this really good for you? Z, what do I do?"

"You can continue, maybe gently cup my balls, or, ah, lick your palm so you slide better..."

So, licking my palm, I take his balls in one hand, and continue stroking him with the other. Oh, my... His testicles are kind of squishy, but firm too. This whole area is weird feeling. Z is standing still but making little sounds in the back of his throat, so I think I'm doing okay for him.

Z slowly moves his hand down my waist, in between my legs. Opening my folds with his fingers, he moves around my entrance, teasing me without entering me, and it feels good. I find myself moving closer to his hand, almost cupping myself in his hand. I wish he would touch me harder or something. I want more. *Wow...* that's a first for me.

Looking at Z's penis, I see a little liquid coming out of the tip. It's glassy and I start moving my hand over the top, pushing it further down his length with my movements. Z moans a little louder, and I'm feeling bold. What does that taste like? Should I try? Tugging on him a little, I try to make it clear that I want him on the bed, and Z understands.

Removing his hand from me, he gracefully crawls on the bed, as I turn to look at his body.

"May I taste it?" I'm blushing again, I can feel it, but I don't really care. "*Please...*"

Taking Z into my mouth slowly; I'm surprised by his taste. It's not

gross, or over-powering. It's kind of salty, but not really unpleasant. Moving a little over the tip, my tongue begins flicking at him. When Z's left leg suddenly lifts and bends outward, I want to explore more of him. Putting his penis in my mouth, I slide my tongue and mouth up and down the shaft. He fills me, and I'm not able to take the whole thing, but Z's body tenses a little, so again, I think I'm doing this okay for him.

"What else do I do?" I whisper.

"Ah, what you're doing is good, maybe a little faster and... ah, try sucking a little." Okay.

Taking him back in my mouth, I suck him in and take more of him deeper into my mouth, but Z suddenly jumps.

"Um, maybe suck a little less hard, Sweetheart. You're going to make me cum quicker than I want that way." I am? I want to... or maybe not. Do I really want his stuff *in my mouth?*

"Isn't that a good thing? Don't you want to do that to me?"

"I don't want to *do* anything to you. We can do this together though. Would you like to feel pleasure, while giving it to me as well?" Yes. How? Oh, and then it hits me, the 69-thing Marcus wanted to try once. Yuck.

"Come here, Sweetheart. Place yourself over my mouth. I *need* to please you as well. I want to taste you..."

So, climbing awkwardly over Z, I kneel over his face. This is so, so embarrassing. I hate this. He can see everything and I can't hide myself down there when I'm like this. This is too much, and I can't hide at all.

"Sweetheart, stay with me. If you don't want this, we stop now. Do you want this?" No. Not really. But I want Z.

"Whatever you want. Do whatever. I'm fine. Honestly."

After an uncomfortable silence grows between us, I move away from his mouth embarrassed. Sitting on the bed beside Z, I'm mortified. I can't do anything right. I swear to god, I'm just useless with this sex stuff.

"What did I do wrong? I'm sorry," I whisper through my embarrassment.

"You didn't do anything wrong, but I don't think you're very comfortable with this, and I don't want to make you uneasy. Come back to me. Come here and kiss my lips." No!

"I'm fine..." and quickly taking Z back into my mouth, I suck him down deep, as I throw my leg over his face. Feeling his whole body jump makes me smile. Ha! Maybe I am okay at this. And then...

"Oh *god!*" I moan around him in my mouth. He has licked me down there and inserted a finger at the same time. It feels amazing, and dirty, and sexy, and... *REALLY* good. Z does it again. That is... *ah...* my knees start shaking already. *Christ!* He's good.

Taking him back in my mouth, I find it really difficult to concentrate on him. Everything he does, I want to imitate on his body. I feel Z flicking his tongue, and I flick mine in return. When we both moan at the same time, I can't help but smile as I feel myself writhe on him again.

Holding my hips, Z slightly lifts me up and down, back and forth across his mouth. One thumb is merciless on my clitoris. My moans are frequent and sometimes very loud. I can't stop. Trying to focus on him, I keep up my movements, but it just doesn't feel the same, as what he's doing to me. He isn't as loud, or moving as much.

"Am I doing this right? I'm sorry... I don't know what I'm doing..."

"You are doing *more* than alright. But if I don't stay in some kind of control I'll cum, and I don't want to yet. Relax, love. I'm very much enjoying giving *and* receiving." Was that his smile-voice?

Z moans again, and I relax further. He is working me so good; I start to feel the internal pulling thing- that movement and tightening inside that means I'm close. I wonder if he is close too. I wonder if I can actually make him release with just my mouth.

"Sweetheart, I don't want to cum in your mouth. I don't think you're ready for that. Please stop now. *Please...*" he begs with another moan. This is great! I guess I *can* make him release. I love making him moan like that.

Z impales me harder with 2 fingers, and I feel all my muscles tighten up around him. Everything is getting tense again. Everything feels tight, as he works me with his mouth and fingers. *Ahhhh...*

And suddenly I find myself on my back, as he twists out of the way, moving lower to take me again with his mouth. *Oh my god!* My legs are raised over his shoulders and his one arm holds my stomach flat. Uncontrollably, my hips jump and my back arches. Everything is so tight, I feel like I'm going to lose it soon.

"Z? I'm getting that *feeling*... It's happening again... Um, I want you..." Shit! *Hurry up.*

I don't know what he does next, but the pressure is incredible. And before my mind can process what he's doing to me, my body convulses and I hear my own screams echoing in the room.

When I am slightly coherent, I see Z pulling a condom onto himself. Watching him, I realize I *want* him inside me so badly, even as I try to pull his thighs closer to me.

"Hold on, Sweetheart..." as Z begins lifting me toward him. Pulling me into his lap, Z kisses me so tenderly, I moan into his mouth. Wrapping my legs around his waist, Z maintains a kind of crossed leg, sitting position, with me straddling him. This feels so intimate. I hate eye contact, and this position demands it. I'm starting to feel a little overwhelmed by the position.

"It's just you and I, Sweetheart... And I want to kiss you, and watch you as pleasure consumes you. You are so beautiful, and sensuous, and *brave* with me. I want you to feel this between us. Can you try, love? Can you be here with me?" God, I want to. *Sensuous?*

"Yes..."

And taking my lips again, Z lifts me once more, gently over his penis, as he starts a slow, up-down motion. Feeling him enter me slowly is exquisite. With my breasts rubbing against his chest, and my arms around my neck, I feel him... *all* of him entering me.

Pulling away from our kiss, Z smiles at me while staring hard into my eyes. I have to remember to breathe. Please, I don't want to freak out over this closeness. This is Z. This is Z here with me.

"You feel like a dream, and you look like an angel. Do you know how stunning you look right now, all flushed, and ready for me? Your eyes are beautiful blue pools of hunger and your lips are swollen and darkened from my kisses," Z says while continuing his slow up and

down motion.

"No... I don't feel stunning... or, ah, *beautiful....*" Blush. *Shit.* Don't do this!

"But you are. If you trust nothing else I say to you, trust that. You are beautiful to me right now... *always.*" Oh no! My eyes are filling with tears again.

"Oh, Sweetheart... I wish you had known this before me. I wish you had felt this kind of intimacy. You were made for tenderness and adoration. You were made for sex and passion. You were made for... *me,* I think."

Bursting into tears at his lovely words, I try to hide my face in his neck. I can't stand this intimacy. I almost want the bad sex I've had, so I know how to handle it. At least with the bad 'Marcus-sex' I know what to expect. This is too lovely, too intense. I don't know how to handle this.

"Please don't cry. *Please...* You're breaking my heart here. Sweetheart... I want you to feel only pleasure..."

"Oh, I do. You just overwhelm me with your words, and your kindness. I, I don't know what to do or say to you. You are just so... *so much,* but in a good way."

Lifting my hips again, pulling me harder- faster back onto his body, my breath hitches.

"Just feel *this.* Please don't think about anything but you and me, right here, like this."

"Okay... But this is so wonderful; I don't know what to do. *You* are so beautiful, Z. You make me sad because I, I want you so badly." More tears falling. *Dammit.* I can't stop.

"You have me. I'm going nowhere until you tell me otherwise. I'm here. Just feel me, love."

Z starts a harder movement, up and down, dragging himself through my body. I try to calm my tears because I don't want to cry, I *want* to feel all this, this goodness, this pleasure, this... *love?* I feel like I kind of love Z. I feel like I wish he was mine forever. I feel like I wish I could *keep* him forever...

Bending my legs so I sit on my chins, I have more mobility. My back is still a little tender, but in this position, I can help Z now. I can move easier with his gentle thrusts.

With his hands still on my bottom, and my legs in better use, I can take him in faster and harder. He feels so good inside me. He is a gentle stretching, and a deep impaling.

When Z takes my lip's once again, I feel an urgency to get into him, to devour him with my mouth. I want to devour him so that I'll never forget this feeling. Z kisses me just as intensely as I want to kiss him.

Speeding up our movements, Z pulls away and watches my face closely. He seems to want me to feel good. He looks closely to make sure I'm still here, still okay with this.

I'm okay. I'm more than okay, I'm actually *happy.* So smiling at him, I take his lips once again.

Z pulls away again after forever, and holding my breasts in his hands, he begins pushing me into a position on my back. Uncurling my legs underneath me, Z does the same. My spine throbs on my back, but not too painfully.

Sitting on his chins now, he pulls my hips until my body is on the incline of his thighs. I feel so exposed in this position, and as Z looks down at my body I realize I am just that; very, *very* exposed to him.

Touching my nipples, rolling them in his fingers, Z gauges my reactions closely. I can only watch him, as my body tenses and tightens inside. When he looks down at where are bodies are joined, I want to cringe at the intimacy, but Z just stares with a kind of stunning lust on his face.

"I love watching as I enter your body. You were made for me, Sweetheart. Look. Watch your body take me in. It's beautiful to watch."

Holy *shit!* Watching; I see what he means. He *was* meant for me. Watching my body open up to him is beautiful. It's not gross, or mean, or even painful. It just looks right somehow. So, lifting my knees higher and further apart against his sides, I see more, and feel more. He is so deep inside me, and yet again, there is no pain.

Seemingly hours later, Z grasps my hips, lifting me further up his body as his movements increase in speed and intensity. My chest and breath start to mimic his. We are panting and sweating and writhing and grinding.

I can feel the now familiar pull that Z creates inside me. I can feel it tightening up my body. My legs are shaking and my stomach is contracting.

Z alternates between watching my face, and watching our joining. He looks so handsome, and intense, and... *controlled.* I feel no fear of him. I feel only pleasure and security with Z. This is such an amazing feeling. I feel as though I'm kind of free of something, though I'm not exactly sure what that something is, but I don't care. This is amazing.

When Z slides his hand in between us, I watch as he spreads his hand against me while his thumb starts working my clitoris. *Oh my GOD!* The reaction is instant. My whole body jumps into his hand and my breath explodes from my chest.

"Breathe Sweetheart. You're almost there. I can feel you grasping me inside."

"Z... *please...*"

"Does it feel good, love? Do you want more?" Oh, *god...* YES!

Increasing the pressure, my whole body writhes on his lap. This is incredible. I feel it happening. My head starts moving back and forth on the pillow. My stomach is so tight, I feel the muscles being pulled. My insides feel stretched and full. Z is too big now. I'm starting to struggle a little with his size inside me. This is taking on an intensity I'm unfamiliar with. It's too much this time.

"Sweetheart, relax for me. Just breathe... and feel the building of pressure."

Moving my hands to my sides, I grasp the sheets while my body continues to writhe. This pressure is killing me. It's too intense.

Opening my eyes, I look at Z, and he looks like he's in pain. He is so beautiful, but he's struggling to hold onto his control. Let go for Z! Everything tightens to that incredible tension, and then I just snap.

Screaming, my whole body jumps and convulses, as Z holds my hips steady against him. Staring at his face, I see his control shatter, as he punches into me once, twice, three more times, with corded neck and

strained stomach muscles until finally he groans... and releases one final gasp. His release is spectacular to watch. *He* is spectacular to watch.

Moving his legs quickly, Z collapses on my body, kisses me, and rolls me onto his chest. My stomach lands on his erection, and he groans again with a little writhing motion against me. Catching my breath, I try to sit up, but my arms are too weak. I want to look at him. I want to see his face. Trying to sit up once more on my forearms, I finally see him.

Sweat-covered, flushed, and panting heavily, Z is the most beautiful man I have ever known. He makes my heart actually *hurt*.

"I wish I could love you, Z. I wish I could love you forever..." I whisper.

Z lowers his chin to stare into my eyes, and whispers, "Why can't you Sweetheart?"

"You know I can't. I'm not meant for this... I'm meant to go back to them. But Z, this will *always* be the best week of my life." And grinning to burn the intensity and sadness away, I add, "The best *sex* of my life."

Wrapping me tightly in his arms, pressing me back onto his chest, Z whispers in return, "I wish you believed you could have this. That you *were* meant for this... *meant for me.*"

"I wish I could believe that, too." God, that's such a sad thing to admit but I know it's true. I know I could never have something like this, and certainly I could never have *someone* like this. I don't think someone like me is meant for a happy ending.

In the long silence that follows between us, my eyes grow heavy. Glancing at Z's clock, I see it's nearly midnight. Z and I made love for hours, and it was amazing, and kind, and... beautiful. It is a memory to hold forever. A memory I will pull out whenever I need something good in my life.

Z is a memory I will always hold tightly as the greatest of my life. He will always be the man who gave me everything, without taking anything from me. Z will always be this special memory of time in which I felt happiness for the first and probably only time, in my entire life.

"You are the best thing that has *EVER* happened to me, Z. Thank you."

And squeezing me tighter to his chest, Z whispers, "Sleep, Sweetheart. I'm going nowhere, and you aren't leaving me..."

No, I'm not leaving you, but I will be taken away...

Wednesday, June 1st

CHAPTER 19

OW! My body hurts. Over and over. Bang, bang, bang. What *IS* that? Everything hurts so badly. There is pain everywhere. What the hell is happening to me?

Opening my eyes, I see Marcus above me. NO!! Where's Z? What is Marcus doing here? Oh, *NO!*

"Please stop Marcus! Please! You're ripping me open again!! Please stop!! Fuck! I don't want this anymore! No more! I hate it! I hate sex! I hate you!"

Oh the pain is too much! Pushing against his body, I try to fight him again. God, this is agony.... Bang, bang, bang.

"Why don't you ever stop when I say NO?! Stop Marcus!! You're *KILLING* Me! *STOP!!*"

And then I scream when Marcus covers my mouth with his hand. Biting it, I push again with my hands, until suddenly the weight is lifted. Marcus is off the bed. I can't even see his face anymore.

Why is it so dark? Where is he? Oh, god. Is he going to take me from behind again?

"No! Not there! Don't take me there! It hurts so bad back there. Please! Stop hurting me! I don't want you to do me BACK THERE!"

I'm screaming at him. I'm screaming as he looms over me. I know I'm screaming, over and over. But I'm blinded by the darkness until suddenly the world erupts in light.

"No! Don't look at my body in the light! No!" Christ, I can't stop screaming!

"Look at me! Look! Sweetheart! Look at my face! *NOW!*" *What?*

Turning my head, back and forth, I look. Trying to adjust my sight to the blinding light, I look for the voice. What's happening?

"I'm right here. I'm right beside you. Look at ME!"

But I can't see. I can't see anything, but light.

Begging and gasping, "Who are you? I, I can't see. There's too much light."

"Sweetheart, it's Z. I'm standing beside you. Look to your left." *Shit.* I see NOTHING!

"I don't see anything but light. Please turn the lights off."

"The lights *ARE* off. There's only a little sunlight in the room. It's still mostly dark. Look at me."

Staring hard to my left, I see nothing. There is nothing but brightness; a kind of blinding glare in my eyes. I feel like I'm staring at the sun. And then, I suddenly feel the pain.

My head is pounding so hard, I can barely breathe. Turning to my side, I hold my head tight in my hands, desperate for relief, but there's no relief. There is nothing but this excruciating, blinding pain.

Oh my god. I'm going to throw up. Leaning to the side of the bed, I vomit violently. I can't help it. The pain is so intense- blinding in its intensity, I gag and wretch. More vomit. Outside my agony, I think I hear Z speaking gently to me. I think I sense him leaving me.

"I'm sorry. Please don't leave me."

"I'll be one minute, just hold on."

There's more vomit, and more agony. More everything. What's happening?! I think I feel Z close to me again. Actually, I'm sure he's beside me, but... I Can't *See* Him. Oh, *shit*. More vomit.

After forever, there is finally a pause in my vomiting.

"I can't see you. Are you here?" I beg.

"I'm here. Can you see me at all?" Z sounds so anxious.

"No... Oh, *god*... What's *HAPPENING* to me?!"

"I'm right here beside you. I'm holding your hair out of the way. Can you feel me beside you?"

"Yes, I think so... Why can't I see you?" I gag.

"I don't know. I think you may have a migraine. Just relax, Sweetheart. Do you still feel you need to vomit?"

"I don't think so. Did you really hold my hair back, like a gentleman would?"

"Yes, I did- Like a gentleman..." I can hear his smile-voice again.

Smiling back, I whisper, "Thank you."

==========

However long later, Z shifts beside me. I still can't see him, but I *feel* him.

"I'm sorry I threw up on your floor."

"I don't care about the floor, Sweetheart."

"Why can't I see, Z? Everything still just looks like bright light. It really hurts my head and my eyes."

"I don't know. But when you are a little better, I would like to take you to the hospital to get you checked out. Okay?" *The hospital?!* NO!

"No! I can't go there. Marcus and my parents will take me away. The hospital is bad for me. I *remember* that. Z, please don't take me to the hospital."

"Would you allow a physician to visit you here? Please?" Oh, his voice is so lovely.

Finding and holding Z's hand, I feel sad. This is so sad, I think I'm going to cry again. Ooops, I think I already am crying.

"Please don't be sad, Z. I hate hearing you sad. I'm so sorry... I wish I could see you... I think you're breaking *my* heart..." I can feel my tears dripping down my face, and I can feel Z squeeze my hand tighter.

"I'm good, love. I don't like any of this, but please, think about you right now. Can you try to open your eyes again for me?" He asks as I feel him wipe away my tears with a cloth.

When I try to open my eyes, the light is so bright; I instantly flinch from

the agony. Gagging, I wretch, as Z holds me tighter, pushing something into my lap. I think I'm going to vomit again. I need to get it out of me. I'm so nauseous, I feel like I'm swaying in his arms.

"Easy, Sweetheart. Throw-up if you have to. Don't worry; it's just you and me here."

"Thank you, Z. I'm so sorry about all this. I don't know why this is happening. But I feel like I *should* know why."

"Don't worry about it now; you can think yourself to death later."

Ah, *that* was his smile-voice, for sure.

Once the nausea passes, I try to lean back down on the bed, but Z stops me.

"Just stay here with me, Sweetheart. I like you in my arms. And I don't really want you falling asleep right now."

"Z... I'm really, *really* tired. Can I please just have a little rest?"

"No, Sweetheart. Please, just trust me. Stay right here, okay? I'll be back in one minute. I just want to reach my phone, okay?"

"All right."

==========

The second Z leaves my side, I'm instantly frightened. Oh. My. *God.* I'm alone, and I can't feel anything. I can't see anything. What's going to happen to me? I'm defenseless here.

"Z? *Z?!* Where are you? PLEASE!" Well, that sounded like a scream. Gasp. The pain!

"I'm here. I'm right here! I told you I would be back in one minute. I'm not leaving you. Please, don't panic."

"Sorry..."

"It's okay, love. But I need you to stay calm. I'm worried about your lack of vision, and I don't want you stressed any further. Can you do that for me? Can you try to stay calm?"

"I'm trying, but it's so hard. I can't *see* anything. I don't know if you're here, or away, or if you're mad at me. I don't know *anything.*"

"Just know that I'm here, I'm going to try to make you well, and you need to stay calm. I'm going to make a call in the bathroom to a physician friend of mine, and then we'll go from there. Here... let me prop you up against the headboard."

Moving me slowly, Z settles me against the pillows. Once I'm fully upright, the pain in my head and back is just excruciating.

"Z... I'm sorry... But my head and back hurt too much like this. Please, can I lie down on my side? *Please?*" I beg, knowing I sound slightly manic and crazed.

"Here, let me help you rest on your side, upright. If you're going to throw-up, the bowl is on the bed in front of you. I'll be just one minute."

"Why do you have to leave? Please, just talk on the phone right here."

"Just one minute, Sweetheart."

It takes only seconds for me to get that panicky alone feeling again. Christ! My head is killing me. I don't think I've ever had a headache this

bad in my life. Trying to stay calm, I listen for Z's voice. His lovely voice is muffled, though angry sounding through the door. What the hell is he saying?

Listening closer, I hear certain words in certain sentences, all mumbled together. I think I hear the words 'hospital and Marcus and fever and psychotic, and the Beaumonts...' And then I hear Z yell, 'Get here now!' Wow, I heard that one clearly.

Shit! None of that sounds good. I have to get out of here now. I think Z is trying to have Marcus and my parents meet us at the hospital. Dammit! My parents will take me away as soon as they find me.

Standing, I feel for the bedside table. GOD! My head feels like it's going to explode. My back hurts less in comparison to my head, which is good, I guess. I don't know where anything is. I don't even know where my purse or keys are. What do I do?

Z is going to help them take me away. I knew it. I *always* knew. I think he knows my parents. I think he knows Marcus. Maybe Marcus told him to follow me around. *Shit.* I wonder if he's working for my parents. He said he wasn't scared of them. He said they couldn't hurt him. Maybe he *IS* with them.

Making my way to the bedroom door is hard, but finally I feel the doorknob. Pulling it open and feeling out, I realize I'm in Z's closet. *Fuck!* I'll just hide here. Maybe Z will think I left, and he'll leave to look for me, *for them,* and then I'll be alone.

Sitting on the floor, I curl my knees up to my chest and rest my pounding, throbbing head on my knees. Quiet. Don't panic. I'll just rest for a minute until he leaves.

==========

"Sweetheart. Open your eyes. Can you see anything?" Marcus whispers. *Flinch.*

With my eyes closed tight, I respond, "No Marcus, I still can't see. I'm sorry." Did he just gasp at me?

"What are you doing in here? Were you running away from me?"

"No, *Honey.* I know better. My parents told me I could never get away, and you've told me a hundred times that I couldn't leave. So, *no.* I'm going nowhere. I just needed some privacy."

There, that sounded like the truth. Ha! Marcus is quiet, probably trying to think of something else to accuse me of.

"Sweetheart, I would like you to come back to bed now."

"Please don't call me that. *That* is someone else. I really don't feel well, and I don't want to have sex... okay?" I whisper and hope. Please, please, *please.*

"Okay, love. No sex today, but I really need to get you in the bed." No sex? Yeah, right.

"Is this a trick Marcus?"

"No. No trick. I'm just going to get some clothes to put on you, and

then I'll put you into bed. Is that okay?" *Clothes?* SHIT! I'm naked again. What is *WITH* that?

"Yes, please. But no peeking..." I can't help but giggle.

"No. I won't peek, I promise." *Really?* That's a first.

Slowly Marcus helps me stand. Walking, he leans me against his body. This is nice. This is the first time Marcus has ever touched me nicely, or even held me.

"You're never nice to me Marcus. You're always mean, or you ignore me or you just *hurt* me. But this is nice. Why are you different now?"

"I just feel differently toward you. You are wonderful, and I wanted to show you that I think you're wonderful. Come on now. Sit down, and I'll help with your clothes."

"Thank you. You've never dressed me before. You usually only scratch and pull, or tug and bruise to get my clothes off. Why are you being nice now?" Did he just *flinch?* What the *hell?* "I'm sorry I won't say anything else. I know you're a good man. You and my parents told me I was lucky to have someone like you, so I'll be quiet. I'm really, *really* sorry, Marcus." Will he be mad at me anyway? Oh, probably. "Please don't be mad at me?"

"I'm not mad at all. Come on lift your bottom... there you go. Now I'm going to put this t-shirt on you, okay?"

"Oh, yes. Thank you. I feel better now. I wish I could see you. I would like to see what you look like when you're pretending to be nice to me."

Marcus is so strange. This isn't like him at all. What's he doing? Should I be nervous? *Shit.* Maybe he *is* tricking me.

"Please stop touching me now. I'm fine. I'm just going to have a rest. I'll prepare a proper meal shortly. Thank you for your attention, but I'm fine now. Please leave me alone."

"Sweetheart, are you here now?" *Huh?*

"Yes, of course I'm here. Thank you. Please leave me for just a little while. I'll be down soon." Oh, *god!* Just GO!

Marcus must be gone now, because everything is so quiet. I need to rest while I can. I need to recover while he lets me. I need to sleep for just a little bit because the pain always makes me so tired.

==========

"Listen Sweetheart. My friend will be here very soon, and I don't want you to be frightened, okay? I'll stay with you the whole time if you want. He's just going to talk to you a bit." *Uh huh.*

Here we go. It's always *just a friend.* It's always someone *special* who wants to meet me. It's always someone *nice,* until they're *NOT nice.*

"Are you going to take the pictures?" *Jeez...* is his body shaking on the bed?

"Um, no. Should I?"

"If that's what you want. How should I know? Whatever you want. I won't be any trouble for you or your friend. Can I just rest my body a

bit before he gets here? *Please* let me rest up." I'm so tired.

"Why does your body need to rest up?"

"Because of what you do to it. But it's fine. If you let me have just a little rest you can do that stuff again. I'll be fine."

"Why do you need to rest, Sweetheart?"

"I'm sorry. I don't understand. You *know* why. When you're done, I get a little rest before you start again."

Is he moaning? What the *hell* is he doing? I've never heard Marcus make that awful noise before. It's a sad, ugly sound. I really don't like it much at all.

"I just need a little rest. I'll be good in a few minutes, I promise."

"Okay, Sweetheart, you can rest while we wait for my friend to arrive."

"Please don't call me that... *Sweetheart* is someone else."

CHAPTER 20

Am I awake? Voices talking scare me. Why can't I open my eyes? Why aren't my eyes working? *Shit!* Open your eyes. Open Your EYES! *FUCK!*

Jumping from the bed, I am stunned by the pain. Screaming, I sink to the floor on my knees.

"No! Stay still. Don't move, Sweetheart. *Fuck!*"

"Who are you?"

"Sweetheart, it's Z. Do you remember me?" Well, *duh.*

"Of course I remember you, what's happening? Why are you asking me that?!" I snap at him.

"Are you in pain?"

"Yes. My back is killing me, but it's my head! The pain is blinding. Oh, that's *too* funny. I'm actually blinded by the pain, Z. *Holy shit!*"

I can't help but burst out laughing at the agony. What else can I do? My head is pounding so badly with my laughter I can do nothing but keel over and hold my temples with my palms. This is **AGONY!**

"Stop! Stop, now. Listen to my voice. Listen to me, Sweetheart. I want you to stop laughing now, and take a deep breath."

"Okay. Sorry. But that *was* kind of funny... *in my defense.*"

"Yes it was, and maybe tomorrow we'll have a good laugh over it." Ah, his smile-voice.

"Do you know how much I love your smile-voice? I look so forward to hearing it. It makes me happy." I shouldn't have said that.

"My *smile-voice?*" And there it is again. Z is just so adorable sometimes.

"Yes, *that* voice. Right there; the voice with the smile attached to it. I love it, but please don't stop using it now that you know I like it, okay? Please?"

"I wouldn't dream of it. I like that my *smile-voice* pleases you."

"Thank you." I heard it that time, as well.

"My friend would like to meet you now, if that's alright." *Flinch.* Shit. Here we go...

"Um... I'll be good. Please don't hurt me this time..." I hate waiting for this to begin.

In the silence while I wait for the *friend,* my whole body begins shaking. Even my teeth are chattering loudly. I hate this. The wait is always the most brutal part for me. At least when it's happening I try to think of something else, but when I'm waiting for it to happen, all I can think about is what's *going* to happen. *This sucks!*

"I'm Dr. Michael McDonald, but you can call me Mack if you'd like. It's nice to meet you." *Mack?*

"What name do you want me to call myself?" Please not a bad one. I hate those. *Please.*

"Um, what would you like to call yourself?"

"How the hell do I know?" *Flinch.* "Sorry, sir. Are we going to play *doctor?* Should I be nurse-*something?*"

"No, we're not going to play doctor. We're just going to talk, and I'm going to examine you a little, okay?" Yup, here we go.

186

"You always examine me first, I know."

What does he want me to do? I can't tell. Whispering, "Z? Z, what does he want me to do? I can't tell. Please tell me 'cause I don't want to make him mad at me."

"Mack isn't going to *do* anything to you, Sweetheart. I promise. I won't let him or anyone else hurt you." Yeah, right. "Do you trust me?"

"Do you want me to?"

"Yes. Very much." Oh, well, that's easy then.

"Okay. Then tell me who I should be before he starts."

"Just be yourself, love. Mack just wants to ask you a few questions." Uh huh.

Turning around, I sit on the edge of the bed. Lifting my shaking hands, I remove my t-shirt quickly. No bra... good. But before I can slip my pants off, Z grabs my hands.

"What are you doing?"

"Getting ready. Does Dr. Mack want me to undress myself, or does he want to do it?"

"No. Mack, *my friend,* wants to talk to you *with your clothes ON.*"

Why? I don't get it. They never want my clothes on. Well, not after they first examine me, anyway. God, these days can be so long. I wish this was just over already.

"What is your name?" I jump.

"Who are you? I can't see."

"This is Dr. McDonald, or just Mack. Can you tell me your name?"

"I don't have one. Um, whatever you want. Please, just tell me! I'll be whatever name you tell me to be! I'm sorry, but I don't know who you want me to be!" Fuck! What game is this? No one is speaking. What are they waiting for?

"Call her Sweetheart. That's a good one, isn't it?" Z asks.

"Yes. I like that. I haven't been hurt when I'm her. Ha! You can't hurt me Mack if you call me Sweetheart! So there! Right, Z?"

"That's right. Mack wouldn't hurt you anyway; I wouldn't let him hurt you. And when you're Sweetheart, *nobody* can hurt you." Oh, thank god.

"Thank you..." I whisper, as tears of gratitude start falling down my face.

"May I look in your eyes, Sweetheart?"

"Yes. But they don't work. I don't know why, but they just won't see anymore."

"That's okay. I'm just going to open your eyelids slowly and take a look, okay?"

"Okay, but no peeking, *down there...*" giggle "...Sorry. I'll be good."

"You *are* good, Sweetheart. Can you relax your eyes for me? Just stop holding your eyes tightly closed..." *Whatever.* "That's good. Just relax your facial muscles."

"Am I doing what you want? Am I a good girl?" Ahhhhh! FUCK!! *Flinch.* "What are you doing?! You're hurting me! Z! He's burning my eyes! Please make him stop! You promised you wouldn't let anyone hurt me! You promised!"

"Mack isn't hurting you, Sweetheart. He's just shining a little light in

187

your eyes. It'll be over soon." Jesus *Christ!*

Hey! I see shapes now. Wow. Everything is really fuzzy and bright, but there are definite shapes now. Turning my head, I kind of recognize Z beside me. Raising my hand, I try to touch him. Finally, my hand lands on his face. He is stubblier than before.

"I can see you a little. Well, not see- *see* you, but you're kind of a blurry shape now."

"That's good, Sweetheart. I'm pleased. Can you try to focus on me better?"

Turning my head again, I see another shape. Oh, it's another man. Here we go. "How do you want me?"

"I'm sorry?"

"Um, where should I be? Just tell me, please. I'll be good. I'll do whatever you want."

"I don't want you anywhere but sitting right there beside Z." Uh huh.

"Z, how should I be?"

"You should be right here beside me. I told you no one is going to touch you, or *hurt* you today. Just relax beside me."

Relax?! RELAX?! God, as if I could relax. They're really starting to piss me off here. Why won't they just do it already? *Christ!*

"Fuck! Can we just do this! I hate the waiting! Look, we have to hurry. The staff will be back soon and I'm not supposed to be in here. Can you just do it? I have to hurry. You have to hurry up! *Which way do you want my body?!*"

"Sweetheart, listen to me carefully, Mack and I are not here to have sex with you. We don't want that. We're just here to help you get better. That's all. That's all we're going to do today. Trust me. We. Will. Not. Hurt. You."

"They always say that at the start, and then they hurt me. I don't trust you, so please JUST. DO. IT!!" I scream in his face.

"Stop! Listen to me. Mack and I..."

"No!"

Jumping up, I rip my pants down, turn, and throw my knees to the floor. With my stomach on the bed, my ass is right where it should be, even though my back screams in pain.

"There! Do it! I'm ready. Please! We're almost out of time."

"Jesus *CHRIST!* Stop this NOW!!" Z is screaming at me and I feel him shaking the bed.

Turning my head I ask, "Mack are you fucking my ass, or taking the pictures? Hurry up! Which *one?*"

"Um, neither. Z and I aren't going to hurt you, *or* take pictures. You're safe, Sweetheart. You. Are. Safe."

I am so sick of all the lies. They always say I'm safe. They always say it won't hurt when I whimper. Well, not this time! I'm not whimpering this time. FUCK *THAT!*

"Hurry up and start fucking me! My birthday party is starting soon, okay?! My parents will be back soon, and the staff is probably already preparing upstairs! Just fuck my ass! Do it, Z! HURRY UP!!!"

"I'm sorry, Z. I won't talk anymore. Please don't be angry with me.
I just though you wanted me to do that with Mack too." I whisper.
"It's okay, Sweetheart. Mack doesn't want to do anything sexual with
you, and I don't want him to either. Is that okay?"
"God yes. I never want them to do this to me, but I'm not allowed to
say no, unless they try to put their dicks in my dirty hole..." Shut up!
This is a secret.
"Who are *they*, Sweetheart?"
"Um... I'm not allowed to tell. But PLEASE don't be mad at me. It's all
my fault for being a slut, and I'm not supposed to tell on them because
it would embarrass everyone."
"Okay. Maybe you'll tell me some other time, when you trust me..." but
I shake my head no, even as he finishes speaking.
Sitting back onto the edge of the bed, I decide it's time to close my legs.
If Mack and Z aren't going to fuck me, what's the point of being spread
out...
"You know Z, you don't fuck like Peter did."
When the whole bed jumps and my arms are grabbed hard, I know I'm
in big trouble now. OH NO!
"Oh god, please don't hurt me. I'M SORRY Z! You fuck really good!
You're the best actually! *I SWEAR!* There's no one like you. You're the
best Daddy I've ever had! I'm sorry, I'm *really* sorry! I didn't mean to say
that. Peter is a secret too. I just forgot for a minute. You were kind of
mean to me and you made me do things I didn't want to do like Peter did,
but you weren't mean like Peter was!"
"Let her go, Z..."
"It's okay. Z can do whatever he wants to me! I've been waiting for
him to hurt me!"
"Z *cannot* do whatever he wants, and Z *wouldn't* hurt you. *Would you
Z?*" And suddenly as Z releases my arms, I'm sorry again.
Moaning, Z says, "No. I would NEVER hurt you, love. I'm sorry I
grabbed you."
"*Oh, Z...* It's okay. You can do whatever you want to me. I shouldn't
have said anything. You're a really good daddy. You are very, *very* good
at fucking. I just meant you don't fuck my ass hard, like Peter did. You
only ever take my cunt-hole. It's okay though... you can do whatever you
want to me, *wherever* you want to do it."
I'm so scared suddenly. I like Z. I love being with Z. I don't want him to
be mad at me anymore. Turning to face him, I try to see his face. It's still
really blurry, but he looks really angry at me. Oh, no. I've ruined
everything again. Fix it!
"Z? I'm so, so sorry. I promise I'll never speak again. I can't have you
mad at me... You're the only one who's nice to me- The only one! It's
going to destroy me when you leave. Please don't leave yet. *Please?* I'll
do absolutely *ANYTHING* you want, if I can keep you for a little bit
longer. *Please...?*" Christ! I'm desperate, "Please stay a bit longer. I won't
ruin anything else. I won't be bad anymore. I will *be* and *do* anything you
want. Z? Please stay... I WON'T be bad anymore, I promise," I sob.
But there is nothing but silence. Both men are so quiet, I can hardly
breathe. Why won't they talk to me? Am I in big trouble? Usually when

I beg and sob and apologize they just ignore me and continue. No one ever stays mad at me; they just do their stuff to me. *Oh, no.*

Now, I'm sobbing loudly. I'm so scared he's leaving me now. Fuck! I am such an idiot. Everyone was right. I *am* a moron!

Falling to my knees on the floor again, I wrap my arms around Z's waist. Resting my head on his thighs, I can't help but sob uncontrollably. When Z starts stroking my hair gently, I cry even louder. No one has ever been kind to me before, AND I'VE RUINED IT!

"Z isn't mad at you, Sweetheart. Z cares about you very much, and he's not leaving you. Are you Z?"

But there's still more silence. Is Z shaking again? I think I feel the bed moving.

"No... I'm not leaving you," he says in a quiet gravelly voice. He sounds really sad now.

"I'm sorry I made you sad. I'm just going to go to the bathroom okay? I'll just be a minute and when I come back I'll do anything you want. I won't ruin anything ever again, I promise."

Standing, I make my way against the wall to the bathroom. Everything is still blurry shapes but I can see enough to know where I'm going. When Mack starts following me, I panic. Where's Z? Looking I see him still on the bed, with his head hanging in his hands.

"I've ruined everything, haven't I, sir? I always do..." I whisper.

Mack whispers back, "Z still cares for you very much, I promise. You haven't ruined anything. I just want to freshen up, while you use the bathroom. Nothing's wrong, at all."

It's a little weird, I mean, *jeez*, can't I have any privacy... but whatever. I promised I would do anything to make Z not mad at me anymore, so I have to let Mack follow me.

In the bathroom, I walk behind the little glass privacy blocks and start peeing. Mack also runs the water, just like Z did. Z was so nice to me. He always did nice things. I didn't even have to ever ask him, he just knew and did them. I'm going to miss him very much.

I feel my tears falling on my thighs. Christ! I'm naked again. For someone who hates her gross body, I seem to be naked... *a lot.* I feel kind of dirty and used up, too.

"Um, excuse me, sir, but what time is it?"

"It's a little after 10am. Are you okay? You sound like you're crying over there, and you've been there for a while now. Can I help you at all?"

"No, thank you. You're nice like Z was. I wish I could keep him, you know? I was trying so hard to be good for him. I wanted to make him happy. I didn't want to disappoint him, too. But I failed again, I think."

"You didn't fail anyone. You're a very good girl, and Z is *very* proud of you."

Yeah, right. He is just saying the pretty words I used to want to hear. But now I know. I've always known the truth. Everyone just always thought I was too stupid to know, but I always did. I remember that now. I remember knowing they were just pretty words when I disappointed them.

"Can I have a bath, sir? I would really like to wash all the dirt off. I feel

kind of gross. Please?"

"Yes, of course. Would you like Z to come in, or would you mind if I stay with you?"

"Um, no offense... But I'd like Z, if he still wants to look at me, but I don't think he does."

============

When Mack leaves the bathroom, I feel my way to the sink to wash my hands. When the water is off I can hear Z and Mack talking about me. Z sounds really angry. He's yelling at Mack, and I hear my name again. *Shit.* He's talking about 'Peter' and 'disgusting', and 'ugly', and 'a fucking pig', and 'lies', and 'hate', and 'remembering', and 'photos', and... *ME.*

Oh, god, this is too much. I knew I was disgusting and ugly. I knew he would hate me eventually. *I knew it.* I knew Z would hate me soon. It's time for me to leave. I have to take a deep breath.

This isn't a shock. I knew it would come. I knew it was *always* going to come. Z would know and he would hate me, and now he knows and he *does* hate me. It's all over. My special time with Z is over and he's going to give me back to them for use.

Opening the cabinet, I see my freedom from all this pain and sadness. I don't know what, and I don't care. I can't read them anyway because my eyes are still too blurry. Hiding the pills in the towel beside the tub, I start the water and jump in before they can see me.

Using the faucet for water, I empty the pills into my hand, use the Jacuzzi tap and drink down everything. Christ, there was a lot. It was hard to swallow, but I did it. I did something right, *for once.*

Hiding the bottle again in a towel, it's done and finally I can relax. Finally, I can exhale. Finally, it will all be over soon. Z won't have to send me back to them, and I'll be free of all of them, and then we'll all be happy.

============

When Z enters the bathroom minutes later, he asks, "How are you feeling?"

"Fine. Thank you, Mr. Zinfandel. I really am sorry to have caused you all this trouble. But it will be over soon. I'm really, very sorry." I think I saw Z flinch again.

"Why did you just call me that, Sweetheart?" He asks while walking to the side of the Jacuzzi, kneeling on the little step, placing his forearms on the edge.

"It's nothing. I'm sorry... Z. I won't slip again. Please, can I just be alone now?"

"But I want to be here with you, love. So does Mack. He's waiting outside the door to talk with you again. Is that okay?"

"Not really. I just want to sit here quietly for a while in private. Okay?"

"No, Sweetheart. I really want to be here with you. You don't have to talk to me if you don't want to. But I need to be near you. You are very beautiful and good... Do you know that?"

"I don't think so. And please don't lie to me anymore. I don't lie to you... Well, *not really.*"

"I'm not lying to you."

"Oh, shut up! *Okay?!* Of course you're lying. I am NOT good. And I am NOT beautiful. You're just bullshitting me until I trust you, so it's more fun for you to fuck with my head later. Just leave me the fuck alone! You're just like them! All of them! You all think I'm so fucking stupid. You think pretty words *fool* me, well, THEY DON'T! I'm not a fucking moron. *I never was!* I just pretend to be, because it's what everyone wants me to be... A stupid, slutty, cock-sucking moron, who always does as she's told! FUCK! Just give me some privacy, okay?"

Looking in the doorway, I see the shape of Mack. "Oh, and here's the other one. Do you like looking? Does it turn you on to see the ugly, scarred up naked chick? Do you like looking at my pussy or something? Fuck! Just fuck me already, or FUCK *OFF!* I would like some mother-fucking privacy. Why won't you both just leave me the fuck alone?!" Gasp. *Shit.* Not now. *Please...*

"Sweetheart. Breathe slowly with me... come on. I want you to calm down, and take a deep breath with me."

"Z... Please? Just leave... me alone. I know you th-think I'm a fucking pig, and a disgusting whore. I know. I know what you *really* think about me. I heard you, and it's okay, 'cause I know it's true. So please leave me alone now. Just go- go away."

"I'm not leaving you, and I DO NOT think you're..."

LIES!! And then I just feel myself SNAP!

Jumping at Z, I start slapping his face and punching his chest. I claw at his face and try to bite him. Mack suddenly grabs at me with Z. They're restraining me. My hands are held. My head is held still. Z is yelling, and Mack is yelling. I hear 'stop'. I hear 'Sweetheart'. There is so much noise and water, and noise and anger, and noise and desperation. *I'm* desperate. I *need* silence again.

After screaming in their faces, I abruptly stop, and everything else suddenly stops as well. Total silence, *thank god.*

Z is breathing hard, and Mack is covered in water. Oh, my vision is back. Nothing is blurry anymore. I can see now. *Yay me!*

Mack is looking a little shocked by me. Mack even has water dripping from his chin. Oh, how funny. I can't help but burst with laughter again.

"Wow. I'm sorry. If I told you I've never hit anyone before, would you believe me Mack?"

But its Z who answers. "No. Not really. You're kind of a natural, Sweetheart. You have quite the right-hook."

Looking at Z, I'm shocked. He is bleeding, and shaking, and covered in water and blood, and his shirt is torn at the collar. What did I do? What the *FUCK* did I DO?!

"Oh, my GOD! I'm so sorry Z. I didn't mean to, but you wouldn't leave.

I didn't know what to do. You wouldn't listen to me. No one listens to me because I'm invisible. I'm always invisible..."

Gasping, my whole body begins sobbing. He looks terrible. I did that to him. I. Did. That! He is nice and good, and I tried to destroy him.

"I destroyed you. You were the first good thing ever, and I destroyed you. I hope you can forgive me one day. It won't be long now. It will be over soon, and I'll be gone. I hope then you'll forgive me."

"You're not leaving New York, or me, anytime soon. And there's nothing to forgive. I should have listened to you, Sweetheart. You are NOT invisible, and I should have listened to you. I just wanted to spend more time with you, because I *like* spending time with you. I don't think you're bad or disgusting, or anything else, other than a wonderful woman who I want to spend more time with. That's all. Please don't cry. Mack and I are going to help you get better. And then you won't feel invisible anymore. I promise."

Z actually has tears in his eyes. I can't believe it. This beautiful, successful, kind man has tears in his eyes. Tears *for* me? Or tears *because* of me?

This is the worst feeling I've ever experienced in my life. This sadness is oppressive in its strength. Everything hurts again. I can't believe the depth of the despair I feel. This feeling is so powerful, there's nothing left of me that doesn't ache with the intensity of this despair.

"Please Mack... help Z. He needs help. I'm not good for him, and he is so good, he needs to feel happy again. Please help him feel happy. I want to know he's happy when I leave him. *Please...*"

"Z *IS* happy with you. *YOU* make him happy, but we want to help you feel happiness too. Would you let us? We could go to my office and talk some more, maybe take some medicine to calm you a little. Would you let us take you from here, just for a little bit?"

"Oh! Of course. How embarrassing. I'm sorry I stayed so long, Z. You could have just asked me to leave. I would have. I would have gone back to them. I'm sorry you had to ask your friend to get me out of your life."

And shaking his head, Z replies sadly, "That isn't what Mack is asking. He wants you to come to his office *with* me. I'm not leaving you. And I don't want you out of my life for good. I don't want you out of my life at all, unless you tell me otherwise, I promise."

==========

Reaching out my hand, I touch Z's cheek. Wiping away the blood, he leans his face into my palm.

Has anything ever hurt me like this before? Has there ever been a greater pain in my life? I don't remember feeling this much pain, ever. It's everywhere. It's in my skin, and in my bones, and its inside me, *everywhere.* My heart aches with this pain. I can feel nothing but this intense agony as I look into his eyes. I'm going to leave feeling only this agony, *forever.*

Whispering, I breath into his mouth, "I'm so sorry, Z. I wish I didn't cause you any of this. I don't want you to feel any of this, anymore." As my tears fall, I continue, "Please know that I will always hold your memory with me when I'm gone, and I hope you will at least remember that I *wanted* to be good for you. I think I love you, and I want you to know that I've never felt this way before. Please remember me as I *wanted* to be when I'm gone, not as I *actually* was for you."

Sighing my sadness into him, I gently kiss his lips. I will remember this moment for eternity.

After I kiss him, Z and I just stare at each other. I don't know how long we stare. I can feel time passing, but neither of us move. Mack is stationary in the doorway I can see, but I have only eyes for Z.

His dark brown eyes look so beautiful to me. *He* looks so beautiful to me. There will never be another for me...

The water is freezing, and I think time has really passed for me. This is it. It's over.

Letting Z's face go, I try to stand on shaky legs. I need to lie down now. I'm so tired from this soul-consuming sadness and gut-wrenching pain. I think I'm honest and truly... *heart-broken.* My heart doesn't really beat right anymore, it's kind of thumping painfully and erratically with the sadness I feel.

Z stands as well, but I don't want his help. I don't want to take from him anymore. He's almost free of me and all this drama.

"May I just lie down for a few minutes before I leave? I want to sleep. I don't want you to help me anymore... My heart hurts very badly, Z. I feel like it wants to die now. Can you keep it though? Can you keep it here in New York when I'm gone? I don't want *them* to have it. I don't want it to end up in Chicago. *Please?*" I beg in a pitiful whisper.

"Sweetheart, you're going to be okay, I promise. Let me help you to the bedroom. I *want* to help you. So does Mack."

Walking with Z's help, my knees feel like they're going to buckle. Gripping his arm tightly, I ask for a towel, and suddenly...

All hell breaks loose!

Mack starts yelling with the bottle in his hand. Lorez... *something.* My knees buckle with the shock of sound in the room. Everything begins shaking, as Z starts screaming in my face again.

"What did you do? Oh, *god,* Sweetheart... What the *FUCK* did you DO?! FUCK! Mack! HELP HER!!"

Everything turns to chaos. Everything explodes all around me.

Mack is yelling at Z now- 'It's been too long.'

Mack has me on the floor on my back. Mack is listening to my heart. Mack is straddling me.

Z is yelling and slamming things. Z is screaming into his phone.

Mack is hurting my chest. Mack is carrying me to the bedroom.

Z is still screaming into the phone.

Mack is yelling in my face, as I try to watch Z.

'It's been too long!' Mack yells at Z while sitting beside me on the floor.

With my head heavy and tilted to the side, I just watch and try to

soak in all of Z. I want to keep him a beautiful memory forever. Z is just so good and lovely. Even angry and frantic, he is so lovely to watch. My eyes are really very heavy now, but I'm desperate for more of him.

Mack is yelling at me again, but I don't really hear the words anymore. I don't know what he wants from me, and I don't really care.

My heart is throbbing, and it feels kind of fast. I don't like this. This hurts again. My eyes are closing and I can't really keep them open anymore.

"STAY HERE! Stay here, Sweetheart!! KEEP YOUR EYES OPEN!" *Oh, Z.*

"I'm sorry Z... but it's just a broken heart... "

I hear Z again, but I feel Mack. Mack is kissing my mouth, and hurting my chest.

Opening my eyes is hard, but when I do, I see tears falling from Z's eyes, as he holds my hand to his lips. Z is rocking back and forth. Oh. How pretty he is. His eyes look like shiny marbles.

"You are so lovely. I wish I didn't have to leave you..." I don't know what Z is saying to me, even as his lip's move. Everything is humming too loudly now. It's all I am in this moment- throbbing and gasping, pain and noise.

I am so tired. This exhaustion is so great, I can't fight it any longer. I need to sleep now.

With a final glance at Z, I close my eyes as he grabs for me. I can feel him shaking me, but suddenly, I'm just too tired to care.

Whispering, I say my goodbye.

"I wish I could love you, Z.
  But I am gone..."

PART 2

DEATH

FRIDAY, JUNE 17

Sarah Ann Walker

CHAPTER 21

"Open your eyes, sweetheart. I know you're here. I know you can hear me. Just open your eyes. If you want me to leave, I will. If you want me to stay, I will. Please, love. Open Your *Eyes* for me..."

I can't. I don't want to see you. I said goodbye. I said it to you especially. Please leave me here, alone. I want to be alone now. I want to be alone... *forever.*

"Open your eyes. Talk to me. I'm trying to help you. If you don't talk to me or Mack, we'll lose you. Your husband and parents want you with them in Chicago. They want to take you away, so you have to Talk To Me. I need to talk to you, to help you." Oh.

They'll do it anyway. They'll take me. I knew they would. I can't fight them. They *always* win.

"Open your FUCKING eyes. Right now! Do you hear me?! I'm very disappointed in you. You're being very bad. Open your eyes! *NOW!*" *Oh god.*

Z's disappointed in me? He sounds so angry. He hates me. I should apologize. He should stay away. I'm not trying to be bad. I want to be good for Z.

"I'm s-sorry..." Was that out loud or was that whisper in my head?

"Oh, *FUCK!*" *Flinch.* "You're here. Open your eyes, sweetheart. Look at me! Look at me please!"

I can't, but I'm trying. My eyes are so tired, I can't lift them. *Please...* Z is mad at me. *Please*, open. Slowly, I feel the need to blink. Oh god, the light.

"It's too bright... hurts..." I hear movement.

"Fuck, sweetheart. There. The lights are off. Come on, open your eyes again. I need to see those gorgeous eyes of yours... *Please.*"

"My head hurts..." I choke.

Looking around again, I try to clear my head. I feel so slow and my brain feels like its smashing up against my skull with each movement I make. Actually, I feel like I have a nasty hangover without the previous night of fun. It's just too much for my eyes and head. It's just too much to look at Z.

"What happened to me?" I whisper with my eyes shut again.

"After you collapsed, Mack and I brought you to the hospital by ambulance..." HOSPITAL! "... No! Wait. You're okay. Mack is one of your physicians at the moment, and he's been taking good care of you. It's okay. Listen to me before you freak out. Please."

"I'm trying. Does my family know where I am?" I ask squinting. God, I would kill for some sunglasses right now.

"Yes. They've been here."

"Do they know about you and me?" What *are* we? Are we even a *'we'?* No. I don't think so.

"No. They know I was with you when you were admitted. That's all. The story is we ran into each other, *accidentally* near my apartment, I could

tell you weren't feeling well, I invited you to my home so you could call your family, and it was there that you collapsed. It's all a little too *coincidental* and quite frankly, pretty lame as far as stories go, but neither your parents, nor your husband have questioned me further. Actually, your *husband* shook my hand and thanked me for helping you. Fuck. I wanted to punch him in the face, but sadly, I didn't."

Even through my squinted eyes I can see Z looks like he's going to throw up after telling me that. He really doesn't seem to like Marcus much. You and me both Z.

"But I didn't meet you before."

"And *conveniently*, your parents don't remember me NOT meeting you at some function or other over the years. They were just so thrilled that a 'Williams' helped you, and therefore, *OBVIOUSLY* understands the Upper Class *code of silence*, that they didn't seem to remember I hadn't in fact met you as a child. Their relief in my name created their ignorance."

Z is shaking his head and smirking a little. He really does appear to dislike all things Upper Class.

"So what happened to me? I don't remember anything."

"Look, Mack's going to be here any minute, and he would like to talk to you about it all, but just know you're going to make a full recovery, and you're going to get better."

"Z. What happened? Please tell me." I try to open my eyes wider so I can really see his face, but it just hurts my head too much.

Z seems to be thinking about what to tell me. It must be bad if he's pausing to think. Z is always the type who knows exactly what to say, and when to say it. This must be really bad then.

"You had surgery, sweetheart. You had a small aneurism rupture in your brain, but you're fine now. You've been in a medically-induced coma for over 2 weeks while your brain recovered, but you're much better now. You'll heal. Your vision will be fine, and you'll feel much better soon." Wow. *Really?*

"An *aneurism?* That's weird; I didn't feel like I had one." Oh, *duh.* What a stupid thing to say.

"Listen to me, I will tell you anything and everything, but just not right now. I need you to try to focus, as hard as you can."

"I am focusing as hard as I can. I had an aneurism, ya know?" Okay, he didn't like that joke much. Too soon? *Apparently,* going by Z's look.

"Come on, sweetheart. We're running out of time here. Once your family knows you're awake, they'll move you back to the hospital in Chicago. You need to talk to me, quickly."

"I'm sorry... I'm trying. My head feels so heavy and kind of like I'm drunk or something." I can't open my eyes fully, but I can still talk.

"I know. I'm sorry. But it's crucial that you talk to me before they find out you're awake. Please, try very hard. I'm going to ask Mack to come here, okay?"

"Who's that?" *Mack?* That seems familiar, but not really.

"Do you remember anything about the last time you were at my house? Do you remember what happened there?"

"No... Oh! Do you mean when we were *together?*" Oh, I can still blush, even with my eyes closed.

"Ah, no... Not that. Though that *was* pretty unforgettable." Oh god! His smile-voice.

"You sound the same. I love your voice..."

"Focus, sweetheart. My friend met you at my home. He helped you. He brought you to this hospital and he's been monitoring you before and after the surgery. Do you remember Mack at all? He was very nice and very *kind* to you. He's my friend. Do you remember anything?"

"No. I'm sorry."

"Okay. That's okay. But I'm going to call him to visit you. You'll like him. You liked him when you met him. Just let him come see you, okay?"

"Okay...." God, I'm tired. "I need to sleep now."

"NO! Stay awake, love. This is very important. Please stay awake. Mack will be here in a few minutes. He works at this hospital."

I think Z is calling his friend. I'm in a hospital? What did Z say about my brain? Oh! Is my hair gone? I wish I could get my arms to work better. I hope my hair isn't gone.

"Do I still have my hair?" *Please.*

"Um, not all of it. But it'll grow back. It's just a small part near the front that's missing." I hear Z in the background. Is he talking to his friend?

My hair is missing? My mother will be so thrilled. She'll try to force me to cut it *all* off now. She hated my hair. She hated my short frumpy body. She hated my clothes. She hated so much about me. My mother really did hate me. I think I'm crying.

"Why are you crying, sweetheart? Mack and I are going to do everything we can to help you. I promise."

"It's not that. My hair is missing..."

"What? Yes, but as I said, only a little bit near the front. It'll grow back. I need you to focus. Mack and I have to ask you some important questions."

Whispering, "I know my hair will grow back. I don't really care about it. It's just my mother. She hated my long hair... she hated me. *Always.*"

"I don't think she hates you. I just think she isn't a very nice person, or a very good mother."

"That's not it. She told me she wishes I was dead..." *What?*

"What? When? Tell me when."

"I don't remember when, but I know she did. I can remember what I was wearing."

"Hi. Welcome back. How are you feeling?" *Flinch.*

"Who, who are you?" That voice...

"It's Dr. Michael McDonald. Mack. Do you remember meeting me?"

"Um, no. I'm sorry. Z? Who is he?"

"Sweetheart, this is my good friend, Mack. I asked him to join us here. He met you at my house a few weeks ago. Can you try to remember him? Mack is your friend."

"I don't have any friends."

"Yes, you do. I'm your friend, and so is Mack. We want to help you."

Nope. I have *no* friends. I'm not doing this anymore. I'm too tired, and too sad. I don't want anyone tricking me anymore. I'm done with them all.

"Could you please leave now? I really don't want to talk to either of you anymore. I just want to sleep."

"We have to talk to you, to help you. You're in a potentially bad situation with your family, and Mack and I want to try to help you."

"I want to see my family now. Please? I want my parents and husband. Can you please leave?"

"Listen to me very closely. Right *now*, I am your doctor. I am trying to help you, but if you push me away, your family will take you back to Chicago, and it will be very difficult, if not *impossible* for Z and I to help you at all. Do you understand what I'm saying to you? Listen closely. I need you to stop pushing us away. I need you to speak to no one else. I need you to talk to us, so we can help you. Once you are taken to Chicago, I won't be able to help you. Your family has a different doctor waiting to put you in his care. Do you know what I'm saying to you?"

"I'm sorry. I'm confused."

"Sweetheart, please. Your parents and husband want to put you in a special hospital with Dr. Simmons, and he'll keep you away from Mack and I. We won't be able to help you once you're gone." *What?* Oh NO! Dr. Simmons. Oh! He'll hurt me again. Breathe. Gasp.

"*What?!* What do you remember? Breathe, love. Come on. In and out slowly. Breathe with me. Tell us what's wrong."

"He... he's bad. He h-hurt me. I remember. He hurt me, lots. *Oh god.* He's awful." Come on! Not now...

"Listen to my breath. Listen to my voice. Calm yourself. Please stay with us."

"I'm trying. *Really...*"

"I know you are. You're doing very well." Almost there. My breath is slowly returning.

"How did he hurt you? What did he do? You can trust Mack and me."

"Um... I don't know *exactly*... But I *feel* what he did. I just *know* he did bad things. I'm sorry... I'm trying, but I can't remember what it was..." *Shit.* What did he do?! "My brain is all slushy."

When there is nothing but silence, I realize they're waiting for me to remember.

==========

"Listen. I have to go. Your family will be returning very soon, but Mack is going to stay for awhile. You can talk to him when I'm gone, or wait until I return to talk to him. It's your choice."

"I'm not going to tell your family that you've woken from the coma... *yet.* I just don't *actually* know you've woken yet... *understood?*" A doctor will lie for me? "That buys us a little time. Your parents and husband are returning to Chicago this evening for your mother's birthday party tomorrow night. So, if you pretend to still be asleep when they visit, I

can keep you here until they return on Monday. Can you play along? For Z?" I can do anything for Z.

"What do I do?"

"Ironically... *nothing.* Just sleep, or pretend to sleep. I'm going to give you a heavy muscle relaxer, and a sleeping aid which should knock you out while they visit. They're going to be here any minute, but they won't stay more than an hour. Just lie there and don't move. I'm going to schedule an MRI while they're here, to kill more time for you."

"I have to leave, sweetheart. But I'll be back once they leave. I promise. I'll be back very soon." And leaning in, Z kisses my forehead. *Oh god, no!*

"Please don't kiss my forehead. That's what Marcus does and I hate it."

"No problem. I prefer your lips anyway." And kissing me on the lips, I hear his smile-voice.

Grinning, "Thank you. Please come back soon."

"I promise." Z smiles back as he walks out the door.

==========

"He's gone now. Can you open your eyes for me?"

"I tried, but it was so bright, and it was really hard to open them. They feel very heavy and sensitive to light. Can I have a pair of sunglasses?"

"Okay. You can open your eyes later, and I'll get you some glasses to wear. Listen, this is very important. Do you think you can *act* comatose while your parents are here? I'm going to give you some medicine to knock you out, but it might not take affect for at least fifteen minutes or so. Therefore, you *must* act comatose initially. No moving at all, no matter what they do or say, otherwise they'll know, and you'll be taken back tonight to Chicago. Your family already has transport on call."

Tonight? Why do they want me back so badly? My mother hates me. My father ignores me. Marcus tolerates me. As a trio, they are the most uncaring, *unfeeling* group I have ever known... Why do they care if I'm here or in Chicago?

"No. No medicine at all, I'll pretend. I think I'll be fine. I've been pretending my whole life Mack... I know what to do."

"But this is different, it's about movement. One flinch or blush, and they'll know you're awake. Are you sure? I would feel much more comfortable knowing you were medicated and *actually* asleep during their visit."

"But I wouldn't. I don't know why, but I don't really trust that they won't hurt me when I'm sleeping. I can't explain it, but..."

"Stop. Sleep. I hear your mother. I'll stay as long as I can, and I'll be back as soon as I can for the MRI."

Walking from me, Mack leans against the back wall with my charts. After a quick movement of my legs and turning my head toward the window, I settle into my deep '*sleep*'. I'm *very* tired anyway...

CHAPTER 22

Waking, I hear their voices. Oh, god. Don't flinch. My mother is as usual... Complaining about the cleanliness, the rude staff, the wall color... Christ! *The color of the walls?* Get a little perspective, would ya? Ooops. I almost giggled.

I hear Marcus talking. What's he saying?

"... I don't understand. She was supposed to be awake by now. The medication for the coma was stopped 48 hours ago. There's no brain swelling. There shouldn't be anything wrong with her anymore. So, tell me, what *IS* wrong with her?"

"The surgeon told you patients *generally* wake up within 48 hours, but not always. She had such a sudden rupture and surgery, that her brain went essentially into a kind of shock, if you will. She also had the further complication of the other medication making her slip into a coma on her own, so the surgeon and Neurologist monitoring her had to base the medication on what her brain was already doing to itself. She'll wake up when she can, but more importantly, she'll wake when her brain is ready."

"Will she be normal? I know I keep asking that, but I'm just so worried she won't be normal anymore. If she's still strange like she was before, I don't know what I'll do."

"In my medical opinion, she..."

"Marcus, she'll be fine. Dr. Simmons guarantees he can fix her."
Flinch. Shit. My mother's voice can still scare the hell out of me. Don't move. Don't move. *Oh. My. God.* My mother is holding my hand. Even her hand is cold. *Ew....* Gross.

"She's my daughter, and I know she'll be fine. She always bounces back from her little *episodes.*"

"Mrs. Beaumont. She has had more than an 'episode'. She has had major brain surgery, for a major aneurysm. She may need intensive therapy, maybe even rehabilitation before she can recover from this *episode,* as you call it."

"I know that, Dr. MacDonald! And I will see that she gets it. I just don't see the need to stress poor Marcus out with all this drama, when it will all be over soon. She'll return to Marcus *normal,* and their lives can pick up where they left off. I will have it no other way." Jesus *Christ.* Did her voice just scare the doctor as much as it scared me?

"What if she doesn't want to pick up where we left off? She was really upset about my little transgression. She ran away. She even did what she did to get away from me. I think I really hurt her this time. Maybe she..." You think? *Asshole.*

"Marcus, *believe me*, what she did wasn't about what *you* did. She was always so dramatic. She was always looking for attention whenever she didn't feel she had enough. Her father and I were so embarrassed by her, weren't we darling?" Huh. My father *is* here. Nice grunt... *daddy.*

"...She always acted strangely around our friends and associates. She was just so, so *ridiculous* when she was a teenager, but her father and I thought she had it out of her system once she grew up. This isn't her first time doing something like this, but I promise you, dear, it will be her

last. When Dr. Simmons is through with her she will be perfect for you. Please, don't worry."

What the hell is she talking about? Not my first time? Of course it is. She's crazy. And a liar. God, I hate her so much. I wish she would stop touching me. I wish I could pull my hand away. I want to smack her face so badly. *Shit.* I think I've started shaking a little.

"She's moving." *Shit!*

"Yes, just muscle spasms. I have an MRI booked, and I need to take her now. Please say your goodbyes." Is that Dr. Mack?

"Goodbye, honey. I'll be back Monday evening, after work. I hope you're awake by then. I hope you're much better." Aaaah... *how sweet. Asshole!*

"Oh Marcus, don't sound so sad. She'll be fine. You just concentrate on you. Are you sure you want to return Monday evening with us? We can take care of her. You could just enjoy yourself back in Chicago, without all this upset."

"Yes, I want to return. I *should* be here. If it wasn't for me, she would still be in Chicago. She would still be the woman I love..." *Flinch* again. *Dammit.*

"I really need to get her to the MRI station. MRI scans are booked solidly, and I shouldn't be late for the technician, especially on a Friday evening. I'll take good care of her this weekend.... Enjoy your party, Mrs. Beaumont."

"Oh, yes. Thank you, Dr. MacDonald, we certainly will. My parties are something of a Chicago tradition. Isn't that right, darling? Mr. Beaumont spoils me every year, don't you?"

"Of course. Why wouldn't I? You are a treasure in my life." *Oh. My. God.* **Gag.** Hello, father. No kind words for your *comatose* daughter? Am I a treasure in your life? No? But I never have been, have I?

"Goodbye, darling. When your father and I return Monday evening, I expect you to be up and well. We have a nice stay with Dr. Simmons planned for you... to help you mend from this little *incident.* I just hope no one has the inclination to ask about your whereabouts at my party. We've decided to tell anyone who may ask that *regretfully* you had to attend a business trip in Florida this week."

God. Even her breath in my face is foul. Fight the *flinch! Fight it!*

"If you don't stop all this *shit,* I will punish you severely. Do you hear me?" She whispers in my ear, while kissing me on the cheek. **FLINCH!**

As if I could hold *that* flinch in. *Holy shit!* Did anyone else hear that? Shit! I hope the Doctor heard her. My mother swore... *AND* threatened me at once. *Christ!* She's just so EVIL.

==========

"How're you feeling?" Mack asks while suddenly wheeling my bed down the hall.

"Um..."

"Yeah, I get it. Your mother is wicked, huh?" *Wicked?* Giggle.

"I was thinking she's more of a raving fucking bitch, but wicked

works too, I guess." Ooops. More giggles. And a swear.

"Well, I didn't want to say anything so rude about the *lovely* Mrs. Beaumont, but your description certainly works better than mine."

Laughter pours out of me. My eyes are still closed to the lights all around, and tears seep from them, but it feels kind of good to laugh. I even hear Mack chuckling to himself.

"Did you hear the last threat?"

"No. But I could tell she whispered something while kissing your cheek. What was it?"

"'If you don't stop all this *shit,* I will punish you severely'. Isn't she amazing? No one would ever believe my mother capable of such bad language and threats. She has everyone fooled- just like I do. I don't swear out loud either. I'm not allowed to, but I swear in my head all the time." She really does have everyone fooled, doesn't she? I am sooo *fucked!*

"Does she talk to you like that often? Has anyone else heard her?"

"Um... I *think* she does. I can't remember an actual time though, but I just *know* she does. And her threat didn't surprise me. It just seems like something she *would* say to me. Does that make sense?"

"Yes. Your mother would hide that side of herself thoroughly, because of her lifestyle and position in her society. And because you can't remember specifics, it would make it seem highly unlikely to anyone else if you told them. But I believe you, I assure you. Your memories seem to be buried behind something, and we need to figure out how to get to them."

"I don't know about that. I just know nothing she does or says surprises me. No matter how mean." Huh.

===========

After the MRI, Mack stays with me in my room, and even manages to get me a pair of dark glasses to wear. He told me he was finished his 'rounds' and he could spend as much time with me as I would like. Do I want that? I think I do, but I'm not sure why.

There is something about Mack which just relaxes me. He's easy. He doesn't look at me like I'm gross. He doesn't look like he pities me. He just behaves like a normal person would *with* a normal person, though I feel anything *but* normal.

"Z will be back soon. He hasn't left your side often, unless, of course, your family was visiting. Would you like to talk a little while he's away, or would you rather wait for him to return?"

"I don't know. What should I do? What do you want me to do?"

"It's not about what I want. Would you like to talk to me in private?"

"I don't know." *Shit.* I'm so confused.

"Okay, no worries. How about we talk a little, and if you get uncomfortable and want to wait for Z, we stop. Just like that."

"Will you be mad at me if I need to stop? I really don't want you to be mad. Please, just tell me what to do. What do *you* want?" Christ! I

hate making decisions. *Really?* I've never realized that before.

"Listen to me closely- I need you to understand something very important. Please believe me when I say, *absolutely nothing* you do or don't do, nothing you say, or don't say is going to anger me. I'm YOUR doctor and I'm Z's close friend, but you are the one here with all the choice, and I will respect your choices with absolutely NO repercussions, I promise. Do you trust me?" Um.... "Okay. Can you at least trust what I just promised to you?"

"I'll try."

"Okay." This is going to be horrible, *I know it.*

"What is the last thing you remember?" Oh. Blush.

"Ah, I remember when Z and I... um, *you know.*" Another blush.

"Had sex?" *Flinch.* "You remember when you and Z were together. Z told me that was the night before I met you. Do you remember meeting me the following morning?"

"No, I'm sorry. I'm sure I should remember. I'm really sorry..." This seems bad or something. Is he offended?

"Listen to me. I am not angry or offended. I told you I wouldn't be. You were suffering at the time. Medically speaking you were suffering an acute brain trauma. You were suffering immensely; your *brain* was suffering immensely, so if you don't remember anything the morning we met, it's absolutely understandable, even typical. I'm just trying to assess what you do and don't remember. Please just relax. We're friends too, and I want to help you. That's all."

"Okay. I'll try to relax. I just don't remember you, but I kind of *feel* like I know you. Does that make sense?" Big inhale.

"Yes. You did meet me, so you feel like you know me, though right now you have no cognizant memory of meeting me. This is all very normal."

"Oh, well... good then. Thank you." Exhale.

"So you remember when you and Z were together. How do you feel about that?" *The sex?*

"I feel fine about it. Why? Shouldn't I? Oh, I shouldn't, right? I'm still married. Oh god, I guess I'm a whore now. I'm sorry Mack. I don't feel good about it. I really don't. It was a mistake. I didn't mean to do that with Z, and I'm sure he's sorry he was with me..."

"Actually, I'm NOT sorry, At All," Z states walking into the room.

"Hello, Z. Perfect timing. We were just discovering her last memories... Would you like to continue with Z in the room, or would you like him to leave? The choice is absolutely yours. Isn't it, Z?"

"Of course. Whatever you want sweetheart. I can wait in the hall until you're finished, if you'd like." Oh, god. What should I do?

"Um... please leave. Just for now! Please, I'm sorry... I mean, I want you to stay, but... *NO,* it's okay. You can stay, I'm fine."

Walking to me, Z takes my hand, and leans over the bed. Kissing my lips gently, Z seems to exhale into my mouth.

Ew. When was the last time I brushed my teeth? *Gross.* Pulling away, I can't help but just stare at him. He is so handsome still... So, so beautiful or something. I feel that pull toward him, but I also feel such sadness. Why does looking at his face always make me so sad?

"Please don't cry, love. I'm going to go out into the hall, but I'll be back as soon as you want me to return. I told you before; I'm not leaving you... unless you ask me to."

"I don't want that. It's just; you make my heart hurt or something. I can't really explain it."

"And *you* make *my* heart happily beat faster." *Oh god, that was so lovely.* More tears.

"Thank you for saying that. No one says stuff like that to me. No one feels that way about me. No one..."

"It's okay, sweetheart. Talk with Mack for a while, and I'll be waiting for you to finish."

"Okay. Thank you." Another big exhale. When was I holding my breath?

"There is one thing I *must* say first though. Sweetheart, I do not regret our time together, and I do not regret making love with you. You were amazing, and I enjoyed every minute of it. I don't feel badly about it, and I wish you wouldn't either. As far as I'm concerned, you were separated at the time, therefore, you did not commit an infidelity. You may see it however you like, but that's how I see it. I did not feel badly then, and I do *not* feel badly now. Okay?"

"Sure..." Was that convincing? I doubt it.

"Talk with Mack, and he'll come get me when you're ready."

"Thank you."

Watching Z leave makes me exhale again. Why is that? I want him here, I really do, but I can't really talk about the sex stuff with him here because he makes me want *more* or something. God, I'm so confused and I can't help crying again. Oh, Mack is watching me now. Stop crying!

"What's wrong? What are you feeling right now?"

"I don't know..."

"Could you try? Please? Just look at your feelings, and try to explain them to me." How? I have nothing but silence in my head.

==========

Oh, he's waiting for me to speak. *Dammit. Fine.* I'll talk.

"I don't know what I feel at the moment, Mack. Z is wonderful, and handsome, and, and so *good.* He's way out of my league. So, I know I should tell him to go away and never come back, but I don't want him to leave me. I want him here, which is selfish and wrong. He should be spending his time with someone else who is good, and beautiful, and wonderful- *Not* with me. I *know* that. Plus, he makes me want things I'll never have, and don't deserve, so he really should go. But then my heart starts hurting when I see him, and my heart hurts more when I don't see him, and I don't know what to do. If I was a *good* person, I would make him go away, but I'm **not** a good person, so I want to beg him to stay. It's back and forth, kind of."

More silence. *Jeez...* Is Mack ever going to speak?

"I don't know what you want me to say. I feel like I kind of love him or something, and I know I shouldn't, and I know he doesn't feel the same way, and I know he *shouldn't* feel the same way. I know I'm going to have to go back, and Z will be this, like, really amazing memory that I'll always have, and always pull out when I'm so sad and lonely I could scream. But that's it. Z will be no more to me than a memory. I don't want more than that, and I know he doesn't. I'm not even sure why he's still here. He is too good for all this. I mean really… what if I'm brain-damaged or something…" giggle "…Sorry. That's not funny. I just don't understand why he's here, and I don't really want him here anymore. He should just go home, or go back to work, or go have sex with some wonderful, beautiful, *good* woman. Not me. Not that we're ever going to have sex again, but if we were going to, I wouldn't do it. I have 2 memories of sex with Z to last me a lifetime…"

And more Silence. Come on! Say *something.* Don't just stare at me. *What the Fuck?*

"Why aren't you speaking? Why are you just staring at me? Am I a big joke to you? Why do you ask me to tell you things, and then just mock me when I do? I thought you were a nice doctor, *Mack*… Not a fucking asshole! Stop staring at me like that! What the fuck is your problem?! Is this funny to you? The short, round chick crying and tortured over the hot guy she can never have or keep? Am I fucking funny to you?! Say something! For fuck's sake… SPEAK!"
"Why are you so agitated right now?"
"Because you're being a total Fucking Asshole!"
"How?"
"Oh, FUCK *you!*"
"Please tell me how I'm being a 'fucking asshole' right now?"
"Finger *'air* quotes'? You just used fucking finger quotes? Are you fucking mental, *Doctor Mack?* Who *the fuck* still uses air quotes when speaking? I thought that went out in, like, the 90's!" How fucking funny.
Great howls of laughter burst forth from me, and I can't stop. What a fucking loser Mack is. Honest to god. This is the person who's supposed to *help* me- *This* idiot!
My laughter continues. Great rocking howls of laughter… Oh funny. Ah, I can barely breathe for the laughter. Gasp. More laughter. Gasp again. *Shit.* I can't breathe.
"Breathe slowly. You're starting to hyperventilate. Just take a slow, deep breathe in, and release it slowly."
"I… I can't. Oh, god, *h-help me.* I can't get a… breath… in."
"Nice and easy. You're having a panic-attack. Look at me. Just look at me and breathe slowly."
"Help me… *please.*"
"Can I touch you? I just want to rub your back. Is that okay?"
"Yes, please…" Gasp. Oh *god.* "It hurts… my head… so bad."
Walking to me, Mack sits on the side of my bed. Pushing me forward so my head hangs, he begins rubbing slow circles on my back. It feels okay, kind of good, actually. He's not creepy, or *pervy.*

209

"Breathe as slowly as my movements. The panic attack is fading now. Breathe slowly. Would you like me to get Z? He told me he has often helped you through these..." *What else has Z told him?*

"Yes, p-*please.*"

Leaving my side, Mack walks to the door, and I suddenly panic again. *Shit!* Is he coming back? Oh god, please come back... But seconds later, Z pushes the door open. Striding to me quickly, he practically jumps onto the bed, and takes my face in his hands.

"Breathe slowly, sweetheart. Listen to my voice, and breathe with my breaths. Okay?" I nod.

"I didn't think M-Mack was coming b-back. I didn't think you... would be back." Gasp.

"Stop, love. I will always come back, and Mack wouldn't leave you when you're in trouble. He *is* a doctor after all." Is he joking with me?

"He's a d-doctor who uses 'f-finger *air* quotes...'" Giggle.

"Ah, yes... *those.* I've often told him about them, and how they went out in the 90's, but sadly, they persevere." Z smiles.

"That's what I s-said to him!" Another giggle.

"Um, hi. I *am* in the room." Mack says, with his own kind of smile-voice.

"We know. I think I'm just hoping you drop the 'quotes' finally, if we keep mocking you for a bit. Right, sweetheart?"

"I think so. I'm really sorry Mack, b-but they have *got* to go." More giggles escape between my gasps.

"Okay. I'll work on it, I promise." Now, he's laughing with us. This feels great.

"Thank you Mack for staying, and for trying to help me, and for being nice and rubbing my back and everything." Big long breathe in and out. "I'm sorry I got so angry with you. I'm not sure why I did that. It's weird, but I didn't really feel like that was me, at all. I just know your silence was bothering me very much. I hated the feeling of talking and having you just sit there, staring at me. I hope you can forgive me? Please, don't be mad at me, Mack. I like you, I think."

"Of course I forgive you. But I have to say, for this to work, for Z and I to help you, you're going to have to talk to me. You're going to have to access memories I think you have buried deeply within your unconscious. You will have to trust us, or rather *me*, specifically, because I'm the doctor who can *and will* help you. You have to realize and believe that no matter what you say to me, no matter what you remember, I am NOT going to judge you nor will I think badly of you. Z can stay for parts, or all, or none at all. Whatever YOU are comfortable with, but I *need* your honesty. I need you to trust me with your honesty. I cannot repeat anything you tell me, unless you allow me to do so. And I cannot betray your secrets, or your memories, unless you let me use them to help you. But Z is not held by the same standard..." Z suddenly jumps from my bedside.

"...Wait! Let me finish, Z. I'm not suggesting for a moment that Z *would* betray you either... *However,* Z is not *legally* bound to keep your secrets as I would be, as your physician. Z is emotionally invested, and as such,

he may find it difficult to keep your secrets. He may want to lash out at the individuals involved. Isn't that right, Z?" Shit. Z exhales and nods, but doesn't speak. "...I am a doctor, and yes, your friend, but a doctor first, therefore, absolutely *anything* you tell me stays between us. It's called 'Doctor/Patient Confidentiality'. Period. Unless again, you allow me to use anything you tell me to help you work with, or against your family."

So, I can tell him anything? I've never done that before. I don't think I've ever talked to anyone ever about stuff. I just kind of hide what I'm thinking.

"Can you trust me? Can you trust me and/or Z with your secrets, so that you can be helped? You can think about this if you need to. You can do whatever you want to do. I am *only* your Doctor while you're here in this hospital. Once you leave I will no longer be your physician, but I can be, if you trust me, and *choose* me to be... which I hope you will."

Wow. Mack sounds so sincere. He held eye contact the entire time with me, and I barely squirmed. He seems so nice and real and safe, I think. I don't actually think he'll hurt me, like Z hasn't. I don't think Z will hurt me, and I don't think Mack will hurt me. What a strange feeling. I have never felt this before. I'm not anxious to lie, or omit information so that they like me. I feel like they honestly *do* like me. I want to ask, *why?* but I won't.

This feeling is new, and kind of *good.* I want to just trust them. I want to jump. I want to have two friends, who *want* to be my friends. This is all so new and very strange.

As a nurse walks in, she begins checking all my monitors. Taking my temperature, asking a few questions, she's nice enough that I don't feel bothered when she touches me. The room is silent while she tends to me. *No, I'm not hungry. No, I don't need anything. Ew, I have a catheter.*

I try to answer her as best I can, but I'm thinking too much. Do I? Don't I? What do I do? Once she finally leaves my room... *Jump!*

"Okay. I want you to be my doctor, and my friend. And I'll try really hard to be good for you Mack."

"You don't have to try, you *are* good. And I'm honored that you trust me enough to allow me to be your physician. You're going to get through this, I promise. But honestly, it's going to be hard sometimes, and you're going to want to stop, but you can't stop. Can you do that? Can you continue with me, even when it's difficult?"

"I'll try really hard, Mack. I promise." I will try this time, *for real.*

"Good enough. Look, it's very late, and you must be exhausted. I have to start all the medical proceedings, and I have to begin the transfer injunction, so I suggest you sleep now. I'll be back early in the morning to speak with you. Is that okay?"

"Yes, please. I feel very tired."

"Okay, good. Sleep well tonight, and I'll see you in the morning. The surgeon on call will be by a little later with the MRI results for you. You may as well sleep in the meantime."

"Okay. Thank you, Mack."

As Mack rises from his chair and makes his way to the door, there is

a giant *elephant* in the room- Z. I'm not sure what to say or do, even Mack looks at Z, like he's uncomfortable with him staying in my room. This is so awkward suddenly.

"I'm just going to stay a few minutes. I want to see you rest, and then I'll leave, okay?"

"Um, sure." Looking at Mack, I see him nod at Z, and then he smiles at me as he leaves the room.

"Don't worry, sweetheart. I'm not staying. I just wanted to tuck you in." He's grinning?

"Okay... Thank you."

"I'm very happy you're going to work with Mack. He is a wonderful physician, a very good man and a very good friend to have. I trust him completely, and I think you'll come to trust him as well."

"I hope so, Z." Oh *god,* I hope so.

"Can I get you anything before I leave?"

"No, thank you. I just want to sleep now. Okay?"

"Absolutely. I'll be back in the morning, but should you need anything, or if you wake in the night and need to talk, feel free to call my cell, anytime. My cell number is beside your phone, here."

"Thank you... for *everything,* Z."

"No problem, sweetheart. Good night." And leaning in, Z gives me a light kiss on my Lips. Oh. I miss kissing Z. How long ago was that? When did I kiss him last? I can't remember what day it is. Should I ask? No- that'll make me seem weird, I think.

"Always thinking... You really need to rest, love. Can you try? For me? I have a feeling tomorrow is going to be a big day for you, and you should be well rested. I'll be here, or I'll leave according to whatever you want or need. But I beg you to try to sleep now."

"I will, I promise. I feel absolutely exhausted."

"Sleep well, sweetheart. I'll see you tomorrow."

As Z stands to leave me... Wow! PANIC! Please stay! Oh, I don't want to be alone. *Shit.* What if my parents return to get me in the night? What if Marcus returns and demands my release? *Shit.* How will I fight them? I don't even think I can walk properly yet. *Please Z! Don't leave me.*

Looking at Z, I can't ask. I want to beg him, but it isn't right. He should leave and rest himself. He should go back to his large red and burgundy bed. He *should* leave. Oh god, I want him to stay with me so badly, it kind of hurts actually.

"I have an idea. Why don't I just rest in this chair here tonight? It isn't the first time I've slept in it during the last two weeks. I even have a spare blanket in your little closet. Would that be all right with you?"

As tears begin falling from the glasses, I whisper, "Yes, please... Thank you."

"Sleep, sweetheart. I'll just pull up my favorite faux leather hospital chair. It's remarkably comfortable, I'll have you know." Is he grinning again? "Close your eyes, and no more tears tonight, okay?"

"Okay. Good night, Z."

As I watch Z settle into the chair, tossing the blanket over his legs, I am stunned by him. He acts like he isn't even doing me a kindness, but I know he is. I am very aware of his kindness toward me.

"I will never, *EVER* forget all you've done for me, Z. No matter what happens, you will always be the single most wonderful person I have ever known..." I whisper.

"Nothing will happen that you don't choose. And I am kind to you because I want to be, because I *need* to be. I owe you that, at least. Please close your eyes, sweetheart. For me?"

"Okay. Goodnight."

And closing my eyes, I think of my awakening today. So much is still fucked up, but it seems like maybe there can be a little hope somewhere.

I think Mack understands what my family is *really* like, and what I'm up against. And he seems like he's ready and willing to help me fight them, too.

And then there's Z. He's still here, for whatever reason. Still smiling, and still laughing with me. He's still kissing my lips, and acting like he actually wants to be here. He's still calling me 'Sweetheart' and he's still kind and wonderful.

Why is he here? What did he mean by 'he owes me'? He owes me nothing, but I owe him *everything*.

"Stop thinking. Sleep, sweetheart."

Grinning I close my eyes tightly, exhale, imagine the Relaxation Response as Z taught me, and slowly feel the pull toward sleep.

I know I'm almost there. I know I'm falling...

Saturday, June 18th

CHAPTER 23

My night was filled with endless interruptions. Many doctors and nurses constantly in and out of my room with many, many questions, followed seemingly minutes later with many, many follow-up questions. Apparently my surgery was a complete success, and things look good for me and my recovery. Blah. Blah. I just wanted to sleep.

Every time I was interrupted, or the door banged open, or the lights from the hall momentarily blinded me, Z was there. Every time I looked to his chair, he was watching me until I made eye contact and then he smiled at me in reassurance. He never left. He was always right there beside me.

God, Z would be so *easy* to love, I think. He would always make me feel special, I think. He would always make me *feel*, I think. Z would be the happiest my life could ever be.

I know deep down it can't happen between us, and I'm sure he wouldn't really want it to... but just thinking about loving Z makes me feel such happiness and pleasure, it's like I'm light, or elated, or whole, or something that resembles all those words together. I can't even describe it properly.

I just know that if there was ever a moment in my life when I could love Z completely, I would want to die in that exact moment of pure bliss and completion... Just so I could take his love with me when I'm gone.

Unlike the lover of Porphyria, I wouldn't want to kill him if he loved me completely, but *I* would want to die, at that precise moment of complete love and adoration, just so my last memory of Z, was of him loving me completely... Of him being *mine* forever.

At that moment, I would leave this earth fully alive with my true, healthy, beautiful love for Z, surrounded by the only happiness I had ever known. Because I would know that there would never be anything more or less than Z's love; to stay with me, *forever.*

===========

When I awake, Z is still here, whispering with Mack and they're having a yummy looking breakfast together. I wonder if they were talking about me. I wonder if it was bad. *Shit.* Maybe Mack and Z have changed their minds about helping me. Should I ask them?

"Relax, sweetheart. Mack and I were merely discussing the superiority of the Knicks, over the tragic Celtics. That's all." Oh.

"I lean toward the Celtics myself. Sorry," I whisper.

"Ha! Sucker! Two against one. We win!" Barks Mack.

Oh, funny. I can't help but laugh at Mack. They're like kids or something. I think Mack said something about knowing each other for years. They seem like it. I think Mack must have even brought Z some clean clothes, because he's changed this morning. I wonder if Mack brought his breakfast too.

"You break my heart, love. That is the deepest cutting remark you could have ever said to me. And to think I had Mack bring you your own clothes, *and* a delicious breakfast... all before even 8:00am. But you slice me deeply with the *Celtics...* You have GOT to be joking! *The Celtics?!"* *Jeez...* Z even places his hand over his heart with that one.

"I really am sorry, Z. But we Chicago girls would never, ever be a fan of the Knicks. It's entirely against our religion." Oh, this is neat. I'm like playing or teasing or something.

"I *knew* you were awesome! From the moment we met, I just *knew* there was greatness in you." Ha! Mack has his hand on his heart now, too.

"You boys are highly dramatic little girls it seems... At least where basketball is concerned."

"We are..." Oh my *god.* They just said that in unison. *Too funny.*

Bursting out laughing, the *boys* join in, as Z rises, kisses my lips gently, and begins moving a tray of food toward me. Oh, it looks good and I'm absolutely starved.

"Dig in. We ordered a bit of everything. I didn't know what your typical breakfast was, and I couldn't find Apple Jacks on such short notice but there's almost everything else." Yum-*my...* It all looks so good.

"Thank you. I think I'm starving."

"You probably are. You've been on a drip for 2 weeks now, so you haven't had a single thing in your stomach. It's probably shrunk a little, so don't overdo it. Plus, eat and swallow slowly. Your throat and gag reflex needs to adjust as well." *Really?* I wonder if I've lost weight? "You've lost some weight as well, but you could gain it back in a few weeks, I'm sure." *What?* Cool. Why the *hell* would I want to gain it back? *Christ!* What a *man* thought!

"Ahhh, I'm good. I could stand the weight loss, and I'll take it easy on the food- though it does look amazing. Thank you very much Mack for all this, for me and especially for Z."

"No problem. Eat up."

As I eat slowly, chewing and swallowing with a daintiness I don't *actually* possess, I listen to Mack and Z change arguments from basketball to golf. *Golf?* Ugh. Now that's a boring sport.

Oh god, I used to hate when I went to my father's Country Club to watch the *fine art* of golf. What a pretentious ass he was. I hated going there. I hated my mother and her nasty two-faced friends, and I hated my father and his stupid fucking friends. Golf is such a boring, pretentious, useless *art,* if ever there was one. Fucking *Idiots!*

==========

"What's wrong? What are you doing? *FUCK! WHAT ARE YOU DOING?*" Z yells.

"What?" I jump.

"Sweetheart, talk to us. What's bothering you?"

"Why? What do you mean?" What the hell is he talking about?

"Sweetheart, give me the knife... *Now.*"

Oh, shit. What have I done? Opening my hand, the knife is imbedded in my palm. *Shit.* Even as I try to pry it open, my skin tears and peels with the knife. *WOW!* How hard was I gripping the knife? It looks like I'm nearing the bone, actually. *Ooops.*

"Jesus *Christ!* Mack! HELP HER!"

Open my hand quick; like a band-aid. "Ow, *SHIT!*" I can't help but yell out as I open my palm fully.

"It's okay. Let Mack look at your hand." Fuck. There's blood *pouring* from my hand.

"Sorry... I didn't mean to... I didn't know I was holding it like that. Sorry," I apologize to Mack.

"Please give me your hand to look at. Z, I need you to get a nurse at the nurses' station. Tell her to bring a prep-kit and sutures."

As Z leaves, I look at Mack closely. Is he mad at me? But Mack just smiles, while holding my hand in a strange, kind of upward position, as the blood continues pouring down my forearm.

"What were you thinking about? Why were you so tense a moment ago?" Um...

"It's nothing actually. I was just thinking about my father and mother and his Country Club and golf and their stupid friends, and how much I hated it. You and Z started talking about golf, and I just remember how much I hate golf." Oh, it does sound stupid.

"Good to know. I'll tell Z how you *really* feel about golf. Between golf *and* the Celtics, he'll be devastated."

"Are you teasing me?"

"Just a little," Mack says with a wink. Oh, how fun.

"Thank you."

"For teasing you, or for talking about the one sport guaranteed to make you stab yourself?" Oh. *What?!* I can't help but laugh.

"You are very *un-doctorly*, Mack." I giggle at my lame word.

"I know. Isn't it awesome?"

God, Mack is so cute, I just reach out and hug him. I can't help it.

"What's wrong? What *happened?!*" Z yells while walking back into my room.

"Well, she hates golf so much, she stabbed herself. It's sad really." Mack says direly shaking his head back and forth.

Just as Z yells 'WHAT?' Mack and I both burst out laughing. Oh, Z looks really mad at us. Ooops. I stop laughing almost at once.

"Sorry, Z. I didn't mean to make you angry."

"*YOU* didn't. Mack, however, is being a real idiot right now." Another little giggle escapes.

"We were just joking Z. Mack was distracting me from the pain, I

think. Weren't you?"

"I was. And I succeeded until a certain hyper-sensitive golf aficionado killed the mood," Mack says winking at me again.

"Could you PLEASE stop joking, and *help her.* She's bleeding everywhere!" Oh, another clipped tone toward Mack.

"Z, I'm fine."

"You're NOT fine. That looks very bad. The nurse is on her way. Is it bad, Mack? It looks like it's bad. Is it?" God, Z sounds very tense right now. I don't really like tense Z.

"It's bad, but I've seen much worse, and I'll have it fixed up in minutes. So, why don't you *sit down* and relax, Z." Mack seems to impart his own tone into the room.

"Ah, sure. How do you feel, sweetheart? You barely touched your breakfast."

"I'm fine, and I'm stuffed. Before I did this, I did actually eat enough."

As the nurse walks in, she seems to take in my room with a strange mixture of shock *but* professionalism. It's like she wants to say something insubordinate to Mack, but she can't. Oh, I know how *that* feels. I've been biting my tongue since I was born... frustrating, isn't it?

The nurse prepares a bowl of water with something else, while Mack puts a needle deep into my palm. Exhaling a long breath, I wait for the needle pain to end. Once he has finished with the needle, the relief is almost immediate. My hand no longer burns.

Mack and the nurse take turns doing *stuff* to my hand, while I turn my head away on my pillow and relax as best I can. Every once in a while, or actually, fairly frequently, I try to sneak a glance at Z, but I always meet his eyes. He's sitting in his chair watching my face closely. We smile at each other from time to time. God, he is still so beautiful to look at.

A while later, Mack is done. My hand is wrapped up tightly in gauze, bandages are applied, and a sling is placed around my neck, holding my hand high against my chest. Apparently, it was a deep, long wound requiring more than 20 stitches. That seems like a lot to me, considering I've had 6 to 8 stitches before. *Weird.*

Deciding to change my gown and bedding, the nurse asks Mack to assist. As Mack lifts me gently, while keeping me covered, the nurse quickly and quite efficiently removes the bottom sheet and replaces it just as quickly. Placing me back on the bed, the nurse and Mack begin adjusting my wires, and catheter bag again- ugh, still *super* gross.

Without being asked, both Z and Mack turn their backs to me, as the nurse unties and lowers my gown from the back. God, I would kill for my own clothes, but sadly they aren't exactly catheter friendly. Once I have a new gown on, she again adjusts certain wires and tubes, props my pillows, raises the bed again, and draws a clean sheet over top of me. Yay. All done. She even managed to retie the sling around my neck.

Afterward, the nurse makes a few notes in my chart with Mack signing a few papers and initialing the chart. With a nice smile at me, and a little pat on my thigh, the nurse finally leaves. And then there is nothing but silence.

"Um... sorry, again. I didn't mean to be..."

"You weren't bad. It was an *accident*... clearly. But I would really like to discuss what happened? Would you like Z to stay or leave? Remember, everything is your choice to make."

"It's really not a big deal. I told you I was just thinking about golf and my father's Country Club. Z can stay. There's nothing to really discuss."

"Are you sure?"

Mack looks so serious suddenly. Oh, I don't like serious Mack as much as silly, teasing Mack. Looking over at Z, he nods at me. What? What does the nod mean?

"I can go, sweetheart. I'll just be outside if you need me. It's nothing. Would you like me to stay or go?" I already said stay. What the hell?

"Stay." I think that sounded a little snarky, so I tack on, "Please." Again, he just nods and says nothing more.

==========

"Z and I were talking about golf, and you began thinking about... *what?*"

"Golf. Then my father and his friends. And my mother, and her nasty friends, and his Country Club, and the 'art of golf'. That's all."

"What about golf bothers you?"

"I don't know. Nothing, I guess. Golf is just... *golf*. Boring. Who cares? It's not like a *real* sport. It's just kind of a place to network or something."

"Who would network?"

"My father on the course, and my mother in the Clubhouse." Why?

"And where were you while they were networking?"

"I don't know. Around, I guess. I just kind of hung out and waited to go home."

"Where did you hang out?"

"The lounge, mostly. Sometimes, in the gift shop. Sometimes, I went for a walk. Sometimes, I waited in the car and read if I was super bored. Why?"

"I'm just trying to understand your reaction to the Golf Club." *What reaction?*

"I don't have a reaction. It's nothing. It was just so boring for me. That's all. I heard the same lectures time and time again. The importance of golf in *proper society*. The importance of golf as a corporate outlet. The importance of *wheeling and dealing* during such a *civilized* event. Just crap like that. My father would lecture me the whole way to the Club, and my mother would lecture me on the return trip."

"How did their lectures make you feel?"

"Bored enough to take a golf club to my father's head?" Giggle.

"And your mothers lectures?" Oh, no longer teasing Mack. Right! Gotta remember that.

"She drove me crazy. She was such a nasty, judgmental, two-faced bitch at the Golf Club. She would speak with every woman there, turn her

back, and trash every woman she was *friends* with minutes later. She never stopped. She was all delicate Mrs. Beaumont and an evil wicked BITCH, moments later. It was almost amazing to watch, but I hated it. I used to listen for a while, and then I had to leave because my stomach hurt from all her meanness. She was truly horrible. I'm surprised to this day that she maintains the very large circle of friends, acquaintances and *followers* that she does..." Oh NO! "...Shit! What's today's date?"

"Saturday, June 18th... Why?"

"It's her birthday today. She loves it when her birthday falls on a weekend because she gets to go double-time on her lavish parties. If she could, I swear she would change the Gregorian calendar each year to place her birthday on a weekend... like it's a national holiday or something." She really is ridiculous.

"Can we talk about the Club a little more?"

"Um, sure. But that's it. There's nothing more to tell."

"Okay... just bear with me. When you wandered around the Clubhouse, who did you talk to?"

"I don't know. Lots of people. Everyone spoke to me because I'm a Beaumont. Ah, I think I actually hated being a Beaumont. It was kind of exhausting. I had to always speak a certain way, and act a certain way. I always felt like if anyone saw me do anything wrong, even just for a second, they would run and tell my parents. I could barely breathe at the Club... My mother's friends all spoke to me like I was some fat little embarrassment for my dear, sweet mother. And my father's friends hit on me all the time." *What?!* Huh. I forgot that. Holy *shit!* They did, didn't they?

"They hit on you... *how?*"

"Um... They would hug me, *a lot*, and talk to me... Oh, *oh shit!* I remember Mr. Allister talking to me about gross things. I remember wanting to get the hell away from him, but my mother's friends were watching, and I couldn't get out of his hug, without causing a scene. I was kind of trapped and he knew it. Actually, I think he *liked* that I was trapped."

This is so awkward. Don't look at Z. Don't look. I'm so afraid he is looking at me like I'm gross. Just keep looking down. No eye contact!

"What *gross* things was he talking about? You can tell me, it's okay."

"Um... I remember something about his... p-penis. Something about the size, or something. It was gross. I was young, like twelve. I barely knew what a penis looked like at the time, but there he was talking to me about his, holding me at the bar in a tight side-hug."

"What else did he say?"

"That's it, I think..."

"Could you try to remember back? Could you try to remember if there was anything more? Anything else that you can remember?"

"I'm trying. I don't know. It's like I remember, but not really. It's kind of fuzzy in my head. I remember his smell, his cologne, and his hug... But the words are kind of like an echo, or something. Dammit, I'm so confused right now."

"What you're experiencing is typical of a kind of traumatic *'tunnel vision'*. Sometimes in a stressful situation, we process the events

incompletely, or even strangely. We may remember scents and feelings, but not all the details. You're doing fine, and just know that this is completely normal. We're just going to have to figure out a way to get all the information."

"I d-don't think I really want to. It was just creepy to me."

"I know, but we really need all the pieces of the puzzle. I'm trying to help you, and without ALL the information, I can't help you. Can you keep trying?"

"I guess so."

Ick, I feel so gross suddenly. Thank god, Mack seems to understand and he gives me a minute to settle this gross feeling a little.

"Do you remember anyone else at the Club speaking to you inappropriately?"

"I don't know. Maybe..." Oh! "...Um, Mr. Stephens used to talk to me about my baby tits..." *Flinch.*

"You're doing really well. What else did Mr. Stephens say to you?"

"I don't know. That's it, I think. He would rub them and say he loved my *baby tits...*" Oh, *SHIT!* What the FUCK was *THAT?* "I remember that! He actually touched me." Breathe, Dammit. Don't do this.

"Breathe, sweetheart. You're okay. Mack and I won't let anyone touch you, I promise. May I come closer to you?" Um...

"No, thank you. Sorry, Z. I just d-don't really want to be touched right now. I don't want you to see me." Huh. As if he can't see me.

"No problem. Just take a few slow, deep breaths, okay?"

"Yes...."

Long silence. God, the room feels so heavy on me. I'm trying to breathe slowly, but the room feels more like a weight on my chest.

===========

"What are you feeling right now?"

"Well, Mack. I feel pretty *grossed out,* actually, and this silence is killing me. How do you think I'm feeling?"

"Do you remember anything else from the Clubhouse?"

"Should I?" *Ooops.* That sounded a little bitchy. "Sorry, Mack."

"It's fine. Do you remember anything else happening at the Clubhouse?"

"Um... not really." Keep breathing.

"Could you try hard for me?"

"I am! What do you want from me?!"

"I would like you to try to remember. I would like you to *tell me* what you remember. And then I want you to tell me how you felt at the time, and how you're feeling now about it."

Feelings, feelings, *FEELINGS!* Jesus Christ! Shut UP!

"Would you like an alphabetical list, Mack? Would that make you happy?"

"Would it make you happy to give me an alphabetical list?" *Asshole.*

"Yes, Dr. MacDonald... I believe it would."

"Then please, tell me your list." What?! What a total *ASSHOLE!*

"Fuck you, Mack! I'm not playing your game right now. Go fuck with someone else… Okay?"

"I'm not *fucking* with you. I would just like to know what else you remember about the Clubhouse."

"You want details?! You fucking pervert! You want to hear what I did with them?! Would that turn you on? Do you have a hard-on Mack? Yeah… I'm sure you do…" Pause. Breathe.

"How are you feeling right now?"

SNAP!

"Fucking *horrible*, Mack. Thanks for asking. I have all these *feelings* screaming in my body, and all these *thoughts* grossing me out. And you keep making me remember!"

"What is grossing you out?" *Seriously?!*

"Oh, I don't know, Mack. Remembering Mr. Salmons dick in my mouth gagging me, or Mr. Sheehan's hands bruising my hips as he slammed me against his cock. Or, actually, I remember an awesomely horrendous ass-fucking I took in the sauna by Mr. Philips, followed immediately by Mr. Williams. That was particularly painful, and I remember Peter thanking me for 'being such a good girl' afterward, as I crawled to the door because I couldn't even stand up or walk when he was done with me…"

WHOOSH. All the air is just *GONE!* OH. MY. *GOD!* **OH FUCK!** Don't look. DON'T LOOK AT HIM!! Just close your eyes.

The silence in the room is deafening. I can't breathe… At. All. Take a breath! Inhale! Do it! But I can't. *Nothing is happening.*

Turning my head slightly, I see Z. He is still and expressionless. He looks like he's in a coma or something. *Shit.*

This is too much! I need to leave. Can I walk? Can I even get out of the bed? Can I please just LEAVE?!

Turning toward Mack, my mouth opens and I try to speak, but a sudden great horror fills my gut. Mr. *Williams.* Oh. My. *God!* I have fucked Z *and* his father, *Piggy Peter.* That's it. I'm done. My mouth closes on a gasp.

Throwing myself to the opposite side of Mack and Z, I vomit… *everywhere.* Huge heaves of vomit, followed by wrenching gags of bile, followed by loud dry-heaves. The sheets, my gown, the floor… *everything* covered in my vomit.

I think Mack is beside me, holding me onto the side of the bed. I think I hear him talking to me. I think he's aiding me. *I think…* but all I *feel* is Z's horror.

Oh god. There's more. More heaves. More noise. More everything. Will this ever end? Will *I* ever end?

==========

After forever it seems, I finally exhale. My stomach is burning, but now it's with pain, not nausea. Pain is better. Pain, I'm comfortable with.

"What are you thinking about right now? Can you tell me?" Mack practically whispers beside me. Oh, I think I've been holding his hand

this whole time. That's nice.

"Um, I love pain, because it can be measured. Just like time and numbers. Pain is either really bad, or not so much. Like a 'one to ten scale'. I can gauge anything on a one to ten scale. Pain is always measured, and it always feels less painful afterward. I just remind myself of that when I'm *in* pain. The memory of the pain is never as painful as the pain was. And I've never hit a 10 yet. There were a few 8.5's, and even a 9 once, but never a 10. Ten is unbearable pain. I bear pain. I have always been able to bear pain. I can bear this pain."

"Are you in pain now?"

"Yes. Everything hurts in my body, probably from the vomiting. But my head hurts quite badly. My head is actually throbbing, I can feel it. But it's my heart that's killing me. May I have a little rest, Mack? *Please?*"

"Of course. Lie down and rest while I have the nurse issue more pain killers. I'll have someone clean this up and help redress you, as well. Would you like Z to stay with you, or would you like him to leave with me? We'll return as soon as you've rested. We will return to help you, I promise."

"Could I just be alone for a little while?"

"Of course. We'll be back shortly. Please try to rest."

When I hear Z at the door, I call out to Mack quietly. "Mack?" I whisper as he comes closer to me.

"Yes?"

"Please take care of Z."

"Okay, I will. And I'll be back soon to take care of you."

"I don't care about me. Just please take care for Z, okay?" And turning from him onto my side, I finally exhale all my pain and tension.

I couldn't even look at Z as he left. Oh, what he must think of me. I can't believe how humiliated I feel. It's like a wash of disgusting humiliation is drowning me.

To think, I've slept with Z *and* had his father fuck my... It's just so disgusting and twisted, or something. Z must despise me now. *Finally.* I've been waiting for it to happen, and it finally has. I'm almost glad it's here, so I no longer have to worry about what was *always* inevitable.

Once the door closes behind Mack, I close my eyes and desperately try to rest. I can't believe I remembered the Country Club. Where the hell has *that* memory been? I had totally forgotten what it was like for me there. No wonder I've refused each and every offer or invitation to attend some party, fundraiser, or function at the Club for years. No wonder I hate golf. Giggle.

When my reverie is interrupted by a nurse, I stop thinking. She asks a few generic questions, writes some notes, checks me over, helps to redress me *again,* and finally, *thankfully,* hands me 2 little pills.

Five minutes later; sleep is almost here, I can feel it. I feel the in-between... I'm slowly falling, falling...

I'm done.

CHAPTER 24

Waking, I feel absolutely atrocious. Everything hurts. Everything is pressing together. My head is pounding in rhythm with my face and chest. My stomach feels like I've pulled all the muscles. My hand and legs are cramped. My other hand is on fire. If possible, I swear my *hair* hurts right now.

Waking, I'm in *agony*. What the hell is wrong with my face? It's all tight and rigid. Reaching up, I feel a mask or something around my jaw. What the *hell* is this? *Silence of the lambs, much?*

"Don't panic. It comes right off." *Flinch.* "You were grinding your teeth so badly; Mack put a mask over your jaw to prevent movement. Would you like me to help you remove it?"

"No, thank you..." I mumble.

Pulling at a strap near my right cheek, the mask instantly falls away to the left. Good. Wow. My jaw is killing me. Opening my mouth slowly hurts like a bitch. This is definitely a solid 4 on my pain scale.

I don't want to open my eyes yet. I just don't want to see Z's face of disgust. Even though I love being around him- right now, I would give anything for him to leave. I just can't face him.

"Can you open your eyes for me, sweetheart?" Sweetheart? *Still?*

"Yes, but I still have a bad headache. May I keep them closed for now?"

"Can you please open your eyes for me, for just a minute? *Please?*"

Opening for Z, my lids begin blinking rapidly. Argh. *Flinch.* I hadn't realized he was right beside me looking down.

"Please don't be afraid of me, sweetheart. I would never hurt you, I promise." *What?!*

"I know."

"Do you?"

"Of course. You haven't so far, and I'm sure you're leaving soon, so..."

"I am NOT leaving soon!" Oh! Another flinch followed by Z breathing heavily.

"Fuck, I'm sorry. I didn't mean to frighten you. I'm just so fucked up right now. Listen to me, please. Look, I don't know what to say. I guess I'm just so sorry, *so* fucking sorry that my *father* ever hurt you. I can't believe it, and yet I totally believe it. I believe he did those things to you... And I AM SO SORRY. I want to kill him, and I can't... the fucker is already dead."

"Z..."

"No. Please, let me finish. I will never be able to make this right for you, and I can't make it right. But I need you to know, that I didn't know what he did to you. I knew he was a pig, I saw pictures once..."

"Of *ME?!*"

"Oh, fuck no! Some other girl, a young brunette. When I asked him about the pictures, he was so cavalier about it, so dismissive, that I became disgusted by him. After that, we had very little relationship left. My parents died maybe 2 years later. And yes, I mourned for him, but I didn't know the extent of his depravity. But if I had known..."

"It's okay, Z. I'm sure I deserved..."

"If you say you *deserved* what he did to you, I'll lose it. This is *So Fucked Up.* I wanted to help you because I care for you. Now, I *have to* care for you because my fucking father hurt you. I am just so messed up over all this. I NEED to make it right for you, somehow."

"Z, I'm really sorry about all this..."

"Sweetheart, if you apologize one more time, I'll..." *Flinch.*

"Z! That's enough. That sounded like a threat, and she doesn't need that added weight or pressure to her situation right now. Stop."

"Shit. I didn't mean to sound like that... I was just trying to say how sorry I am. I don't want you frightened of me. I just meant that I, ah, *fuck!*" Z is shaking, badly.

God, I want to touch him. I would do anything to make him happy again. I wish I had never met him. I wish I could just walk away and never see him again. I *want* him to be happy again. My heart aches for him. My heart *breaks* for him.

"Oh, sweetheart... *please* don't cry. I wasn't trying to make you upset. And I could NEVER be angry with you. I just wanted to apologize for my father having any part in what happened to you. I don't know how to make you believe me. I don't know how to make this go away for you. I always know what to do, about anything, about *everything,* but I don't know this time. I can't make this go away, and I'm so sorry about that."

I have no words to give him. I don't know what to say, even if I could speak. There is just nothing but silence.

"Z, you didn't do this. You had no part in this. So you need to leave her alone, so she can process her own memories. She needs comfort right now, but you are adding to her upset. There is a time for apologies, if you feel the need to make them... *later.*"

"You're right, Mack. I'm sorry, sweetheart. I didn't mean to make any of this about me. We can talk about this later. Please forgive me."

"There is nothing to forgive. I just wish you weren't unhappy right now. I don't like it when you're unhappy. It hurts my heart."

"I AM sorry for that. That wasn't my intention. What can I do to make your heart NOT hurt?" Don't say it! DON'T SAY IT!

"I think you should leave, Z. I don't really want you here anymore. I don't blame you for anything **at all,** I promise. But I just don't want you to hear anymore of all this... *stuff.*"

Wow. Z actually took a step back from my bed. He looks really hurt. *Shit.* I was trying to prevent him from feeling anymore hurt. Looking between Mack and myself, Z seems to collect himself after another moment.

"Um... Are you sure, sweetheart? I'll just stay in the corner like I did this morning. I'm okay now."

"Yes, I'm sure. I just want to talk to Mack alone for a while. It's not you, I promise. I didn't mean to hurt your feelings." Fix this! Please.

"You didn't hurt my feelings. Its fine, love. Whatever *you* want, remember? I'll just go home for a little while, freshen up, and if you decide you want to talk to me, or you need or want me to come back, just call my cell. I can be back here in an hour or so. It's whatever *you* need,

sweetheart. I know that."

"Thank you Z, *for everything.* And I'm really sorry for all this drama. It just never seems to end with me, does it?" I give him a weak smile, which he doesn't return. Ouch, that hurt.

"I'll see you later. And Mack, please call me if she needs anything."

"Of course. We'll be fine."

Looking toward me once more, Z touches my shin over the sheet, smiles at me, nods once, and makes his way to the door. Wait! *Shit!* I don't want him to go. Too late.

Once the door closes, I lose all control. Great lunging sobs tear from my chest. My head hurts so badly, I hold my head with my hands, ripping my bandaged hand free of the sling. Holding my head tightly seems to help. Grasping and pulling at my hair seems to help, as long as don't pull the hair too close to the bandage on my skull.

I just can't stop crying. The pain is shocking again. I know he will return if I ask, but I'm not going to ask. He shouldn't be here anymore. He gave me Mack, and he should be free of all my drama now. I had really wanted to keep him. But now, I just want him free.

I know there can never be a 'Z and I', so I have to let him go. I won't see him ever again. I can't. It hurts him too much. And it hurts me too much. I had him for a little while and it was amazing, so I'll just keep my memories, and I'll move forward without him in my life.

God, I wish I could stop crying. *Please,* stop crying. And almost immediately my sobs taper off to little hiccups of tears, and breaths of pain. This time, I really, truly am *heartbroken.* But it's good. It's as it should be.

I wish I had said a memorable, heart-felt goodbye to Z, but I didn't. And now I can't. Seeing him again, even once more, will kill me. He is free now. And I want him free. I want him free of... *me.*

"Goodbye, Z...

I think I love you."

==========

When I wake up, everything still hurts. *Christ.* Will my head ever feel the same again? I need to get well, so I can get out of here. I need to walk. I need to change my clothes. I *need* to leave. Where do I go? Where am I safe from all this? What do I do?

"How are you? Would you like more pain medication?" Oh, Mack's still here.

"Yes, please. I'm sorry, but my headache is so distracting."

"It's not a problem. You've had major surgery AND much stress, so you're supposed to be on pain killers. Let me just speak with the nurse. I'll be right back."

"Okay. Thank you."

When Mack leaves, I wonder if this is what it feels like to be really, truly alone. This is a first in a long time I think. Actually, it's a first, period. I've never been alone in my life. I've never lived alone. I've never bought

my own groceries. I've never had my own place. I've never been by myself. I've never *been* myself...

"What are you thinking about?" Mack asks while holding out the little cup of pills.

"Um... about being alone."

"You're not alone. I'm here, and Z can be back in..." I have to cut him off.

"That's not what I meant. I mean, I was thinking about being alone in the world. I've never been alone, Mack. I lived with my parents, even in college, and then I married and moved into the house with Marcus. The house he purchased without me- the house I help pay for, but didn't choose. It's weird, but other than one love seat, and a matching chair in my sunroom, I have chosen nothing in my life. Oh, actually, that's NOT true... *sorry.* I choose to wear black clothing, and I choose to keep my hair long, though my mother hates it. But that's it...

"...I didn't pick my friends growing up; my mother did. So I just stop having friends. I didn't even pick which college I went to, my father did. I didn't choose to marry Marcus, my parents did. Marcus didn't even ask me. He just worked it out with my parents, prenups and all, and that was it. I was married on the date they said, with the guests they chose, in the dress my mother designed...

"... I have never been alone, Mack. Alone scares me, but it might be okay for me to try. I think I *want* to try being alone. Is that okay?" Oops. Did it again. Giggle. "I realize I just asked you permission to allow me permission over my life. Pretty absurd, huh?" *Idiot!*

"No, not absurd. If you have never had control over your life, taking control is going to be hard, and sometimes confusing. But you don't need to ask permission to do so, from me or from anyone else for that matter. Not even from Z. *You* choose what you want from now on. You can do that. I want to *help you* do that."

"Thank you. But I don't really know what to do." What a loser I am. *Honestly.*

"Why are you smiling right now?"

"I was just thinking about what a loser I am, and somehow that makes me smile. Kind of silly actually, but if I can call myself something in my head, and it's not a *dirty* word, I seem to smile." *What?!*

"Why is that? Do you often think of yourself as a *dirty* word?"

"Yes, I think so. I don't know, it's weird because I hear myself as dirty words, and it's sometimes *my* voice but sometimes it's other people's voices speaking. I can't always tell who is actually saying it to me." That made sense, right?

"You have other voices in your head? Do they always talk to you?"

"No! Not like that. Not like I'm a Schizo or anything. It's like the memory of *them* saying bad names to me, and my memories of saying bad names to myself get confused or something. So, I'm not sure if it was actually me, or them who said it."

"Who are 'they'?"

"You know, *the men*, I guess. The men who did stuff, and said stuff to me." Dammit. I hate this.

"Who were the men?"

"I told you some already. Why are we talking about this?"

"I would like to know about the men, and the *stuff* they did and said to you."

"*Why do you care...?*" I practically whisper.

"I want to help you process these memories. I want to help you *deal* with these memories. Once you do, I think you can have the life you want, or at least you can take the necessary steps to create the life you want." Pause.

Shit. I'm feeling so sad again. It's like a never-ending cycle of pain, sadness, despair and desperation.

"I know what I want, but it isn't for me."

"You can have some things you want. You may even be surprised at how easy it is to ask and receive whatever, or *whoever* it is you want in life."

"I disagree. Nothing in my life has been easy. And I don't believe asking, or *willing* life to change for me now, is going to happen. It's too late for me."

"It's never too late." Oh, he is SO wrong.

"Mack, thank you for your kindness, and I guess, for your friendship, but on this you are dead wrong. Once my mother realizes I'm awake, she'll take me away. I'd be surprised if she doesn't know by now, even though she's probably busy preparing for her party. She'll come here, tell me what's going to happen and it will happen. Just like that. Really, there's no sense in me wanting or hoping for anything, I'll just be disappointed in the inevitable."

"*Maybe,* but don't you want to try? Don't you want to make a decision that's clearly yours to make?"

"Of course I do, I always did. But it's just too hard to fight all the time. It's much easier to simply do what I'm told."

"That's right... It's *easier.* You aren't even trying anymore. When was the last time you fought for what YOU wanted? When was the last time you *really* tried, and didn't merely live through the motions of trying?" *Asshole.*

"You don't know me! You don't know, Mack. They're brutal and suffocating. They tell me what to do. They have always told me what to do... But I DID try. When I was younger I tried to stand up for myself. I tried to tell them no, but NOBODY listened! They even laughed at me when I said something contrary to their demands. They always laughed at me. I have always been an inconvenient little joke to them...

"...I once asked my mother why I was born, and do you know what she said? She actually told me she had to have at least one child to secure herself within the family fortune. That's it. When I looked at her in shock she laughed at me. She fucking laughed, pouted her lips and said 'Ah, did you think I actually wanted you? Poor baby. I never wanted you- you're fucking fat, and a whore.'" OH GOD! *What?!* "Oh. I, ah, forgot about that. *Shit.* That's pretty bad, isn't it?" Giggle. Why do I giggle? I really AM insane, I think

"I would say that's 'pretty bad', yes. In my non-medical opinion, your mother sounds like a complete fucking bitch." *What?!*

Both Mack and I erupt into laughter. It feels good to just laugh with Mack. He is so easy. I don't have feelings for him. He is just kind, because he is. Instantly, I feel so sad though, and my laughter has quickly turned to tears again. Christ! I'm sick of crying. I spent a lifetime *not* crying, and now it's all I do.

"May I give you a hug?" Mack asks me kindly.

"Yes, please."

Walking to me slowly, I think to appear non-threatening, Mack sits on the side of my bed, and just takes me into his arms. He doesn't hold back. He just holds me so tightly, I melt into his chest. He is so warm, and kind, and my sadness spills over.

"I'm sorry I'm crying all over your shirt."

"I don't care, it's not mine. It's Z's. I grabbed it this morning when I picked up his clothes for him. I'm sure he won't even notice it missing. That boy has a serious obsession with clothing."

"I know... I snooped in his closet." *Flinch.*

"No worries. I won't tell him about the snooping, if you don't tell him about the grand theft dress-shirt. Deal?" His smile-voice is almost the same as Z's.

"Deal." I smile in return.

In the silence that follows, Mack stays right beside me. He even makes himself more comfortable on the bed, but not in a creepy way. He just leans back, and keeps his one arm wrapped around my shoulders. He doesn't touch me gross, or even seem like he wants to. Why? Every man I've ever met wants to...

"Why aren't you touching me dirty, Mack?" Shut up!

"Do you want me to?"

"Oh god, no! Oh! I'm sorry, that sounded rude. You are very attractive. I just don't really want anyone to touch me right now... But if you need to..."

"Stop. I do not *need* to, nor *would* I. Just hugging you like this could be seen as fairly unethical, but I wanted to offer you *comfort*-that's all. We are patient and doctor... and friends. I would NEVER touch you, or even *think* of touching you inappropriately.'

"I'm sorry. I haven't really known a man who, ah, didn't..."

"Touch you inappropriately? Violently? Abusively?"

"Pretty much."

"Did Z hurt you?"

"God, NO! He was amazing, well, after the first time at the hotel. He was always so kind and sensitive, and loving, and really, *really* good at all the sex stuff..." Big blush. *Argh.*

"That's good. What do you mean about the hotel?"

"Um, he was a little forceful with me... BUT ITS OKAY! He can do whatever he wants to me... Well, he *could.* I don't think he will now."

"How was he forceful with you?" Mack asks so calmly, it makes it easier to just talk.

"He kinda made me, um, have an or-gasm..." I whisper.

"Forced you? Did you tell him to stop? Did you ask him to stop and he refused?"

"Not really… I did say stop a few times, but then I kind of gave in and then kind of wanted him to continue, I think."

"Did you ask Z to stop, and he refused?"

"Not really, I guess. I didn't really want him to tie up my hands like he did, and I didn't want him to touch me where he did, and I didn't really want to have an orgasm… but then I guess I must have wanted him to, because I did have one. So it all worked out. I'm fine, right?"

"Do you feel like it all worked out well?"

"Yes, I think so. I mean it doesn't feel like Z did anything *wrong* to me, just more like I was uncomfortable with what he did to me. But then the after was awesome, so it's good now, right?"

"Do *you* think it's right?"

"Yes. Z didn't hurt me. He did things to me that I didn't want, but then I did enjoy myself, so it's okay. I like what he did to me, and I *really* liked what he did to me afterwards."

"Okay. But you can tell me if you change your mind, or feel like Z went too far, or didn't stop when you asked him to. I'm YOUR doctor and there is nothing you can't tell me, about Z or anyone else for that matter. Understood?"

"Yes, but Z didn't do anything wrong. I *feel* he didn't. I only feel good about all the things he did to me."

"Okay, good. Now I don't have to kick his ass." That was such a nice thing to say.

"Thank you for that. No one has ever defended my honor before."

"No problem. You deserve to have your honor defended. Plus, it would've been fun to kick Z's ass." Big smile. God, he really isn't like a doctor at all.

Mack slowly sits up, and moves back to the chair beside me. Z's '*faux leather'* chair. Squeezing my hand, Mack settles into the chair and extends his legs under my bed. He looks like a teenager, or something.

"Is your husband violent or sexually abusive? Does he hurt you?" Gulp.

"He's not violent or *abusive*… He's just not very good at sex, so he kind of hurts me when he does it to me. I don't think he means to hurt me. He just doesn't listen to me when I tell him it hurts, or when I ask him to stop. He gets pretty excited about sex. I guess I'm lucky he only does it like once a month-ish."

"Do you understand that you just said you *both* tell him he hurts you, *and* you tell him to stop, but he continues to hurt you, and he refuses to stop? Do you not see how your husband is both violent and sexually abusive toward you? If you were anyone else, and you heard those statements, wouldn't you feel as though the person were being violated and abused?"

"Well, yes, but Marcus is my *husband,* so he's supposed to…"

"Supposed to abuse and violate you?"

"Um, no. But it's not like that. He just likes to do sex fast and kind of hard against me. I honestly don't think he means to hurt me, it's just me. I can't really get, ah, *prepared* for sex, so I'm not really ready *down there* when he starts doing it to me. Honestly, it's my fault." Annnnd, another blush.

"Actually, it is NOT your fault, at all. There are many sexually incompetent men out there. There are many men who like sex hard and fast. There are many men who can't even maintain an erection for more than a few moments. There are countless pills on the market for it. And there are countless books on how to become a better lover for men...

"...There is NOT however, a widespread acceptance that a woman should be torn apart, ignored, violated and abused sexually, just because *her partner* likes it hard and fast. Do you understand what I'm saying to you? Listen to me closely. Whether you are unprepared for penetration or just don't *feel* like having sex... when you say 'stop', or 'you're hurting me'... everything is *supposed* to stop. Period. Just like that. Your husband did abuse *and* violate you, each and every time you spoke up, and he continued to penetrate you. That is reality. And I really need you to understand that reality. You have choice and options, and you are *allowed* to make sex stop. No matter whom it is with."

"Okay, but..."

"Listen to me. There are no buts, I *know* you know this. Z told me you once said your husband 'takes you against your will'. Why are you fighting this reality now?"

"I'm not *fighting* it, I'm just trying to say that it's not always that easy. Sometimes Marcus was just excited. Maybe Marcus didn't really hear me. Maybe he meant to stop but was caught up in the moment or something."

"If Z was caught up in the moment right now, if Z didn't really hear you say stop, or if Z was really excited... Would it be okay if he continued penetrating you after you said he was hurting you, or if you even said the word stop? *Shit.* What do I say? "Fine. If *I* did all those things, and you told *me* I was hurting you, and you told *me* to stop but I ignored you and continued penetrating you anyway, would that be alright? Would that be acceptable behavior?"

"Well, no. You're my doctor." *Duh.*

"Forget I'm your doctor. Pretend I'm just a man. Is. It. Okay?"

"But we aren't lovers, so..."

"So Z can hurt you because he is your lover? Marcus can hurt you because he is your husband? But if I was really excited, and I ignored you, and I wanted to..."

"Um... If you *really* wanted to, I guess. I mean, if you were *very* excited..." What the hell is the right answer here?! *Christ.* This is annoying.

"Is it okay if I *rape* you?" *Flinch.* **What?!** *Fuck!*

"*I don't know Mack,* IS IT? Fucking *DOCTOR* Simmons thought it was fine to RAPE ME! Why not *YOU?!*" Gulp. Whoosh. *There goes my air...*

Shit. Here I go. Jesus *Christ!* I can't get any air into my lungs. Grabbing my own chest, I try to will the air in but nothing is happening. *Fuck.* This one is bad. This one really, *really,* hurts.

Mack is talking to me, but I can't hear him. There is so much noise in my head. I'm screaming I think in my own brain. Shut up! What is that noise? It's like a train, or a loud truck engine... There's something in my head and everything is spinning now. I can barely keep my eyes open.

Oh. My. *God.* This is it, I think. My heart is pounding. I think I'm having

a heart attack or something. *Shit.* I've felt this before. When? What did I do to stop this before? *Think!*

Mack is in my face again. I still can't hear him. There are others here now. What are they doing? My bed suddenly drops, and I'm flat on my back. Why? I'm still gasping, but nothing is coming in. My lungs are dying, I know it. I can *feel* it.

Ouch, my arm. There's a nurse beside me now. What did she do? What the *hell* is Mack saying to me? I see his lip's move, but there is still only this loudness in my head. What's on my face? What are they doing to me? Just help me! Please, *HELP ME!*

God, I'm tired. I just need to sleep. I need this to stop. I need silence. And closing my eyes, I feel the pull. I think this is death coming for me finally. I think it's here. Oh, thank you. I can't stand this anymore. Just take me. I'm *so* tired...

Sunday, June 19th

CHAPTER 25

Waking, I'm alive... and I can breathe. Yay! Everything is so quiet. Looking around, my body doesn't really hurt right now, but my head still throbs. I wonder if I'll ever have a pain-free head again?

Where is Mack? Maybe with Z? Maybe Mack has finally washed his hands of me. Maybe I finally said too much. I knew it would happen. I knew I would make him leave. I just didn't know how, but now I do.

I can't believe what I said to him. Jesus *Christ!* I remember Dr. Simmons now. I remember my mother insisting I visit with him at the hospital. I remember fighting her. I remember him showing up at our home. I remember fighting him. And then I remember *his* hospital.

Oh god. It was brutal. I remember his words. I remember his breath. I remember how gross he was, and I remember how many times I tried to stop him. He was so fucking gross!

Oh! I remember meeting him at one of my mother's parties with Marcus. *Shit.* Dr. Simmons introduced himself and told Marcus 'he was a lucky man'. What a fucking pig! Yes, he *knew* what Marcus was getting, *didn't he?* Ick. *Oh shit!* Here it comes...

Leaning over the railing, I dry heave again. When was the last time I ate? I wish I had some food in my stomach so barfing wouldn't hurt so much. *God*, more dry-heaves, and more gagging. More nothing, but pain.

Suddenly, there is a nurse beside me with a bedpan, like I need a bedpan. I'm vomiting... *nothing.* There is nothing inside me. I have nothing left to barf. I am nothing in this moment.

"Thank you. I'm sorry for all this."

"No problem. It's my job," she says with a grin.

"Um, my head is *killing* me. Do you think I can get some of those pills of yours?"

"Absolutely. Are you okay for a minute? Can you hold this bedpan?"

"Yes, I'm okay."

"I'll be right back," she smiles.

Once she leaves I try to get comfortable, but nothing works. No matter which way I lie, my head pounds. This is honest *agony.* I think I would cut off a limb or something, just to ease the pain in my head for a while. Maybe if I distribute the pain evenly, I could handle this pain better. Giggle. How sick was that?

"Why are you giggling? Most people cringe after dry-heaves."

"I was thinking about cutting off a limb, to evenly distribute my pain."

"Oh, sadly, I don't think that works. You would just have 2 types of pain. But it was a good and thorough hypothesis, nonetheless." Is she teasing me, too?

"Are you teasing me?"

"Absolutely. Does it bother you? I just thought you could use a little

humor. Am I wrong?"

"No. I like to be teased. It kind of makes me feel like I'm a part of something, or that someone likes me... I can't explain it, but it feels good."

"Well, that's good then, because I'm kind of the local smart-ass among the nurses here. Actually, my colleagues don't like me all that much, but I seem to get on quite well with my patients, so there's nothing anyone can do about my *smartassedness*." What? How funny. She makes up words too.

"I make up my own words too. Thank you for being nice to me..." and looking I see her name is Kayla. *KAYLA?! Seriously?!*

"I'm nice to everyone; unless, of course, you piss me off- then I make your life a living hell. Being a nurse makes for an easy Sadist."

I just pause, look at her, and burst out laughing. She is so cute. I don't even care that she's really tall. She is just so, like normal, or something, but still really nice and beautiful. Actually, she is just like my *old* Kayla. And suddenly, I miss 'Chicago Kayla' very much.

"Why are you crying?" Am I? Yup. Again.

"I have a Kayla in Chicago. Actually, I *had* a Kayla in Chicago, and she was tall like you, and funny like you, and a real smartass too, with a crazy sadistic side as well. You just seem so much like her; it's like a cosmic joke or something." More tears.

As nurse Kayla hands me the pills, she continues moving around wires and cords beside me. She seems to be thinking about something. God, I hope it's a good thought.

"Maybe it's the name. I've known one other Kayla, and she and I hated each other because we were exactly the same. We even knew that's *why* we hated each other, laughed about it, then continued hating each other anyway," she says laughing.

"Maybe it IS the name then."

"Do you miss her?"

"Yes, but it's complicated. She slept with my husband."

"Oh. What a bitch!"

"No! She didn't actually *know* he was my husband at the time."

"Huh. That *is* complicated. Do you believe she didn't know?" Do I believe her? Yes, I do.

"I believe her."

"Can you forgive her?"

"I'm not sure. Yes, I think. It's just so weird. How do you sit with a friend you know has had sex with your husband...? What would YOU do? *Honestly*."

"Well, after I punched them both in the face, I'd forgive her, but I'd dump his sorry ass. *He* knew he was married, after all."

"Kayla said that! She actually said I could punch her in the face, and she wouldn't even hit me back! I can't believe you just said that!" Holy *SHIT*. It's like the freakiest déjà vu, ever!

"It really *must* be the name then."

"Can I put my normal clothes on now? I just feel so, like, fat and naked in this gown."

"We can try later this afternoon, certainly. You just took more pain

meds. The *awesome* ones..." she winks. "So you'll be too unstable to stand for a few hours. But I promise later, I'll help you walk around a little. Once you can walk around on your own, I can remove the catheter, and then you get your own clothes. Sound good?"

"Yes. Thank you so much, Kayla. You are just so, so awesome or something. Sorry, that sounded stupid."

"Nah, it's good. I love hearing how *awesome* I am," she says laughing.

The meds are already hitting me. *Jeez.* How long have I been awake? Like an hour, and I already feel like sleeping? That's a first. Maybe I should stop taking these pills.

"Before you sleep, I *HAVE TO KNOW*... which tall guy is your husband? I saw the tall dark and yummy who visits you in the evenings, and I know the tall dark and yummy who used to stay overnight. Which one is your husband? I'm *dying* to know. And ah, *way to go*, by the way- *Two* dark and yummies? *Sweet.*"

What? I feel a little trampy when she says it like that. No! Don't go there. Kayla is teasing and having fun. Don't get all sensitive and judgy.

"Um, the tall one in suits is Marcus my husband, *I guess*. And the other one with the bright crazy colorful shirts is Z. He's my, ah, *friend*." Blush. *Shit.*

"Well, the husband looks yummy, and the, ah, *friend* looks *delicious*."

"Kayla! It's not like that. I swear. It's just so complicated and weird and uneasy and unsettled and..."

"No worries. I'm not judging you, I'm just jealous, *I swear*. Relax. It's time for you to rest now anyway. I'm sure the happy pills have kicked in- And lord knows with those 2 men around, you're guaranteed *sweet* dreams..." Again, she smiles, but now she winks as well.

"Thank you. I am tired again. I just want to sleep for a little while, okay?"

"Yup. I'm here all day, so I'll come back in a hour or two to check on you."

"*Promise?!*" God, that sounded so pathetic and needy.

"Yeah, I promise. But there's one more thing..." And here it is! I've been waiting for it.

"What?" Big inhale. Hold breath. Wait.

"There has been a Kayla from Chicago who calls each and every day since you were admitted. She has irritated every single nurse in this department, and I think a few nurses from other departments as well. I even told her to fuck off once, which could have cost me my job, but thankfully, she just laughed at me and thanked me for the information. If this is the same Kayla, and I'm sure it is... You really *do* have a good friend there. She misses you terribly, anyone can tell. And she is worried sick about you." Wow. Big exhale.

"Oh... um, thanks..."

"I just wanted you to know, in case you were unsure of her intentions, or you didn't know if you still had a friendship left. I suggest you take her up on her offer and punch her in the face, then hug her for a long time, and then get absolutely hammered together and trash talk everyone and *everything* you can think of. That should clear everything up nicely."

"*Seriously?!*"

"Absolutely. And that's not just my medical opinion talking."

"God, you're just like her. I swear, I love having you here. Thank you so much." *Shit.* More tears.

"Just relax, okay? I don't think anyone could handle 2 Kaylas at once, but I'll gladly substitute for your *Chicago* Kayla while you're here. Sound good?"

"Yes, thank you. Does that make you my *New York* Kayla?"

"You betcha. Sleep now, okay? I'll be back soon."

Walking out my door, Kayla looks back, winks at me, and then she's gone. She really is Just. Like. Kayla. How is that even possible? Maybe I'm hallucinating or something. I mean, they don't really look that much alike, other than they are both really tall, but that's about it. If I was hallucinating, wouldn't my two Kaylas look the same?

Why am I even thinking about this? Christ, I'm weird. Go to sleep, now. Close your eyes. Ah, there it is... the pull. I'm already almost there.

"Let go, love."

Oh! *Z.* God, I miss your voice, but I'm letting go...

CHAPTER 26

Waking however long later, I see Mack in the corner working on some paperwork. He doesn't see me watching him. He really is quite handsome. He is tall like Z, but much thinner. Actually, he looks too thin.

Maybe he doesn't eat enough working at the hospital. God knows, hospital food is gross. Actually, he does seem to work a lot. Maybe he doesn't have enough time to eat regularly. I should make sure he eats. Ooops. He caught me looking.

"Hi. How are you feeling?"

"Good. You?"

"I'm well. I read that you had more vomiting earlier and more pain as well. Are you comfortable right now?"

"I think so, though I haven't moved my head yet. It's usually only my head that hurts. Oh, and my hand, and sometimes my heart..." Shut up! *Jesus!*

"Your heart?" Nope. I'm not talking about Z.

"Where's Kayla?"

"The nurse, Kayla?"

"Yes. She said she would be back to check on me."

"She was here. She filled out the notes on you. It seems you two had a nice conversation. She didn't leave details, but she did state that you were very lucid, with 'a charming personality'. She wrote that she enjoyed her time talking with you, and that you seemed to enjoy your time with her as well." She did? She liked me?! That's awesome!

"Oh, good. She was really nice to me. I liked her a lot. She is just like my other friend Kayla in Chicago."

"Your other friend? Z mentioned what happened with your other friend Kayla. Have you chosen to resume the friendship, then?"

"I think so. 'New York Kayla' thinks I should punch 'Chicago Kayla' in the face, give her a big hug, and then get hammered and trash talk everyone and everything. She's amazing."

"Is she? Well, I don't know that a nurse should be prompting patients to physical violence, or even rendering a medical opinion, or otherwise, but I'm glad you were comfortable with her enough to talk to her about some of your issues." Gulp. That sounded bad.

As if on cue, Kayla walks in. *Shit!* I didn't mean to get her into trouble. What do I do? *Christ!* I'm panicking again.

"Mack! Kayla was just joking, I know she was. So was I. Of course, she wasn't telling me to do anything wrong. I'm sorry if it sounded that way. Kayla! I'm sorry. Mack is mad at you, and it's all my fault. I didn't mean to get you in trouble."

"Relax..."

"No! Mack is going to PUNISH you and it's my fault! I'm really, really sorry! I was just telling him how nice you were, how you are like my other friend Kayla, and I told him what you said to do, but I WAS JOKING! Mack doesn't understand."

"Stop! It's fine."

"No! *Please.* Oh, *God!* I'm sorry, Kayla. I wanted to be your friend. I wanted to keep you."

I can feel the tears pouring down my face again. I can feel my head throbbing. I can feel the upset in the room. I feel everything, and I just want to go back a few minutes, and never say anything to Mack. I fucking hate Mack right now.

"Listen to me. Look at me."

"No! Fuck you, Mack! I fucking hate you for taking Kayla away!"

"Listen. To. Me! I am not mad at Kayla, and I most certainly am NOT going to *punish* her. I was merely going to suggest that she keep your conversations slightly more professional, or at the very least, have your unconventional conversations while I'm in the room, so that I may spot, or witness any potential triggers for you. That's all. And, I wouldn't begrudge either of you a friendship." Oh. But...

"But you said you didn't want her 'prompting me to physical violence, or rendering a medical opinion, or *otherwise*'. You sounded very angry. You sounded like you would hurt her."

"I would never *hurt* anyone- especially a woman. And I certainly wouldn't *prevent* a friendship from forming. I just want to be apprised of your conversations, so that I can monitor you. You are *my* patient, and as such, I need to be aware of anything that upsets you, or even something that pleases you. I'm trying to help you, but I can't do that if I don't know what you're thinking or feeling from one moment to the next. That's all. I have no ulterior motives, I promise you. You are safe. And your 'New York Kayla' is safe."

In the stillness of the room, I finally exhale. Kayla hasn't moved from the doorway. Mack hasn't moved from the end of my bed. They both just seem to be waiting for something... waiting for me to do or say something, I think. What should I do?

"Um... I'm sorry I told you to fuck off Mack. I didn't mean it. You're always so nice to me. I was just really scared."

"I understand. And please don't worry; most patients want to tell us doctors to *fuck off* from time to time." *What?*

"And I'm sorry I almost got you in trouble Kayla. I just wanted Mack to know how nice you were to me."

"No problem. And it's true, most patients *and* nurses want to tell the doctors to fuck off *most* of the time." *WHAT?!*

Oh. My. *God!* I have never wanted to laugh so badly in my life. Holding it in as best I can, I look over at Mack and his smirk does me in. He wants to laugh too. I can tell.

I can't stop it. My laughter bursts forth. I am howling with laughter. Even though my head feels like it's going to explode, I can't stop it. Actually, I just kind of snorted too- disgusting and funnier. Kayla looks at me with such a comical look of disgust on her face at my snort, I laugh even harder, as she joins me.

"Real *lady-like* there. And to think you snort like that, AND have two hot guys wanting you... Jesus! What the *hell* am *I* doing wrong?!" Too. Funny.

"Please stop! *Seriously,* Kayla. My head is going to explode. Please?"

"Okay. But *honestly.* You have got to tell me your secret with men when

Dr. MacDonald leaves the room. Promise me."

"My *secret?* Yeah, right. If you were a scarred up, sexually repressed whore, who repeatedly got fucked in the ass as a kid by many men, *and* her own doctor, even as her daddy took the pictures... then I could help you. As it stands now, you have *GOT* to be WAY better off than I am..." More laughter. This is too funny.

As laughter tears fall down my cheeks I look to see if Mack is still laughing and I am stunned into silence. My laughter just stops dead. Everything in the room stops dead. What the hell is happening? Gasp.

"*What?* What's wrong?!" Gulp. *Shit.* What did I do now? Looking at Kayla, she is frozen- just *frozen* in the doorway.

"Do you know what you just said? Do you remember what you said?" Mack asks me all serious and kind of angry looking.

"Um, about Kayla?"

"No. Just now. About the men?"

"When? I don't know. What did I do wrong?"

"Do you know what you just said? Can you remember your words? Think." Um...

"I snorted and Kayla looked at me like I was gross, but in a funny way... I don't know. Why?"

"What did she say to you after that?" *When?!* I have no idea!

"Kayla... What does he want? What should I say? *Please...*" I whisper desperately.

"Do you remember me asking you to tell me your secret with men? Do you remember I wanted to know how you managed to get two hot guys?"

"Yes. But, what's wrong? I thought you were joking. WHAT'S WRONG? Just tell me. *Please*, Kayla."

"Um..." But Kayla just looks at Mack. And Mack looks like he is thinking of what to say.

"Listen to me. Do you want Kayla here right now? She can stay if you want, or she can leave. It's your choice."

"Why would she leave? What did I do wrong? Just tell me."

"I'll stay. May I sit beside you?" Kayla says walking toward me.

"Yes, of course. Kayla, what do you want me to say? Just tell me. *Please?*"

At that moment Kayla looks over at Mack, and he nods. He actually nods at her, like I'm not even here. God, I hate that! Everyone does that to me.

"I *AM* here you know! Just fucking tell me, Kayla. I don't care which one of you talks, but somebody FUCKING SPEAK! I get so sick of everyone talking about me behind my back. Whispering and talking... Oh, look at *her*... How did *SHE* get the hot husband? *She's* the Beaumont heir? That's *her?* What. Is. It?!"

"Um, you mentioned that you were repeatedly..."

"Say exact words Kayla. She needs the exact words she used..."

"Oh, yes, Kayla. Please say my *exact* words to me. Heaven fucking forbid you don't get it right?! *WHAT IS IT?!*" I practically scream in her face. *Christ!* I'm so sick of their shit!

"You said, um, you repeatedly got fucked in the ass as a kid by many men, and by your own doctor, even as your daddy took the pictures..."

Whoosh. Again. Holy SHIT! Where the hell is my air?

"No! Breathe. I want you to listen to me. Look at me, RIGHT NOW. I want you to breathe with me. Slow and deep. You are not doing this again to yourself... Do you hear me?!" Um....

"I'm t-trying... it's..." gasp "... hard."

"I know, but I want you to look at me, and breathe with me. Do what Z taught you. Slow, even breaths. There you go. Stay with us. Look, both Kayla and I want you to breathe slowly... *right* Kayla?"

"Yes... Of course. You can do it. Breathe with Dr. MacDonald."

"Mack. He's M-Mack."

"Yes, that's right. Breathe slowly with Mack. You're doing really well. You're barely shaking now and your breaths are evening out. How do you feel?"

"Better. Th-thank you. I'm sorry for this. I, I'm not sure why this happens to me..."

"Don't worry about it. I have panic attacks from time to time myself, especially when I'm shopping at Macy's during their yearly shoe sale." *What?!*

"I did too! A few w-weeks ago!"

"Well, anyone would. I mean come on, Manolos, Jimmys, and Wangs... Who wouldn't panic during a 60% off sale...?" She says with a huge smile. Oh. My. *God.* She is so amazing.

Breathing, I'm doing better. I can *feel* my lungs working. My hands aren't really shaking anymore, and my heart is beating slower. This is good. I'm almost back, I think. I just can't believe what I said. It's too much.

"No. Come on. Breathe slower. No thinking at the moment. I just want you to breathe slowly with Kayla. I don't even know what a 'Wang' is, but it seems pretty important..."

"*Vera* Wang, Manolo Blahnik, and Jimmy Choo... *Come on* Dr. um, *Mack...* these are very important shoe *Creators.*" I swear she added 'duh' to the end of that sentence.

"Oh, of course- forgive my ignorance. I must have missed that while in school forever, *becoming a doctor...* Can't you girls give a guy a break?" They're teasing each other? Oh, fun.

"You two would make a very cute couple. Mack you have that serious doctory, good looking, but dorky fun thing going for you. And Kayla you have that total smartass, awesome in bed, sexy thing going for you..." Ha! They both blushed!! I can't believe it, I just made someone else blush!

"Sorry..."

"That's okay. I've been trying to get his attention for over a year now. Maybe you just got his attention *for me* with that whole 'sexy AND good in bed' comment." *What?!*

Wow. Mack is positively RED. Now, I feel a little bad. I hope he's not mad at me.

"I'm not mad at you, if that's what you're wondering. I enjoyed your description of me way too much. 'Serious, good looking, *and* dorky fun'. I can't think of a better way to be described. Thank you for that."

"You're welcome and it's true. I mean it, you seem like you are just so

good, Mack, and I love having you in my life, for however long I get to have you."

"Listen to me closely. You will always have me in your life, if you want me. Both as your doctor, and afterward as your friend. You and I are going to be friends for a long time, I think." Oh!

"That was one of the nicest things anyone has ever said to me, Mack. I hope that's true. I would love to have a friend like you. I've never really had any, and you just seem like the perfect kind of friend. You don't hurt me, like, ever."

Dammit. More tears. I really wish I could stop this crying all the time. It's beyond embarrassing. Kayla leans in and actually wipes away my tears with a tissue. Oh. I remember that.

"The *other* Kayla did that for me once. It's okay, I'm fine. For some reason I cry a lot now but I never did before. Actually, I couldn't cry. I tried a few times. I thought of horrible things, really bad things, but I couldn't cry, I just had no tears. It was like I didn't even feel sad or something... I only cried once when I chopped an onion, but that was like a physical reaction or something, I looked it up... Anyway, now I seem to cry all the time. Do you know why Mack?"

Looking at him, Mack just seems so kind, and thoughtful, and like he knows everything. I bet I could tell him anything and he wouldn't get mad at me. That would be a really nice feeling to have- to not be afraid to talk to someone.

"Actually, I do. You have all these memories of very *bad* things in your brain. Things that you have repressed for so long as a survival tool, I believe. Once you suffered the bleed in your brain, your brain itself was no longer able to hold onto these repressed memories... And as you started remembering these things, you were no longer able to repress *all* your feelings as well. Basically, in layman's terms, you held onto *all* emotion to cope with your childhood trauma, and once you became sick a few weeks ago, you couldn't hold onto those emotions anymore, because you couldn't repress the actual memory of the events any longer. Now, you don't really know how to control your emotions at all. That's why you cry often, or you become enraged and lash out, or why you feel such suffocating despair, from one moment to the next. If I tell you your reactions are *sadly,* completely normal under the circumstances, it's not to minimize the effect they have on you. They affect you horribly, which is *very* real, but it is actually normal for someone with as much trauma in their life, to experience these emotions, as you have so far. Did that make sense?" Um...

"May I, Mack?" Kayla asks him.

"Sure." Mack looks a little taken aback, but Kayla just ignores him and turns to me.

"Look. You had a totally fucked up childhood from what I'm gathering, and for whatever reason you wouldn't, or maybe *couldn't* deal with it all, so you just didn't deal- *Period.* Now that you're older, and you're remembering everything that happened, you're finally reacting to it all. So, it's perfectly okay to cry, or scream, or freak out, or even have panic attacks. There's nothing wrong with anything you feel, no matter how embarrassing or uncomfortable it makes you feel at the time. Now, do

you understand?" Yes, I nod.

For a minute I think Kayla is going to gloat, but thankfully, she just asks Mack if she did okay. When he nods, both Kayla and I seem to exhale. Suddenly, I am very tired again. I can barely keep my eyes open. Why am I always so exhausted?

"Mack, why am I so tired all the time?"

"You just had major brain surgery, so your mind likes to shut down to regenerate. And you're on an emotional roller coaster right now, totally out of your comfort zone, so again, your body needs to shut down, to 'recharge' if you will... How did *I* do Kayla?"

"Not bad, *for a doctor*," she shrugs. God, they are so cute. I hope they go out together.

"Would you like to rest for a little while? It's only 3pm, so there's still a lot of time to talk later. You seem to only sleep for an hour or two at a time."

"Yes, thank you. Mack, I promise I'll talk when I wake up."

"No problem. But I have to ask, may I record you when we talk? I know you probably hate the idea, but it would be very helpful if you were recorded relaying certain information regarding your choice of Psychiatrist, rather than me merely repeating it- It's kind of a hearsay element I don't want working against me when I try to help you against your family tomorrow."

Oh *shit*. Record me talking about that *stuff*? "Um... Who will hear it?"

"Just you and I... Or anyone you give me express permission to allow to hear it. Until you do, it's just you and I, like I've told you from the start. Remember the 'Doctor/Patient Confidentiality' I told you about? That applies to any recordings as well."

"Okay. I guess. I mean if you think it will help."

"I do." Well, that's that then.

"I'll check in on you later, okay? And no worries, I won't ever tell anyone about anything you have or *will* discuss with me. I like you, and I'm not a bitch, I'm just a smartass... So your secrets are safe with me, okay?"

"Thank you, Kayla. Um, you're very kind."

"Just don't tell anyone..." and smiling she leaves my room.

I am so tired now. I don't even feel my body anymore. Hey! Why haven't I eaten in like, forever?

"Ah, Mack. I don't think I've eaten in a long time, like early yesterday, I think."

"You're back on a drip because you can't hold anything down yet. If you can make it through to tonight without gagging or vomiting, I'll feed you real food, I promise. Anything you want. You name it, I'll get it. Sound good?"

"Very."

"I'll see you soon. Rest well. I'll send the nurse with more pain medication for you."

After mere minutes, swallowing more pills, and a deep exhale, my body instantly feels the pull for sleep. Closing my eyes, I know I'm done.

Sarah Ann Walker

CHAPTER 27

Waking, my room is silent. Looking around, I see I'm alone again. I'm starting to like alone. I don't have to say or *do* anything when I'm alone. No one makes me tell them things, and I don't even have to think about all that awful stuff when I'm alone.

I really need to get out of here though. I need my own space; somewhere to just think, *alone.* Somewhere other than this hospital, or Chicago, or even New York, I guess. I need a get-away, something that is just for me. Somewhere that's all mine. That's all I need for now. I'll deal with all this other stuff after I have a little alone time.

Leaning over the side rail, I finally figure out which button actually lowers the bed and rail. It's amazing how complicated it is. All the tubes and wires are on my left side, so I turn to my left. Damn. My head is still pounding, and I'm a little dizzy from just this slight movement too.

With my feet nearly touching the floor, I look at the tubes. *Ew.* Catheter tube and bag of pee. That is just so gross, but I don't really know how to remove a catheter, so I'll have to wait for Kayla to do it later.

Looking at my hand, I decide to pull out the intravenous wire. How hard can it be? Holding my breath, I pull the needle out of my hand, and watch as a small dot of blood forms. Huh. That wasn't bad.

Opening my gown, I see the little heart stickers, which are also not a big deal. These are just stuck to me with adhesive. Pulling both off, the machine makes some noise. The monitor has many buttons, but only one that actually has a 'heart' picture on it, so holding my breath again, I push the button and... *silence.* Yes!

My bandaged hand is hurting, and my head is screaming from all this *work*, but I feel kind of excited too. I just want my own clothes. That's all. I hardly think that's too much to ask for. Right? *Christ!* Who the hell am I talking to? Myself? *Shit.* I'm still doing it. Stop. Focus on the job at hand.

I'll leave the pee bag on the sides of the bed, for now. Looking down, I gently push my hips closer to the edge, and let my left foot touch the floor. Oh. It's freezing. My feet love this! Pushing further, I force both feet on the floor. I'm standing. This is easy. Holding onto the railing, I put all my weight solidly on the floor, and I actually hold. I'm fine. Now I just have to take a step or two.

Slowly, I push my right foot forward and it holds. Following, with my left foot, it works too! I'm steady enough to move across the room I think. I'll just go slow, and try to use furniture and my arms to hold me up safely. So far so good. At least now I know I *can* walk. Another potential disaster averted. My mother would freak out if I couldn't walk.

Unhooking the pee bag and holding it tightly at the *un-peed* top part, I slowly, tentatively, make my way around the room. Gripping the chair, and then the walls, I'm going to make it. I'll try the skinny little closet where Z kept his blanket. That's got to have my clothes.

When I finally get there, which honestly feels like it took me hours, I'm

just exhausted. What the hell do I do now? I don't want help, but I can't even imagine walking all the way back to the bed. I'm just too tired. Opening the door to the skinny closet, I see my clothes. Yes! There's my blacks. All neatly hung up. All beautiful. God, I love black clothes. They hide every nook and cranny, every cellulite bump, and any extra fat I own. Black clothes can even make flabby arms seem toned. Black clothes are awesome!

With the catheter, there is really only one option. Though it seems silly, what else can I do? Sliding down to the floor, I grab my clothing and reach to untie my hideous green and white striped hospital gown. Bye bye, baby. I wish I could reach the garbage, or even a fire-pit.

Dressing as quickly as possible so no one sees my breasts naked, I slip on my clothing and finally exhale. I don't have to worry about the rest of the hospital gown until I stand up again, which should be in about 5 hours, give or take. God, I'm so tired. I feel like sleeping right here on the cold floor... my favorite.

Inside the closet I notice Z's blanket again. I'll use it for a pillow, just for a few minutes. I need a little rest, and then I can make it back to my bed. Placing the blanket under my head is remarkably comfortable. The blanket even smells of Z, like I knew it would. I hoped it would, and it does. His cologne still lingers, and it's so wonderful, I can't help but breathe him in deeply.

I'm going to leave the hospital with this blanket. I'm going to wrap it tight in vacuum-sealed plastic, and open it every once in a while when I need a reminder of Z... NOT that I'm ever going to forget him. But it'll be nice to have his scent to remind me of how good he was. I'm so excited to steal this blanket when I leave, I squeeze it tightly and smile.

Smiling, I know it's time to rest now. I'm going to rest for a few minutes, get up, slowly make my way back to my bed and wait for Kayla to remove this gross catheter. That's my first plan- my first independent action. I chose it, and I'm doing it- No pee-bag! GO ME!

===========

When I wake it is to the scent of Z. He is all around me. Oh! His blanket. I'm so glad I thought of it. Now, it's mine to keep... *unlike* Z.

"Can you open your eyes for me?"

"Hi, Mack," I smile.

"What are you doing down here? Did you fall?"

"Nope. I just needed a rest, and I love sleeping on cold floors. The cold always feels good to me."

"Would you allow me to help you stand?"

"Yes, thank you. Walking was a bit hard, and I'm not sure if I can get up again."

"Here, let me help you."

As Mack places his hands under my arms, he feels a little too close or something. Closing my eyes I force myself to *not* panic. Mack won't

hurt me. I know it, but I still don't like him touching me so close to my breasts. Cringing, I just try to keep breathing until I'm back on my feet.

Moments later, Mack is walking me back to the bed. Leaning against his chest, with his arm *safely* around my shoulders, I'm okay now. His hands aren't near my breasts, and he didn't grab me, or touch me bad or inappropriately. Mack is safe. I *know* that. I just forget sometimes.

Once I'm back at the bed, I see Mack hook the gross bag back on the side. Ew! He had to carry it. This is so embarrassing. I know I'm super red and I can barely breathe for the blush, as he helps me sit on the edge of the bed. Gross.

"Why are you upset right now?"

"Um, I'm sorry you had to carry that bag. Could you please, please get rid of it? Please."

"The bag is needed to..."

"No! The catheter. I need it out. I don't like it, and I don't need it obviously... I walked!"

"I'll just have a nurse come and remove it for you, okay?"

"Can't you do it?"

"No. This is more of a nurse's job. Just give me a minute."

I think he must be grossed out by me *down there*. I know it's a bit messy and scarred but it still works fine. Well, actually, I just learned it still works... Z taught me that it works. But I'm still embarrassed that Mack thinks I'm too gross to look at.

"I'm sorry I'm so gross down there. It's really not my fault. Sometimes they just got a little excited and did stuff to me, but I tried to stop them. I did! Well, until I realized I couldn't stop them, then I just closed my eyes and counted till it was over, or until someone helped me get up or until I woke up afterwards." I think Mack just flinched. Ooops.

"Let me go get a nurse and I'll be right back." Mack says with a kind of ashen face. I hope I didn't upset him talking about that *stuff.*

"Please Mack, could you just do it? I don't want to wait. Plus, I really want you to see me. I don't know why. It's not perverted or anything... I just feel like you should see it. Maybe so you know what it looks like down there. Maybe if you see it all, I won't have to talk any more, I don't know. Can you please just look?" What the hell am I asking?

"Listen to me. I cannot look at your vagina..." *flinch* "... It is highly inappropriate, given the circumstances, and I don't need to look. Plus, I know you wouldn't be very comfortable with me looking at you so intimately. Also, I *need* you to talk to me- me looking at your body is not going to change that, therefore, examining the damage inflicted upon your body will not change the fact that you and I need to discuss what happened to you. Do you understand what I'm saying to you?"

"Yes. I understand." I'm used up and too gross to look at. I understand, *totally.*

God, this sadness is oppressive. The weight on my chest is so heavy, I can barely breathe. I really wish I hadn't asked. I wish I was just like, *normal* or something. I can't explain any of this anymore.

Before my brain became sick, I at least knew what I thought and felt. Before, I was in complete control of myself. Before, I acted the way I should for everyone, but at least in my head I knew what I actually

wanted to do, and say, and feel... whether I did, said, or felt it, for others to see.

Now, I know nothing but I *feel* everything. I feel too much, and I hate this. This remembering and feeling is suffocating and nauseating, and honestly, just horrifying. I prefer my *Before*.

My Before was hard... but easy too. It was hard to always swallow everything down, but at least I had all the choice taken from me. I just knew I had to swallow it all, or I would get into trouble. Period. That's all. That was easy, because there was no choice, or decisions to make.

Now, I'm supposed to choose. I'm supposed to act on my own. I'm supposed to do, say and feel whatever I can at all times. I hate this *Now* that I'm living in. Now is hard. Now is heavy. Now is depressing. *Now*, I'm sad, lonely, scared, and kind of *desperate*, actually.

I really hate my life Now. I hate all this feeling, and sadness, and confusion. I know now, I like my *Before* better. I think I need the Before... when I didn't feel anything, but simple frustration. I think I want to go back to my *Before*.

==========

"Why are you crying?" Mack asks gently.

"I don't really want to do this anymore, Mack," I confess through my tears.

"What don't you want to do?"

"Um... *This*. All of it. I'm not really good at this, and I don't want to do it anymore."

"What don't you want to do anymore? What is upsetting you?"

"*Life*." Oh, that actually felt good. I said it. That's what I've meant all along. I don't really want this *life* anymore, and I don't want to feel this way anymore.

"I'm really tired Mack and just *sad*. It's very heavy, and I hate feeling this way. I don't want to feel this way anymore. I *can't* feel this way anymore. It's just too much. This hurts too much, *all the time*."

"Listen to me. You are depressed, and you're very stressed out. There are actual physical, psychological, and physiological reasons for this depression, but it can be helped. I can give you medication that will help. I can talk with you and help you understand what you're feeling, and how to cope with what you're feeling. You *can* and *will* get better in time. I promise you; you will not always feel this way."

"Um... thank you, Mack. But I, ah, don't really care why. I'm just too tired to care anymore."

Squatting down, Mack puts his hands on my knees and looks up at me, so kindly, I can't help but sob. He is so special. He is just, like a *delight* or something.

"Mack. I will take your memory with me too. I will, you know? I don't have *those* kind of feelings for you, but I think I love you very much for your goodness. Even right now, you're touching my knees, and I feel only *good*. You are so kind, and beautiful. And I really do love you, I think."

245

"Thank you, but..."

"Please listen Mack. You didn't do anything wrong. You're a really good doctor, but I don't want to do this anymore. I really don't. I've thought about it... all the bad, and even the few *goods,* but they're not enough. I don't want this anymore. Please understand that it's not you, and I really hope you believe me, but I have to go. I just have to leave all this *awful.* I really do want to die now, it's time for me." There. I said a heart-felt goodbye to Mack.

"Well, I can't allow that, I'm sorry. As your doctor, but more importantly, as your friend, I WILL NOT allow that. I have to step in, and take that choice from you." No!

"Please, Mack. I have to. You don't understand how much I hurt. God, everything hurts! My head is filled with pain, and memories of pain, a lifetime of pain... and my heart hurts so *badly.* It's agony to continue. *Please?* Please understand? I have to go. I have to. I have nothing good and I *feel* nothing good. There is only awful, heart crushing agony. Please let me go... I don't want to live anymore, I really don't. I really have thought about it, *I have.* I'm not making a hasty decision, and it's not something to regret. I need to do this. I *want* to do this... I *want* to die. I want to be dead now." And in nothing more than a whisper, I beg, "Please Mack, let me do this. *Please,* let me go..."

For one long moment Mack just stares at my eyes. Shaking his head suddenly, Mack exhales a hard breath and says, "I can't, and I won't let you go. You are going to live, I'm going to *make you* live. And you've just given me the power to ensure that you live. I have to take your will from you, *for now,* until you're better. I'm really sorry about this, but I WILL do this."

And rising, Mack begins walking to the door. *Shit!* What's he going to do? "Please, Mack! Please don't do anything to me. Please! I like you, please don't hurt me."

Shaking his head, Mack calls for someone in the hallway. I hear a code of some sort. I hear his name paged overhead. What's happening?

"Please Mack... You don't understand! *Please!"*

Ignoring me, Mack waits at the door. With his back to me, I see him talking and nodding to someone in the hall. What's he saying?

This is so stressful. What the hell did I do? I should have just pretended. I should have acted happy, and then done this later, or on my own, or somewhere else, or, or *LATER. Fuck!* Why was I so *stupid?* Why did I trust him? I knew he'd screw me over. I *knew* it. Fix this.

"Mack! *Mack!!* I'm fine. I've changed my mind. I'm good. I won't do anything! I promise! I'll be good, and do, and say, and, ah, *feel* whatever you want me to, I *promise!* Mack! Please listen to me! Please! I won't be bad again, I swear! PLEASE!"

When Mack turns to me, he actually looks sad. It's weird, I want to comfort *him* or something. I want to make him not sad. He kind of looks like Z did. *Shit.*

"I'm sorry, Mack. I was just being silly, I promise. I'm good, honestly. Don't be sad or anything, I'm not, ah, worth it, I'm really not. I'll do

whatever you want."

"Actually, you ARE *worth it*. And I'm going to help you *feel* worth it," Mack says as he walks toward me, while 2 nurses and a man walk in the room.

Oh FUCK! Here we go. *Shit.* What have I done? What did I do? *What the hell is happening?*

"MACK! Please don't hurt me... *please...*"

My chest is pounding. And my head feels like it's going to explode again. And I can't breathe very well. Where's Kayla? These nurses are mean looking. They don't like me, I can tell. The man is big-ish and he's not looking at me at all, he's just standing at the end of my bed, looking at Mack.

"I'm going to give you a needle. Please don't fight me. I want you to stay calm. I want you to get better, and this medicine will help you, I promise."

"*FUCK YOU,* Mack! I don't want a needle, and I certainly don't want your help! You're being such an ASSHOLE right now! I promised I'd be good. I promised I'd do whatever you want. Why are you being so mean to me?!"

Pushing myself as far up my bed as possible, I practically climb onto the pillows. What the *fuck* am I wearing? Oh, right. I had to put on my black, backless cocktail gown because of the catheter. Wow. It made sense at the time, but it looks really stupid right now. Giggle.

"Sorry for the outfit... But I couldn't put on pants with this stupid tube sticking out of my snatch. **See!**" And spreading my legs wide, I hope everyone understands I'm not mental. I had to wear my beautiful gown, or I'd still be stuck in the ugly hospital gown.

"There Mack! Now you can see the damage. See. It's pretty gross, but my hole still works. Wanna try?" Ooops. Another giggle.

"Stop this now. You're not doing this again." Mack says as he tries to take my arm. The nurses grab my arms, and the guy seems to pull my legs down the bed, all at once. NO! NOT AGAIN! FUCK!

"STOP!! PLEASE DON'T FUCK ME! PLEASE!!"

I know I'm screaming and fighting. I know my one leg got loose and I kicked the guy hard. I know my arm got loose and I hit the nurse to my left. I know it, but they still hold on. In one last desperate attempt, I break free and get Mack's face. Punching and scratching as hard as I can, I know I connect with his face! Yes!

Ouch! What did he do to my arm? What did Mack do? Fight! Fight more!

"You PROMISED! You promised you would never hurt me! You're a fucking liar Mack. Just like them! You said you wouldn't hurt me, AND YOU ARE!! STOP HURTING ME!!"

Screaming at the top of my lungs...I can barely breathe. Don't look. Keep screaming! Maybe someone will hear me? Maybe someone will help? Maybe this will be over soon? Maybe someone will hear me screaming and I won't be invisible anymore?

Opening my eyes, I look around and there's... Z.

Oh my GOD! Whoosh. I just stop and there's nothing but silence in

the room. *Z* came to my rescue...? *Yeah right.* Z gave me to Mack.

With my voice hoarse and broken, I whisper, "You lied to me Z. You said he was good. You promised he wouldn't hurt me, and now he's going to fuck me and you're all going to watch and take pictures, and take turns fucking me. You lied to me..."

Z actually steps forward, but I hate him. He's bad. He gave me to Mack. He made me *available* to Mack.

"**DON'T** touch me! Don't even look at me!! I really did trust you, you know? I didn't want to and it was hard to trust you, but I did anyway, even though I knew it was wrong. I trusted you Z, but you gave me to the men anyway, just like my mother did. *You* did this. When I'm dead, I want you to remember that. I Know What You Did To ME. You did this. I think I love you, and you did this to me anyway. That's why I never love, and that's why I never feel."

Z is still beautiful to look at. He is still handsome, and just so amazing... But not to me now.

I think my arms and legs are restrained. I can't seem to move them anymore. Not that I really want to. I just don't want anything anymore. God, my body is tired.

"I really wanted to keep you. Just once..." My words are broken on a sob. "...I wanted to keep you, but you were never mine to keep, were you? I knew that, but I hoped so hard anyway. Just once. I wanted someone to want *me*. I wanted to be *special* to someone. Just once..."

"You ARE special to me..." Nope. I'm not listening anymore.

"You're a liar. Go away, please. Please don't watch Mack fuck me. Please don't watch it. I only wanted you. One more time. I think I love you, and I wanted someone to love me too, *just once*. But I don't anymore. I don't want any of this anymore. I want to die, I really do. I don't want all this pain anymore. Please leave, Z. I never, *EVER* want to see you again." Sobbing in agony, I stop speaking. I stop everything and the room is still and silent except for the agony inside me.

I can't fight this anymore. I don't want to. Maybe I'll die in my sleep, but I doubt it. Mack wouldn't do that. Maybe I can get better, and then I can do it. Maybe? *Whatever.* I just want this life to be over with. I don't want to feel this life anymore.

Sleep is here, I can feel it. I am being sucked into sleep, not a gentle pull, but a soul sucking exhaustion- and I wouldn't fight it if I could. Asleep, I won't know what they do to my body. Asleep I won't feel the thrusting and the ripping. Asleep, I won't see all the red. Asleep, I won't know how bad it was. And when I wake up, the memory of the pain won't be the same as it actually was. I won't know and I won't remember.

Looking at the monster who gave me away, I take in his beautiful eyes for the last time. Clouding over into an abyss of pain and loss, I see his eyes begging for me. In no more than a final breath, I whisper the words I have always wanted to say.

"I wanted to love you, Z.
   But I am gone..."

PART 3

PURGATORY

Saturday, September, 4

Sarah Ann Walker

CHAPTER 28

Mack should be here within minutes for our breakfast meeting, as I call them, and today's meeting is going to hurt, I think. It's time to talk about my *attempt.* Mack and I have skirted around talking about it for months now. We have almost spoke of it, but neither of us fully commits, and we each pull back from the discussion I'm dreading.

I don't know what I did, *exactly,* though I know pills were involved and I know I did it at Z's apartment. I need the details now, I think. I need to know how bad it was because the raging hypothetical's in my mind are making me mental.

Waiting, I'm obsessed with images of what I did. Some are okay, but some are horrendous. I know better than to let my mind wander. I know better, but I find myself unable to stop the exhausting back and forth, rapid train of thought. I'm becoming more and more anxious as the minutes tick by. Where the hell is Mack? It's 8:31, and he's never late.

Waiting, I'm scared suddenly. What if something happened to Mack? What if he was in an accident? *Oh my god!* What if he's dead? I'll die- plain and simple. I'll curl up and my heart will just give out, I think. I can't live without him. He's all I have. I have no family left, and I threw *him* away to save him, so Mack is all I have in the world.

Suddenly, the pain I feel is unbearable. I can't stop the steady track of tears from falling. I can't help the hitching of my breath as I struggle. There is nothing left for me now. There is no one to love. There is no one to trust. I have nothing. I *am* nothing without the one person I do have- *Mack.*

"Why are you crying? What's happened?" I hear the soft whisper as a warm hand strokes my head in comfort.

Gasping, I look up into Mack's soothing face. Springing from my bed, I grab Mack and throw myself in his arms. Kissing his cheek and pulling his hair so he's closer to me, I wrap myself all up in his arms, as he holds me tightly. Choking, all I can whisper is "you're alive..." again and again, as I sob and hold him tighter.

Minutes or hours or *days* later, Mack gently pulls himself free of my death grip and looks at me with questions all over his handsome face. Sitting beside him, I can't breathe for my joy. My post adrenaline rush is making my hands shake and I feel slightly nauseous. Actually, I'm *really* nauseous. *Shit!* Turning my head quickly, I throw up beside us on the floor, as Mack jumps out of the way.

Returning to my bedside seconds later, he hands me a blue bowl and towel, while he continues stroking my head as I gag and wretch in the bowl. *Jeez...* The sound is amplified and echoey in the plastic bowl. It sounds kind of funny actually. Trying to contain my giggles, I fail miserably, as a few gags and following giggles escape.

"I'm sorry. I'm not crazy, but my gags sound really loud and echoey in this bowl. Oh, actually that sounds crazy, but I swear I'm okay. I'm just happy you're alive, that's all."

"Why wouldn't I be alive?"

"You were late."

"I was 6 minutes late, which by Manhattan standards is actually 24 minutes early. You should know that by now," he says grinning at me.

"I'm sorry, you're right."

"What happened?" Mack asks, giving me his special 'talk to me' look, and on a dramatic exhale I talk.

"Um, you were late, and I started panicking, and then before I could control my thoughts you were suddenly dead, and I realized how lost and alone I would be without you, then I was totally overwhelmed with despair and I couldn't stand the pain anymore, and then I realized that basically, I'm totally screwed without you, and then I realized I want to die too, if you're dead." There. I spoke.

"That's a little extreme, don't you think?"

"Not really. Well, the 'you were dead' part because you were 6 minutes late was extreme, but the rest wasn't."

"The 'Mack is dead, so I should be dead too' part wasn't extreme?"

"Not to me."

"Well, it is to me. I want you to live a long, happy life, whether I'm around or not, *THOUGH* I very much plan to be around for you for quite some time. However, should something happen to me, you are not *ALLOWED* to give up. I would be very angry at you if you gave up just because I'm not here with you, 'cause I'm dead." I think he's smiling at me, though I don't want to look at him just yet.

"But you'll be dead," I smile.

"Yes, but I can haunt you."

"You're too nice to haunt me."

"Don't count on it. I can be scary, you know? Just ask Z..." *Flinch!* Ouch! "I'm sorry, I meant..."

But it's too late... the spell is broken. I'm not relieved with Mack anymore. I'm just filled with the oppressive weight of loss and the heartbroken sadness I've learned to dread throughout each of my days.

My heart is pounding, and my hands are shaking again, and I just feel *bereft.* There is no other word. I feel like death is all around me.

This is the grief that fills all of my days and nights. A grief so powerful, I can't function some days, and other days, I simply function on autopilot with no thought or action of my own.

"Mack, um, I'm really *off* this morning. I think I just need to lie down for a while, okay? Maybe just an hour or so? Maybe I'll wake in an hour, and start my day all over again? You could go see Kayla. Maybe she's on her break or something?"

"I'd rather stay here with you if you don't mind. We could watch some of your ridiculous TLC shows together?"

"I really want to be alone for a bit. I'm not going to do anything bad, I don't feel *that* way anymore, if that's what you think. I don't, I promise. I just want to close my eyes, and wash away all this heaviness from my chest."

Turning, I push the bowl to the bedside table and lie on my side with my back turned to Mack.

"I'll just stay in my corner while you sleep, and you can ignore me completely, okay?"

"*Please...* I'm *begging* you. I just want to feel this alone. I'm sure I'll be

fine in a little while. Please Mack, just let me feel this alone, just for now-just today. I can't be with you, and I don't want you here with me. I'm fine, but I just need you to go away for now. *Please?*"

"Okay. I'll be back in an hour or so."

"Thanks, Mack. And I'm really happy you're alive..." I whisper as I listen to his footsteps walking towards the door.

"Me too. Kayla would be lost without her doctor to torture and harass."

"I love you Mack, and I really want you to be happy..." The 'without me' goes without speaking. I can't say it, but I know Mack knows what I mean. He's a smart man, and he has to know where I'm headed. This is too much for me. This despair is too great.

Thank you Mack for trying so hard. God, that man truly is an angel sent just for me. I love him so much. I love him until he *almost* fills all the places where I hurt so badly inside.

When I start crying again, I know I'm going to be awhile. These are the tears I cry when the pain lashes at me, and knocks my breath from my lungs. These are the tears that I fight, and don't show anyone if I can help it. These are the tears of agony and loss.

These tears explode from my heart for a mother and father who abused me, and never loved me. These are the tears for a husband who abused me, and never loved me. These are the tears for a man who *never* abused me, but who should *never* love me either.

These are the tears for the life I wanted to live but didn't, and for the life I did live and never chose. These are the tears for the choices I didn't have, and for the youth that was stolen from me. These tears pour out every hurt I've ever felt, and every hurt I now remember I have suffered. These are the tears for the life I dream of living, but will never have.

It is when I release this stopper on the agony that everything I know of pain, and even the pain I repressed for fifteen years spills like a deluge from my emotional reservoir. This is for them and... *for him.*

This pain is for all I ever wanted and for all I'll never have. These are my tears of agony and loss.

===========

When I wake, it's nearly noon. The floor has been cleaned and new flowers are beside me. My head is pounding, my eyes feel dry and swollen, and my throat is scraped raw. I need to sit up and take a drink. I need to rise and shower to wash away all this misery. I need to function again.

"Would you like a drink of water?" I *knew* he'd be here.

"Yes, please." I croak.

"You sound terrible. Lunch will be here in a few minutes. Did you want to shower before we eat?"

"Yes. I'll just be a minute. Thanks, Mack."

"No problem. I'll be in the hall," he says smiling while handing me a plastic cup filled with ice cold water.

"Thank you Mack, for everything, *always.*" I whisper as he leaves my room once again.

Mack knows I like to shower after every particularly difficult session, or upset. I don't know why I have to, and Mack doesn't question me or even explain it; he just knows I *need* to shower and he always gives me the time alone I need, and he accepts it.

I like to think my need to shower it as simple as me enjoying the scent of my vanilla-jasmine, though I'm sure there's some deeper meaning behind it. Regardless, I always have to rise and shower whenever things have been intense and painful.

Whenever I have cried hard, or whenever I have panicked fully, I have to excuse myself and go shower. Sometimes right in the middle of the painful conversation, I leave to take a shower. It's a little odd, I think.

Actually, I seem to remember there have been days when I've had like ten to twenty quick rinse-off showers in one day. That seems a little obsessive, no? Huh. I didn't realize just how much I shower here. I should ask Mack if it's normal behavior for someone like me.

After another quick rinse off shower, I dress in my standard blacks, and keep my hair pinned loosely to my head. I remember the first time Mack saw my hair down. Mack had this lovely look on his face, while kind of shocked by my hair, I think.

For one split second I remember feeling nervous of his reaction. I was scared he would be *attracted* to my hair and then to me or something, but he wasn't. Mack just smiled, said my hair was beautiful, and then continued talking as if it my hair was pinned up. I remember the instantaneous relief I felt knowing I was still safe with Mack.

Walking out of my room, I spot Mack immediately by the nurse's station talking to Kayla. She is so gorgeous with her black hair and dark brown eyes, and her long, stunning eyelashes which every woman would kill for. Kayla is tall with an average body, but somehow on her, the average body looks killer sexy. Maybe it's her height that makes her look great, or maybe an average body IS just right on her, I don't know. I do know that she's gorgeous, and I think she's finally making headway with Mack.

Seeing me, Kayla says something to Mack who turns with a shrug and a cute little boy grin aimed at me. Kayla gives me a wave and a smile as Mack walks toward me with our lunch. With his back to her, Kayla signals a very enthusiastic thumbs up, smiling from ear to ear. I can't hide my return smile and nod to Kayla, even as Mack raises a questioning eyebrow toward me.

"I'm not telling you, so forget it," is all I say as Mack pouts.

"Fine. I'll feed you, and then maybe slip you some meds... Whatever works, whatever I have to do to get you talking."

"You wouldn't dare." I scowl. "I could have your Shrink badge revoked for misuse of your position and prescription pad, quite easily you know."

"You wouldn't dare," he scowls back, "I could have you committed to a padded cell for the rest of your life, quite easily *YOU* know," he says with his most smug face.

"Dammit. You win. Will I ever have the upper hand with you?"

"Oh, *Christ,* I hope not. You're insane, remember?"

Bursting out laughing, I push open my door, and hug Mack from the side. Wrapping, my arms tightly around him, I just breathe in *my* Mack. His comfort and strength has gotten me through some of the worst days of my life. There is nothing I wouldn't do for Mack, and thankfully, after all these months talking with him, I'm pretty sure he feels the same way about me.

Sitting down at our little corner table, Mack begins pulling out our lunch. It's still warm enough that I see steam rising from the styrofoam. I love styrofoam meals; they're usually greasy and yummy, and thankfully Mack and I only indulge in these kinds of meals once or twice a week, so I don't get too fat. Usually we only indulge when I've had a particularly stressful day.

"Cheeseburgers and fries? Is this because I've already had a wretched day? Or because my wretched day is going to get worse? Yum, by the way." I can't help smirking.

"Both, I think. This morning was hard for you, I know. I was in the corner while you sobbed for over an hour…"

"What? You *were?*"

"Yup. And today is just going to keep *sucking*, I think," Mack says deadpan.

"'*Sucking*' is that from the newest psychiatric compendium? Or an older addition?" I ask dryly.

"The newest addition of course."

"Of course. Um, can I enjoy this greasy yumminess before I have to delve deep?"

"Certainly. I wouldn't dare spoil a delicious cheeseburger. Just relax and enjoy your lunch." *Uh huh.*

After eating in a comfortable silence with Mack, I finally crack. I hate a comfortable silence with Mack. I hate any silence from Mack. I think that's why we work, there are rarely silences that I *have to* fill. If I'm quiet, Mack starts talking, until I'm talking again. So far, it's always worked with me. I wonder why he's being so quiet today.

"What's wrong? You're never quiet unless we're watching TV. Just tell me. Look, my cheeseburger is finished and I couldn't eat all the fries anyway. Please Mack, just tell me what's wrong."

"Nothing's *wrong.* I'm just trying to think of the best way to get through today. Sometimes I need to think too, you know? I'm awesome, but even *I* need a minute once in a while."

"You *are* awesome, Mack. Just tell me what you want to- it's okay. I'm okay."

Standing, Mack collects all our styrofoam, the empty cans of soda, and the used cutlery. Dumping them in the garbage, Mack walks into my bathroom, which he rarely does, as I listen to water suddenly running. I'm starting to get really, *really* nervous now. Mack isn't acting like himself at all. This is weird, and upsetting. I hate this, but I wait for him to return. If Mack is acting strangely, than something must be bothering him, so I should give him the same courtesy he always gives me when I need a minute. I *know* that, but I'm just so nervous I can't help shaking.

Exiting the bathroom, Mack motions with his hand to join him in our chairs. Once I'm seated, Mack releases a long exhale, something again, he never, ever does. *Oh, shit.* This is going to be really bad.

"Okay. So first things first; you scared me this morning. I felt like you were pushing me away, and I felt like you were on the edge of hurting yourself again, though I wasn't sure of the means this time. I do understand, and even recognize that once in awhile you need time to yourself to digest whatever we've discussed. And that need for momentary solitude is quite normal under the often stressful circumstances you find yourself in. And that is why I always encourage you to take your showers to have your momentary time alone...

"...But never before have I watched you become so taken with your despair. And never have you pushed me away so completely. Well, never since your *actual* suicide attempt. I was very frightened this morning, and though I'm not telling you this to upset you, or to further burden you emotionally; I do need you to understand that you too, are very important to *me*, and I don't like the feeling I had this morning."

Before I can speak, Mack raises his hand to silence me, as he continues.

"Within minutes of me being late, you were ready to shut down completely, and within minutes of that, you *did* shut down, effectively shutting me out at the same time. Again, I understand that there are times when some of the more graphic details we discuss upset you and you need time to collect yourself, but you have never outright pushed me away before as you did this morning. And coming on the heels of your confessed suicidal thoughts surrounding my hypothetical death, you, well... essentially, *scared the shit out of me...*" Oh!

"I'm sorry Mack," I sigh.

"I don't want your apologies... what I want is an assurance from you that you will never again go there. Now, I realize asking you to promise me that you won't have suicidal thoughts is fairly ridiculous and impossible, but what I'm asking from you, is an assurance that you will not follow through in hurting yourself. I want to hear you promise me that no matter what happens, what we learn together in session, or even if something happens to me, like, *my death*- I want you to promise me that you will not attempt suicide again. Period. A kind of life-long contract between us."

"Um... okay."

"*I mean it!* I want you to promise me that you will never again attempt suicide. Promise me!" Holy *shit!* He sounds really mad at me.

"Okay, I'm sorry. I promise. It's just..."

"Listen to me. There is no *it's just*, there is no *'back-out clause'*, no *buts*, and no anything else. This is it. Period. I want you to say it, and mean it, and know that for the rest of your LONG life, you promised me, your friend Mack- *ME*- who would move heaven and earth to help you- I want you to promise that you will never again attempt to commit suicide- no matter how bad it gets, and no matter how hard it is to continue some days. I have never asked anything of you ever, except for your honesty, and I have been here for you continuously, but this- *this* I'm asking. I want your promise to me, *right now.*" Exhaling again, Mack looks simply exhausted.

"Um, I promise Mack. No matter what happens, no matter how hard it gets, and no matter how badly I feel, I won't attempt to commit suicide again. I'm so sorry. I didn't mean to scare you, I was just overwhelmed this morning. It just hurts so badly sometimes, the pain and memories are like an agony that won't stop. Please don't be mad at me," I beg on a whisper.

"I'm not *mad* at you, I'm *scared* for you. There's a huge difference, a difference I'm sure you can't understand at this point in your life, and in our relationship as doctor and patient, and as *friends*. I understand that you have never had anyone you trusted before to simply care for you, therefore, it's an alien concept to you. But I do care for you, *deeply*. I love you dearly and I will help you always, but this love and care must go BOTH ways. You have to give to me as well, because that's what people who care for each other do. YOU promise you won't do anything to hurt yourself, and I promise I will do everything I can to help you not *want* to hurt yourself. Do you understand what I'm saying to you? Do you understand what I'm asking?"

Mack is so agitated; I can see his hands shaking on the table top. Reaching over, I take his hands into mine, squeeze them gently, and make eye contact as I promise him I won't do anything to hurt myself, ever again.

Mack stares at me forever, then finally exhales, pulls me into his arms for a tight hug, and thanks me.

This is such a strange feeling for me. Mack seems so sincere, and for once I just *believe* in someone's sincerity. I believe Mack loves me, and wants me safe. I believe him completely.

This is so foreign for me but suddenly I feel warmth all around me and *inside me* for this special man. *My Mack,* my friend, my doctor, and someone I can count on not to hurt me, ever. With tears streaming down my face, I feel happiness and relief and trust in this moment, for the first time in my entire life.

"Oh. And I've agreed to a date with your New York Kayla."

Smiling, I whisper, "She's a very lucky woman, Mack," as I hug him tighter.

"I know, but maybe you could remind her for me later." I can hear Mack's smile-voice again, though I can't see it.

"Absolutely, I'll tell her. But I think she already knows..."

Saturday, October, 12th

CHAPTER 29

Marcus will be here to talk to me tomorrow. Mack told me that he spoke with Marcus extensively over the last 8 weeks. Mack also told me Marcus has even *agreed* to 'continued therapy'.

Marcus in therapy? Marcus admitting he needs help? It's just so strange to think of Marcus admitting he isn't perfect and that he needs help as well. It's kind of a relief, too.

I hope Marcus received counseling about sex as well. I don't know for sure, because Mack can't tell me anything about their sessions, but I hope so. I'm sure Marcus still thinks he's god's gift to women *sexually*, but now *I* understand differently. After all those years of pain and sexual brutality, I finally understand Marcus was wrong to treat me like he did. Marcus was the problem... at least in part.

I understand now, I too, hold some of the blame because I could have left him. Had I understood at the time that what he was doing to me *was* sexual abuse, I *should* have left him. But I didn't understand, and I didn't leave, and therefore I hold part of the blame.

I don't know, but I'm sure Mack would have brought to Marcus' attention the fact that he was sexually abusing me for six years, and hopefully Marcus is aware now, and will never do it again, to either me, or to some other woman in the future.

I don't know what's been said between them. Mack can't tell me because of *their* 'Doctor/Patient Confidentiality' agreement, but Mack did say that I may be surprised by what Marcus has to say to me. And that's all I know, which is kind of frustrating, actually.

We'll see. I've only had to talk to Marcus a few times since mid-July, and they were very short, very precise conversations. It was all very *civilized*. It was all very standard for Marcus, but not so standard for me anymore. I found myself wanting to just scream after our 'civilized' conversations.

In a strange way, I actually feel badly for Marcus. This certainly wasn't the life he signed on for, nor was it the life he would have chosen for himself. Marcus likes calm and order. Marcus is a stickler for routine and control. Marcus wouldn't have even recognized that he *was* abusive, therefore, he probably lives now in a state of shock, that his actions toward me may have actually contributed to my emotional breakdown. Marcus honestly believed he was the blameless *good guy* in all this, I'm sure. And it is this ignorance of his actions that makes me feel badly for him, not that I feel him blameless for the actual abuse I endured by him.

We'll see what tomorrow holds for Marcus and me. It should be interesting at the very least. I just hope it's not brutal between us, not that I think Mack would let it get that far.

==========

The last three and a half months have been anything but easy. It still amazes me how far I've come in the last three and a half months. It amazes me even more that I *survived* the last three and a half months.

This hospital room has seen me at my absolute worst, I know that. I am more than aware of what I did now, and what I was even planning to do. I am still shocked to learn I attempted suicide on June 1st, and that I wanted to commit suicide by the end of June as well.

I remember when Mack told me. I remember the feeling of shock. I remember not believing him, until slowly the memory returned to me. So slowly, like a tangled mess of memory and unreality, wrapped in horrific pain... the memory merged into a crisp recollection of my last night at Z's apartment.

I clearly remember the ambulance ride now. I remember Z talking to me the whole time. I remember Mack and the ambulance attendant having to restrain Z from holding me in his arms. I remember his tears and his apologies. I even remember the complete and utter despair I felt watching Z's desperation and sadness.

It was such a strange ride to the hospital. I continued to fall in and out of consciousness; hearing Z speak to me, then Mack speaking to me, then Mack trying to calm Z, while still trying to soothe me. I remember both men fighting so hard to keep me alive. I remember both men promising to help me. I remember just staring at Z's beautiful face. And that's all I remember seeing; Z's beautiful tear-stained face throughout the ride to the hospital as I fell in and out of consciousness.

Apparently, in a twisted view of my actions, I actually survived dying *because* of my suicide attempt. If not for my attempt, I never would have been in the hospital when the aneurism fully ruptured.

Apparently, the medication I ingested causes a person to fall into a coma when an overdose occurs, and lucky me, I fell into a coma from the overdose. While in the initial coma, the doctors in the ER preformed an MRI and a neurologic brain scan, and that's when the bleeding aneurism was found.

Had I not attempted suicide, overdosed, and fallen into a coma I would have had a slow brain bleed probably alone in the hotel room in Chicago. Likely, I would have just fallen asleep, never to wake again, I've been told.

God, hearing these facts with my new clearer head is remarkable. It was *so* close- closer than I could have ever imagined, closer than anyone could have imagined. I lived, because I wanted to die. So. Messed. Up.

And of course, if not for Z, I would be dead right now, buried in the ground. Without Z's insistence that I accompany him to New York, or Z's insistence on taking care of me, or Z's insistence on having Mack come to his apartment to meet with me...without any of those actions, I would be dead. Everything he did- all of it- saved my life. Whether he knew that at the time or not becomes totally irrelevant. Z's actions saved my life. Period.

Even now, Z remains my staunch, true supporter, though now it is from a distance. We haven't spoken, and I haven't seen him since that last horrible encounter, because *I've* needed to maintain my distance. I have to stay distant. I *need* the distance while I try to put my life back together. But I know he's always there, in the background. I can feel

him there.

I do need to thank him, I know that as well. And I will. I've been working toward it. With Mack's help, I'm getting really good at saying what I think, and recognizing what I feel, *when* I feel it.

I don't really hide anymore- Okay, I *try* not to hide any longer, but I still have to fight the overwhelming urge to retreat and hide each and every day. That 'survival mechanism' is still strong, but with Mack's help I can pause for a moment *before* I turn to retreat. It still happens from time to time, well, pretty frequently, actually... But I'm working on it. Every single day, I work on it. Mack helps me work on facing each day without retreating back into my head, alone.

===========

And then there's Mack- Another whole story in of itself. Mack is my Angel. I tell him often and he just grins. He knows how I feel about him. Though we have, and will *always* maintain a completely platonic relationship, we love each other very much. I'm sure I love him more than he loves me, but when I ask him, he always says that's simply not the case. He swears he feels just as strongly for me, as I feel for him. Honestly, his kindness knows no end.

Mack even took a leave of absence from the hospital, so that he could devote his time to my care. My Estate pays him because I insisted on it, when he refused. And after a big fight between us, I refused to see him, if he didn't accept payment from me. He hummed and hawed, but eventually recognized it was the only way for me to trust him completely.

I needed the small barrier of Doctor/Patient to truly trust him. And once he accepted my financial proposal and he took his leave of absence, we picked up right where we left off; Doctor and patient, and dear, *dear* friends. And so far, Mack remains the only person on the entire planet who I trust implicitly.

I even know Mack was brought up by the Psychiatric Review Board after taking my case on. Mack had to explain what he was doing, how he was doing it, and why his methods were so necessary to 'my recovery'. Eventually, he convinced the Board that he wasn't breaking any ethics laws by becoming my private physician. He finally convinced them, and I finally exhaled.

If not for Mack, I would have died. I know that. The despair, both caused by my brain injury, and by my past, would have inevitably killed me. I absolutely know beyond a shadow of doubt that I would have killed myself, had Mack not been there waiting for me.

And Mack waited. He was so patient and kind. No matter what I did or said. No matter how I tried to hurt him. No matter how I tried to hurt myself... Mack stayed right beside me. He refused to leave me, and he refused to let me *slip away,* as he said it. He did what no one else has ever done my whole life- he chose to help and protect me, day and night, period.

When I was still too messed up to even speak for myself, Mack spoke for

me. When I was too weak to fight, Mack fought for me. When I gave up, Mack refused to allow me.

At one point, a few weeks after my complete breakdown, I remember Mack losing it. *Finally.* Thinking about it now, it's almost funny.

Mack was always professional, always a *Doctor.* But in this one moment, he told me afterward, he honestly believed he was going to lose me, and he just… *snapped.*

After a particularly grueling session, after which I basically had nothing left, all I did was cry to die, while turning away from him and life. I was nearly catatonic with my despair, and that's when Mack SNAPPED completely.

Grabbing my arms hard while shaking me, Mack actually begged me to come back. He yelled in my face. He was so frustrated, and scared of my complete decline into madness and depression… And then he cried.

I think it was that exact moment when I finally felt *something.* I realized I didn't want Mack to cry, or to hurt *ever,* especially because of me. I just couldn't stand the thought of such a wonderful man hurting because of *someone like me.*

Looking at his tears and wanting to comfort him, I just grabbed hold of him and hugged him as tightly as possible. I remember really sobbing for the first time since my breakdown in Mack's arms. We both just cried and then he whispered…

"Are you back, Suzanne?" And that was it.

Suzanne.

He said it. He said my name and I sobbed in his arms for hours. Every time I thought I was finished crying, Mack would whisper *Suzanne* in my ear and I would sob again. For hours he did this. Just held me, whispered my name, and let me cry, often hysterically, in his arms.

And that was the day I *became* Suzanne- complete.

That day I put to rest all the other names. I will never again be anyone but Suzanne. I refuse to be. In my shock and confusion, Mack told me it was okay to REFUSE to be the other names.

So, that day I actually put to rest; *Slut, Whore, Cunt, Dirty Hole, Cock-Sucker, Bitch, Pig, Darling, Honey, Sweetie, Babe,* and sadly… *Sweetheart.*

Mack told me I *am* Suzanne. And I can be *any* Suzanne that I want to be. I can rebuild her, and make her whatever I want to be. There are no more rules and no one to demand I be what *they* want her to be. It's up to me now to make Suzanne into the woman I always wanted her to be. It is finally my choice.

I am now Suzanne.

Mack even described the Suzanne he knows, and she was pretty good. Of course, I can improve her, and I have to start really *feeling* her, but she is me now. I am her and she is me, any *me* that I want to be.

And I'm working on it. Suzanne and the *old* me are trying day by day to

261

get acquainted with each other, and we're trying to live with each other. Every time a different name or feeling surfaces, we inhale and state that 'I am Suzanne now. No one else.' And it's slowly working.

Slowly, I feel more and more like *Suzanne*. Slowly, I am *believing* I am Suzanne. Slowly, I am *becoming* the Suzanne I always wanted to be.

===========

I'm expecting Mack any minute now. He always arrives by 8:30am on Saturdays. He is always here. Mack is a light for me. My angel. Mack is truly an amazing, remarkable man.

If I could wish to have a romantic love, it would be with Mack, or rather Mack's exact replica. But I don't want a romantic love, and I don't want Mack. And we never will be romantically involved, and we're both okay with that. We need that sexual/emotional distance. *I* need it, especially.

Having no romantic attachments has been the only thing I could rely on during this last three and a half months of hell. Because of this romantic *disinterest* and detachment for Mack, I could talk to him openly about all the bad sex stuff, in detail. I could talk to him without fear of judgment or even disgust by him, because he is *just* my Doctor but *mostly* my friend.

Not that I *could* disgust him. Lord knows I should've by now, but he never has been. Once in a while he would choke up, or suddenly take me in his arms to comfort me, though I suspect some of the time, he needed some comfort as well. Most of the time however, he could seem completely immune to the horrors I recounted and relived with him, and it was this appearance of emotional detachment to the horrors, which allowed me to tell of the events honestly and freely without fear of judgment.

Mack can stay sane and impartial when I need it. But he also seems to know, or to understand when I need him to react, and he does so accordingly. He seems to *always* know what I need, *when* I need it. Even when I have no clue what I need from one moment to the next, Mack always does. Mack seems to always know when I need *him* and when I need my solitude.

Now, months later, we are so comfortable with each other and our friendship, we can joke and talk about *normal* stuff too. He even sits and watches TV with me in my room, or sometimes Mack even talks about his own life with me, like friends would. We have an actual *friendship* with each other. He even confides in me, and trusts me with a few secrets of his own, and I love him all the more for his trust in me.

Once, after a particularly grueling session early on, I jokingly threatened to report him to the Psychiatric Review Board for being 'inappropriate', when he had taken me into his arms for a huge, comforting hug, (which I had desperately needed at the time.)

Pulling away from me, Mack grinned and said, "I dare you. I'm the Doctor and you're just the *crazy* patient. Who do *you* think they'll believe?" And that was it. He issued a threat with humor, and I wasn't

afraid of him. I just *understood* he was teasing me. We broke the Doctor/Patient barrier, and became honest friends.

Mack and I have even talked about my 'neediness'. I was afraid I was making him too important in my life because I've never had a real, good, loving friend before. And as usual, Mack was okay with my neediness and all the attachment I place on him. Mack explained that, yes, I was in fact holding onto him tightly and yes, it could develop into an emotional dependency, but that he would monitor it closely, and make sure I didn't become 'crippled' by my emotional attachment to him.

I remember exhaling and thanking him for being smart enough to know when I was panicking, and when I was too needy. Mack just smiled and said "Why wouldn't you want me close? I'm doctorly serious, good looking, and dorky fun... What better guy to want by your side?" And it is *that* Mack that I love.

Mack is my 'forever friend'. I actually *have* a 'forever friend' in Mack, which is awesome. He is *'my person'* too. I remember watching Grey's Anatomy with Mack one night, a show I had never seen before that particular night with Mack (to his utter horror.) After I told him I liked it, he ran out and bought a small TV/DVD combo for my room, and the first 6 seasons of the show for us to watch together.

When I first heard Christina call Meredith '*her person*', I burst into tears. Crying, I just stared at Mack. He said not a word, just smiled and nodded at me, which of course, made me cry harder. Mack just knew, understood, and accepted his role in my life, as 'my person'.

Mack has even told me he *loves* being 'my person', and after that night we made Relax Night. So, every Sunday and Wednesday we watch two, sometimes three episodes of Grey's Anatomy together. We're up to season 6 now, and Mack is excited to buy all remaining season box sets for us.

I love Mack. Honest and truly. He is everything to me, without all the romantic, sexual, or physical *stuff* getting in the way. And though he tells me I'm attractive when I'm feeling particularly low, or vulnerable; Somehow he manages to say it convincingly, without freaking me out, without making me *sexually* nervous or scared of him.

Mack is an attractive, *tall* man. But somehow he has made himself 'my person', my doctor and my friend, while never threatening me, or making me fear him. He is truly an amazing man, the only truly good man I have ever known, and I thank god every day that he was brought into, and *chose to stay,* in my life.

CHAPTER 30

"Good morning, Suzanne. How was your night?"

"Very well, Dr. MacDonald. How was yours?" I grin. I'm practically bouncing in my chair. Come on. *Come on!* Tell me!

"My evening went quite well. Thank you for asking." *Dammit!*

"FINE! I'll beg... HOW WAS IT?!"

"Good." He smirks.

"Ugh! You're such an ass! Mack spill it, or I'll hit you, I swear to god! You know I will. You know I *can*, actually..." I giggle.

"Yes, I know. Don't remind me." He says laughing.

Dammit. I can't take it anymore. I charge him. Running for him, I grab him around the waist and squeeze tightly.

"I swear to god, if you don't talk I'll go *postal* all over your ass, and then you'll have to start all over again with me. Tell me!"

And pulling away from me, Mack finally smiles. Like a real smile. Oh, this is going to be good.

Walking away from me, Mack sits in his chair, leans back, calmly crosses his legs in front of himself at the ankles, takes a long, slow sip of his coffee and studiously *ignores* me. Jesus *Christ!* I'm gonna kill him! He's totally messing with me right now. The bastard!

Finally, he speaks. "Last night went very well. Kayla and I had a great time. She was charming and funny, and she has a truly *wicked* sense of humor. She actually kept me on my toes all night, but it didn't feel exhausting, it felt very exciting."

"AND...?" *Jeez...* I'm *dying* here.

"And *what?* We had a very good time. She said she wants to see me again. She thinks I'm a perfectly 'respectable' doctor, though she said she hopes to make me a little *un-respectable*."

"Holy *SHIT!* SHE SAID THAT?!"

"Yup." He's smiling so big now that he's absolutely adorable to me.

I have wanted Kayla and Mack to hook-up for months now. Actually, it seems like I have wanted Mack and Kayla to get together forever. I was just shy of obsessed with the idea. But he insisted *I* was his priority at this point in time, no matter how much *I* insisted otherwise. I was really feeling bad about it. I wanted Mack to have a life, but it felt like his whole life revolved entirely around me and my drama.

Finally, after secretly talking to Kayla, I convinced Mack to call and ask her out. Apparently she teased him right from 'hello', and Mack was smitten immediately. God, I hope this works out. It seems like it could. They are both just so great, so it seems like they should be great *together*.

When my phone rings I jump, but reach for it anyway. Old habits die hard apparently.

"Hello?"

"Is he there? Don't say anything if he is! Is he?" Oh, *shit*. It's Kayla.

"Yes, um, thank you."

"Do you know how to play this game? Come on Suzanne, have you ever played the *'answer all the questions without answering a single question obviously'* game?" *What?!*

"No, but thank you for asking." Was *that* good?

"Dammit. You *suck* at this." Giggle.

"I'm sorry, I *am* trying. This is my first time you know," I say as another giggle escapes.

"Oh, shit. You're gonna give me away, I know it."

"Thank you. I'm sure I can handle that..." I can't stop smiling. This is so much fun. Do people actually play this game?

"Fuck. Fine. Did he say he had fun? Did he like me?" Kayla begs.

"Yes, that's right. I'm sure that's what was said at the time."

"Okay, you're not *too* bad at this game. Is he looking forward to seeing me again?"

"Yes, thank you again. It was *wonderful...* ah, hearing from you."

"What the hell does *that* mean? Are you hanging up on me?!"

"Ah... no. It was wonderful, as I said."

"Oh. That's good. Did he say he had a good time with me, um, in bed?"

"*WHAT?!* NO, he didn't!" *Shit.*

"HE DIDN'T HAVE A GOOD TIME WITH ME IN BED?!"

"No! No, that wasn't what I meant."

Shit! Mack is right beside me now with his doctorly face on. I can tell he's just itching to grab the phone. He always gets involved when I get the bad calls. *Dammit.* This is too stressful. He thinks I'm freaking because of someone bad. Kayla's freaking because she thinks he didn't think she was good in bed. Argh. What do I do?

"Um, one moment, please." I hear Kayla yell *what?!* as I cover the phone on my chest.

"I'm fine Mack. It's nothing. Would you mind if I had a little privacy for a minute. Just a few minutes, I promise."

"Suzanne, you are obviously getting stressed out. Who is it? What are they saying to you?"

"Ah, it's...." Oh my god. I can't think. I've totally drawn a blank.

"Suzanne. Let me handle this for you."

"No! It's fine! I'm fine!"

"Suzanne... What's wrong? Please tell me. No secrets, remember?"

"Um..."

"Suzanne, I can't help when you don't tell me what's going on, and how you're feeling. I need to know. You *know* this."

"It's not like that Mack..." Crap. I can't lie to him. "Okay, fine! It's Kayla, and she's playing a game called something like *answer all my questions without letting him know you're answering my questions obviously*, or something like that. I don't know. I think I suck at it, but in my defense, I've never had a friend before, so I've never played it before, so it's not *really* my fault if I suck at it!" There! I spilled. Big exhale.

Smiling, Mack asks, "May I?" as he takes the phone from me. *Shit.*

"Good morning, Kayla. No. No she didn't tell on you. Suzanne was feeling a little stressed out because she was playing the age-old game of 'tell me without sounding like you're telling me', as we *men* like to call it. Uh huh. Yes, that's right. Yes, she is aware that she sucks at it, but I'm

sure with some practice you and she will have the perfectly sneaky, underhanded, often manipulative game down pat. Oh, *I see.* You would like me to shove my head *where?*"

What?! That's it. I'm done. Sitting on my bed, I start howling with laughter. They are too funny. I love these two together. I can't wait for their first fight, it's going to be hilarious to watch. God, I hope I'm there to see it.

"... Yes, I *very* much enjoyed myself. I'm glad you enjoyed yourself as well. I look forward to Tuesday night as well... Yes, all night. Yes. Okay. See you Tuesday. Pardon? Yes, I'll relay the message. Bye Kayla."

He's smiling again. *God,* Mack is just so cute. "Apparently, though you suck at the game, being as it was your first time, Kayla promises not to kick your ass, and she's sorry she stressed you out, and she's going to call you later for *proper* details, as she put it. Oh, and she said I had better give you *proper* details, so that you can tell her later... behind my back."

This is just too funny. At least I don't throw myself into a panic anymore at the mere thought that I may disappoint someone, or that they may be mad at me. That's growth, for sure. I can even handle little bouts of stress now without throwing up, or crying myself into dehydration.

"So? What should I tell you? What are you comfortable hearing, do you think?"

"I don't know. It's not about me. It's not *my* stuff, so I think I'll be okay. What do you *want* to tell me?"

"Well, Kayla and I had a lovely meal, followed by only 2 drinks, so sobriety wasn't an issue, and when we were about to leave, Kayla suggested I follow her to her apartment. Which I did, gladly." Smirk. "Once there, we talked, listened to music, made out like teenagers on the couch, and then moved to the bedroom. I'll spare you the specific details, but please relay to Kayla the fact that you were right, she *is* really good in bed." Annnnd another huge smile from Mack.

"Okay. That's what I'll tell her. I'm glad you had a good time, Mack. You should. You're awesome, and you spend way too much time with me. I, ah, actually really want you and Kayla to work out because you're both really good people." Exhale.

I'm okay. I'm good.

============

"Where are you, Suzanne? What's going on?"

"Nothing. I'm nowhere. This isn't about me, at all. I'm glad you had a good time last night, honestly."

"I know you're happy for me, well, *us,* but there's more."

"There isn't. Last night was about you two. You even had sex. Wow. How long has it been, Mack?" I smirk at him.

"You're deflecting. But to tell the truth, it's been forever. Thank god, I wasn't *rusty* at it." He says grinning.

"Oh, I'm sure it's like riding a bike or something."

"Oh, it's like riding *something*, all right."

"Mack! You dirty bugger. I'm going to tell Kayla you said that!"

"Please do. Something tells me she would enjoy the analogy." Grinning, I agree with him- Kayla *would* love that sarcasm.

Moving from our chairs, I start refolding my t-shirts.

"Okay, Suzanne, deflection time is over. Yes, last night wasn't about you, *at all*, but today IS about you. This is our time. You and me time- so talk."

"I don't know. I just feel sad, or lonely, or something. I can't explain it. I was so happy about playing the game with Kayla, like friends. And I was also happy for you. I was bouncing all night, waiting for details, I almost called your cell 500 times. Oh! *Thank god* I didn't... that would've been embarrassing. Anyway, everything was good. I wasn't even panicky about Kayla maybe being mad at me, but then I just suddenly felt sad."

Breathing a big exhale, I turn to Mack. Mack waits, like he always does, in case I have a little more to say after these big confessions. Nope. That's it I think. I don't feel anything else wrong right now.

"When did the sadness hit you? At which point?"

"Um...after I was laughing. When Kayla told you to shove your head up your ass, I assume. I was sitting laughing, and then you got to the sex stuff with her, and that's when the sadness hit."

"Very good. That's probably exactly when it hit. Sex."

"No. Not like that. I'm not thinking about all my bad stuff. I was just thinking about you and Kayla having sex. That's what makes me sad."

"Kayla and I being intimate makes you sad, like in a jealous sort of way? Are you jealous of *us* having sex? Or are you jealous because *I* had sex with Kayla?" *What?!* Oh, I get it.

"No, it wasn't the *you* part. I'm cool with that. No worries. I haven't slipped from needing your love and friendship, to needing you like *that.* The you and Kayla part I want really badly. And I don't think of you like that, still. Thank god, 'cause I'd be a total mess if I did. It was just maybe the *make out like teenagers* thing, or just the happy sex thing... I don't know."

"Maybe it's a combination of both, Suzanne. You have really never had either. You were never touched appropriately as a teenager, so you didn't live through and enjoy the kind of sexual rite of passage that teenagers experiment with. And you've never enjoyed sex, or thought it was good, except during a time when your life was falling apart. You really have no true, real experience with it, therefore when I describe it so comfortably, so *normally*, you really don't know how to process it. Sex is NOT *normal* for you."

Total silence follows his words. I think Mack is waiting again for me to participate in the conversation. Shit. I don't know what to say. I don't even know what I feel right now, other than sadness.

"I know sex isn't *normal* for me Mack. But will it ever be?" I whisper.

"I hope so. I want that for you. I want you to have normal experiences, under *normal* circumstances. But do *you* want that?"

"Of course I do... *in theory*. I just really don't know how to get there."

"It'll take time, Suzanne. It'll take time and much trust with yourself and with your potential partner. You'll know when you're ready, and you'll hopefully know how to ask for what you want from your partner."

"I guess so. Time and trust. Okay."

"Suzanne, do you know what you want? Sexually?"

"No. Sex is broken down to the three categories so severely that I don't know how to get one or the other or even which one I want."

"The three categories?"

"You *know*, Mack. You're just trying to get me to say them. I *can*, you know? I *can* say them now."

"I'm sure you can. Would you like to?" *Dammit.*

"You're being really Dr. MacDonald right now."

"Imagine that." Shithead! *Honestly.*

"You're a real shithead sometimes. You know that?"

"Yes, I do. Many people seem to tell me that. Thank god, I'm too much of a shithead to care what others think. Stop deflecting. Say them Suzanne."

"Fine! Fucking. Sex. And making love. There! The Big Three. Are you happy?"

"Are you?" *Argh...*

"No. Not really, but that's the point, right? Make me say the things I don't like, so you can make me talk about why I don't like them, and then I can *grow* and learn how to get through the obstacles, right?"

"That about sums it up, yes," Mack says and waits during this long silence.

"What are you thinking about, right now?"

"Z, actually." *Dammit.*

"What about Z, specifically?"

"Just the sex, I guess. It was just sex, I think, though he said *making love*... I don't know that it really was. I don't know. I'm confused."

"Was it sex or making love for you?"

"I don't know. It was really good- like awesome good. I remember that. There was no *bad* involved and I even enjoyed myself. That was the first and only time I have ever enjoyed anything with sex..."

"But...?"

"But he doesn't love me, so it couldn't have been making love even though he said so. I remember Z asking me once 'in general, would you call your marital relations making love, having sex, or just fucking' and all I could think at the time was 'Christ! I don't know. It's not like I was an active participant.' And even now when I think back on Z's question, I still don't know anything about any of the three...

"...Well actually, I think I have 'fucking' down, because being wretchedly fucked was all that was done to me when I was young. But I don't know what Marcus did to me, other than fucking me until I hurt, even though I think he loved me, in his own way. And I have absolutely NO idea what Z did to me, because *I* loved him, I think, but he didn't love me, and he didn't hurt me so 'fucking' is out, but then we couldn't have 'made love' because he doesn't love me, so that leaves just sex, but it feels like more than 'just sex' I think, at least for me. So I'm confused... and just *sad*."

Waiting for Mack to respond, I take many slow deep breathes to keep the panic at bay. I really am getting much better at this. Controlling the panic is becoming easier and easier by the day. If only I had known how to control myself a few months ago, maybe I wouldn't be here now. Then again, maybe I needed to be here. Or maybe…

"Suzanne, stay with me. I see you thinking in circles, and struggling with one reality and then the next. Let's just try to focus on these questions for the moment, okay?"

"I'm trying. I did stop an impending panic-attack Mack, so that's good, right?"

"Absolutely. You're doing very well considering the topic."

"Thanks…" I mumble.

"Okay Suzanne, I'm going to speak to you person to person here. There will be no clinical terms, and Dr. MacDonald has left the building, okay?" When I nod, Mack continues, "I want you to try to think of 'The Big Three' not in terms of three *types* of sex, but rather as simply sex with three different elements, or even styles, or intensity…

"…For example, a typical man can fuck a woman he loves, or cares very little for. He can also have plain sex with a woman he loves or cares very little for, depending on his mood, or even hers. And a man is absolutely capable of making love with a woman he either cares for, or truly loves. Making love requires, generally, either strong affection for, or love for, but sometimes can occur without either of those emotional attachments, though that is somewhat rare…

"…Sex can happen with any emotion. A male or female can just have sex for sex's sake, whether they love, care for, or even like the partner involved. Now 'fucking' is the tricky part, and the one I think you struggle with the most…

"…Fucking isn't necessarily about abuse, though to you it always has been. For the average person who hasn't experienced the abusive atrocities that you have, fucking can be just that- *fucking*. People who fuck are people in a consensual relationship who enjoy fucking, some of the time, or all of the time. They are not abused because they participate in the enjoyable, wild, often intensely satisfying experience of fucking. When both partners are feeling highly sexual, fucking can occur, even though they may or may not love or care for each other strongly. Some couples madly in love even *fuck* from time to time, or even *every* time. Fucking is generally just a speed and intensity difference from normal sex, and love making…

"…I think you confuse what was done to you as fucking. You weren't *fucked*, Suzanne. You were raped; repeatedly, violently, and against your will as a child. You may see it as fucking, and you may *need* to see it or categorize it as 'fucking' because the word rape makes you uncomfortable but the fact of the matter is this; You were RAPED. You were sexually abused as a child, you were never fucked as two consenting adults may or may not do within a relationship at any given time. You were raped as a child by grown men looking to hurt you. You were not *fucked*, Suzanne…

"…So, "The Big Three' as you call them, is really all the same- sex, but with varying degrees and edges. As a man, I can make love, have sex

with, and fuck a woman without abuse of any kind, and I can do all of this without *hurting* her. There is no such thing as sex against someone's will that is *not* rape. You have known very little sex in your life without rape, or at least a form of sexual abuse attached, therefore, again, I think you confuse what was done to you with what an average man, or even average couples do with one another. To you, everything seems so cut and dry. Am I correct?"

"Yes..." *Dammit*, I'm kind of crying again.

"Suzanne, it's okay to feel like this, given your circumstances and how old you were when all the abuse occurred. I'm not telling you you're wrong to confuse fucking with rape; I'm just trying to put your feelings into another context for you to think about."

"I know. I'll think about everything you said Mack."

God, I feel crappy. All tired or something. I don't know how I feel, but it's not pleasant. I'm all, like, dirty feeling, and itchy or something. My skin feels like it's actually crawling.

"Mack, I don't really feel like doing this today. Okay?"

"Suzanne... We always start on this path, at least a dozen times or so, but every time you stop. And every time I allow you to stop. But this time, I think you should continue... Can you try to continue?"

"Mack... I really don't want to. *Please?* Not today, okay?"

"Suzanne. It's time, I think. Z was a very important, though short-lived period in your life..."

"I know! Mack, I'm *very* aware of how important Z was at the time, and even still is, I guess. But I just can't. I'm going to see Marcus tomorrow, and you and I are supposed to go shopping this afternoon, and, and I just can't! It's just too much today. It still really hurts, and I want to be strong for tomorrow. Please, Mack? Please, not today?"

"Okay. We'll talk about all this another time. But we **will** talk about it, understood?"

"Yes, of course. I will. Just not today."

Exhaling, I know I've won this round. Mack always tries, but he stops when I just can't go further. That's the good thing about Mack, he doesn't force me to do or say things. He just tries to push me in a certain direction, but if I can't go there, he backs off until another time. Mack once told me it was counter-productive to *force* me to talk about the things I was *forced* to do.

I have to get ready anyway, Mack and I are going shopping soon.

CHAPTER 31

I've been living in the private clinic section of the hospital for two months now. And though I have many freedoms, I'm still not allowed to *officially* leave, until Mack (and I) decide... which we finally have.

Next Saturday, I'm leaving the hospital. I have two options, or rather two *choices*, and depending on Marcus tomorrow, I'll make my final choice. It's time. I'm doing much better, and Mack and I agree that I *should* leave the hospital.

Leaving today for a 'cardio-round' of shopping as Mack calls it, I'm excited... and nervous. I really want to buy some clothes, but I'm still a little freaked-out by the whole 'Macy's Incident', as I call it. But Mack will be with me, and he has promised not to grumble *like a man* the whole time. He even promised to carry my bags if I promise to let him go to a Best Buy. Mack is such a *man* when it comes to electronics. *Honestly.*

With all the proper paperwork filled out for my day pass, Mack and I are off. Walking me to the parking lot, I'm still bouncing a little, though trying to calm down. Smiling at Mack maybe a little *too* frequently, he returns my smile with a gentle side hug. God, he is just so good to me.

I love Mack's car. It's awesome. It's such a 'man car'. The first time I saw it I was totally overwhelmed. It's a candy apple red Porsche Carrera. *Seriously.* When I stopped still, he smiled, laughed, and explained that after all the years of medical school, all the jobs he worked throughout, and all the years of no sleep, he felt he *deserved* one real Doctor thing- his Porsche.

And then I saw the license plate and burst out laughing. Mack is a really good Psychiatrist. Mack is amazing, and funny, and warm, and *normal.* I laughed for a good ten minutes as we drove away from the hospital for the first time. It was wonderful to just laugh away all the stress of leaving the hospital for a quick bite to eat for the very first time since I broke down.

And there it is again, and I still grin. I'm finally relaxed now, as I buckle in and prepare to shop. I'm in the gorgeous, fast, *manly* candy apple red Porsche Carrera, with the funny amazing Shrink, with his very funny license plate... 'U Think?'

===========

Five hours in, two thousand dollars spent, and 3 coffees later, *I'm* doing well. Mack, however, looks totally *spent.* I almost feel bad for him, but he insisted he come with me for moral support, even after New York Kayla begged him to let her take me. Now, he looks like *he* wants to kill himself. Oh! Funny.

"Why are you laughing?"

"Because you look *cooked.*"

"I'm fine. Honestly. Is there anywhere else you want to go?" He looks like he's pouting.

"Mack, you're pouting."

"Am not." He says with a very dramatic pout.

"Are to." I laugh.

"No, I'm good. Let's go. Where to next?"

"Best Buy?"

"Oh, thank *GOD! Honestly*, Suzanne, I don't get it! How the hell can you try on basically the exact same blouse, in four different stores, and still not purchase it, until you try on the exact same blouse in the fifth store? Its madness, I tell you... *Madness!*"

Grinning, I take his hand and lead him out of the mall. The poor bugger. He looks totally drained, and that was only 5 hours of shopping. New York Kayla and I had planned a 12 hour, 9 to 9 shopping marathon.

After Best Buy, which I found ridiculously boring, until I bought myself an iPad that is, we finally leave for food. Mack is so starving; he doesn't know that he can even drive. But when I offer to drive his 'baby', he suddenly comes to life again. *Men.*

==========

When we arrive at the restaurant and take our seats, Mack instantly looks all *doctorly. Shit.* Here we go. He was just my friend Mack all day shopping. He complimented me when I needed it. He even weighed in on a few skirts or blouses when questioned. He was very relaxed and friendly... No Dr. MacDonald in sight. Now, he's here, looking anxious to speak.

"Go ahead Mack. Say it, or ask it."

"Let's order first. Then we can talk, okay?"

"Ah, okay." *Dammit.*

After we order there is an *uncomfortable* silence between us. This is rare. Mack and I can and *do* talk about everything. Rarely is there a silence, especially an uncomfortable one. I find myself stressing out.

"What did I do wrong, Mack?" Ooops. *Flinch.* Old habits, again.

"Suzanne... You know you did nothing wrong, at all. Please don't revert."

"Sorry. But you're stressing me out. What's wrong then? Just say it."

"I apologize. I'm not trying to stress you out, though I'm very aware of the fact that I'm doing just that. I'm merely trying to formulate my thoughts to best present them to you." *Shit.*

"Mack you're speaking very *doctorly* right now. Just say it. Don't worry about it. I'm good."

"You are *more* than good, Suzanne. You were wonderful today. I rarely saw you come close to panic. And when you did have that one tear-filled moment by the dressing-rooms, I watched you work through the moment until you could function again. I watched you struggle with the present and past, and inevitably, you came out of the past, with no help from me. You did amazingly well for your first real time out since May."

"Thank you. But...?"

"There is no but. I'm just concerned about tomorrow for you. I'm worried that today and tomorrow will be too much in such a short period of time. Believe me, *I* have faith in you and *I* think you can handle it, but I'm concerned that you won't think you can handle it."

"Me too, but you'll be there, right? So if I need a minute or if it starts going badly, you'll be there to help me, right?"

"Of course. I'll help you, or even stop the meeting if it becomes too much. I hope it won't become too much, but I'm not sure of Marcus and his motivation. He didn't tell me what this is about, so I'm going in as blind as you are, and that's where my nervousness for you stems from."

Oh *Shit.* If Mack doesn't know what Marcus wants, I'm screwed, I think. I assumed Mack did know, and therefore, he could prevent anything bad from being said, or from happening. Huh. This makes tomorrow even harder now. I kinda wish he hadn't told me any of this.

As our food arrives, I try to eat, I really do. Mack keeps prompting me to eat, but I'm just too worried now to handle food. Chewing, the food even tastes gross in my mouth.

"Suzanne, I really am sorry. I see the error I just made. I wanted to prepare you for any potential upset tomorrow, but I did it poorly. I don't want you stressed out all evening, but I realize I have done just that to you. Again, I'm very sorry. *Doctorly* mistake?"

Laughing, I nod, "It's okay, Mack. I know what you were trying to do. I'll be fine. I just hate *unknowns* now. I'm trying hard every day to accept the fact that I can't control everything in my life, but I still hate it. Honestly, I know you'll be there, and I trust you to intervene if it becomes bad, so I'll be fine."

"I know you'll be fine. I know you can handle whatever comes at you. We'll handle everything that comes at you, together. I'm just a little nervous myself about Marcus." Ha!

"Me, too. Marcus freaks me out, but I think I just want to get all this over with."

"Good. Okay. Now, can you please eat a little, so we can get out of here. I think you and I need a Grey's Anatomy night, don't you?"

"God, yes."

===========

When we arrive back to my room, New York Kayla is waiting for us. I was recently granted a key for my room. Mack, of course, has a key, and there is an emergency key at the nurses' station down the hall, but I still get to lock my door now. That was a big step.

Seeing Kayla, I'm so excited. She's going to appreciate my new clothes. She's going to love ripping open my bags, upending them on my bed, rummaging through them, oohing and aahing as required.

Pulling me into a hug, Kayla turns and very *seriously* extends her hand and says *way* to sternly, "Good afternoon Dr. MacDonald. I do hope you had a pleasant day shopping with Suzanne."

"Why yes, Kayla. Shopping in a mall for *5 hours*, debating the exact same clothing in 9 different stores is a secret love of mine... Thank you for asking."

"As I suspected Dr. MacDonald."

Oh, come on! They are too funny, and silly and actually kinda stupid right now. God, just kiss her or something. Unlocking and opening my door, I shove Kayla inside, and turn to Mack as he walks in.

"Kiss her! Right now, Mack! Give Kayla a kiss. I won't look. I promise." Both stare at me like I'm insane (again). But I don't care as I turn my back, tap my foot on the ground rather dramatically, and hum the Jeopardy theme.

"Suzanne. He kissed me. You can turn around now."

Turning to them, Kayla's lipstick is a little messy, Mack's wiping his mouth casually, and Kayla and Mack are both blushing. Ha! That was fun. I love, love, *love* making other people blush.

"Okay, good. Though I must say, that was *highly inappropriate and unprofessional* Dr. MacDonald. Now, could you please leave Kayla and I alone for maybe a half hour so she and I can go through all my new clothes. Its kind of a Chick-thing, from what I've recently been told."

"Of course. I'll just run back to my car and read the instructions to all my new *guy* things. Call my cell when I can return. We have some Grey's Anatomy to watch."

"Thanks, Mack," I say hugging him.

"*'Highly inappropriate and unprofessional'* huh? You are *so* busted for that later, Suzanne." Mack whispers as he kisses my cheek and leaves grinning.

"Kayla. I'll talk to you later."

"I look forward to it, Dr. MacDonald." Kayla salutes him. A *salute?*

Mack actually pauses, gaping at her for a second, before laughing as he walks out the door.

Okay. Done. Man gone. Girl time. I gotta get the goods from Kayla about last night.

Walking to my bed, Kayla upends all my bags, just as I knew she would. Lying out all the clothes by type, she makes neat little piles while still not looking at me. Blouses, skirts, pants, and even a few sweaters are neatly piled on top of each other. Holding my fabulous new pair of heels, Kayla finally turns to me with the biggest smile I've seen from her yet. Wow. She looks amazing.

"He was AWESOME! Honest to god! He was *incredible* in bed. I didn't know how good he would be. Actually, I kinda thought I would be better, and I'd have to, like, teach him some moves, or something, but NOTHING! He did everything, just, *awesome!* Holy *shit*, Suzanne! He's like a *Sex-God*, or something!"

"Wow. *Really?*" *Mack?*

"I'm not kidding you. I think I thought because he's a doctor, or maybe because he doesn't act like a sexual Dynamo, or like a player or something, that he'd be just *okay,* or something. I thought he was probably just a standard kind of 'missionary man', but *missionary... HE WAS NOT!*"

"Wow. *Really?*" *Jeez...* Can I speak?

"Really. He was **AWESOME**! Mack is like, all *skilled* or something. He was totally all about me, and *my* pleasure... and he didn't even ask me, or talk about it, or like have to fumble around to see what turned me on, he just *knew*. He was incredible, right from the first kiss to my last orgasm."

"Wow. REALLY?!" Oh, come *on!* Say *anything* else!

"Suzanne, is this okay? You seem to be a little weirded out or something. If this is too much...?"

"No. I'm fine. Honestly. It's just... I kinda thought the same way- NOT that I really ever think about Mack and sex, but when I do... I mean, I thought Mack would be really kind and gentle in bed, maybe very slow and romantic, but I didn't really think of him as the *Sexual Dynamo* type. That's all."

"I know. It was a total shock to me, too. *Believe me.* But Mack was just so *good* in bed. I didn't want him to leave. I knew he had to, and it's a little early for overnighters, but I really, *really* wanted him to stay with me. But he says he's staying all night Tuesday, and I can't wait!"

"Good. I'm glad. Mack was fairly smitten this morning as well. I think he really likes you too. He didn't kiss and tell like you are, but he didn't really have to. He was extra smiley this morning."

"So was I! My god! What that man can do with his hands and mouth was incredible..." *blush* "... Mack definitely has the moves and experience of a *real* man. Like a man who gets off on the woman's pleasure or something. He was so thorough and attentive, and sexy as hell. He's like a *Lover,* something you read about but think doesn't really exist outside of a novel." And another blush for me.

"'A *novel lover'?* Wow! I hadn't thought Mack could be like *that."*

A novel-lover? I had a novel-lover once. I knew a novel-lover. I remember feeling my novel-lover touch me. I remember my novel-lover. I still feel him sometimes. Where is he now?

"Suzanne? *Suzanne,* are you okay? Fuck! I'm sorry. Suzanne, why are you crying? *Shit.* I'm going to call Mack, okay?"

I have no words. I have only my silence. I think I'm frozen. I'm not having a panic-attack. My breathing is fine. I can *feel* everything in my body. I know I'm here, but I just can't move. Nothing is moving...
I'm stuck.

CHAPTER 32

"Suzanne? Can you talk to me? Suzanne?"

"Hi, Mack." Finally, *words.*

"Suzanne, are you here with me?"

"Yes. She's here."

"Suzanne. Are *you* here with me?"

"No. Not really... I'm *stuck* Mack." *What?!*

What the hell is happening? What does that mean? What the hell is *stuck?* I don't know how to stop this. *What's happening to me?*

"Suzanne? It's Kayla. Can you hear me? Can you talk to me?"

"No. I just really want to sleep for a little while, okay? Please, Kayla?"

"Suzanne, Mack would really like to talk to you a bit. Can you talk to Mack for me? I really need you to talk to Mack. Please?" Kayla sounds all hysterical or something.

"Suzanne, I need you to talk to me before you sleep. You know that's *our* rule. Talk to me first, sleep second. That's what we do, and I really would like you to follow our rules, okay?"

"Mack, can I please be alone?"

"No, Suzanne. I would like to sit here with you for awhile. Maybe I'll just watch Grey's Anatomy while I wait for you."

"Mack... *I'm stuck,"* I whisper.

"How are you *stuck,* Suzanne?"

"Um..."

I don't know. What is this? I was fine. My brain is working. Everything is working just fine. Why can't I speak properly? Why can't I say what I mean? Why do I feel like this? I really, *really* don't know what's happening to me this time.

"Suzanne, I'm going to talk with Kayla about what you and she were discussing. I'm going to try to understand the trigger for you. I need you to listen to Kayla and me. I'm watching you and I'm right here. Nothing will hurt you, and no one will touch you. I am right here beside you. Can you feel me holding your hand?" Oh. He *is?*

"No. I can't feel you. Sorry Mack."

"Do you feel me rubbing your palm with my hands?" Oh, there it is.

"Yes, I feel you now. Thank you, Mack." *Christ,* I sound like a robot or something. Why can't I speak properly anymore?

"Kayla, what were you discussing with Suzanne when you noticed her retreat?"

"Shit, *Suzanne.* I'm gonna *kill you* for this!"

"Kayla! No threats, please."

"I'm just joking, and I *know* Suzanne knows I'm just joking."

"Kayla, what were you talking about, specifically, when you finally noticed Suzanne's retreat? Exact words, please."

I can't even see where Kayla is standing. I think she's beside me, but I can't really see anything. It's kind of like a tunnel or something I'm looking through.

"*Specifically*, I had just told Suzanne about having sex with you. I told her how much I enjoyed myself, and I told you were very good at sex."

"Okay. What did you say specifically about the sex?"

"Nothing about the actual sex. I said you were really good, attentive, you knew what you were doing, and how I was *pleasantly* surprised. I called you a 'Sexual Dynamo', and that's it…"

Oh, I can't see her, but I think I felt Kayla's blush- the room just got really hot suddenly.

"Suzanne? Are you still with me? Can you talk to me?"

"She's here." She? *Shit.* "I mean, I'm here. I am. This is Suzanne. I know I'm Suzanne."

"Suzanne? Can you tell me what has you so despondent?"

"No, I can't. I'm stuck. I think I just can't move forward, physically, or mentally, or something. I'm stuck here now. There is no back, and no forward. I don't know what went wrong Mack. I can't really see or feel. I'm just stuck."

"Suzanne, move your hands for me. I want you to move your hands and feet. Right now." I'm trying. "Suzanne? Move your body, right now. You are NOT stuck. Physically, you are okay. You are fine. Move your body. Now, Suzanne."

Move body, *Move….* There. My hands and feet are moving. I'm fine. I am NOT stuck. I *can* get out of here.

===========

"Oh *god* Mack, I'm so sorry. I really am sorry for all this. I was fine. I *was.* Kayla and I were just *normal.* I don't know what's wrong. I hate this feeling. I can move, see? I can. Please don't be mad at me…" *Shit.* Here come more tears. *Dammit.*

"Suzanne, listen to me. I am *not* mad at you. I'm not mad at all. I'm here and I'm working with you. We're figuring this out, together. Suzanne, do you need Kayla to leave? Would that make this easier for you? We could just talk, you and me. What would you like?"

"I'm sorry Kayla to have embarrassed you. I'm so sorry for all this. I wanted *girl talk*- I really did. I'm not sure what's happening, but I just can't really move or something. I'm so sorry. I promise you didn't do anything wrong. I *wanted* to talk. I wanted to hear about your night. *I wanted you to trust me.* I'm sorry I failed…" Here I go. Honest to god, I am such a LOSER!

"Suzanne. Stop! You did nothing wrong. You didn't fail me at all. I just wish I knew what I said that made you this way. I'm very sorry. Would you like me to go? I'm not mad at you, and I won't be offended. I know you need to be alone with Mack right now to talk. I'm absolutely fine with it. No worries Suzanne, I promise."

"Thank you, Kayla. Will you still be my friend?"

"*Forever* Suzanne. I'm not going to stop being your friend, just because you've embarrassed the hell out of me with Mack." Oh, I hear *her* smile-voice.

"Thank you. And I hear *your* smile-voice. I love that Kayla. I love yours and Mack's, and Z's..."

OH FUCK!! Complete bodily reaction. Huge flinch and giant jump on the bed. My whole body just revolted against me! *HOLY SHIT!* Oh this *hurts.* Shit. Here it is. I can move now.

Z! It's *always* about Z!

Now I can move. Vomiting right on the floor, and partially on Mack's shoes, I nearly fall off the bed. If Mack wasn't holding me upright I would have landed on my face.

Trying to catch my breath, slowly the vomiting and nausea subside. Mack is still holding me, and I see Kayla moving around the room. My head is pounding and humming loudly. I am absolutely exhausted.

"Mack. I'm so sick of all this Z *shit.* It never goes away. No matter what I do or think or say, Z is *ALWAYS* there. He never goes away. I'm never at peace. I can't stand it anymore. It's making me crazier, I think. Please tell me what to do!" I yell in between gags.

"What about Z is bothering you? What is it specifically?"

"I don't know. I can't... explain it."

"Suzanne. You were talking with Kayla about sex, and something set you off. Can you tell me what it was? Please. If I know what the trigger words are, we may be able to help you better deal with them."

Moaning my words, "It's always him, Mack. I hate this. I HATE IT!"

"What do you hate Suzanne?"

"Kayla said you were *amazing* with your hands and mouth. You were *awesome.* You were *incredible.* It's you Mack! I know it's you. It's not *him. YOU* were amazing and Kayla thought she was in heaven *with YOU. YOU* are an amazing lover, Mack. It's *you* now, I *KNOW* that, but it's all twisted. Oh, this hurts..."

"What hurts Suzanne?"

"I'm done now Mack. I need to sleep. I'm done, and you can't force me to talk. Remember? It's counter-productive. You said so. You said it. I'm tired now Mack, and I'm done."

"Suzanne...?"

"Good night, Mack. I need to sleep for a while. I have to. I just can't... be."

"You can't be what, Suzanne? Talk to me. Tell me what you can't be."

I'm not talking anymore. I'm not, and Mack can't make me. I don't want to talk anymore. This hurts, and I feel gross inside. Everything is painful and confusing. I can't talk about it; I don't know what to even say.

Lying on my bed, I push all my new clothes to the floor. Actually, without thinking I pushed them to the other side of the bed, thank god. Puke-covered brand new clothing would have been *really* sad. Unlike *this* sadness, which is just, like, crippling or something.

"Suzanne. I want you to stay with me and I would really like you to talk to me about what you're feeling right now."

"I can't Mack. I. Am. Done. Go play with Kayla. Use your *amazing* hands and mouth on Kayla. Please *her* like a *lover from a novel*. Be amazing again. I don't care what you do, but please just leave *me* alone."

"Suzanne. Please, I didn't mean to upset you. I was just talking to my friend. I didn't give actual sex details, so I thought we were okay. Please forgive me. Suzanne?"

"Kayla, there's nothing to forgive. You should have been able to talk to me. If I wasn't such an insane asshole, you *could* have confided in me, but I am, so you can't. I'm very sorry, but I just want you and Mack to go away. Go touch and love each other some more. Go fuck. Go have sex. Go do whatever you did last night that was so *amazing*. I don't care, just don't make me watch. That's all. I just can't watch it."

I think I just heard Kayla gasp, but I don't really care anymore. The quicker she's mad at me, the quicker she's gone.

"Suzanne…"

"Mack did you fuck her last night, have sex with her, or did you actually *make love* with Kayla? *Seriously.* WHICH ONE?!"

"Suzanne, is that truly what you want to know? Is that what you need to ask? Will knowing that make anything better for you right now?"

"Yes, I believe it would Mack. Why? Are you too *ashamed* to answer the question? Are you embarrassed that you *fucked* her?" I hear another gasp. Is that *Kayla?* "Sorry, if this is too *vulgar* for you Kayla, but maybe you *should* hear what Mack has to say. Maybe you *should* know what you *actually* mean to him. Maybe if you knew you were no more than a dirty cunt **HOLE**, he wouldn't seem like such a *lover from a novel* anymore!"

"Suzanne!" Ha! They yelled in unison. *Too cute.*

"Or maybe you should just leave Kayla, before you find out the truth. Whatever. I don't really care anymore what either of you do. I just don't care, but I want both of you out of my fucking room. Please just get the fuck away from me, I mean it. I'm done with you both."

Christ! I hate the silence. Just leave me alone, but neither will leave. Neither will leave me in hell, alone. What the fuck are they waiting for?!

'What did you do, Mack? Did you FUCK her? Did you HURT her? Was it *GOOD* for you? *WHAT DID YOU DO TO HER?"*

"Jesus *Christ! Suzanne!* We had SEX! Mack didn't *fuck* me, and he certainly didn't *hurt* me! We had amazing *SEX,* but if he plays his cards right, I have a feeling we'll be *making love* in the future. That's it! There was nothing bad between Mack and I. He was a gentleman, and really, really good at sex. HE was **NOT** *them*, Suzanne. And Mack didn't hurt me, *AT ALL!!* MACK WAS…"

"Kayla!! That's enough. Suzanne doesn't need you yelling at her."

"But she was accusing you of…"

"These are her questions, and these are her feelings Kayla. This is how Suzanne expects things to be. Right, Suzanne? But Suzanne and I will discuss all these feelings and then she will process reality differently. Isn't that right, Suzanne?" I can't even answer him. I have nothing to give but silence.

"You are not helping Suzanne, Kayla, though I suspect you very much want to."

"I'm sorry. I'm going to go now, but I want you to know Suzanne that I'm not angry with you, we're still friends, I'm going to call you later, and I love you still. Please listen to Mack and try to get better. I'll talk to you soon, okay?"

"Good bye, Kayla. Thank you for everything. I liked keeping you for a while…" I whisper.

===========

Christ my chest hurts. It's like on fire or something. I haven't felt this before, I don't think. Maybe I'm dying. Maybe I'm having a heart attack. Maybe all *this* will finally be over. *What?!*

Shit. I haven't been here in a while. I've been really good. I've wanted to be better. I've *wanted* to get better. I really did. Now, I seem to want to let go again. Mack will be so pissed if I do though.

"Suzanne. What are you feeling right now?"

"I want to let go Mack. I'm tired again, and don't really want to keep fighting, but I don't want you to be angry with me. I know I promised you and I'm sorry." *Dammit.* Here come the tears again. Within seconds, I'm sobbing.

"Are you telling me you're having your suicidal feelings again?"

"Um… I don't know. I'm just so tired Mack. I want to exhale again. It's been so long since I just exhaled. Why can't I? Please. Just let me *let go.*" I say on a gasp.

"Not this time, Suzanne. You have just hit a roadblock, but we'll work through it. We will get through this, just like we did with everything else. We will get through it together, and you will come out stronger than before. Today we went shopping, in *a mall,* no less. We went shopping, and you had fun, and you were strong. Could you have imagined doing that four months ago? No. You couldn't. So today is what we Shrinks like to call *'A Bad Day'.* That's all. Today has been a bad day, and tomorrow may be worse, or it may be better. But we have to get through today, together. *You* have to get through today."

"But I don't want to Mack. I'm going to sleep now. Good bye, Mack. I'll call you later, okay? I promise."

Just go. Why do I always have to beg for solitude? Everyone else on the planet gets to be alone when they want to be, but not me. I always have to talk to someone, or look at someone, or just sit beside someone. I am never allowed to be alone. I just want to be by myself.

"Go ahead and rest Suzanne. It's okay. Go to sleep, and we'll talk later."

"Thank you, Mack. I'm sorry I suck. I love you very much."

"I love you too, Suzanne. And you don't *suck.* You are a wonderful woman going through a particularly bad time in her life. Sleep well, Suzanne." And leaning in, I feel Mack kiss my cheek as I close my eyes.

Good night, Mack. You really are my Angel. I know you'll be waiting in the hall for me to fall asleep. I know you'll sneak back into my room then. And I know you'll curl up in the chair in the corner and read a book while you wait for me to come back to you.

I wish I was yours to love, because you *are* the beautiful, romantic, caring, attentive man in the novels. I wish I was someone who could love like that. I hope you find that kind of 'novel-love' with Kayla, I truly do.

Sarah Ann Walker

CHAPTER 33

When I wake up, it's dark. Looking at my clock, I see its 10:16pm. Wow.
I've been asleep for a few hours. Sadly, I feel like I want to sleep for a few
more.
Where's Mack? I know he's here. He would never leave me alone on a
bad day. He rarely leaves me alone on *good* days. Maybe he's getting
something to eat. I *hope* he is.
 I've lectured him about eating before. He is too thin. He makes enough
money now, through my *Estate* to eat out 5 times a day if he wanted to. I
made sure of it. But I haven't seen Mack gain any weight. Maybe he is
just one of *those* lucky people who eat all the time but never gain any
weight. *I hate those people.*
Mack promised me after he became my personal physician that I was
allowed to boss him around. I loved that conversation. He looked at me
like I was crazy, which I guess I *was* at the time, but regardless, he
agreed. I loved pointing out to him that as his Employer I could tell him
to 'Fuck off' as needed, and sadly he couldn't do anything about it. Of
course, Mack agreed, we both laughed, and I proceeded to tell him to fuck
off the first chance I got.
It's a very strange thing to have an Estate. It was given to me by my
grandfather, who crawled out of the woodwork when this all hit. My
grandfather, whom I hadn't seen or spoke to in over 15 years, since my
grandmother's death actually, came to see me.
 At the time, I was completely loopy. I was often incoherent, and often
so emotional, I couldn't breathe from one moment to the next. During
that time, Mack continued to champion me, and intervene when
necessary.
 Upon learning of what happened, my grandfather was apparently so
appalled at my parents' behavior that he flew to my side immediately.
Apparently, my grandfather always knew my mother was *warped* (my
word, not his), but he never thought for a moment that it extended to
me, 'their *innocent* daughter', he said.
He and Mack had a long talk, a huge fight, and finally, my grandfather
took Mack and the hospital to court. I think he was trying to take me to
some other hospital, but Mack fought him desperately to keep me where I
was. I don't know the exact details, but I vaguely remember a side court
battle happening between the two of them, with Mack and the hospital
winning, *barely.*
 Afterward, my grandfather, who I have seen twice since, and spoke to
four times on the phone in the last three months, gave me my 'Estate'. I
guess, the Estate was going to my mother, but due to the *circumstances*,
it was quickly, and *legally* changed so that the bulk of the money went to
me. And strangely it's mine *now*, as opposed to when my grandfather
dies.
 I often wonder if he gave me the money *now* because he felt guilty about
his daughter's behavior toward me- his granddaughter, or if he just
wanted me to have it in case I needed the financial help. Maybe it's
simply because I *am* his granddaughter and maybe he just loves me,

though I doubt it most days. I don't think I'll actually ever know the reason why, so I should just let that question rest.

There was another hearing issued because I was not 'legally of sound mind', and therefore, I had to have a Legal Executor for my Estate. Mack once again came forward. And again, I was told by Kayla, Mack had to also battle another Conflict of Interest hearing, which he won, *by a hair.*

My grandfather apparently hated the thought of my doctor having all medically legal *and* financial control over me. Inevitably, it was decided that a panel of three lawyers, subject to Mack's approval, weigh in on my *financial* Estate. Therefore, Mack has the final say on my mental health; but he does not have full control over my finances. At that point, Marcus even came forward, but was quickly told to move on by my grandfather, which Marcus did, I found out later.

I guess if I didn't trust Mack with my life, that all makes sense. As it is, I could care less what Mack does or doesn't do with my money. He has proven himself to me time and time again. Mack is singularly the only person who has never hurt me, even once, my entire life.

It's all a little intimidating, but Mack has fought non-stop 'to ensure I have my freedom', as he put it to me one night. I remember asking why he was even bothering with me, and he told me that he promised me he would never hurt me, and walking away from me would be tantamount to hurting me, but more importantly, because he likes me very much. He even grinned and shrugged, and told me I was *'a total pain in the ass',* but *'totally worth his time and effort'.*

I remember balling my eyes out. I wanted to tell him to stop. I knew he was exhausted from dealing with me, and his other patients, and the legal proceedings, and the lawyers, and the Prosecutors, and an endless list of other things poor Mack had going on at the time. I knew his life was spiraling out of control, even as he tried to help my life *gain* some control. I know, because Mack looked exhausted though he would never say a word about it.

I remember begging him to let someone else help me, and he just sat beside me, took me into his arms, shrugged, and said "I won't ever leave you to fight alone. I'm here, like I promised I would be, and I'm staying."

After the Estate was changed to make me the sole heir, I read in the New York Times newspaper that my mother was suing me, my grandfather, a group of lawyers she said *illegally* had the Estate provisions changed, and finally the hospital, and Mack as well.

Under the circumstances, my mother was 'advised' to drop the lawsuit because apparently it would bring too much bad publicity to her *other* legal matters. And as a side note, she was also advised to drop her lawsuit because it would further victimize her poor, *'mentally incapacitated'* daughter.

It's so strange to read about yourself in the paper. I remember reading eight stories about myself, in six different newspapers. Apparently some of the people involved in my 'bad stuff' were quite unhappy with the turn of events, or rather, in being *caught* finally. They were even more pissed that their precious reputations and societal influence was diminishing.

Under Illinois State law, there is no Statute of Limitations on statutory rape. And somehow the Prosecutors managed to take possession of a

very incriminating black school book filled with photographs from my parent's library. I'm not too sure of the *exact* contents of the book, but I have memories of some of it, so I know it's pretty bad. Subsequently 6 predominant men from Chicago, two women, AND my *beloved* parents are being prosecuted by the State of Illinois.

I read that Mack and I were being threatened. I read that Mack had had his home and office trashed. To my horror, I read Mack had been assaulted outside the hospital one evening. I finally learned the depth of all that was taking place outside my walls. I learned of the threats and was scared to death, but not for myself... I was *horrified* for Mack.

I was so frightened of Mack being hurt because of me, I screamed and cried to anyone who would listen. I wanted a different doctor. I wanted- and quite fruitlessly- *demanded* to be released. I wanted them to let me go so no one at the hospital would be hurt because of me. I tried everything I could, but eventually, I was just restrained and sedated.

It was when I awoke from the sedation that Mack sat beside me, took all my newspapers away, and told me I could ask him anything. Mack promised to answer my questions truthfully but said that it was not in my best interest to read the hyped up, often misleading account of events from the newspapers...

And so I asked. I asked him what the hell was happening outside my little room and Mack told me, truthfully, and in a completely straightforward non-hysterical manner, though *I* was quite hysterical at the time.

Mack told me that originally when the allegations were made by him against Dr. Simmons, no one believed Mack. He was questioned repeatedly, and was nearly prosecuted himself for false accusations. However someone leaked to the press what was being said about Simmons and after an article appeared in a Chicago Times, eight women came forward to talk about the abuse they suffered by Dr. Simmons hands, in *his* hospital.

One of the women was actually a girl I knew from elementary school, whose parents also hung out in the same circle of friends as my parents. This coming forward by some of the other victims, prevented anything further from happening to Mack, and subsequently Dr. Simmons is in jail, without bail because he is a serious flight risk, while the Prosecution team formulate all their evidence. Simmons awaits his trial, which is to begin next year.

Next, I was told that though Mack and I, and I guess my parents, are aware that many more than six men were involved in my sexual abuse, the famous 'black school book' only *clearly* showed six men and two women's faces. The Prosecuting team however is still looking to identify more of the men based on physical traits, and markings or characteristics in the photographs. I think they're mostly waiting for me to remember more of the men, *specifically.*

When I asked how they found the book, Mack said he wasn't sure, but he WAS very happy about it. Mack said it became a slam-dunk case against my parents because my mother is spotted in a few of the photos and my father's handwriting is on the back of most of the photographs. And because of all the evidence, my age at the time, and the content of

the pictures; my parents are being prosecuted the hardest, with at least 30 felony charges apiece, with only the slimmest, most *unlikely* chance of acquittal for each.

Apparently, my mother is already trying to plea down her potential sentence, and is setting a rather different scene than *I* recall, against my father. According to my mother, my father was an abusive monster who she feared every day of their married life. Blah. Blah. I can't wait to testify otherwise…

Not that I have to testify in court. Mack and the lawyers worked out a kind of closed testimony where I get to tape my testimony in a different room with only the Judge, Mack, the lead Prosecutor, and the lead Defense attorney present. There are always ways the Defense Team can make this closed testimony *not* happen as I've been warned by the Prosecution, but I just have to hope for the best. The trial doesn't begin until next year anyway.

I asked Mack if he knew why my parents did this to me, and sadly he had no explanation. Mack admitted to me that my mother seems so indifferent toward me, that it's like there is something missing in her personality. Mack even suggested that she may have severe mental health issues as well, because of her complete lack of compassion and reaction to the events in question. Mack hugged me and told me quite honestly that I would probably never know why she abused me, and that I should maybe just accept the fact that I would *never* know the answer.

Mack did offer to accompany me to the courthouse to speak with her, if she would permit it, but I decided not to even try. I mean really, what the hell is she going to say that she hasn't already? My mother has made no secret of the fact that she hated me, so why listen to her say it once more. I'm done. I'll never know *why* it happened, and it really doesn't change *what* happened to me anyway.

I have heard however, and there are stories floating around about my parents trafficking in young girls, and there are other stories that suggest they were just singularly screwed up and evil toward me, only.

And of course, there are the few stories circulating that I am a total nut job head-case who made the whole story up for attention. I'm almost positive my mother started *that* particular rumor.

After Mack and I sat and cried and talked about all this, Mack finally came clean and admitted that he has had a bodyguard stationed outside my door since the beginning, and that he himself had his own bodyguard for a few weeks. He also admitted that he *was* in fact, attacked outside the hospital in an 'attempted robbery', and his house and office were also trashed and searched. He admitted to being absolutely terrified something was going to happen to me at the time.

Mack then told me it was actually my grandfather who wielded his wealth and *significant* power and influence, as soon as he found out about the threats against me, (and Mack), and suddenly everything stopped. There were no more threats from Dr. Simmons, (not that Mack or the Police could prove that) and there were no more threats from the wealthy Country Club set of Chicago proper. Everything just stopped.

Later Mack admitted he does still pay someone to watch me if and when he and I leave the hospital on our day trips… *just in case.* The police

agree with him, and apparently my grandfather *insists* upon this security measure, as a provision in my inheritance.

And that was it. The end. Mack hasn't left me since, no matter what I've said or done. Mack always comes back, and acts like it's perfectly *normal* for me to cry, scream, and fight him and his help at every turn.

But now that I'm awake I need to apologize again. I didn't mean to hurt him, or to make him into a bad man, like the *other* men were. I didn't mean to make him and Kayla bad, or to make their new relationship *ugly*.

This time I *really* need to apologize. This time, for whatever reason, I attacked him personally. And it is *so* wrong; I can hardly breathe for wanting to beg his forgiveness.

I don't know what happened earlier, but it's like my sleep washed away all the upset and desperation. I barely feel what I felt earlier. I hate how quick and violently those feelings come on, and I hate how quick and violently I react to those feelings. Strangely, I'm embarrassed when the feelings leave me just as quickly, because it's so hard to explain to Mack just how intense, and how strongly I had felt them at the time, when mere hours later I feel totally calm again.

===========

Rising from my bed, I first notice that all my vomit has been cleaned up, and second that all my new clothes are folded on the chair. Did Mack fold my clothes? If so, he is honestly going for sainthood.

In my bathroom, I brush my nasty teeth, and take another quick 'rinse-off' shower. I'm still not allowed a razor, but who cares if my legs are shaved? It's not like anyone touches me there. Actually, with the exception of Mack's hugs, no one touches me at all.

I remember the first time I saw 'Chicago Kayla' after I was admitted. Apparently, New York Kayla broke hospital policy by telling Chicago Kayla what I had done; and how badly I was actually deteriorating. This Kayla was even brought up by the Hospital Disciplinary Committee, when one of the other nurses reported her.

This Kayla fought it, and then Chicago Kayla denied it, and both Kaylas walked away relatively unharmed. I remember apologizing to New York Kayla for her involvement with me, and she just laughed and said, "Do you *really* think this is my first time in trouble? Pu-lease..." And that was that.

Chicago Kayla walked into my room, began a fifteen minute tirade about Marcus, the men, my life, and then she winded down with a very heart-felt apology with tears and everything. Finally she took me into a huge hug. At the time, I still cringed from physical contact, but after a few seconds in her arms, I just exhaled, and grabbed her tight.

I cried a lot that day while Mack stayed in the room and monitored me from the corner. Chicago Kayla was awesome, and very easy to be with. I had forgotten in my anger and hurt just how awesome Kayla actually was. She asked many questions I couldn't or wasn't ready to answer. And she forgave me when she received no answers. She said she didn't

care what she knew or didn't know, what I could or couldn't tell her, she said she just wanted back in my life… in any way I would have her.

When she left later that evening, I was really sad to see her go. Forgiving Kayla, when *honestly*, she didn't know she had done anything wrong, sleeping with Marcus at the time… was easy. I was glad to strike her off the very long list of people to hate.

A few days later, both Kaylas asked me if I was okay with them talking to each other, and I agreed. Looking back on it now, I was pretty drugged up at the time, so they kinda pulled one over on me, but there it is anyway.

My two Kaylas are friends, and they talk on the phone, and though I know I'm more often than not, the center of their conversations, *which I hate*, they actually get along fabulously.

The last time Chicago Kayla visited, a few weeks ago, she even stayed at This Kayla's apartment. The following morning when they walked in, they talked about their night, and even joked that they didn't throttle each other, or even really feel like it. It turns out Chicago Kayla also knew another Kayla, and she hated her guts too. Both Kaylas said "It's got to be the name."

I remember feeling a momentary bang of jealousy that they got on so well, but then they each turned their attention on me, and I realized it was *because* they cared for me that they were friends. Both my Kaylas. 'This Kayla' and 'That Kayla'. Fairly confusing for Mack some days I know, but kind of funny as well.

Chicago Kayla and I talk on the phone every second night now. She has even called me while on a boring date. She still has her sexploits, I can tell, but thankfully, she doesn't discuss them with me. I'm not too sure if she knew not to, or if Mack, or maybe even This Kayla explained not to, but for whatever reason, Kayla mentions going out with men, but she no longer *gags* me with all the sexual specifics.

Chicago Kayla even fixed my hair for me. Well, it's not like I had much choice in the matter- she just walked in with a bunch of hair paraphernalia and began. When I attempted to protest, Kayla gave me her damn pout, and before I knew it she had called New York Kayla, and I was done. There was no fight, just a kind of resigned submission to the insanity that is 'My Two Kaylas'.

When it was over, like an hour later, Chicago Kayla had created this kind of swept-over, fluttery bang which covers the scar and lack of hair on the front of my skull. I actually really like the look. The bangs are adorable with my hair up, and even on the rare occasions when my hair is down, the bangs still work.

When New York Kayla saw the final look, she was totally awed by Chicago Kayla's work. Beaming, she yelled, "Yeah! Total Farrah Fawcett Fuck-Me Flips!" And then the room went dead silent.

I didn't know where to look. Chicago Kayla just gasped and stared. The long pause that followed was so comical, I nearly died with laughter. New York Kayla actually stammered- She had *nothing*. I think for the first time in her life, she was completely and utterly *wordless*. Chicago Kayla stared like she too had no idea what to say. Finally, I let her off the hook.

"How about, Farrah Fawcett, '*DON'T* Fuck-Me Flips'… will that do?"

Thankfully, New York Kayla recovered herself quickly, wrapped me into a tight hug, whispered she was so sorry, then agreed, "Don't 'fuck-me flips' *more* than works."

Crisis avoided. Amazingly, I kept it together the whole time *and* I actually kept my two Kaylas reasonably relaxed through the whole funny, but potentially devastating ordeal.

I really like having two friends. God, I hope I didn't kill my friendship with This Kayla this afternoon. *Shit.* I probably did. How can she forgive me for being so rude and disgusting toward Mack and her budding relationship? *Shit!* This might be really bad.

I need to figure out what I'm going to say to her. I love having This Kayla in my life. All the other nurses are afraid of her; therefore, they stay the hell away from me. I really, really like having This Kayla. She has been so kind to me, for months now. No matter how bad I got, she always came to my room to visit me. She always made a point of talking to me, even when I could barely talk myself. And she always just tried to be here whenever she could, and I will always be grateful to her for that.

=========

Twenty minutes later all my new clothes are hung up in my tiny, cramped little closet. Mack even somehow managed to wheel in a 'rolling bureau' as he called it, but it's still not enough space.

Both Kaylas seem to just *always* stumble upon some sale or other, and they just *had to* pick up whatever was on sale for me. Originally, I refused and fought them, but again, I just became tired, because quite frankly there is NO use fighting *two* Kaylas. Inevitably, they have filled my two spaces to capacity with the most amazing clothes.

Argh... *where the hell is Mack?* Okay, I've stalled long enough, I have to call him.

Dialing, I'm quite nervous. I hope he isn't too mad at me this time. I know I really pushed it today, and though it wasn't my intention to go after Kayla and him, I did anyway. Mack is usually so forgiving, but today I think I crossed over a very dark line.

Okay, now I'm really nervous. He isn't answering, which is an absolute first. Four rings in, I go total meltdown. Oh. My. *God.* I **have** ruined it. Jesus *Christ!* I can't lose Mack! I just can't! *FUCK!*

When his voicemail picks up, I'm done. I know it. I can't have this. Not now. I am so close.

"Mack! MACK!! Please pick up! Please call me back. Please! I'm Sorry..." *Shit.* I think I'm screaming. "...MACK! Please don't hate me! *PLEASE!*"

Suddenly Mack is in my room calling my name at the door. Spinning toward him I'm almost dizzy with my upset. Thank god! He's here. Running for him, Mack opens his arms and looks like he's bracing himself for impact. *Oh,* that's kinda funny actually.

"Mack! I'm sorry. I was such an asshole this afternoon, I know it. I didn't mean those things to you, and I'll apologize to Kayla too. I was just messed up. Please! Please don't leave me yet." *Yet?* Ooops.

"Suzanne, stop. Breathe. Look at me. I'm not mad at you. We'll talk about this afternoon, but I am not mad at you. You and I are fine. And I wouldn't leave. Not yet. Not ever. You really need to start believing that." *Exhale.*

"Sit down by the table. I have food arriving any minute for us. I was down the hall when you called, so I just walked here instead of answering. Had I known you would panic, I would have answered. You know this. When do I leave you? When have I *ever* left you, *especially* after a particularly hard day? *When* Suzanne?"

"Never…" I whisper.

"That's right. *Never.* I don't leave you, and I won't leave you. Try to remember that."

"Sorry. *Ick…* now I feel like a child." *I hate this feeling.*

"Suzanne. I'm not lecturing you like a child. I'm trying to brow-beat some sense into you. You know I won't leave you, I *know* you know that. Yet you instantly go to your place of abandonment each and every time you have a bad day, or a grueling incident. That's why I'm repeating myself. I don't mean to sound like I'm lecturing you; I just hope that if I repeat these words often enough you'll eventually believe them. Okay?"

"Okay, Mack. I'm really sorry."

"Suzanne, you could try a Saint with all your apologies, you know that?"

"I know. Z used to say that too. But my family and Marcus couldn't get enough apologies from me. 'Old habits die hard', remember? You told me that once."

"Yes, I'm well aware of my own words of wisdom."

"You should be, there are so *few* of them." *WHAT?!* Giggle.

"That was very quick and *very* cleaver Suzanne. Thank you for slaughtering my intellect. I do so enjoy being intellectually slaughtered, especially by a crazy chick such as yourself. It cuts deeper," he says grinning. Oh. Thank *god.*

Grabbing Mack in a tight hug, I finally breathe properly. I hate feeling insecure with Mack. I feel it so often with so many, that feeling it with Mack is just too much. I can't handle it, and I can't stand it. I *want* Mack to always feel safe.

"I really am sorry for everything I did and said this afternoon, Mack. *Really.* I feel awful, just sick over it…"

"I know. But we have to talk about it tonight. We have to. But I would like to wait until after dinner, okay?'

"Okay." And with perfect timing there is a knock on our door.

Jumping up, I receive our food, from the nursing staff. Mack always orders our food from an 'outside source' as he puts it, to maintain our health. It's always delivered to the nurses' station, no matter where he buys from, and the nurses and any patients who happen to see and/or smell our food *always* resent us. Mack just shrugs.

========

After our perfectly delicious Italian dinner, at nearly midnight, Mack stops, turns to me, and gives me the 'doctorly' look I have come to dread, and maybe even sometimes fear. I don't get away with nearly as much shit when he's in doctor mode, as I do when he's in friend mode.

"Okay, Suzanne, you're off the hook tonight. I can tell you're absolutely exhausted, and I know you've made yourself sick with worry all evening over everything that happened earlier, so I suggest we pack it in for the night. Go to sleep, and I'll return early in the morning so we can talk. Marcus isn't expected until 2:00, so we'll have more than enough time to talk, work through any issues, and then prepare you for Marcus' arrival. If things don't go well tomorrow, I'll simply cancel with Marcus, and reschedule for another day. How does that sound to you?" Ex-*hale*.

"It sounds great. Thanks Mack."

"Suzanne you are off the hook for *tonight*- ONLY. Tomorrow morning I will be here by 8am, and we ARE talking about everything that happened and what was said today. Understood?"

"Yes, Dr. MacDonald. I promise." I even place my hand on my heart for emphasis with a solemn head nod.

"I think your 'Here and There', or 'Then and Now', or whatever the hell you call your 'Two Kaylas' are having a terrible influence on you. You are quickly becoming quite the smartass, Suzanne. I may have to speak with New York Kayla about it."

"Don't you dare! I love having two smartasses. And if they teach me to toughen up a little, all the better, right?"

"Yes. You're right. Okay, I won't say anything, *yet...*" He grins.

"Good night Mack. Thank you."

"Good night, Suzanne. You're welcome. Sleep well."

I think I will sleep well. Pasta always fills me and makes me tired, plus I've had a crazy up and down day today, which always exhausts me. Making my way to my bathroom, I brush my teeth and wash my face.

Pulling on my comfy pj's, I head for my cozy bed. The sheets aren't those crisp cold hospital kind; I have real sheets, and a real blanket- Z's blanket in fact.

I still sleep wrapped in Z's blanket even though his scent is long gone, and it's been washed dozens of times. But I still have it, and I still *need* to sleep with it. Sleeping with Z's blanket is the closest thing I'll ever have to sleeping with Z, and I'm honestly okay with that now.

Sunday, October, 13th

CHAPTER 34

When I wake, I *feel* Mack in my room. This used to creep me out, but now it's nothing to me. Mack has seen me so hideous over the last few months, that a little bed-head no longer worries me. Plus, he's usually reading in the far corner, not even physically close to me, nor is he watching me like a stalker or something. Mack just sits in the corner and waits for me to wake.

"Good morning, Mack," I croak.

"Good morning, Suzanne. Could you *please* get your *ASS* out of bed? Its 9:30 and I'm bored to tears," he smirks.

"*Really?* Wow. Sorry. Just give me a minute."

Jumping from my bed, I grab some clothes, and head for my bathroom. Kayla bought me an electric razor to use on my armpits, the one thing I refused to deal with after I was told I wasn't allowed any razors. So every morning, I quickly use the electric *poor substitute* razor, because I hate having stubbly underarms. It's just gross.

Back in my room, I see Mack has a whole breakfast spread laid out on our table. Everything looks really good. I'm starving again, even though I had a huge dinner only like, ten hours ago. If I keep this up, I'll gain back the twenty-five pounds I've lost in the last four months.

Handing me a plate, Mack starts dishing out all the things I love. Huh. This seems like a ploy. He even has blueberry jam, which I know he hates. Holy *shit.* Mack even brought the jasmine honey I love, the kind that's next to impossible to find. *Uh oh.*

"Mack. You're really freaking me out here."

"With breakfast?" He grins.

"Yes, with breakfast. You have *my* jam, and *my* honey. Both of which I know you hate. This screams of *'Butter up Suzanne, then nail her ass with something brutally thought-provoking and make her talk…'* Am I wrong?"

"Nope. You're not wrong. I do want you happy and relaxed. I want to have a tough conversation, and what better way to get through it, than to make sure you're all happy and satiated with your favorite *gross* jam and ridiculously expensive, impossible to find, and not *nearly* worth the effort, honey?"

"Okay then. I guess I better dig in, so I have something to barf up later." I grin in return.

While spreading *my* jam, I can't help but ask, "Is Kayla really, *really* mad at me?"

"No. She *really* isn't. She understands that there are some triggers that happen, out of your control, and she also understands that you try very hard to keep it all inside, and sometimes it just bursts forth. She is a good nurse, and she has dealt with many people and their issues. So, no, Suzanne, Kayla is not mad at you. She does however think you and I

need to have a talk about personal boundaries, but more importantly, she thinks we need to talk about "The Big Three" as you refer to intercourse, a little more thoroughly." *What is she, my doctor now?*

"Personal boundaries?" Gulp. I DON'T like the sound of this.

"Yes. *I* think, and Kayla agrees, she made a mistake talking to you not only about sex, but about sex *with me*. You weren't ready for sordid sex details, and you certainly shouldn't have had to think about *me* in that way. You and I work because there is no *sexuality* between us. Yesterday, Kayla made me *sexual* to you, and you lost your balance. I believe that's what made you lose it, if you will."

"Um... I don't know. I was fine. I was happy for you both. I just..." I have no words to express what happened. I don't *know* what happened yesterday.

"You couldn't handle thinking about me in an act of intimacy because I'm supposed to be safe for you, sexually *non-threatening*, and yesterday you became aware that I am a man who *has* sex, therefore, I became a threat to you?" Um...

"Maybe. I don't know. You became not only a man who has sex, but a man who is *amazing* at sex, a *Sexual Dynamo*, a man who is *really good* with his mouth and hands. I don't know Mack, that's a pretty awesome description coming from Kayla. I shouldn't feel any threat from that. I shouldn't, right?" I am so confused. *I hate this.*

"No, you shouldn't feel threatened by me, because I am **not** a threat to you. But that doesn't mean that you don't *feel* like I'm a threat. Who have you ever known sexually who didn't threaten to hurt you, or who just hurt you sexually anyway? You have NO experience with anything other than brutality, Suzanne. You know nothing of normal, loving, erotic, healthy, beautiful, *amazing* sex. I don't know that you can even imagine it at this point. Can you?"

"Yes, I can imagine it sadly. I had it once, well actually two times, but then I didn't and I won't again, but I remember thinking it was really, truly, amazing and just, like, *wonderful*. I think I was so shocked, that I couldn't even believe it was *real* sex. It was like a dream or something."

"Suzanne, you're crying. Do you know that you're crying?"

"No. Sorry Mack. I don't know... anything, anymore."

Putting down my toast, I can't make eye-contact with Mack right now. I'm getting that feeling of chest pain again. I get so tired of this feeling. It's all I know when I think of Z. Everything about Z hurts my chest. I hate talking about him. Shit, I hate *thinking* about him, because pain is all I know when I think of him. I am such an idiot over all this.

"Suzanne. What are you thinking about at this exact moment? Say it, please."

"I'm thinking I'm an idiot for having such painful feelings over someone who I barely knew, and who I shouldn't know at all. He was so good, and I make my time with him into something so good, but I know it wasn't real. I do know that. It just makes my chest hurt when I remember him, because I shouldn't think about him, at all." Let *go* of him.

"Who are you talking about?"

"Z. *There* I said it. I know you were waiting Mack, I'm not stupid, you know?"

"I know you aren't stupid. But I think it's important for you to say his name out loud. You rarely do, and when you do, you have a tendency to vomit." *I do?!* Oh, funny.

"Maybe you, ah, shouldn't tell him I barf when I say his name. That sounds a little insulting," I giggle.

"As much as it pains me **not** to torture him with the fact that a beautiful woman barfs at the mere thought of him, I will refrain Suzanne… but *only* because of our damn Doctor/Patient Confidentiality agreement, which I'm bound to… *Not* because I wouldn't love to see my best friend's shock at such a statement." I hear his smile-voice.

"Mack you are such an ass. *Honestly.* You think The Kaylas are a bad influence on me? You're worse. You have a real nasty streak covered in gentlemanly, *doctorly* humor."

"I do. But The Kaylas are still worse than me."

I can't think of anything else to say. I don't talk about Z ever, I don't want to. It really is like a never-ending agony. And Mack always tries to make me talk about Z, but I refuse. I wish I could have some closure or something. Isn't that the word Mack always uses? *'Closure'?*

"How is he, Mack?" *What?*

"Z is good, Suzanne. He has accepted the fact that you won't or *can't* see him. He tried for quite awhile, but you refused so many times, that he and I decided it was in *your* best interest if he stayed away. I'm sure however, if you would like to see or speak with Z, he would be more than willing."

"No. No, thank you. He's too painful for me. I just wanted to make sure he was okay. I didn't know how all of this stuff had affected him. Was he okay with it all? *Is* he okay with it all?"

"Z did suffer greatly in the beginning. He hid nothing of his father's involvement, even going so far as to give up any files, photographs, and an old laptop of his father's to the Police in Chicago. Z was adamant about helping the Police and Prosecutors."

"Does he know everything Mack… you know, all the *really* bad stuff?"

"Not that I'm aware of. Z only knows what has been publically reported, and about the few details you told him when you were unwell in his apartment. He has enough information to know he wants everyone involved brought to justice. And I know he has used some of his own resources and connections to make this happen."

"Why? Why would he do that? It doesn't make sense. He isn't Peter. I don't get it."

"He was doing it for you, Suzanne. Z wanted to try to fight for you somehow *now*, because he didn't know what was happening to you *then*. I'm sure if he had, Z would have stopped his father years ago. He cares about you Suzanne, deeply. Z wants…"

"Mack stop! *Please.* I don't want to know what Z wants, and I don't want to know how he does or doesn't care for me. I just wanted to know how he was. That's all. I don't want to go there Mack. Not today. I still have Marcus to deal with today."

"I understand, Suzanne. We'll focus on your visit with Marcus. Are you comfortable at the table? Did you want to move to the chairs where we usually talk?"

"All right." And moving to our chairs in the opposite corner from our table, I try to focus on today's problem... *Marcus.*

==========

I haven't seen Marcus in close to a month and I'm dreading seeing him. Whenever I *have* seen him I become emotional, enraged, and horribly depressed.

Marcus represents the 'middle' part of my life, so far. He was the 'in between', and as such, he carries some of the weight and responsibility for the way I felt as an adult, but he also holds none of the responsibility of making me the way I am. Therefore, I pity him *and* I dislike him too. It's really quite confusing.

"What do you want to say, Mack? You seem extra irritated about Marcus coming here today. Why?"

"Suzanne. Marcus hasn't told me why he wants to be here today, but he did say it was really important, and he had to get answers. When I pressed him, he wouldn't tell me anything more. So, clearly, I'm a little nervous for you. I don't like the *unknown* either Suzanne and I won't tolerate Marcus putting any pressure on you, whether *he* needs answers or not. That's my only concern for you today."

"Okay. What do we do now? What do we talk about?"

Mack actually pauses. He rarely does that. Mack is just too smart to ever need a minute. He seems able to think, speak, and act on the fly, and everything usually ends up right.

I envy that about Mack. I wish I didn't have to over-analyze and fear every single thing I do, say, or feel from one moment to the next. I wish I could just be a person who doesn't fear *everything*, every single day.

"Suzanne. We need to talk about your "Big Three". We have to. Should Marcus talk about your marriage, or your sexual relations, I don't want you confusing Marcus' and your sex, with the brutality of your past."

"Sometimes, they run very close, Mack. I don't think Marcus really knows the difference."

"The difference in what?"

"You know... The Big Three. Marcus wasn't very good at sex, as I've told you before, but I seriously think he has confused what the types are."

"Maybe he doesn't know the types, Suzanne?"

"Oh, he knows. He always knew. He just didn't care." *He NEVER cared.*

"Suzanne. Before you explained 'The Big Three', even I didn't know about them. Of course your Big Three make sense, just as they are, but there are variables, and I didn't place certain sex acts, or experiences, or even positions into a category of 'three' like you have. It's nearly impossible Suzanne..."

"No, it isn't Mack. It's very easy. I know it is. *Everything* fits into my theory of 'The Big Three'."

"Okay Suzanne, here's a hypothetical for you; A very loving couple, who have been together for years, *make love* frequently and are very happy with each other in life and within their sex-life. One night, the wife is feeling a little *frisky*, so *she* decides to have sex with her husband. It's a different experience, maybe even a different position then they usually *make love* to. When it's over, both are thrilled, and they still love each other very much. Nothing changes between them; nothing changes even for a moment throughout the sexual experience. Now, which of your Big Three did they have?"

"Easy. She's a slut who fucked her husband, and of course he went along with her for the ride... Oh, *literally,* I'm sure." Giggle.

Ooops. *OH FUCK!!!* I HATE that!!! I forgot to think first. *SHIT!* I forgot to think before speaking.

"Never-mind Mack, my mistake. They made love of course and nothing changed between them. Sorry. I forgot to think, um, I forgot to use my *brain to mouth* filter. Sorry." *Argh*

"Do you use your 'brain to mouth filter' often with me Suzanne?"

"Of course." *What?!* SHIT! "No! I really don't Mack. I'm fine. Sorry I just get confused when you talk about that kind of sex, I mean stuff. That kind of *stuff. Shit.* Mack, please don't touch me." *Dammit!* I'm losing it. Breathe.

"Suzanne, I would like you to take a deep breath and look at me. I'm not moving near you and I'm not touching you. I'm just looking at you. I want you to remember that I won't hurt you no matter what you say or do. You are safe with me Suzanne."

"I know. I just need a minute to breathe Mack. Okay? Just don't talk for a minute... *please.*"

And as silence continues, I realize Mack is right- I always think of everything *badly.* Everything is 'The Big Three'- *always.* Even non sex is somehow categorized into my head as 'The Big Three'. It's gentle, mediocre or brutal, *always.* Everything is, and every person is gentle, mediocre, or brutal. That's it. Period. I seem to place all events and even *people* into these three categories.

"Mack. I think I may have just had an epiphany of sorts, but I'm begging you to let me talk about it later, AFTER Marcus leaves. I just can't do it yet. It has to do with everything, and Z, and everyone, and how I *do* categorize everything and everyone. I know I do it, and I'm sure there is some perfectly *shrinky* reason for it, but I just don't want to do this right now. Its 11:25 and I really need a little nap before Marcus arrives."

"Suzanne, you just woke up..."

"I know, but I'm most strong and, like, clear or something after I wake up. I just want to rest for an hour, that's all. You can stay or go, maybe find Kayla. Oh, is she here this morning? If she is, go find her, fake a doctor emergency, and then take her to the gross cafeteria for breakfast, or I guess lunch now. Yes. Do something like that. Mack?" Why is he just staring at me?

"Suzanne, you're behaving a little erratically at the moment. Can you tell me what has you feeling so stressed out? I know you, and I know when you're pushing me away, or deflecting, and right now that is *exactly*

what you're doing. What is it? Just tell me Suzanne, and we'll work through it together."

"I can't Mack. I really can't. If I start now, I'll start crying, and I won't be ready for Marcus. And we both know I *need* to be ready for Marcus. Please just give me until 1:30, and then wake me. I'll be ready quickly for Marcus, and we can get it over with. *Please,* Mack?"

"That's a little longer than a quick nap Suzanne, but if you honestly believe you need it, then certainly. I'll entertain myself elsewhere, and be back by 1:30 sharp. Are you sure Suzanne? That doesn't leave you much time to prepare yourself for Marcus."

"Yup. I'm good. I know what I'm wearing already, and my shoes are picked out. All I need to do is brush my teeth, reapply my lipstick, get dressed and we're on our way. Mack, honestly, you're wasting my nap time. Go. I'm fine."

"Okay Suzanne, I'll see you shortly."

CHAPTER 35

At 1:55 Mack and I leave my room, for the more impersonal conference offices. Mack's residual hospital privileges allow for him to book the room for the next 2 hours. God, I hope this meeting with Marcus isn't going to take two hours. *Argh...*

When we enter the room, Mack pulls a chair in the middle of the table for me, nearest the door. Sitting two seats over on *my* side of the table, Mack settles in with a kind of 'it's going to be okay' smile and shrug. God, I love him. He *always* knows what to do in any given situation, at any given time with me.

"Mack? I just want to tell you how much I love you, and how wonderful I think you are, no matter what happens." I whisper, and almost choke up. *Dammit.*

"Suzanne, you're going to get through this, and I will not let anything or *anyone* hurt you. I promise. Oh, and I love *you* very much Suzanne." Mack winks, shrugs, and grins.

"Thanks, Mack." Big exhale.

Seconds later, there is a knock on the door. Jumping, my head whips around a little frantic looking at the door. *Shit.* What did I think was going to happen? Marcus magically appears in the chair across from me? *Christ.* Get a grip.

When Marcus enters, I just freeze. I have no breath. I don't have a single thought. I don't even think my heart is beating. Everything is just still. *SHIT!*

"Marcus. Please take a seat."

Mack offers the chair across the table from me. Dammit. Now I have to look at him, or at least in his direction.

"Thanks. You look lovely, honey. It's so..."

But already everything is wrong. Shaking my head, I can't help but start pulling at my hair. No names. NO NAMES! He isn't supposed to call me names. *EVER.* No one is allowed to call me names anymore. Mack promised. No one gets to call me a name.

"Marcus! As I discussed with you, countless times, this is SUZANNE, your wife, and I must insist that you use her proper name, *SUZANNE.* Do you understand?"

"Ah, yes. Sorry. I just always called her, hon..."

Christ, I actually hear myself moaning. What the hell is that? I'm *moaning?* *JESUS!* I sound psychotic. It's just a word. It's actually a good word. Most people don't think of that word as a bad word. It's really not that bad. Stop acting like a psycho. *Shit.*

"Suzanne? Suzanne can you talk to me? Would you like Marcus to leave the room for a minute so we can talk privately? Suzanne? Can you answer me?"

Mack gently reaches out, and takes my one hand into his. Oh, smart. Holding my hand stops me from pulling my hair out. Giggle. Shit. Don't start this. Not now. Marcus will hate me for sure. Then where do I go? Ooops, and there's another giggle.

"Suzanne. I need you to talk to me. Right now. What are you thinking

about?"

"Well, Mack, I was thinking how smart you are holding my hand so I don't rip all my hair out, then I was thinking that Marcus must despise this kind of behavior, which makes me giggle a little. Then I thought, where do I go when Marcus decides he wants a divorce?" And another giggle escapes.

"I don't hate you! And I, ah, don't want a divorce. I came to see when you were coming home with me."

"*Coming home?* With *you?* To *Chicago?* Are you *INSANE?* Why the hell would I go *anywhere* with you, Marcus?"

"What? Ah... I thought you wanted to come home."

"Why would you think that? Because I've been so *keen* to keep in touch with you? Or because I've seen you no more than 4 times in the last four months? *Why* Marcus? Why would you think I want to return to you, *with you?* Because you're *Marcus?*"

"We're married. You're my wife, honey..."

"DON'T CALL ME THAT!! I am not *her* anymore. *Fuck!*" Wow. Marcus jumped at my swear. That's kinda funny actually.

"Suzanne. I want you to take a big breath for me, right now. Suzanne! Look at me! Now! I want you to turn and look at *ME.*"

"Mack, I'm fine. I was just angry. I'm okay now, I promise. But maybe you could advise *him* over there, to not call me *honey* one more fucking time, or I will not be held responsible for what I say or *do* to him."

"Actually, Suzanne, you *will* be held accountable for anything you say or do. I know you're freaked out right now, but that does not give you the right to *physically* react to Marcus. Do you understand me?" Dammit. *Really?*

"Poor sport," I exhale with a giggle.

"I know. I'm in Doctor mode right now. Otherwise, I'd let you have at him..." *What?!*

Looking at Marcus, I'm done. Bursting out laughing, I can't believe his face. Jaw wide open. Eyes kind of bugged out. His hands are shaking on the table. *Jesus.* Is he actually that afraid I'm going to assault him?

"Are you so afraid of me now Marcus?" I ask on a laugh.

"Um, no. I'm more shocked at how unprofessional you and Dr. MacDonald seem to be with each other," Marcus says while glaring at *my* Mack.

"DON'T *ever* go there, Marcus! Mack is the only person who has kept me alive and relatively sane through the absolute fucking nightmare that is my life. Mack is everything to me, and if you fuck with that, I will..."

"Suzanne! No threats. Period," Mack barks at me.

"Sorry Mack, you're right. Marcus isn't really worth me hurting, is he?"

"Suzanne, I don't understand how you could be so angry with me. What have I ever done to you to deserve this animosity? I have been a good husband to you for 6 years. I have always treated you well, with few exceptions..."

What?! I can't take the sound of Marcus' voice any longer or his pretend innocence. I can't take it, I just **SNAP!**

"How many times did you RAPE me, MARCUS? How many fucking times did you rip me open when I begged you to stop?! Oh. My. *GOD!* A *good*

HUSBAND?! You're a FUCKING MONSTER, Marcus!!"

"*Rape you?* What the hell are you talking about? I've never raped you! I only ever did what you wanted!"

"Pardon? What did you just say to me?" I ask so calmly it seems to silence the room.

And before I know what's happened, I've launched myself across the table right at Marcus. Grabbing onto his throat, I feel him falling backward in his chair taking me with him, even as I feel Mack grabbing me around the waist. Kicking at Mack, I continue trying to strangle Marcus.

"How dare you? How FUCKING *dare* you say that to me? I NEVER wanted you! I NEVER wanted you to fuck me! And I NEVER, EVER wanted you to RIP ME OPEN!!"

Clawing at him, hitting his face, pouring every anger I've ever had into Marcus; I feel amazing with my anger and vicious with my vindication. This is AWESOME!

Suddenly, I'm lifted and nearly tossed across the room. Mack has me pinned against the wall, even as I scream and glare at Marcus.

"I HATE YOU MARCUS! I HATE YOU SO MUCH! YOU'RE JUST LIKE THEM! JUST LIKE MY PARENTS! JUST LIKE THE MEN! YOU'RE ALL THE SAME! **FUCK YOU!** I FUCKING HATE YOU! I WISH *YOU* WERE DEAD, MARCUS!"

"Suzanne! ENOUGH! If you don't stop this, I will sedate you! I swear to god Suzanne, one more word, and I'll knock you on your ass! DO YOU *HEAR* ME?!" Mack yells in my face.

"Sure Mack, I hear you. *Save* the rapist and FUCK the victim. I get it..."

"Don't you *DARE* go there with ME, *Suzanne. Don't even think about it!*"

"Fuck you Mack! Have him! Go fuck yourself, or fuck him, or fuck *whoever,* just stay the fuck away from me, and take Marcus with you!!" I scream right back in his face.

"SUZANNE! I don't understand what's happening here! I don't get it. Don't you remember? Don't you remember begging me to hurt you like that?" Marcus pleads

"WHAT ARE YOU *TALKING* ABOUT?!"

"Your *safe word* Suzanne? The word you wouldn't use! You told me you would *only* have sex with me like that! You told me that was the *only* way! And I hated it! I *fucking* HATED it! And you *knew* I did! You used to laugh at me when you would bleed everywhere, and I had to leave the room... You *loved* it! You loved laughing at me! For 4 years, I had to fuck you so hard, I thought I was going to choke on the pain, but you just continued. It was fuck you like I wanted to kill you, or *nothing.* You made me do it! You *made me* MAKE YOU BLEED!! OVER AND OVER AGAIN... AND I *FUCKING* HATED IT!!

Whoosh. What? Am I breathing? *Fuck!* Am I *falling?* There is no air, and there is no light. I feel only blank pain and darkness. *What happened?* I don't even know where I am. Why is everything so still and silent?

=========

299

"Suzanne? *Suzanne,* it's time to come back now. I need you to come back to me. It's just you and I now. Marcus has left the room, and you and I are alone. *Suzanne?* I need you to come back to me."

I feel like there is an echo in my brain. Mack's words are there, and I can understand what he's saying, but nothing is clear, or sharp. There is a humming, and an echo, and I find it super distracting. *Argh.* The humming is very annoying actually.

"Suzanne? Come on back now. Your breathing is better, and I think you can hear me now. Come back now. I want you back with me. *Suzanne?*"

"I'm here... Mack... I think. My head hurts. *Mack?*"

"Suzanne, you're in shock. You just suffered such a massive panic-attack and hyperventilation, that I have you on oxygen. Can you feel the mask Suzanne? Can you feel me holding your hand?"

"Mack?"

Minutes, or hours later, I don't know, I try to open my eyes. Oh, weird, I'm in a different bed in a different room. How the hell did that happen?

"Um, Mack, how did I... What's going on?"

"Suzanne, you had a massive panic-attack, followed by vomiting, until you passed out. You've been unaware for close to forty minutes now. You were placed on this bed and cared for by the nursing staff and myself. You're breathing much better and your vomiting has stopped. Can you try to sit up for me Suzanne?" I don't even remember throwing up. What the hell happened? Marcus!

"Where's Marcus? Did he touch me?"

"Of course not. I wouldn't have let him touch you. Marcus is sitting down the hall, waiting for you to recover some."

"I don't think I want him here. I can't. My brain isn't really good right now, Mack. Can you make Marcus go away?"

"Suzanne. I need you to sit up a little. Here, let me take the oxygen mask from your face."

Once the mask is removed my head is a little less echoey. I seem to hear things a bit better. I seem to feel things a bit better. What the hell do I do now?

"Mack? Mack, can I just have a rest now? Can I please go back to my room? I'm really, *really* tired."

"I know you are Suzanne, but I think it's very important that we continue for just a little bit. I think you were understanding a little about your past with Marcus. I think you were..."

"I remember now. Please ask Marcus to come back."

"Suzanne you can take as long as you need."

"Now, Mack. Please get Marcus, *now.*" Nodding, Mack leaves the room.

After a few minutes I decide to move. Swinging my legs around, I just touch the floor with my toes when my knees buckle. Falling, I am suddenly in Marcus arms. Fuck *NO!!*

"Don't touch me!! Don't ever touch me again, Marcus. I'm not yours to touch!" I yell while pulling myself back onto the bed.

"Suzanne! Marcus was just helping you up. I need you to focus on reality right now. Marcus was not hurting you, he was helping you."

Staring at Marcus, I think I remember. I see it. I think I remember.

"Marcus, what about the women? How many did you sleep with?" I whisper.

"Um, quite a few actually. Especially in the first 2 years." *What?!*

"Did you just say that? Did you just calmly say you have slept with quite a few women while we were married? You're incredible, you know that?!"

"Um, Suzanne, you told me to. Don't you remember? You said I had to get it elsewhere..." Marcus says as he sits in the chair across from my bed.

In the silence that follows, I just pause. What the fuck is he talking about? I said *what?* Does he honestly think I believe this shit? I have to breathe. I have got to keep it together.

"Marcus, could you please explain to me what you're talking about."

"Um, okay. Suzanne when we were first married you *refused* to have sex with me. I mean *vehemently* refused, especially on our wedding night. Do you remember that?"

"Sorry, no. Go on." Man, I'm like awesome calm right now.

"Anyway, you refused, like forever. I wanted to go to marriage counseling but you refused. I tried to get you to see a doctor, even an OBGYN, in case you had some *female* issue, but again you refused. I tried everything and I was so patient. Finally, I just lost it one night. I think I said something like, 'you either put out or I was going elsewhere'. And do you remember what you said?"

"Nope. Not at all." This is *such* bullshit.

"Well, you laughed and said 'thank god. *Please* go elsewhere Marcus.' And so I did. Originally it was just to punish you for not wanting me, but then I realized you actually *didn't* care if I slept around. You even made excuses for my absences and infidelities. You were, like, *helping me.* It was so screwed up, because besides the sex issues, you and I got along so well, and we were so happy... and I just couldn't end the marriage."

"Are you seriously trying to feed me this bullshit, Marcus? *Honestly?*"

What the hell? Looking at Mack I'm absolutely stunned that Marcus thinks he can pull this shit on me. Mack just leans against the window with his arms crossed, and kind of nods at me. I think he's trying to tell me to hold on or something. I don't know. Mack looks just as stunned as I feel.

"Suzanne. We continued like that for 2 years, and then I finally told you I had had enough. I threatened to talk to your mother about all this stuff..." *He did?* "... Actually, I did talk to your mother, and she took you out for lunch and that night you were just, like, *different* or something."

"My *mother...?*" Think! Dammit! Lunch with my *mother?*

"Yes. I don't know what she said to you, but that night you were wearing this bright red, like bustier corset thing with stockings and panties and everything. You even had on red high heels. You looked at me, walked across the room, and just tore at me. My clothes, my hair, even my skin was scratched up." Oh *fuck.* I think maybe...

"Suzanne. Talk to me. Are you alright?" Breathe.

"Yes, Mack. I'm fine. Please continue Marcus."

"Um, you were so aggressive, and you asked me to do... lots of *things* to you, *which I didn't!* But you just kept demanding more and more, and

then, you were fucking *me,* and it was *awful...* like really painful, and not very good, and not something I really liked. And you were a virgin, and I didn't understand why you were doing this, or why you wanted sex like this...

"...And then you explained that that was what YOU wanted, and that was the only way you would have sex with me. You told me you had a safe word, do you remember that? You said it was 'black'. Do you remember *black?"* Um, vaguely. *Shit.*

"Christ, I didn't even know what a safe word was at the time. I had to look it up. I couldn't understand how you knew about safe words and the sex stuff you were doing to me, and asking me to do to you. You were a *virgin,* and such a good girl, and then you were all twisted or something with sex. Do you remember your safe word, Suzanne?"

"Vaguely... *I think.* Please finish Marcus."

"Ah, that night you were torn-up pretty badly. I was just so sick over it. I hated it. Don't you remember Suzanne? I was in the bathroom, ah, crying, and then you were gone. I didn't know where you went. I was frantic to find you. I called everyone, even your parents. Your mother was particularly frantic to find you. I didn't know *why* at the time...

"...Anyway, I guess you took yourself to the hospital and were stitched up. I'm not sure what you said at the hospital, but I was scared to death the police were going to be coming for me. But they didn't. And then you came home, and you were kind of limping, and I saw you were in pain, and I just hated everything, and I told you I couldn't ever do that to you again, and then, you told me, it was the only way. You actually said, 'Marcus, if you don't fuck me till I bleed, I will never fuck you again.' Um, you called yourself a 'Dirty-hole'..." *Flinch.* "... And you told me you would only fuck me once a month, and that it had to be like that, and that you would say 'black' if it was too much. And that was it... *Christ* Suzanne, you had never even swore before, and now you were all intense, saying the f-word, demanding sex acts that I couldn't possibly do to you. It was just so messed up...

"...Anyway, I had a few more affairs, *which you knew about,* and said you could care less about. You told me to fuck anyone and anything, as long as I didn't tell your parents. And that's, ah, that's it. We just continued like that for the last 4 years, until May, when you got really strange, or I guess started remembering your past, or had the brain aneurism. *Christ,* I don't know Suzanne, but we were okay, except sexually. You were a really good wife and actually my best friend. But you were just so weird about sex, and you never used the safe word like you said you would. You just never used it, no matter how awful everything got. It was just so horrible Suzanne, and I didn't know what to do. I didn't know who to ask. It's not like I could have asked my coworkers if their wives fucked them crazy, to the point of blood and agony...

"...Um, I didn't know what to do, so I just had my affairs, and waited until a month or so rolled around and you started to tell me at night that you *had to be fucked.* I even tried to ignore you, but then you became extra violent to yourself, and I would shake for weeks dreading the sex you wanted. Then I just stopped shaking and I would have sex with you

as hard and as quickly as I could so it was over fast. That's it Suzanne. Please tell me you remember some of this. *Please?!*"

"Why did you hit me Marcus? I was so afraid of disappointing you and of being hit by you all the time?"

"*Hit you?!* Jesus, Suzanne! I've slapped you *twice!* Two times *ever!* And both times were at your parent's house during one of her goddamn parties. Both times you were acting insane. The first time you were crying and screaming at me, trying to get me to fuck you in the downstairs billiards room..." Gasp. Oh, god. I remember...

"*That room.* I remember that room... That's the cold floor..." I whisper.

"Suzanne? Talk to me..." Mack begs.

"No Mack. Not now. Please tell me Marcus what happened? What did I do in that room?"

"Oh Suzanne, it was really awful, I don't really want to tell you, but it was..."

"Marcus. Please tell me everything. I need to know. I *have to* know."

"Um... When I refused to have sex with you, I mean, there were people *everywhere,* but you got really angry at me and before I knew it, you started, um, there was a pool cue, and you were moaning like these really bad words, and I had to stop you, and you weren't even, like, aware I was there or something, so I just grabbed your arms and slapped your face, like they do it the movies... *and it worked.* You just stopped. You looked at me like I was a monster for hitting you, and you said something about me fucking you real good later... I don't know, it was so messed up...

"...I didn't know what to do anymore, and then you just straightened your clothes, kissed my cheek, and walked back upstairs to the party like you hadn't just freaked out downstairs. You were like a robot, smiling and nodding, but kind of staying away from most of the people. I made you leave as soon as we could without pissing off your mother."

"And then what happened Marcus?"

"You went crazy when we returned home. You were so sexually aggressive, and you used stuff, and you were tore open again, I think badly, but again, you just ran away from me and went to the hospital to fix yourself. I didn't know what to do anymore."

"*I* remember what happened- Mr. Hampton and Mr. Williams. *Fucking Peter* began whispering filthy things to me. I didn't know why, and I kept walking away, and they kept following. Oh *shit!* I remember Mel Hampton sticking his fingers inside me in the quarter hallway. Oh, he dug in me so hard, right under my skirt that I just jumped and froze, but then Marianne walked down the hall, and I could finally push Mr. Hampton away. Shit Mack! He called me a *filthy cunt-hole.* I remember now. I *WAS* a filthy cunt-hole. Fuck! I remember the feeling... I tried to get away. I tried..."

Oh *GOD...* Hunching over, I vomit everywhere. Jesus *Christ,* I hit Mack with that one. Oh, even Marcus' shoes got a little splash-back. Oh no. Help me. I can't feel this anymore. I can't feel this.

"Suzanne! Suzanne, listen to me!!"

"No! Shut up Mack! I remember. I remember the other time too, Marcus. My mother's birthday 3 years ago. We were there and then Simmons was there! I remember he told you, you were a lucky man, and

then he kissed my cheek and whispered to me, 'I know how that pretty pussy tastes.' He said that!! I remember, I didn't know what to do. I was in the wine cellar screaming when you found me. I remember now. I wanted you to fuck me to make that memory go away. I tried so hard, but you just wouldn't fuck me. I remember begging you!! I needed you to fuck me because you were only bad when *I* made you bad! That was the good kind of bad, because *I* made you bad, but you wouldn't be bad, and then you slapped me!" *Oh.* "You slapped me to calm me down. I remember Marcus. I remember it now."

In the silence, I can't help looking over at Mack. Oh, no! Mack looks really sick, or like in shock or something. *Shit!* Not my Mack. I don't want him all fucked up too. I *need* Mack.

"Mack? Please don't be fucked up. I think I really need you now. I have that feeling all over me, and inside me. It's everywhere. I'm disgusting. I really am just a worthless filthy cunt hole... I..."

"Suzanne! You are not disgusting. What was done **to you** was disgusting. And you are NOT worthless. You never were, and you aren't now. You are a sexually abused woman who is slowing finding her way to her memories, so you can finally move forward. Suzanne, you are amazing, and wonderful, and beautiful, and an absolute delight to know..."

Grabbing Mack's hands when we walks up to me, I bow my head, and whisper, "Mack? What do I do? I feel too much this time."

"I know Suzanne. I'm going to try to help you feel better. I want you to feel better. You were an innocent young victim to many terrible things. But I'm here, and I'll help you from feeling all this pain, all the time."

"That's it Mack. It's just pain. That's all I know. I can't breathe for the pain inside me. I don't think I've ever known anything but pain. I just want to feel nothing again. Nothing was better. I liked feeling *nothing* for 15 years..."

"Did you *ever* love me Suzanne?" Marcus suddenly whispers.

Looking at Marcus, I'm shocked that he's even here still. This is so messy. This is gross, and an embarrassment. There's vomit on the floor, and the room smells of it. Everything is so un-*tidy.* I am UN-*tidy.* He looks devastated... *for me? Or because* of me? *Christ!* I think he's even crying.

"Did you Suzanne? Did you ever love me?" Um...

"Did *YOU* ever love *ME*, Marcus?"

"Yes, of course. I've loved you since you were 14 years old." *What?!*

"I'm sorry? I didn't even know you then. You only came around when I was finishing college."

"Suzanne. Do you remember when you were 14, and you were crying behind the Clubhouse gates, and you were cutting your thighs with a small knife and I stopped you from cutting yourself more? I was 20 and too old for you, but I fell for you that day. You were so pretty and so sad, and you had these beautiful eyes that were, like, *begging* me to help you or something. Do you remember that? Please tell me you remember me saving you from cutting yourself more that day?"

"I, um... *what?*"

Watching Marcus take a big inhale and a slow exhale, I just brace myself. He seems so sincere, but I don't know what the hell he's talking about. Maybe Mack with his *shrink* ways can tell if Marcus is lying to me. I'll have to ask Mack later.

"I found you. You were alone behind the Clubhouse gates saying all kinds of bad words, kind of mumbling them to yourself, and then I saw your skirt was lifted to your panties, showing all the blood on your legs And then I helped you. I used my golf towel and a bottle of water to help clean up the damage to your legs when you wouldn't come inside the building with me. *Please?* You have to remember. I took care of you, and you were so sad, and you cried, and you asked me to leave you alone. And I told you I *needed* to sit with you for a while, and eventually you stopped crying...

"...Suzanne, you *thanked* me, and told me I was a *good boy* and that you wished you could love someone like me. And I wanted you to love me in that moment. I *wanted* to take care of you, so I did. I hung out with you until you needed to go, and then I walked you to your parent's limo, and I kissed your forehead and asked you to please be well and then I gave you my number and I asked you to call me... but you never did call. Suzanne? Do you remember me?" *Shit. I really don't.*

"I, ah, *no...* I'm sorry Marcus, I don't remember. You sound very nice, but I just remember always crying at the Clubhouse. I remember nothing but pain there. Thank you though if you were nice to me that day."

"I was *always* nice to you Suzanne. I wanted to marry you the minute you turned 18, I even asked your mother but she told me you had 'some problems', and that I should wait awhile. So I waited. Do you remember when we finally spoke at your mother's Summer Social Party, and I told you I had been waiting forever for you? *Please* Suzanne? Do you remember?"

"I'm sorry Marcus. I wish I did. You sounded very nice then. I wish I remembered you, but all I remember is sadness and unbearable agony. It was a bad life for me then. I'm really sorry."

Choking, I can't help but sob. Wow. Marcus wasn't always a fucking asshole. Or maybe he was *never* a fucking asshole. I have no idea. I know my head, or rather; *my entire worldview* seems to be spinning at the moment. My total memory of my husband has been upended. I really wish I didn't have to think anymore today.

"I'm sorry Marcus that I'm too terrible to remember all those good things you're telling me. I wish I could remember. It would be nice to have a *good* memory for a change. Maybe I will later, I don't know anymore. But I'm really tired, and I'd like to go rest for a while, okay? Thank you for coming to New York. I'm sure we'll see each other again soon. Thank you. But I really need to lie down now."

"Suzanne. *Please?* Are you coming home with me? I'll make it better for you. Now that I know what was wrong, I think we can be happy. We *were* happy, but this time I think we can be happy *for real*. We'll go to counseling, or you can go alone, whatever you want, I just want you to come home with me. *Please.*"

"Marcus. I..."

"Suzanne, it would make me really happy if you came home with me."
Oh, it would? *Really?*

"Marcus, Suzanne has had quite a few bombshells dropped on her today, and she needs time to process all these events, and even to figure out how she feels about them. Suzanne is going to be..."

"I *KNOW* Suzanne, *Dr. MacDonald.* Better than you, I think. I *AM* HER HUSBAND. I have been taking care of her for a long time. Suzanne, please? Please come home with me?"

"Um... " What should I do?

"Please Suzanne? I *want* you to come home."

"Um, okay, I will. But not yet! I just need a little more time here to straighten out my head a little, okay? Then I'll go back to Chicago with you."

"Okay, good. It's settled- just please don't wait *too* long. I've been dying to have you home for 4 months now."

"Oh, okay. *Home.* I'll try to get better quickly Marcus. Thanks for coming today. I'll see you soon. I have to go. Oh, sorry about your shoes. I'll see you later."

Practically running from the room, I'm dying. I have to get to my bed. I just have to make it to my room. I hear Mack behind me. I know he's trying to help me, but I just can't do it. I can't talk right now. I can't talk about my feelings, and I can't stop this madness from hitting me full force. It's like a train slamming into my brain. *I. Am. So. FUCKED!*

"Please Mack! Please leave me alone! I don't want to talk yet! I just can't! *PLEASE* leave me ALONE!! Just for now. I will do or say anything you want later. Just not yet. I'M NOT READY YET!"

As I make it to my room, unlock, and throw my door open, Mack grabs me, and spins me into his arms. Slamming into his chest, I am shocked at his brutality, and then... I just don't care anymore. Grabbing onto his shirt, I just scream everything out.

I don't know what I'm saying. *Christ!* I don't even know what I'm feeling. I just know Mack is holding me tightly to his chest, and I am hysterical. The grief is pouring out of me. The pain is slashing at me. The agony has torn me completely apart.

What the hell is my reality? I can't tell anymore.

Screaming, and crying, begging, and fighting, Mack just holds me tightly. Time continues as the pain rages inside me.

When I feel Mack shake his head, I look to see my New York Kayla crying in the doorway. With her hand over her mouth, she looks pretty shaken. *Welcome to* **my** *world, sister...* Oh, *funny!*

Pulling away from Mack, I whisper, "It's time for me to rest now. We can talk forever, as long as I can sleep right now. Please Mack. I have nothing left."

"Okay, Suzanne. I'll be in my corner if you need me when you wake up."

"Please Mack, I mean *alone.* I just feel so gross and kind of nasty right now and I need to be alone."

"I'm sorry Suzanne, but I can't leave you right now under the circumstances. And even if I could leave you, I wouldn't. I want to be

here when this finally crashes all around you, and then I'll help you back up. I'm not leaving you, especially after a day like today. You know this, so please don't fight me. Just rest. Would you like anything first? Food? A drink of water? Is there *anything* I can get you?"

"I just want a quick rinse-off shower, than I want to lie down. Mack there is nothing I can hurt myself with in the bathroom, so can I please just have a few minutes alone? I need to wash all this *dirty* off my body."

"Of course. Do whatever you need to do Suzanne. I'll just be waiting for you to finish."

"Thank you," I whisper as I turn for my bathroom.

"Suzanne- Today changes **NOTHING**. You are still the wonderful Suzanne I know and love, and you are still the Suzanne who is fighting so hard to find herself. *TODAY CHANGES NOTHING*. Please remember that."

Pausing in the doorway, I exhale. "Okay, I'll try to remember that. Um, Mack? I'm not ready…"

"Okay, Suzanne."

And walking away from Mack, I think about Marcus, and I think about Z. I wish I could talk to Z just once. I wish I could just tell him before I go back to my life with Marcus. I wish I could just whisper the words I have always wanted to say.

"I want to love you, Z.
  But I am gone…"

Sarah Ann Walker

PART 4

AFTERLIFE

Sunday, November 20

Sarah Ann Walker

CHAPTER 36

Okay, so I'm finally ready to leave. Everything I have is packed and ready. All my clothes, and my Grey's Anatomy DVD's are packed along with the countless ugly, sometimes *hideous* 'I Love New York' trinkets and gift shop crap Kayla insisted on buying me... *in case I forget her.* (Like that's going to happen!)

I'm ready. I finally told Mack 2 weeks ago that I'm ready to return to life in Chicago, with Marcus. After countless hours talking together, Mack and I brought in Marcus so he could understand where I'm at, and where I plan to take myself. To say Marcus was thrilled was an understatement. It was quite touching really to be wanted by Marcus so badly.

I know deep down Mack thinks this is a mistake, but true to form, Mack advised me, and helped me prepare for my decision, without *manipulating* my decision. All Mack did was set up a kind of outreach program for he and I, once I leave New York.

Mack is still on retainer by my Estate, and as such, he doesn't plan to return to the hospital full time until the spring. In the meantime, I am to fly to New York every Thursday morning, staying overnight at Kayla's so Mack and I have each Thursday and Friday together. I'm to return every Friday night to Chicago, so Marcus and I have the weekends together.

I'm not returning to work in Chicago. Financially, I don't have to, and because Marcus has no legal holdings on my Estate, he can't touch my money. The money from my grandfather doesn't fall within Marcus' and my prenuptial agreement. Plus, Marcus has clearly stated that he wants nothing to do with my inheritance. I think he still feels horrible about what my parents did, and especially about how he inadvertently helped them manipulate and abuse me throughout the years of our marriage.

Marcus has agreed to 2- one hour private video phone sessions with Mack a week, and he seems to be okay with continuing his own counseling. Marcus has also agreed to a two hour video phone session with me *and* Mack every Monday evening, so the three of us can discuss Marcus and my weekends together, which truthfully I'm quite nervous about.

It turns out Marcus is suffering from quite a bit of guilt towards me, and *because* of me. But I know Mack is helping Marcus process the *sexual reality* I had created in our marriage. I also know Mack has tried to help Marcus understand that though he was brutal to me sexually; it was in fact *ME* who had created the need for the brutality and abuse, because of my own issues *and* because of my inability to understand at the time *why* I was forcing Marcus to hurt me.

It was such a strange little world I created for poor Marcus, and he is struggling with his part in it all. Once I calmed down in October; Marcus met with Mack and I again, and I was able to apologize to him for the sexual hell I had put him through over the years. Feeling the need to apologize to the man I believed raped and sexually abused me for years, because it turns out *I* forced *him* to do it was, well, *screwed up,* to say the least. Actually, it was *So Messed Up,* I can't believe I survived the whole conversation.

Afterward, Marcus admitted that those 6 years with me were the absolute worst years of his life *sexually*, yet amazingly, the best years of his life because he loved me and our marriage so much. Marcus is trying to recover himself, from the kind of *forced* role in my life that he felt trapped in, and disgusted by.

Oh, and apparently Marcus was never a 'five minute man' with all the other lovers he had throughout our marriage and even before our marriage. He was only a five-minute man with me, because I *demanded* he be quick and brutal. So. Fucked. Up. *Honestly.*

I'm looking forward to seeing Chicago Kayla, and I'm looking forward to reacquainting myself with a Chicago that doesn't hurt me anymore or cause me pain. I know its messed up to blame an entire city for my hurt, but somehow Chicago itself has become a place of hurt for me. Now, I'm going to learn Chicago as just the city I live in, *not* as a place of pain.

When I first arrive, I'm to take 'baby steps'. I'm to settle into my home again. I have to learn to relax. I have to try to find *reason* in my new life. Maybe eventually I'll find another job. But for now, I am to enjoy this time of calm. Maybe I can update my Kindle with new books- dirty *and* otherwise. Essentially, I am going to try to learn how to just breathe, day by day in my marriage, and in Chicago.

That's the plan, and Marcus is totally on board with it. Oh, we've also learned Marcus was only hard on me about working because when I *wasn't* distracted by work, I became more of a Sexual Psycho to him. He actually needed me to be caught up in work and distracted by it, so that I didn't have my brutal sexual *episodes* with him.

And so I have a lot to learn when I return to Chicago tonight. I have a whole new Marcus, and a whole new marriage to learn. I even have a home to learn to love; redecorating at will, based on my needs.

Marcus also explained our living arrangement, and my infamous sunroom furniture. Marcus knew I had issues with *red*. Marcus explained to Mack and I, that I was *always* aggressive and manic where red was involved. Therefore when he saw my sunroom furniture, bright red love seat and bright red chair, he was freaked right out.

It makes sense now, but I never really understood his aversion to my favorite room until he explained it to Mack and I. Once it was explained, a kind of reality smacked me in the face, and I realized he was right. Every single time Marcus put his foot down about something in our home, or demanded that I change to fit *his* tastes, it was because I was wanting something *red*.

I even remembered a full-out fit I had once in a Bed and Bath store with him because I tried to buy an entire sheet and duvet set, with matching pillows and curtains as well, in *blood red*. I remembered shaking in the store so violently when I held the duvet in my arms, that Marcus had to pry it from my hands, and take me to his car. Sadly, I also remembered sexually attacking him in the car, demanding that he *fuck me hard* right then and there.

And so I learned red was a *MAJOR* trigger. It seemed red was an issue after the 'Macys Incident', but now it makes more sense. Mack and I

spent 4 whole days on *red*. From red clothing and red furniture, to red *everything*. Slowly with Mack, memories came back to me. Slowly, I understood *RED*.

Red is everything I knew as painful. My mother began dressing me in red at all her parties when I turned eleven. Yet, my mother also made all her 'red is for sluts' or 'only whores were red' comments at the same time. I was always in red when I was abused at the Country Club *and* at my parent's home.

Apparently, by my mother's *loving* request, my room at Dr. Simmons hospital was also decorated in red, because she told the staff, I liked red, and that red *soothed* me. God, she is such a nasty, *evil* BITCH!

Mack even confirmed my memory of the red when he admitted seeing some of the pictures with the Chicago D.A. In the photos with all the different men, whatever clothing I was in, or had been wearing before the rapes, was red. Red was always everywhere I was hurt; my own blood included.

Mack was sadly very messed up over this himself. Mack even admitted to me how hard it was for him to see me so abused as a child, so much so, that he needed to speak with his own Shrink about it. When I cried over his upset, Mack merely shrugged and said, 'Suzanne remember… I'm a 2 on the crazy scale. Of course, I have my own Shrink". And that was it. He held me while I cried for him *and* for the young girl in **RED.**

So red is a trigger, and subsequently Mack and I have learned that Marcus isn't a control-freak asshole. He was just a freaked-out husband trying to help me the best he could with an obvious insight into me and the color red, but with no information on my past to work with. Sadly, all Marcus had was a pedophile doctor *and* my fucked up parents telling him to behave a certain way toward me and my sexual insanity.

And so with all this new information on Marcus, I have decided to give him and our marriage a shot. I know, as does Marcus, that it's going to be hard. We're basically strangers playing a role we should have been living for the last 6 1/2 years. But Marcus really wants to try, and I feel like I owe it to him *to* try.

Marcus has made no effort to hide the fact that he has always loved me. He not only reminded me of our first meeting when I was fourteen, but he went on to explain to Mack and I how he watched me grow up, and waited patiently for me to become an adult. Marcus tells us frequently about how *in love* he is with me, and always has been.

And Marcus doesn't shy away from emotion or feeling, as I always thought he did. Again, it turns out his lack of emotion or apparent concern for me when we were married, was because *I* wouldn't allow him to show any emotion. I would cringe and pull away from the slightest warmth or physical displays of his love and affection. Marcus said the only thing he was allowed to do was kiss my forehead without me *losing it.*

There was even one tense moment between Mack, Marcus and I when all these discoveries were made. Mack, in a moment of rare, uncontrolled anger, told Marcus to stop *blaming* me for everything. He asked Marcus why he even bothered staying married to me, even bothered *loving* me if I was such a mess? Mack actually yelled, "If you knew Suzanne was '*so*

fucked up', and she needed help so *badly*, why did you just carry on? Why didn't you *HELP* her?!" I remember both Marcus and I gasped at the sudden anger Mack threw at him.

Stunned, Marcus stammered that he *did* try to help. He told Mack that he had contacted Dr. Simmons AND my parents, even meeting with them in private to discuss me, and it was based on their recommendations that he proceeded the way he did. He tried to defend himself by saying he had a doctor *and* my parents both giving him the same advise, to ignore Suzanne *and* to entertain her ridiculous sexual demands. Marcus also said that he really didn't know any differently. It was a little weak as defenses go, but it finally made sense to Mack, once he calmed down.

Mack even apologized to Marcus for his outrage, and explained that he did understand Marcus was another victim in all this as well. Mack always remained professional with Marcus before and after that one incident, but I can tell there are still elements to Marcus' personality that Mack simply doesn't like. And there are things Marcus did that Mack can't or *won't* forgive in the name of Marcus' *ignorance.*

And so I'm here. I'm going home with Marcus today, with my new life all packed up in the beautiful luggage my two Kaylas purchased as a gift for me. I am going home to try to be Suzanne *with* Marcus. Any minute now. Any minute...

==========

Marcus and Mack have arrived together. They probably had a little meeting before Marcus came to my room, but I'm not worried. Mack and Marcus seem to have an understanding where I'm concerned. They both want me happy. Mack wants me healthy enough to grow to simply love and trust *whomever.* And Marcus wants me healthy enough to grow to simply love and trust *him.*

Mack and I have gone over everything so many times, I know exactly what schedules I'm to have. I know when I take my medication for my panic-attacks. I know when to eat and I know when to call him; which is *anytime- ALL THE TIME.* Mack even joked yesterday that he felt a little 'momma bird setting her baby free to fly'.

Mack and I sat for a long time yesterday, watching my favorite Grey's Anatomy episode between Meredith and Christina. Mack joked that he would always be 'my person', no matter what anyone, *Marcus included,* said to the contrary. And I told him he was going to be my best friend forever.

I cried a lot yesterday, but today I feel well. I'm ready. I feel sure of my decision, and sure of where I'm going to end up. I rarely throw up now and my panic attacks are few and far between. And the bumps along the way are for me and Mack, and even Marcus, to work through. And I will. I made a decision, and I'm going to see it through.

"Good morning, Suzanne. Are you ready?" Marcus asks me gently.
"I'm ready. Can I just have one minute alone with Mack?"

"Sure, no problem." When Marcus leaves, I'm struck by how kind and loving he really is.

"Are you sure about this Suzanne?"

"Yes. Marcus IS a catch, at least my bitch of a mother was right about that. He is good looking, successful, and kind, and he *loves* me Mack. He has loved me for a long time, and I owe him for that. I owe him a chance to try to really love him back, I think."

"He does love you Suzanne, but what's not to love?" Mack grins at me.

"You're such a dork, Mack, but I adore you anyway," I grin back while grabbing my purse. Mack just stops and waits for me to speak again. "I'm good, Mack. I really am. I want to do this. I *need* to do this. And I really need your support with this."

"You have *all* my support Suzanne, anything you want or need, I'll give to you. I'm not questioning your decision in the least. I was only questioning the timing. *Today.* That's all."

"I'm ready today. Today, I'm going to jump in. I want to jump into my life... *today.*"

"Okay. Done. Now hug me before Marcus returns and sees your *highly unprofessional* Shrink crying all over your shoulder," he grins again.

"Okay..." Holding Mack around his waist, I lean into his strength, once again, as I feel like I have for a lifetime now.

"I love you Mack, with absolutely everything I have..." I whisper.

"Oh, *Suzanne...* You really are a doll, you know that? I'll see you on Thursday but call me before then so I don't go *more* crazy, okay?"

"Absolutely. You're *my* Mack, and you're also *my* Speed-dial, so it's all good," I grin up at him.

"Okay. I'll get Marcus, and I'll help take your luggage to the rental. But no more goodbyes. This is it. I'll walk you to your car, shake Marcus' hand, kiss your cheek quickly, then I'm bolting, just so you know. It's nothing personal, but I need this goodbye to be over quickly."

"Okay. Thanks Mack. I'll talk to you later, maybe even from the airport."

Once loaded into the rental car, Mack does exactly as he said. After shaking Marcus' hand, he walks to me, kisses my cheek, and walks away from me. I saw the tears in his eyes, and I know he saw mine, but neither acknowledge them. It's done. My day in and day out life with Mack is over. I'm starting my new life, with Marcus as the main player.

"Are you ready Suzanne?"

"Absolutely. Thank you, Marcus... for everything."

"We're going to be good Suzanne, I know it."

"I know we will- Just remember, 'baby steps'."

"Got it."

And pulling away from the hospital, I'm now Mrs. Suzanne Anderson... *again.* I'm Marcus' wife, but *for real* this time.

Sunday, December, 25th

CHAPTER 37

Jesus *Christ,* I'm bored! Marcus and I have nothing to do over Christmas. Everyone is gone. We have no family or friends left, other than *this* Kayla- though it's awkward as hell between her and Marcus when she visits. There is no one here and nothing to do.

Marcus and I are so pleasantly polite; I could stab my own eyeball with a fork, just for a little excitement. We should have gone to New York. At least in New York, Kayla and Mack could have entertained us. Mack and Kayla could have breathed a little life into this... *what?* Maddeningly pleasant, wonderfully calm, outrageously stable, boring little life of ours.

Marcus and I barely talk, and we certainly don't relate to one another. But we *do* smile frequently at each other *all day,* and *all night-* pleasant emotionless little smiles. Marcus and I aren't so much living; we're just kind of *existing* here in Chicago.

There is just nothing here. This house is so quiet. All the gifts are opened and already put away. I went a little overboard, but what else could I do, but shop? Marcus bought me a beautiful diamond pendant with matching earrings. Everything was just so, so *lovely.* And quiet. And calm. And *BORING!*

I have tried everything I can think of to be a wife, and I know Marcus has tried everything *he* can think of to be a husband. Besides having sex, which we **have not**; we moved right back into our roles of silent, pleasant, understanding, BORING husband and wife. I cook, keep house, shop, and read. Marcus goes to work and comes home with more pleasantries from the office. What the hell can we do?

All day, I either read, shop, or talk on the phone. My two Kaylas keep me from screaming from the boredom. I don't know what to do anymore. Marcus has tried everything as well. We even took a little trip together at his suggestion, and it was fine- but *boring and uneventful.*

Marcus suggested I redecorate the house, and I have. You'd think redecorating an entire house would take more than 3 weeks, but it didn't. That's it- 3 weeks! I found, bought, and chose everything. It was delivered a week later, and the movers placed the furniture where I wanted. *Voila.* Now what?! After redecorating the ENTIRE house in 3 weeks, I had nothing left to do but shop for Christmas.

Christmas shopping was probably the most fun I've had since returning to Marcus and Chicago. My Chicago Kayla and I went crazy, pulling a 9 to 9 shopping marathon and then, the shopping was done too. After buying the gifts for *all five people* on my list; Marcus, Kayla, Kayla, Mack, and the grandfather I don't know... I was done.

There was nothing left to do. The decorations were up. The new decor and furniture had already arrived and were placed accordingly. The walls had be painted. The tree was up... and I had one more week to go before Christmas day even arrived.

And now it's here and done, and I'm *Just So Bored!* Boredom can actually make a person insane, I think. And if that's true, then I'm on my way back to padded-room land, for sure. I don't know what to do with myself anymore. Maybe take classes? *Like what?* Take up Tai Chi or Yoga? Ah, *not* interested. A cooking class? Yuck. Knitting? No way!

I don't know what to do with myself, and I'm getting very antsy. I think even Mack can hear it in my voice, and see it in my movements. *Christ,* flying to see Mack every Thursday is the highlight of my week, and leaving to fly home every Friday evening to see Marcus, is the dread of my week.

The problem is; there is NO problem. There is nothing *wrong*, at all. Everything just *feels* wrong. It's like I'm trapped again, but this time not trapped in an abusive nightmare like I was before, but rather, trapped in pleasant *boredom.* And honestly, I feel like a real asshole for feeling like this at all.

I *know* people dream about the financial freedom to do nothing. People dream about having a handsome, successful, kind husband. People dream about having *things*, and a home, and security. I know that! I know I'm an asshole, but I can't help feeling just, like, *awful* within all this boredom, and pleasant *nothingness.*

Maybe I need to give sex with Marcus a try. Maybe it's time. Maybe I should try tonight. Sex as a kind of an extra Christmas present or something? Maybe I'll tie a bow around my, ah... No.

Okay. Decision made. Now I just have to follow through. Should I ask him first, or just try it. I'll try. *Argh.* I can't even imagine talking to Marcus about sex. It's just so weird now.

==========

Okay. Dinner is done. A perfect turkey meal, fit for a perfect Christmas dinner. The kitchen is spotless. Marcus helped with everything. He was jovial and had many compliments to give. He even noticed my new black dress, with the *TINY* red buttons down the back and on the cuffs. Marcus was perfect, during this perfect Christmas, in our perfect house. *Argh!*

In our room, where we sleep every night, side by side, *without touching*, I enter the ensuite for a little girly time. In my vanilla-jasmine scented bath, I make sure my whole body is shaved, scrubbed, smoothed, and scented. I've even repainted my toenails, the perfect pale pink.

Dressing for this most *special* of nights, I don a very pretty floor-length black silk gown, with a low dipped bodice, which beautifully highlights my ample cleavage. This is it. *Shit!* I think I need a glass of Zin... Ah, *WINE,* first. (No need to hash up those memories tonight.)

When I'm significantly buzzed, I decide to jump! Marcus is in the study down the hall, so as soon as I call his name he'll be here in seconds. Get ready. Big breaths. In and out. Nice and easy. Here I go...

Dammit! Should I call Mack first? Ah, no. *Awkward.* How the hell do I ask Mack for advise on seducing my husband? Gross. Kinda funny

though. I can just hear Mack's 'ummms and ahhhs' while he tries to process what I'm asking. Maybe I can call a Kayla? Ah, no. Chicago Kayla would probably gag with the way she feels about Marcus, and New York Kayla would probably tell Mack anyway, which would just prompt *him* to call me, and then I'm right back to being awkward with *my* Mack.

"Suzanne? Um, what are you doing?"

FUCK! Scrambling to cover up, I drop my wine glass on the carpet. God *Dammit!*

"Um... *well,* I was... going to try to seduce you tonight. Um, now." What a loser I am, *honestly.*

"Oh. Okay. Do you want help cleaning up the wine?"

"Yes, please."

"No problem." And leaving, Marcus barely looks at me.

Well, this is certainly **AWKWARD.** I should've risked it with Mack first. Okay, so Marcus saw my outfit. I told Marcus my intention. He didn't acknowledge my *seduction* one way or the other, and now he's headed for carpet cleaning supplies. What the *hell* do I do now?

Sitting on the edge of our bed, I wait. When Marcus returns, he drop to his knees and immediately begins scrubbing the carpet, studiously ignoring me... The big cleavaged- black negligee wearing- slightly drunk-elephant in the room. *Shit.*

"Marcus?"

"Just a second Suzanne. I'm almost finished cleaning this."

"Marcus? Please. Forget the carpet."

"Red wine stains badly though. Just give me one more minute."

"Marcus? *Please...*" I say on a sigh.

Finally dropping the scrub brush, Marcus exhales as he slowly sits cross-legged and turns his eyes to me. God, he looks tired, or sad, or maybe bored? It's just so hard to tell with him.

"Marcus, do you want to have sex with me?"

"Of course, Suzanne. Why would you ask that?"

"Marcus, do you want to have sex with me?"

"Of course. I just told you I do."

"MARCUS! Do you *WANT* to have sex with me?"

"*NO! Okay?* I really DON'T Suzanne." Oh... Whoosh.

"Um, why? Is it because of my body?"

"No, *of course not! You're* the only one who ever had a problem with your body." God, he looks flustered.

"Why then? It's okay. Please be honest with me."

"Suzanne. I love you, very much in fact. I have always loved you, but I just don't like having sex with you. I'm sorry. Do you really want me to be honest right now?"

"Yes. Please Marcus, tell me what you're feeling. I *need* to know what you're feeling." Staring at Marcus, there is nothing but a long pause.

Exhaling, Marcus seems to build up his strength for this bombshell, I think. Oh, this isn't going to be good, I can tell. He's looking directly into my eyes, but seems to wish he could look away.

"Okay, Suzanne. Fine. I'll tell you why, but I'm sure you'll freak out and go tell on me to *your* Mack or something. I'm sure you'll say, and maybe even believe that I'm the bad guy, but it's just not true. I'm really not the

bad guy here. Not that *you're* the bad guy, but I just know that I'm NOT the bad guy." Big exhale.

"Go ahead, Marcus. Just talk. I won't tell on you, or whatever it is you're afraid of."

And another long pause for Marcus. *Jeez...* this is rare.

"Suzanne, sex with you has always been awful for me. Sex was like gross and violent, or something. And I know you're better now, I do know that. And I know it wasn't your fault that you were like that, but I just can't think of sex with you any other way. It's like, I spent so many years dreading having sex with you, that, it's like, the only way I feel about it now...

"...The sex with you was quick and painful, and not just for you. I don't think you ever realized that *that* sex was kind of painful to my body as well. I hated *thrusting* into you when you were unprepared. I hated feeling like my own skin was being ripped off, by *your* body. I hated when it was over, and my own skin was sore and sometimes covered in your blood. God, it used to make me gag- I hated having your blood on me. I hated feeling, well, *used* by you, I guess...

"...Again, I know NOW that you weren't trying to hurt me, or trying to mess with my head, but it happened anyway. You physically hurt me too, but mostly you just fucked with my head so badly that I learned to absolutely dread having sex with you." Wow. *Really?*

"I'm sorry. I didn't realize you felt pain as well."

"How could you? It's not like you've ever touched my penis before. You've never even looked at it, I don't think. My penis- *not me*, was like a means to an end for you, that's all. When you would demand I *fuck you harder*, I was amazed I could even stay erect long enough to *do it*. It was just so awful. I hated you then Suzanne, but only when it came to sex. The rest of the time I loved you so much, I just tried to ignore the sex part of our relationship."

Looking at Marcus' bowed head, I'm stunned. Here's another worldview of mine destroyed. It never even occurred to me that Marcus suffered any physical pain. I knew he suffered emotionally, but physically? I just never thought about it. He's the man. I guess I just assumed his body, or I guess, his *penis,* was meant for that kind of brutality. I didn't realize that if I was tearing open, he might be physically suffering as well.

When Marcus raises his head he's crying. Honest to god *tears* are falling down his cheeks. Wiping them away aggressively (like a man would), he seems to be asking me for something, or, like, waiting for something. Oh, this is just so awful, and twisted, *and sad.*

"I'm so sorry Marcus. I honestly didn't realize any of this. You're the man, and I thought sex was always good or something, no matter how hard it was. It's just, that was my only experience. Men hurt me when I was young, but they never seemed to feel any pain themselves. They *enjoyed* tearing me open..."

"I'm not them, Suzanne! I never was!"

"I know! That's not what I meant. I meant that my *memory* of my own pain never allowed me to think it could have been painful for you, because it was never painful for *them*."

"But *I'm* not them..." Marcus whispers once more.

"I know Marcus. I know that *now* but I didn't know that then. I'm sorry." What else can I say?

After a few much needed breaths, Marcus looks up at me again and seems to resign himself to something. Now, I *really* don't want to have sex. It's not like I *actually* wanted it to begin with, I just thought we should so we had more of a *real* marriage or something.

"Suzanne, I'm just, I don't know. I'm..."

"*Fucked up?*"

"Yes. That's it. I'm totally fucked up over all this," he laughs a little.

"I *am* sorry Marcus."

"I'm not looking for your apologies Suzanne. This is way more *your* fucked up than mine, but I just wanted you to know that all this shit did mess me up too. All of it messed me up. Sometimes, I'm shocked by the depth of the betrayal I feel from you, though it wasn't your fault. But especially I hate the betrayal by your parents. They used me, and hurt me, and made me an accomplice of sorts to everything they were doing to you behind my back. It's just too much sometimes."

"Have you talked to Mack about all this?"

"A little. It's hard. I think I want to talk to someone else because he cares so much for you and you for him. I'm jealous of your relationship, and I'm nervous that he just thinks I'm like this *total asshole* that hurt you for years, because he cares so much for you."

"Would you like to go to a different counselor? Maybe a marriage counselor for just you and I? No Mack involvement?"

"You would do that?" Marcus looks genuinely surprised by my offer.

"Of course. I actually understand what you're saying about the Mack involvement. It's hard for all three of us I think- *almost* a conflict of interest. But at the time we started talking together I didn't want anyone else to know what was going on with me, that's why I begged you to talk to Mack, and that's why I begged Mack to talk to you. But it's okay if you want to talk to someone else. I get it Marcus. Mack IS mine, and he always will be."

"Suzanne? Will *I* ever be the person you love and trust the most? Will *I* ever be more important to you than Mack is?"

"Um..." *Shit!* What do I say?

"It's okay. I just want you to tell me the truth," Marcus says with tears in his eyes again. *Jesus!* This is so hard.

"I don't think so Marcus, I'm sorry. It's not like that. Um, Mack saved me from dying, *twice,* and we have a bond because of it, and also because he has just been so good to me right from the beginning. I don't think I would be alive now had it not been for Mack. So, no... I'm sorry, you won't ever be more important to me than Mack is. But you're still my husband and I'm still here with you, trying *with you.*"

"I hope that'll be enough, Suzanne. I'm not sure it will be though."

"I'm sorry but that's all I can give you, Marcus."

Nodding his head sadly, Marcus whispers, "I know Suzanne."

When Marcus stands to leave our room seconds later, I panic for some reason. Grabbing his arm, I yell, "Don't you want to try sex?" *Shit.*

"No, Suzanne. You look very lovely, but I just don't feel that way about you?" *What?!*

"Like, *ever?*"

"I don't know," Marcus says shaking his head no.

"You never want to have sex with me again?"

"I don't right now. I don't know about in the future."

Wow! What a turn of events. It's kind of funny, and ironic, and tragic and just *FUNNY,* actually.

"Are you going to start having affairs again?"

"God, no. That was what *you* wanted, not me. Remember?"

"Yes. But what will you do? I mean don't you have needs or something?" *Christ!* **THIS** is awkward.

"Not really. Not anymore. Can't we just pretend this conversation didn't happen. I'm happy with the way things have been this last month. I'm happy with you being home. And I'm happy with where we're at without any sex stuff. Okay, Suzanne?"

"Um, sure. Okay. If you're happy..."

"I am. I look forward to each day with you. My days are happy and complete with you back here."

"*Really?*" I think I'm shocked by his sincerity.

"Of course. Why? YOU'RE NOT HAPPY?!" Marcus sounds a little panicky too all of a sudden.

Christ! This whole night of seduction has just turned into a total *clusterfuck,* as Chicago Kayla would say. *Honestly.*

"Yes, I'm happy." And bored to tears...

"Okay, good," Marcus exhales. "Well, I'm going to go back to my study. Merry Christmas Suzanne. I'm glad you're back home with me."

"Um, me too..." I whisper as Marcus kisses my forehead and then leaves our bedroom.

Well, this has certainly been interesting. Now I *have to* talk to Mack. *Dammit.* But first things first... black yoga pants, and black cami are required. I may just have to throw this beautiful floor-length, silk, low-cut bodice, cleavage enhancing black gown in the fireplace later. *Shit.*

Sunday, February 12

CHAPTER 38

Here we go. I hope this doesn't hurt as much as I think it will, though from what I've read, these things always *suck.*

"Um, Marcus? I have to talk to you."

"Okay," he smiles once again. I'm almost beginning to hate Marcus' very nice, perfectly kind, respectable, even *loving,* pleasant smile. *Ugh.*

"I'm, ah, leaving to go to New York for awhile."

"Why? *When?!*"

"Tonight, actually. My flight is at 9:45, and Kayla's picking me up at the airport. I'm renting a car in town though."

"What do you mean you're leaving *for a while?*" *Shit.* Here we go.

"I mean, I'm leaving, and I'm not sure when I'll be back. I have a lot to think about and I can't do that here with you."

"Why? *You're alone all day!* I'm not around to bother you or anything, I'm at work."

"It's not that, and you don't *bother* me Marcus, at all. If anything, you *bore* me." Ooops! *Dammit.* "Sorry, what I mean is, I, ah, need more than this. We're just so, like *pleasant* or something. So automatic. So *lifeless.*" Huge exhale of mine, followed by a long silence of his.

"*I bore you?* Would you rather I *hurt* you? Or maybe *stress you out?* Or *freak you out?* Or, or what, Suzanne? What would you like me to do?!"

"Nothing. That's the point. I don't want you to do anything. You're amazing, but I just don't *feel* anything for you anymore. You're like a friend now. A very comfortable friend, not really a husband, and not even a lover. You're just someone I share space with."

"A *friend?* Would you rather I was an *ENEMY?!*"

"No, Marcus. I just want to be happy, and I'm not with you. Maybe I could have been, or maybe we weren't meant to be... I don't know. All I do know is I'm not happy, and I don't think you are either."

"*Actually,* I AM happy, but *MY* happiness has never really mattered to you, has it Suzanne?"

"*Actually, Marcus,* YOUR happiness was the *ONLY* reason I returned to Chicago. I felt bad for you, and I wanted to make it right, and I thought returning to you, when you thought you loved me so much, WAS the right thing to do."

"YOU pitied *ME?* Are you kidding me?!"

"No, I never *pitied* you, but I did feel badly for all you'd been through with me, so when you begged me to come back, I did. I felt like I owed it to you. I thought because you loved me, I should come back and hopefully I would learn to love you the same way. And I do love you, but not as a wife. I love you like a friend, but it's not enough for me."

"IT'S ENOUGH FOR ME!!" *Flinch.* Shit.

As Marcus screams in my face, he grabs my arms hard. Ouch! This certainly isn't going well.

"Marcus, please let go of me. *Please?*"

"Suzanne, if you leave, don't come back. EVER! I don't want you back. I've had enough of all this shit with you. I've been good, I really have, but I can't do it anymore. I WON'T do it anymore."

"Okay, Marcus. I totally understand, and I'm really, *really* sorry."

"Suzanne- *I mean it.* If you leave, that's it. I can't be with you ever again. I won't do it. Being with you has been so hard on me *for years*, and if you leave I don't want to do it anymore."

"Marcus, my arms... *Please* let go of me."

As Marcus releases my arms rather hard and abruptly, I actually stumble a step backward.

"I'm sorry, Suzanne. I didn't mean to hurt you- I'm just so tired of you, I really am. I'm good, and you're good too, but you're bad *for* me, I think. You make me hate things, and you make me love you, even though I kind of hate you too."

"I understand, I really do. I'm just going to pack some more clothes, and I'll leave very soon. I'm really, *really* sorry, Marcus." Turning, I nearly run from the room, but...

"Suzanne?"

"Yes?"

"I'm going to move on. I'm going to find someone to be a good wife to me. I am, you know?"

"Oh, Marcus... you're not hurting me, if that's what you think you're doing. I want that for you. I want you to find someone who doesn't mess you up like I do. I want you to love someone without all the shit that comes with me. I love you enough to sincerely wish you well. Whether you believe me or not, I *want* you to be happy with someone else. I want you to love someone; someone who you can have a normal relationship with. Someone who adores you and loves you the way you used to love me, and the way you *deserve* to be loved. I'm truly sorry that I wasn't that wife for you."

Turning once more, I'm half way up the stairs when I hear Marcus start running up behind me.

"You ARE Suzanne! I'm sorry! I was just being an asshole! Please don't go. We'll work it out. I won't be boring anymore. Just tell me what you want. Just tell me what to do!"

"Marcus, I'm leaving, I'm sorry. I'll be back for all my stuff in a few weeks, okay? I just have to find somewhere else to live. I'll call you. I'll let you know where I'm going. And Marcus, if you ever need me, or just, like want to talk or something, please call me. I would really like to be your friend."

"Suzanne? Let's talk about this for a minute!"

God, he looks so panicky. I feel just wretched inside for him. This whole thing is terrible and exhausting. Marcus deserves better than all this upset all the time.

"We did just talk, Marcus, but I'm going to go finish packing now. I'm really very sorry for all this pain, *all the time.* You deserve so much better than this."

"Wait! Suzanne, I love you, and we'll work all this out. It's only been a couple months... not even three full months yet. We just need a little

more time to figure this out. I'll do whatever you want. It's okay Suzanne. Just tell me what you want, and I'll do it."

"Marcus, I..."

"Is this about sex? I'm fine with it now. It's not a big deal. We can do it if you want to. Suzanne, just tell me what to do, and I'll do it," he pleads.

"Marcus, this is not about sex. *Well,* it kind of is, but not really. It's just that we aren't a good couple. Or maybe I'm just not a good wife. I don't know anymore. I think about you as a room-mate now. You are a wonderful room-mate to me, but I want more than that. I *have to* have more than that. I didn't struggle through hell, to end up with just *enough.* I want more than just enough. And I honestly want more than that for you too."

"Suzanne, you *are* more than enough for me. I'm not even angry or upset anymore about all the bad stuff. I know it wasn't your fault and I'm not angry anymore. It's okay now. Just tell me what to do. Tell me what you need Suzanne, and I'll do it, I promise."

"Marcus, I need you to let me go now. That's what I need from you. I want to go now. You are amazing, but you're not amazing *with me.* I want to go, so *I* can find more, and I want to go so you are free of all this *awful* from now on. Please Marcus, it's enough now."

"But I can't. You're all I ever wanted Suzanne, and it's supposed to be better now. *We're* supposed to be better. You said it would be. I thought it would be..."

"I'm so sorry Marcus. *I'm* better, but *we're* not better."

"Suzanne..." he whispers finally.

Turning from Marcus' desperate stare takes me an eternity, but I finally leave him on the stairs as I make my way back to my bedroom. I feel so awful and sad inside. I can't help but cry while finishing the last of my packing.

I'm going to be 30 years old in a two weeks and I feel like I'm saying goodbye to half my life- which I guess I am. 30 years of Chicago with 30 years of nothing but pain, loneliness and upset, is too much. I have to finally say goodbye to it all, Marcus included.

I'll just have to spend the next 30 years trying to find out what will make *this* Suzanne honest and truly happy.

==========

When New York Kayla picks me up at the airport, I finally exhale. *Jesus,* I was holding my breath for hours. It feels good to be with just a friend- someone I don't have to try or pretend with.

"Do you want to talk about it?"

"Not really."

"Okay. But you can if you need to. I promise not to trash Marcus, though it'll kill me not to." She says with her best New York Kayla evil grin.

"Does Mack know I'm here yet?"

"Yeah. I *had* to tell him. See, *my* Mack can't go one single night without

a piece of all this," she says motioning to her gorgeous body with a cheeky little grin. "So I had to give him a reason for turning him down tonight."

"Well, Kayla, I'm glad *MY* Mack has you in his life. I love you both, and I love you both together. And after all *MY* Mack has done for me, I want him to be very, *very* happy, he deserves it…um, even if his happiness is with the likes of you…"

"That's exactly what Mack says when he's trying to get me into bed…" she pouts.

Bursting out laughing at This Kayla's pout, I can't decide which Kayla has the better pout. It doesn't matter I guess. I love them both, though I hate when they use their pouts against *me*- I'm doomed when they bring out their pouts.

Slowly my laughter turns to tears, and without saying a word, Kayla reaches over and takes my hand. Squeezing tightly, she ignores me, and just drives us back to her apartment. Throughout the drive I can't help but think of the years and years of awful I've had. My years of horror and sadness just seem to never fully rest. This life of mine has been an absolute agony.

Monday, February, 13th

CHAPTER 39

The following morning, Kayla leaves to have breakfast with Mack. He and I have already spoke on the phone briefly, and we're going to get together later for a person to person chat. Kayla left me the keys to her car, and I'm already antsy to get out of the quiet of the apartment. Strangely, I need noise for the first time in my life.

By 1:00, I'm ready to go shopping. My hair and makeup are flawless, and my clothing is shopping friendly... no buttons, or ties. I'm wearing a quick overhead blouse, and snap fly slacks, with my comfy heels in place. I can be in and out of a change room in less than 2 minutes in this clothing

I'm going to Macy's. It's been almost 9 months since the 'Macy's Incident' and I'm ready to try it again. It's time. Being afraid of a department store ranks fairly high on the '1-to-10 crazy scale', so I'm taking on Macy's with my sanity intact... *And* with Mack on speed dial, *just in case.*

Grabbing my purse, I open the door and I'm stunned! Walking right into Z, my legs nearly collapse with the collision. Grabbing my forearms to steady me, I find myself suddenly motionless on a gasp, as I bow my head and close my eyes.

This is what I remember. This is what I remember Z's hands felt like on me. This is the grip on my arms I remember. This is the scent I remember. This is the warmth I remember. This is the man I *always* remember.

"*Oh god...* I wish I could touch you. I want to know your warmth one more time. I miss you..." I whisper softly.

"Suzanne. I'm here. I'm right here. Open your eyes, love. Open for me." Oh god, his voice. It's the same rich, beautiful darkness.

I can't open my eyes. I've dreamed of this too many times, and I've begged for him forever. I can't open my eyes to reality. He called me 'love' and I didn't freak out or throw-up. He called me a name, and it doesn't hurt. I can't open my eyes to the pain.

"Please Suzanne, open your eyes. I've waited forever to see your eyes on me again. I've been so patient, but I can't wait anymore. *Please* Suzanne, open your eyes..."

"Z, if I open my eyes do you promise not to touch me? Do you promise you'll let me look at you, without fear of you touching me?"

"Oh! *Absolutely.* Sorry!" Z sounds positively aghast as he quickly releases my forearms.

Slowly opening my eyes, I just breathe, and take the sight of Z into my body. Staring, nothing hurts. There is no pain and there is no agony. There is just breath and peace. I feel free of this memory. I *AM* free.

Z's clothes are neat and impeccable, but dark. Black. He's wearing my blacks. Looking; I'm motionless though my breath continues.

Z's face looks sad though, and he's so still. He looks distant. Maybe

he's frightened? God, Z looks different. He seems to have aged some. He seems so tired.

Looking at his lips, I remember their softness. Looking at his eyes, I remember their dark beauty and intensity, and I remember his eyes smiling at me. Why aren't his eyes smiling?

"Z, just breathe for me," I whisper.

"Oh, Suzanne..." he moans an exhale straight into my body.

Z looks so unhappy and I wish he was happy again. I wish his eyes smiled again. I wish his face wasn't so frozen. I wish he was free of me.

"Z, you look so beautiful to me, but *so* sad. I wish you were happy. Your happiness kept me alive. Your light kept me from the total darkness. I wish you knew your light again. I am very sorry for the darkness I've caused you."

"It was never you, Suzanne. You were *always* lightness for me. You made me want to turn all *your* darkness into light. I had hoped I could do that for you."

"You did. You were everything, Z. I had such peace with you, and I held your peace when I would have given up so many times."

"Suzanne..."

When my tears start to fall, I see his concern. Leaning in, I wrap my arms around his waist, and hold him as tightly as I can. Resting my cheek against his chest, I want to feel his light again inside me. Inhaling him; I take in his scent, and his warmth, and his light.

Gently, Z wraps me up in his embrace as well. I know he's frightened to touch me, I know he's scared of my reaction, but it was *never* him. I never feared *him.* He was everything I could have ever dreamed of. He was the only goodness I've ever known, from a man who touched me.

"Z, it was always you. From the moment I heard your smile-voice, I knew it would always be you, whether I could have you or not. I knew no other man but you, and I've wanted no other man but you."

"Suzanne... I'm yours if you'll take me. I was always yours. Everything I've done in the past 9 months has been for you. Everything I've felt in the last 9 months was for you. It was always about *you,* Suzanne."

Breathing him in, there is still no pain. This is the closest I have been to Z since I broke, and this is the first time the pain is absent. I'm holding him and breathing him into me. He will *always* be a part of me. *Forever.* And now I can finally let him go.

"I don't feel pain and agony any longer. I'm better and I'm finally free. *You* are free. I want this for you. I want you to move on and I want you to live a good life *away* from me. I'm better, and I am better *because* of you. You gave me Mack to help me in my darkness, and you gave me your light when I needed it. It was you that took the steps to help me, and it was you who made the choices that helped me get well."

"Suzanne, *please?* This doesn't have to be a goodbye. This can be our start. We never really *started;* we just lived quickly and ended horribly. We can have a start now. I *want* a start with you. I've *earned* a start with you, I think. And you've earned a start to your life. *Please?* Please stay and think about starting your new life with me in it?"

"Z..." Oh, *god.* I've never even pictured this scenario before. Thinking of Z was always going to be a happy memory, not a reality. I don't even

know how to process a reality that actually *includes* Z in it.

"Suzanne. Please, just think about it. No force. No promises. No pressure or manipulation. Just think about it. Meet me at my apartment tonight for dinner. Just dinner, I promise. Nothing but a meal together. I just want to know you again. I NEED to know you *now...* Just dinner. That's all I'm asking. You can come to my home, eat or not, stay or go. It's all your choice. I'm just asking for one hour of your life. Please, come to my home, and share a meal with me? And if you need to leave forever; I'll let you go, forever, I promise. I just need a chance to know you. *Please, Suzanne?*"

Just Jump!

"Okay, Z. One meal. One hour. One..."

"Fine! 6:00. My home. No expectations and no pressure. I'll see you at 6:00. Please, Suzanne?" Z looks all concerned again.

"Okay. 6:00. I'm fine I promise, but I really need you to go now. I just want to think for awhile."

By the end of my sentence tears are already pouring down my face. *Dammit.* I was so strong. Now, I feel so weak suddenly. I can't be weak again.

"Okay. I'll see you at 6:00," Z says with a little smile as he turns and walks quickly down the hallway to the elevators.

Oh, god. *I am so lost.*

===========

As Z turns to leave I hear him whisper, 'I miss you', and that's my breaking point. I'm done. Closing Kayla's door, I collapse and cry.

I've always wanted someone to miss me. I had always *hoped* someone would miss me should something bad happen. But nothing bad has happened to me this time, and I'm actually missed, and it *doesn't* feel good... it feels *sad.* I don't want this for Z. I never wanted this sadness for Z. He is *meant* for happiness, not sadness.

Reaching for my cell, I call Mack. God, I need Mack. I need him to help me know what to do. He loves me but he *knows* Z. If anyone can help me think straight about Z it has got to be Mack. If Mack can't help me, I'm lost. This is the one area of my life where I don't have the ability to work it out on my own.

"Suzanne? What's wrong? Why are you crying?"

"Mack, I'm sorry. Can you come back to Kayla's alone? I need to talk badly. I just saw Z and I'm kind of messed up, or sad, or desperate, or something..."

"I'll be there in 20 minutes. Kayla's at the hospital now, and we'll be alone. Maybe put on a pot of coffee?"

"Okay. Coffee. Thank you Mack. I love you."

"I love you too, Suzanne. We'll work this out, together. Just hang tight for me for 20 minutes, okay?"

"Okay, Mack. I promise."

===========

25 minutes later Mack opens Kayla's door. Walking straight toward me, I rise from my chair and hug him tight. It's feels so good to just hug him. It feels like it's been forever since I had a *Mack hug* though it's been mere days.

"God, I've missed your hugs, Mack. You are the only one who I can hug without even a tiny cringe, still. It's just you. Even The Kaylas make me cringe slightly, but never you. Do you know why that is, Mack? From a Shrink's perspective, why is it only you that I can freely touch?"

"Suzanne. When you had no ability to reason your past from your reality, when you were a scared woman fighting for her life, I just happened to be there. You needed one person to trust and I was the person you *had* to trust. That's why you don't cringe with me. You chose me then to trust when you had no one else you thought you *could* trust."

"No. That's not right. No. I think you're wrong Mack. It wasn't *just because you were there.* It was just because it was *you.* Mack, you are everything to me now because you were everything I could have ever needed then."

"Suzanne. It's a good thing we don't feel *that way* about each other, because I would be madly in love with you after a comment like that."

"Oh, shut up, you ass! You know what I mean," I say while shoving his arms away.

"I do. And you know when I'm just teasing you."

"I do."

Walking to Kayla's kitchen, I pour Mack a coffee- double milk, one sugar. As I hand over the coffee and a few cookies to him, exhaling, I'm not sure where to begin. Walking back to the living room, Mack follows silently until I plop into my favorite big purple 'Suzanne chair', as Kayla calls it, and just pause.

When Mack is about to speak, I hold up my hand to stop him. Nodding, Mack gets comfy on Kayla's *honest to god,* ORANGE love seat... and proceeds to wait while sipping his coffee.

Just do it. Talk. This is Mack. Mack already knows everything about me and he doesn't care about the bad stuff. Mack has said what was done to me in the past, and even what *I have done* in the past is not *who I am,* or *what I can become.* Mack is such a good man... and this is why I love him so dearly.

"Mack... prepare yourself. This one is gonna be long and intense for me, but probably painful, tedious and exhausting for you. You may even walk away from me after my request. I'll be okay with whatever you do or say, or with how fast you run away."

"Suzanne, I will never leave you, and I certainly won't *run* from you. Tell me, or ask me anything. There is nothing you can do that will be 'painful, tedious, or *exhausting*' for me."

"Ha! We'll see..." I say with a grin, as Mack motions with his hands the international sign for 'Bring it on, *sister'. God...* he's just so lovable.

Okay. Jump! And on a long-winded exhale I begin.

CHAPTER 40

"Mack, I want passion. And I don't mean just passion in its most base sense, I mean *PASSION*. I miss not knowing what I want, but knowing I'm about to get it. I miss wanting someone so badly that I crave and tingle with desire and excitement. I miss the passion that manifests itself into a kind of love, so real and so painful that I could breathe within it, and weep while without."

Blushing, I admit to Mack, "I have only had one man do this to me... and though I know he's gone from my life, I'm not really sure if it's Z that I fully miss, or rather the experience attached to him that I miss most in my life, but I do think it IS Z, and I do miss him constantly...

"...Believe me, I'm not suggesting I miss my old life, or that I would dismiss this life- the life I have created finally, on my own, with your help of course, but I do miss the feeling of love- love in its most beautiful, compelling sense. I miss *feeling* love. I miss *feeling*."

Admitting on another blush at my childish sounding words, "My experience with Z was just, like, *beautiful*. Um, I'm not intentionally being ridiculous, and I'm not trying to romanticize this... but that's all I can say. My short time with him was beauty, happiness and passion. I enjoyed waking to his scent, and I enjoyed sleeping in his arms for that amazingly short period of time. Days really, but days that have held me in rapture since. He was funny, tender, and so loving, that I miss him every minute of every day...

"...During that small moment in time together, I didn't care what anyone thought or felt because he was with me and I was momentarily happy. I experienced the 'novel'... the novel every woman reads and yearns for in their *real life*, knowing full well that their love will never be as it is on the pages... the novel of their craving. I fell into that novel and sadly I was ripped from the pages before the last chapter."

My tears are starting to fall slowly- Not the tears of desperation that used to fall, but rather tears of resignation.

"I often wonder if it would have been better that I never had this experience of feeling love with Z, so I'd have nothing to miss. But then I often thank life for giving me that one brief experience... but then the sadness returns and I am filled with remorse once again for the loss of feeling...

"...Mack, I finally want to be touched. I want a man who knows how to touch me. I want hungry, loving, thrilled fingers to caress me. I want romance and fulfillment. I want to be held, so innocent, so completely, that my body doesn't matter. I want a man who shudders as I do when things become too intense and pain-filled, like when the memories of my past torture me. And I want a man who smiles and reassures me of my life *now* when the painful memories slowly fade again. I want him to help me sleep without the screaming nightmares I still have. I want to be touched by a hand, not looking for thrill or mere sexual gratification, but a hand that just wants to feel me breathe in and out, shallow or deep. I

want the hand to soothe and enjoy me. I want no scars, no upset, and no pain. I just want love in his touch…

"…I want him to look at me with knowing eyes. I want to be soft and *unbroken* in his eyes. I want him to *see* my eyes. I want to care nothing of my body, with all its physical short-comings, imperfections and scars. I want him to see no damage- I just want him to see *me*. I want his hands to mirror the happiness and the peace in my heart, when he touches me. I want… I want that with Z, I think."

Sitting forward in my chair with my hands on my knees, I know I must look a little wild-eyed to Mack. I'm sure he's nervous for me. I'm sure I'm starting to scare him, but I need to say all this. I just need to hear it out loud. I don't want all this *stuff* trapped in my head any longer.

"When I saw his face today, I wasn't sure if I could stop myself from hurting again, but I didn't hurt, and I don't know why. I know consciously and with very little effort on my part, I would never, ever hurt him intentionally. But I don't know if I could be myself in his presence, as just a *friend* if I thought I could once again feel *something* resembling what I did feel back then *with* him. This desire to feel with Z is like an obsession for me that I'm not sure I should have. He's like a craving I shouldn't satisfy. Z is a life too big for me to live within, I think."

Shaking, I finally admit my truth to Mack. "I'm just *average*, Mack. And with that knowledge comes the reality that I was not meant for and will never have, the unbelievable love that I crave, each and every day of my life. I am without a piece of me. I am incomplete. And I think I want to see if Z could be that piece for me. But I don't think I should, or rather, I guess I'm scared to death of trying and failing. I just don't think I was truly meant for this thing, this love and this *life* which I desire most. I'm sure I wasn't meant for the *happily ever after,* or for the loving calm of a loving and calm relationship. I'm sure if I try with Z, I'll fail, and I don't think I can recover again from another heartbreak…

"…I am her. I am me now. *I know* I'm Suzanne, but I'm so very different from the woman I have created in others' eyes these last few months. She is growing strong and self-assured, but I am still the me of my youth sometimes, *as you know…* I'm still looking, craving, dreaming, and too often, still in pain. I still want so badly the life I dreamed of- a life with romantic, consuming, peaceful love and adoration from another."

Now there's a long pause while I process my thoughts. When Mack looks like he's about to speak after my silence, I again shake my head no, and his movements stop. I need to finish this. I'm brave right now. I'm talking freely and I want so desperately to finish this once and for all.

"I'm not just looking for physical gratification, Mack. Please don't misunderstand any of this. It's not about simple sex or passion, its more, I just want to *feel* again. I am desperate to feel, so much so, that a pain has settled in my heart, so heavy, that I feel as though I have suffered the death of a love… Um, it's so hard to explain, but I feel as though I live in a constant *mourning…* without the actual death. I can't believe any pain can feel worse than this, well, not until I'm actually proven wrong, I guess. I know no other pain like this; not like the pain from my abusive

parents, or my neglectful spouse, or even the pain caused by the men who attacked me - not this awful life I've had, and not the death I thought I wanted. I just know that I live each and every day with a smothering need to be, like, *free* of this pain. Just for a minute, I want freedom from all this denial and memories and, and *agony*. I want the freedom to live *average*, without feeling the weight of that very word...

"...I want to find Z again. I want to have him hear me in my silence, while he calms me when I'm in pain. I want him. I picture him knowing how to touch me while knowing how to break into me, so that I finally exhale and stop holding my breath as I have it seems for an eternity. I want to be *alive* and not just *living*. I want him so badly some days, that the want *IS* the agony...

"...God, I sound so dramatic, I know. But it's just so consuming, this feeling of loss. I feel like I need to scream, shaking with the pain, so that maybe that one scream and that one tear into my heart of pain and longing for Z will be enough to rip the wounds wide open, allowing me to except my fate of loveless, passionless mediocrity, so that eventually I can either heal or I can repress this need for Z, *forever*..."

Once again, sitting back in my chair, I raise my knees against my chest, and wrap my arms around myself tightly. Looking at *my* Mack, he just nods his head as if to say 'go for it. Finish this.'

"Mack, I've always loved the poem 'Porphyria's Lover' by Robert Browning. *I've loved it.* I remember when I was younger understanding why the lover killed Porphyria. I understood how amazing it would be to actually have someone love you, that intensely, in that one specific moment. I remember thinking, I too, would want to kill someone in that moment, so that I kept their love forever, just for me. I know now, *obviously*, that that view on love is obsessive, psychotic and unhealthy. I know that Mack, so don't worry. But I think when I was young, I just wanted to be loved so badly, that the lover's actions in the poem made sense to me...

"...Then when I met Z, I understood the poem differently. I understood the ugliness of the poem. I saw Z struggling, as I was at the time, and I realized *I* would want to die if I was ever loved as thoroughly as the lover believed he was at the time by Porphyria. And yes, I know that is a sick, *crazy* way to view love, but it's the truth nonetheless. I'm not saying I want to die anymore, and I'm not saying it's okay to want to die, just because you are loved. I'm just saying that when I saw Z looking at me like he *did* love me completely and totally when I thought I was going to die, I actually wanted to die then, in that exact moment, so that Z's love would be the very last memory I carried with me into death. I understood needing love so badly, that I could actually kill myself to hold onto that memory of love, *forever*." Long *exhale*.

I find my arms still wrapped so tightly around my knees, and staring at the safety I have in Mack, I take a few deep breaths and continue.

"I'm begging you to help me, Mack. I know this is horrible, and selfish, and disgusting... but I'm *begging* you to help me. I'm begging you to tell me what to do, so that I can breathe again."

Now I'm openly crying. There is no way to stop it. Everything just hurts, everywhere.

"I'm so sorry, Mack. I'm so sorry to put this on you, but I'm begging you to help me get better. I don't want to feel like shit anymore, and I don't want to cry about this anymore, alone in my bed, *way too often* to even admit to myself. I wouldn't ask this from you if there was another person that I *could* ask, but there isn't anyone else, so I'm asking *you*. You're the only one I trust with my life. You're the only person I trust to tell me what to do. Help me to get over myself, or...tell me to shut-up. Tell me to grow up. Tell me to fuck off once and for all. Just tell me something! Do I beg Z to love me, or do I stop all this shit, and move on forever? I can't think anymore. I have no capacity to reason anything anymore where Z is involved. Please, Mack. *Please.* TELL ME WHAT TO DO!!"

Ooops. That last sentence sounded a little manic, and yet the rest was awesome... figures I'd ruin the moment. *Dammit.* "Sorry for yelling..."

There seems to be a complete pause to everything in the room. Even the air itself doesn't seem to exist. There is nothing but total silence from Mack as he just stares at me for a minute. *Shit.*

Turning his head away from me, Mack expels a large breath, shakes his head slightly, and after placing his mug on Kayla's coffee table, he finally turns back to look at me. Oh my god! Mack has tears in his eyes. SHIT!

"MACK! I'm so *SORRY!*"

"Suzanne... *enough.* Sit there. Shut up. And listen to me." *What?* "Just breathe and Listen To Me."

"*Okay...*" Gulp. *Shit.* Breathe Suzanne. Mack won't hurt you.

"I'm a man, *as you know*, so I'm not prone to cry. However, what you just said to me and asked of me, is the single most beautiful, desperate, eloquent thing I have ever heard. If you had not already broken my heart months ago for the life you were forced to endure as a child, you would have broken it just now with that confession. You are honesty, the most *feeling, non-jaded* victim of circumstances BEYOND HER CONTROL that I have ever met in my life. You are absolutely beautiful; and you make me want to live better, and love harder, just by knowing you. You are an absolute *dream*, Suzanne. And if we were two different people, I would love you like you desire for the rest of my life. But we are *not* two different people, so I can't love you the way you desire, or the way you DESERVE. You are absolutely *astounding* to me... " Mack says with a small smile while gently wiping his eyes with his thumbs.

"Suzanne, listen to me closely... Z loves you like you desire *and* like you deserve. I have had to counsel him for months because he has been absolutely lost since you walked into his life. He has been struggling and suffering every single day since you asked him to leave your hospital room months ago. He has been desperate to love you since the moment he met you, *and* since the moment you asked him to leave you. Z has been asking about you and *for* you every single day since you pushed him away. Suzanne, Z is desperately in love with you, and he wants to be everything for you. The only thing holding him back from loving you was *you*."

"But, Z..."

"I'm not finished. So please be still, breathe, and just listen to me."

"Okay. Sorry..."

Nodding, Mack continues. "Z was the one who set everything in motion. It was Z who searched out and found the 'black school book', as you mentioned to us when you were having your breakdown. I don't even know how he did it exactly, there was something about a 'gratitude luncheon' for his discretion, hosted by your parents, in your parent's home. Again, I don't know the specifics, but he found it, and turned it in. It was Z who went to the D.A. in Chicago, and to the police and D.A. in New York. It was Z who contacted your grandfather and told him our suspicions about your parents and your childhood. It was Z who found the photos on his father's computer of you as a child and gave them to the police and the D.A...

"...God, Suzanne, it was Z who paid for the security and bodyguards, until your grandfather took over your security. It was Z who financially, verbally, and in a rather *colorful* way, threatened all the people either directly involved with, or those who only *knew* of the abuse you suffered as a child, forcing them to either come forward to the Police, or to *renounce* those who were involved, publically. He even went after those who simply knew about the abuse but didn't participate in it, blaming them for not coming forward at the time. Some charges have even been laid against *those* individuals as well, based on Z's insistence with both D.A.'s in Chicago and New York."

Shaking his head, Mack continues. "Z paid all my attorneys fees in the beginning when I was being sued by Dr. Simmons *and* by your parents, and he paid for my attorneys during the Conflict of Interest trial brought on by the New York Psychiatric Committee, and also for the trial regarding your guardianship brought on by your grandfather as well... Essentially, whatever *I* needed to help *you,* Z provided. And whatever was needed, financial or otherwise to help *me,* Z provided. He set up a trust in your name for me to withdraw from for any expenses that might hinder my ability to be there for you *at all times*- whenever you needed me, day or night. Absolutely everything I could do for you was provided for, at Z's insistence...

"...Once your inheritance was made yours, and your Estate began paying me and Z no longer had to support me financially; he refused to end the trust fund. Instead, he kept adding to it, for any and all victims of any abuse brought on by his father, his father's friends, the Chicago Country Club your parents were members of, and finally for any victims of Dr. Simmons."

Exhaling, Mack's eyes are shining with tears I think. This is all a little overwhelming and I find my own tears gently spilling from my eyes. But I'm desperate to keep it together so Mack will continue.

"From the moment you were hospitalized, first for the suicide attempt, then the subsequent brain aneurism, to the complete nervous breakdown, it has been Z at every turn...

"...Z loves you Suzanne, so much so, that he and I have talked about his love for you often and extensively. At first I didn't understand it. Z's love was too quick and too baseless, *I thought*. I tried to reason with him that what he had mistaken for love was actually more of an emotional

reaction to the intense guilt he felt over your attempted suicide, and over his father's involvement in hurting you. I thought what he felt was just a simple attraction that had turned into a kind of obsession *because* of all the drama surrounding your time together. I really didn't understand it, and I tried to explain away Z's *love* as a product of intense circumstance. However, watching and listening to Z, I began to realize, he did in fact love you, *totally and completely*. Just the fact that he stayed away, because YOU asked him to, though it was killing him- making him so sad and desperate... proved to me how much he loved you. I saw what he was willing to endure just to give you peace with your decision to push him away. He wanted to come to you so many times, just to see you again but he always stopped himself. He *always* took a big breath, closed his eyes, and reasoned himself out of doing something *he* wanted to do, because *you* didn't want him to do it. His strength and resolve was truly amazing to watch...

"...My best friend was struggling, and all I could do was listen and let him vent his sadness when he needed to. It was agony for me to support you one hundred percent in your decision to keep Z away, when all I wanted to do was beg you to stop *pushing* him away. I wanted so desperately for you to open yourself up to my friend but I couldn't and *wouldn't* ever ask that of you, and Z wouldn't have wanted me to anyway. Originally, he wouldn't even talk to me at all about you and him, or his own feelings for you, because he wanted *all* my focus to be on you. But eventually I reassured him that I could be a friend to him without betraying my Doctor/Patient relationship, and *yes*, my growing friendship with you...

"...And that was when he finally talked to me. He explained the sex you shared and how he is so scared that he caused your suicide attempt. He told me about the initial intensity of your meeting. He told me about his sexual dominance, and about the things he did with you. Z obviously had *no idea* at the time about your past, but he feels such guilt over the way he handled, or rather, *treated you*, that he has made himself sick over it."

Sitting up in my chair, I need to interject, but again, Mack silences me with a gentle head shake no. Sitting back again, I take as many deep breaths as I can.

"I did explain to Z that your breakdown was imminent. I explained that you were already on your way to that breakdown when you two first spoke, but Z is so stuck on the thought that he caused your decline, that I honestly don't know how to help him anymore. Z has been scared to death that he pushed you too far, or rather pushed you over the edge, if you will. Z is ill over the thought that his sexual dominance hurt you. Though he didn't know about your past at the time, he feels he *should have known* something was wrong. I've tried repeatedly to explain the circumstances realistically, but he is just so consumed with guilt that he can't see a reality, other than the one in which he is to blame for your complete breakdown...

"...You see, Z is very sexually *experienced*, if you will. And before you, every one of his sexual partners knew this about him. Actually, that's what they *liked* about him. You didn't know his sexual nature however, and because he didn't explain himself fully to you before you were

intimate the first time at the motel in Chicago, he feels like he harmed you. He had never had to explain his sexual nature before, and so he didn't with you-not because he didn't want to and not because he was hiding it from you, but rather because it just never occurred to him to do so. Now, however, by not telling you properly beforehand about his sexual nature, and not telling you what he had planned for your first encounter, he feels like he essentially lied to you by omission. He thinks of it as an error which caused you irreparable harm...

"...Slowly, Z explained to me that he actually thought you were just like a typical sexually repressed woman. He believed that you simply hadn't experienced pleasure through orgasm, therefore, he was going to push you into *letting go* of your reserve so that you could in fact enjoy pleasure through orgasm. Z told me he tied your hands, took your control from you, and essentially forced you to experience pleasure. And he admitted that to me while shaking with rage at himself, and cursing himself for a horror he believes he did to you because of the past you were forced to endure...

"...As I told Z multiple times, he *did not,* nor *could he* have known the actual *cause* for your sexual repression at the time, but my arguments have been fruitless. Z believes strongly that he *should* have known that there was more going on with you, and therefore regardless of how I have counseled him, he feels he holds blame, if not entirely, at least *partially* for your ultimate break-down...

"...Z and I have had many debates, arguments and all out yelling matches over our differing opinions on the matter, but in the end, I think he is simply consumed with too much guilt that he is unable to rationalize your breakdown apart from any action he may have taken with you...

"...Suzanne, Z helps anyone and everyone- he always has. But with you he feels as though he harmed you instead. Add the fact that you attempted suicide on *his watch* as he calls it, in *his* own apartment, and he is devastated by what happened. Z has taken the events with you so personally that I can't seem to reach him anymore. He is truly devastated by his perceived part in your breakdown. Z honestly believes that by *forcing you-* by restraining you, in an attempt to make you experience your first orgasm with a partner... with him *specifically*, that he harmed you, and that he harmed his chances with you, forever."

Leaning in closer to me, Mack looks absolutely stricken with something. There *is* something, but I don't know this look on Mack's face. I can usually tell the difference between Dr. MacDonald from my *friend* Mack, but this look is so strange, and kind of *sad* looking.

"Z finally explained the intense emotional connection he felt before, during, and especially *after* you and he were intimate. He spoke in details, only to adequately express to me just how intense you were with each other. For Z, you were his first real, *loving* experience. He had never *made love* with anyone in such a way as he did with you. Before you, though Z had loved women, and had sex with many, many women, he was always content with where they were and where they each ended up. But with you, Z wasn't content, so much as 'complete', was the word he used to describe his feelings after you were together. What Z actually

said was, 'Sex *before* Suzanne was content, sex *with* Suzanne was complete.' And that's quite a stunning revelation for a 34 year old man, I might add," Mack smirks.

Stunned? Such an inadequate word for where my head is at right now. Silent and staring at Mack, I can't even speak. I am just **STUNNED!** This is the most amazing thing I have ever heard in my life. The most amazing thing I could have ever imagined happening to me. Actually, I feel a little sick, or nervous, or shaken, or something.

"Suzanne. To answer your question; GO GET Z. He's been waiting for you to take him. He has been dying for you to realize you feel for him even a tenth of what *he* feels for you. Z is *good* Suzanne, I promise. I can't promise it will always be easy, but I absolutely *can* promise you that with Z, you will never have to feel insecure about being loved ever again. Z will love you for eternity, if you'll let him. Z can and will be anything you could have ever dreamed of wanting, but didn't know to ask for…

"…Suzanne, Z is there *waiting* for you. He wants to give you the love, adoration, and even the passion you desire, and *deserve*. He wants YOU Suzanne, with all the baggage, nightmares, scars, and agonies you can throw at him. He wants to be your partner in all the pain, and your partner in all the happiness."

"Mack, I…" *SHIT!* Pitching forward, I throw up. God *Dammit.* This is not right!

"Suzanne?! I thought you wanted…"

"I DO! This is *happy* vomit, I swear! I'm not messed up or unhappy! This is like nervous vomit or something, *honestly* Mack. Jesus *Christ.* I know this is so messed up. See! I only threw-up once. It was just like nerves or something. That's all."

"*Happy vomit?* Did you just say that?" Mack bursts out laughing, as I push down a last gag and join him.

"I AM crazy Mack, remember? *Happy vomit* makes perfect sense to me."

Still laughing, Mack stands and walks to Kayla's kitchen, presumably for cleaning supplies. Thank god she has hardwood floors.

"I'll do it Mack. Please stop. This is horribly embarrassing."

As Mack hands me the Lysol, floor cleaner and paper towels, he leans down close to me, and then hugs me tightly- just a massive, warm hug. A hug of reassurance and a hug of comfort. Mack doesn't even care that I just threw-up.

"Are you truly okay, Suzanne? *Really?* I told you quite of a lot of information, and you're probably suffering from emotional overload, but I just felt it was important for you to know that you *could* have the love you want from, *and with* Z."

"I'm okay Mack. You did good, and I won't tell Z anything you told me."

"I wouldn't care if you did. You're both my friends and I needed to help you two find each other again. Plus, there was no Doctor/Patient Confidentiality agreement in place with Z, whether he believes there was or not. So he can't sue me *or* kick my ass for spilling to you."

Crying again, I whisper, "Thank you, Mack. You are everything to me, and your kindness has given me my life."

"Suzanne. This journey with you has been the absolute greatest joy of my life, thus far."

"Mack, *please*... You're *killing* me here. Don't say another wonderful thing. Please don't tell me you love me and don't tell me I'm special. Please don't *Mack me* anymore...I'm supposed to meet Z at his home for dinner at 6:00, and I'll still be crying when I arrive in 2 hours, if you don't stop all this amazing, beautiful, crap. Okay?"

"Okay. I won't '*Mack*' you..." he says with a silly grin, *and* with his damn finger air-quotes. "But one last thing; Please take everything slowly, for both yourself and for Z. He has had months of wanting, and you have had a lifetime of wanting, so just go slowly together. I don't want you both to be overwhelmed with your happiness. It's hard, but breathe your way through it and talk to him... *always.* Tell him *everything* you can, *at all times.* Z wants this to be right, and he's going to have to be told when you're overwhelmed so that he doesn't feel like he's screwing anything up with you, or that he's asking you for too much, or pushing you too hard. Believe me, he can handle anything you ask of him, or anything you tell him you need. Okay?"

"I will. I'm going to try to be with Z but I'll definitely talk my way through it with him as we go."

"Then you two will probably make it through to the other side together."

"I want that Mack, I really do. And I'm going to do whatever's necessary to have the life I want with Z."

"Good enough."

"Thank you Mack. Thank you again for *everything*, ALL the time."

Rising, and making his way to the front door, Mack turns to me once more, and opens his arms for another Mack hug. Sliding right into place, I squeeze him as tightly as I can, exhaling all the tension, while breathing in Mack's sense of calm. I'm going to be okay. I just know it.

"So, I'll get going. I'm sure you have all your girly getting ready to do, but know that I'll be with cell phone at the ready should you need to talk, or if you just need a pep-talk tonight. Anything at all, just call me. Kayla and I are going to have a quiet night in so feel free to call, or come back anytime this evening. Oh, and Chicago Kayla is visiting this weekend, so your Kaylas are planning a kind of drunken, trash everyone and everything party for the three of you, minus the face punching I hope. *I,* will clearly be hiding out in my apartment that night though, just in case I've pissed off New York Kayla without my knowledge."

"I'm sure you have at some point, though *your* Kayla isn't really one to hold her tongue, so I'm assuming you already know if you have," I say grinning.

"So, as I said, I'll be hiding out in my *locked* apartment that night." Mack says smirking as he turns and leaves the apartment.

"Oh! Mack? If I leave a letter for Marcus, will you please make sure he gets it? I need to say a proper goodbye to him. I kind of left things uneasy and I want some closure for him."

"No problem. I'm supposed to talk to him on Wednesday. Maybe it's best if I fax it to him then, so he and I can discuss anything he needs to

discuss on Wednesday. Good enough?"

"Yes, thank you. I hate feeling like I've hurt him with all this."

"Suzanne. I don't like anyone being hurt either, but it's time you lived life for you now."

"Thanks Mack. You're the most amazing, good-looking, dorky doctorly man I've ever known."

"I know. Make sure you tell *my* Kayla that as often as possible for me though."

"I will. Good night Mack. Wish me luck."

"Good luck, Suzanne. But I think life is going to be much easier for you, from today forward." And with one final hug, and a kiss on my cheek, Mack pulls away smiling.

Closing the door behind him, I can't help a slight panic. Oh god, I hope Mack's right. I hope life is easier from today forward. I almost believe it will be. For the first time in my life, I feel like I might be happy or at least on my way to *being* truly happy. It's quite frightening actually because I've never had it before, and I never thought I was the type to live with... *happiness*. Maybe I *am* meant for a happily ever after. We'll see.

CHAPTER 41

Marcus,

I want you to know that I'm very sorry for the way things have turned out. You have been a good husband to me; even if I didn't know that until recently. I'm sorry marrying me was such a struggle for you. I know you never wanted to suffer as you have, and for that I'm truly sorry.

You can keep the house. You picked it, bought it, and loved it. I actually want no part of it. I'll just pick up my clothing and shoes only, because there's really nothing in that house of any sentimental value to me.

I really don't know what to say to you anymore. I think I've said it all. You were never the problem, as you always told me, and though I _was_ the problem, it was unintentional on my part. You married a damaged woman, and I know I damaged you along the way, so for that, I'm sorry as well.

You told me to never come back, and I won't. There is a different life waiting for me, I just have to figure out what that life is. And I know there is a _wonderful_ life waiting for you. I know it's just beginning for us, separately, and I look forward to hearing about your future. I honestly would like nothing but happiness and ease in your future. Maybe one day you will find the peace you desire. I sincerely hope so.

Marcus, you are handsome, smart, successful, and kind. You are everything I should desire, and everything nearly every other woman desires... I'm just sorry there's too much bad history for us. I'm sorry that I can't be the wife you want, and I'm sorry I can't love you for the man you are.

If my life had been different, I believe I would have been the kind of woman who could have loved you, as you always loved me. But my life wasn't different, and this is who I ended up being. So go find that woman you deserve. Go find some peace...finally.

I think that's it. Please keep in touch. I want to know how you have fared with all this. I'm sure we'll see each other during the trials next month, but I would like to see you away from the stresses of the trials as well. I want to know that you're okay, when all the dust settles.

I truly, and with much love, wish you well.

Suzanne

Re-reading my letter to Marcus, I'm happy with the final draft. There's nothing more to say. There's nothing more I *can* say. It's done. I have to move on. He has to move on. I trust Mack to help Marcus understand that he *is* a good man, and that he will be a wonderful husband, to *someone else.*

And I hope Marcus eventually understands that he was never the problem as he said all along. He was right-It was *always* me. I was the problem and now I am fixing the problem. But sadly, fixing the problem doesn't involve Marcus any longer.

I really wish him well, and in a friendly, platonic sort of way, I really do love him. I just can't love him the way he has always wanted and hoped I would. I've *never* been able to love him the way he wanted and hoped I would.

I finally exhale and give closure to the tragic Marcus/Suzanne fantasy that was my life and our marriage.

"I'm sorry Marcus, but it's finally over."

CHAPTER 42

It's time to go. It's time to go get Z. I know it won't be perfect, and I know it won't be a fairy tale romance, but I think Z and I have a good start, and that's all he has asked of me. He wants a *start* and I'm more than willing to give him that. Actually, with Z, I want more than a start but I'll begin with that.

The car ride seems long, though I know Kayla and Z live only a few blocks apart. My nerves are high, and I'm glad I haven't eaten this afternoon. Throwing up earlier has evacuated my stomach, so it looks good for me. No vomitus interruptus for Z and I. Oh! Ha! I can still say stupid phrases. At least that tragic part of my personality has remained intact. I'll have to share that one with Mack later. He always enjoys my nonsensical words and stupid phrases.

Arriving at Z's apartment I'm nervous, but remarkably steady on my feet. I'm wearing my favorite, fabulous, Vera Wang, black, 4 1/2 inch stacked heels, and I feel safe, secure, sexy, and *tall* in them.

My black knee high pencil skirt is paired with a stunning black blouse with red piping along the bodice and cuffs. I'm proud to be making baby steps with the color red- just little splashes or embellishments here and there. Nothing too intense, but a little red to keep me moving past the nightmare of my past.

Once I'm in the elevator my hands begin shaking, but again, I feel nervous *excitement*, not the once familiar nervous dread, as I used to always feel. Another baby step for me. I feel like I'm on my way. Just one more baby step tonight... Z.

Knocking on his door, I breathe nice and slow, deep and easy. I actually feel NO panic still, just excitement and anticipation. *Argh.* Hurry *up!* Open the door Z before the excitement does turn into panic. As if hearing me, the door slowly opens and my breath seems to whoosh from my lungs.

God! He is *so* beautiful. All dark, and tall, and so handsome, I want to just grab him and hold on. He is dressed in blacks again, with a dark grey dress shirt under his suit. He looks model handsome. His hair is perfect, and his smile is radiant.

"Suzanne."

"Hi, Z. Um, I'm here." *Duh.* Okay so I didn't get any smarter since we last met. Baby steps!

Z seems to be watching my reaction to him. He seems nervous himself. What do I do? *Shit.* Um...

"Please come in. Dinner will be ready in 15 minutes. Would you like a drink while we wait?"

Entering his apartment, I mumble, "yes, please."

Walking into the huge living room, I'm struck with such a déjà vu, of actual memory, that I'm momentarily motionless and silent. I haven't been here since the suicide attempt and I'm not sure how comfortable Z is with me even here. Is he thinking about it as well?

"Suzanne. Would you like to leave? I completely understand if you do.

We could have dinner elsewhere or another night if you'd be more comfortable. I realize I sprung this on you this afternoon."

"No! I'm good. It's fine. I want to be here. *Honestly!*" Calm down. Catch your breath, *Psycho.*

"Okay. Well, please have a seat. What can I get you to drink?"

"Um, *Zinfandel?*"

"Of course," he grins.

As he walks back to the little bar, I find a comfortable seat beside his large couch. I'm not ready to sit beside him yet, and I need to get my bearings for a minute. While waiting for Z, I notice the room is different. The colors are similar, but different than before.

"You've redecorated."

"Yes. I changed the entire apartment. I didn't feel comfortable here any longer, therefore I needed to either change it or move, so I opted to change the décor, *for now.*"

"Because of what I did here?" *SHIT!* Did I just ask that?

"Yes, partially. I never did like the decor though, and the colors were a carry-over from the previous owners, so I wanted to change the apartment anyway."

"The previous owners? You mean your parents?" Jesus *Christ!* Shut UP!

"Yes, them. I've opted to have very little to do with them, and their history, so a change was definitely needed."

"I'm sorry. I seem to have lost the ability to think before I speak over the last 6 months or so. Please forgive me."

"No forgiveness needed. I truly hope you've lost any and all filters. I always wanted to know what you were thinking, good or bad, so *hopefully* your inability to think before you speak will make that easier for me." And there's his perfect *smile-voice.*

"I've missed that Z- your smile-voice. I always loved hearing it. I know I've told you that before, but I just thought you should know; that even then, it was pretty special to me when I heard your smile-voice."

"And I'm sure you remember me telling you that I like that very much. I like that my 'smile-voice' pleases you."

Handing me a glass of Z's finest Zinfandel I'm sure, there seems to be a giant pause in the room. I don't know what to say, and I don't think Z knows what he *CAN* say. It's very awkward suddenly.

"Um, Z? You can just talk to me. I'm much better now, and being with The Two Kaylas frequently has definitely kicked my ass back into the land of the living. I rarely freak out now, and I won't break easily. You can, like, say stuff to me, if you *want* to. Um, when I *can't* handle something, or when something is starting to bother me, now I actually just say so... I rarely have panic-attacks now, and I rarely go off the deep end... I just thought you should know that you don't have to be careful or anything. I'll tell you if I'm uncomfortable, and I'll tell you what I think or what I feel about stuff. Oh, and apparently I ramble now too." Giggle. Shit, I'm such a dork now.... "And apparently I'm a dork now too. It must be all the time I spend with Mack. His dorkiness has kind of worn off on me some." And there's another giggle.

"Suzanne, I'm very happy to hear all that, without of course the dorky

Mack inclusion. One dorky friend is about as much as I can take, though if he has helped you I'll take any and all of his dorky idiosyncrasies any day. I'm very happy that you're doing so well. I had hoped you would. I wanted you healthy and strong, and you sound like you're making your way."

"Oh, I am. I'm *barely* crazy now. Mack says I'm now like a low 3 on the 1-to-10 Crazy Scale. So that's a definite improvement from the 10 out of 10, I was rockin' a few months ago."

"I see. And where does Mack fit on the '1-to-10 Crazy Scale'?"

"Oh. Mack's a solid 2. He's just crazy enough to get me, but not crazy enough to get kicked out of shrinking. It's a fine line the poor man has to walk... You know, crazy enough that he understands what the hell us previously crazy folk are saying, but sane enough to know how to medically treat us. It's a talent, really. Actually, he should be held to a much higher regard than the New York Psychiatric Association actually carries him by."

"Well, I'll definitely speak to the Board then, based on your reference."

"Thank you, please do. And also, um, thank you Z for giving me Mack. He was exactly what I needed, when I needed him."

"No thanks required."

"Actually, Z, *all* my thanks are required and *deserved.*"

"Suzanne, that's..."

"Please let me finish this..." I plead.

"Okay."

"Z, I know everything you did. I know all of it now. And before you curse Mack, know that he only told me today when I begged him for help and clarity. Mack never betrayed a confidence as far as I know *until* today. Today, he finally told me everything you did, ONLY because it was the right thing to do. He knew it was time for me to know what I was running from. He knew I needed to understand you, and all that you had done and continue to do for me, and even for others, it seems...

"...I know everything now. And though this isn't the time to discuss all the ins and outs of what you've been doing for me, I do think it is the time for me to give you my sincerest, most heartfelt thank you. And I mean it Z, thank you, for *everything*. I'm sure I could say much more, and I probably will say *a lot* more later, but I just wanted to say a simple thank you before we have dinner. Okay?"

"Okay. But we can talk about all this later if you'd like, or not at all. Either way, I'm fine. I just wanted you better and if I helped with that at all, then I'm thrilled and no thank you's are necessary."

"You did help. It was because of you that I became well."

"*Oh, Suzanne...* then I'm very happy. I want you well, *and* fed... Shall we eat?" He's grinning again? God, he's just so handsome.

"Please. I'm starving. I didn't eat all day, so I wouldn't throw up when I saw you... OH! *Because of nerves!* NOT because you make me vomit!" Oh *Christ!* I am such a moron, *honestly.*

"Thank you for the clarification. Not many men can handle knowing they make a beautiful woman vomit, me included. So let's go eat, before you do decide to throw up."

"Okay. Thank you."

Walking beside Z feels comfortable, and yet, there's a tension between us. I feel like I should *do* something or say something. Or just like stop the tension somehow.

Turning toward Z, I simply wrap my arms around his waist again. Breathing in his heavenly scent, I just exhale the tension. Noticing Z so still against me, I whisper, "You can hug me back, Z. I'm okay."

"Oh, *god...* Suzanne..." He breathes as he wraps his arms tightly around me.

Holding me, neither of us move. I just can't. I don't want to break the spell. Z is perfect against me. He *feels* perfect against me. I have never felt such comfort and peace in my life. Mack gives me comfort, but in a wholly innocent, reserved way. Z gives me comfort that is wholly complete. It's like I can feel his life wrapped around me.

"Suzanne... Can we *please* eat dinner now before I make a very *unmanly* ass of myself all over your shoulder...?" *What?* Pause. Giggle.

"No problem, Z. Though I do find it hard to imagine you ever *unmanly.*"

"Believe me, I've had my moments."

"Okay. Well, let me go, and we'll talk about those *unmanly* moments after dinner if you want."

"Good. I hope you're hungry?" He asks, while finally releasing me.

Grabbing his hand, which seems to startle Z for an instant, I make my way to his dining room.

===========

Holy *SHIT!* What did he do?

"What is...? Um...?"

"I didn't know what you wanted to eat so I had a chef friend of mine prepare everything I could think of. We have all the necessary staples, so I figured there had to be something you would want to eat."

"Wow. I'm sure there is."

Suddenly, a very handsome man walks out of Z's kitchen smiling at me, while holding his hand out for an introduction. *Awesome,* I didn't flinch at the sight of a strange man coming toward me. The baby steps are working.

"Marty, this is Suzanne."

"Hi Suzanne, it's nice to meet you. I hope you enjoy your rather bizarre dinner menu, all at Z's request, of course. I wouldn't dream of serving anything so peculiar, but hey, that's Z for you."

"Thank you. It all looks wonderful, and amusing. It's nice to meet you, too."

"Enjoy. I'm out of here. Z? If you ever tell anyone I prepared this dinner, I'll gladly kick your ass. Understood?"

"Of course. Thanks Marty. I'll see you out."

With a smile and nod in my direction, Marty and Z leave me to stare slightly dumbfounded at the dining room table. Holy *shit.* Z has everything. Looking at all the food, I'm starving but I can't even figure

out where to begin.

When Z returns, he motions for the chair at the end of the table. Joining him, I sit as he pushes my chair in. Placing my napkin in my lap, I still just kind of stare at the food. Where do I even begin?

"How long have you known the chef? *Marty?*"

"He and Mack have been my best friends for years."

"Marty, Mack, and Marvin?" I giggle.

"And anyone wonders still, why I prefer Z." No kidding. "So, I had Marty prepare everything. We have steak and Lobster. Mashed potatoes, asparagus, and green beans. We have two kinds of salad; chef and Caesar. There's lasagna, and a delicious cheese and mushroom ravioli. There's chicken parmigiana with fettuccini alfredo, and last but certainly not least, we have cheeseburgers, with fries, *naturally.* So? What do you feel like?"

"Ah, besides laughing my ass off at this absurdity of a meal, and crying my eyes out for your kindness, I kinda feel like a cheeseburger with fries, *of course...* though maybe I'll add a chef salad to balance it out a little."

"Let me get it for you. Excellent choice by the way. I was dying for a cheeseburger myself. Please laugh all you want, Marty certainly laughed at me, but if you start crying over this kindness I may not make it through dinner without crying myself in the most *unmanly* way I mentioned earlier. And I wouldn't want that for either of us. I look simply dreadful after crying, my eyes all puffy, and my cheeks all red..."

That's it! *I'm done.* My laughter bursts forth. Z said that so dramatically, I couldn't help it. He is too funny. He's like this little gift for me. He brings out my *real* laughter like Mack does. The laughter I didn't even know I had for the last 20 years of my life. He gives me light, and some peace within my storm. He is a gift to me. Slowly, my laughter turns to tears of... *gratitude?*

"Z, you are an *absolute joy* and a gift to me, I know that. And I want you to know that I'm aware of the gift you are."

"Suzanne, please... I didn't mean to make you sad, I was just..."

Rising from my chair, I step to him and kneel on the floor beside him.

"I know what you were doing. It's the same as you've always done. Your kindness and light know no bounds when it comes to me, and I'm not sad. I'm crying because of the light, and the peace, and because of the *love* you give to me. I know, Z. I really do understand."

"Suzanne. Please don't kneel. I don't want that. I've never wanted that. I want you beside me only, equal with me, together. I want to adore you, not hurt you or subjugate you. Please stand up, Suzanne."

Rising, I can't stop myself. Sitting in Z's lap, I wrap my arms around his shoulders and squeeze. Squeezing him so tightly because I feel such happiness. I feel completed. I feel closure from the nightmare. I feel peace in this moment.

"Z? Would you please make love *with* me? I can finally say that now. I want you to be *with* me. I *need* you to be with me. I know now, well actually I *understand* now that you never had sex *TO me,* like I always felt before you. I know that when we were together, you thought you *were* with me, even though I was unsure and unaware of the difference at the time. Please, Z?"

"Suzanne, I can't, um..." *WHAT?!*

"You can't?" Holy *shit!* I am such a *loser!*

"I mean, *I can,* but I just can't *right now.* There is so much I have to say to you. There are so many things we need to talk about. I need to tell you things. I need..."

"Z, please. We can talk forever if you want. Please don't do this to me right now. I'm feeling so insecure right now. I want to... actually, I'm just going to go now, if that's alright?"

And standing I try so hard to keep in the pain. I don't want to cry again. I don't want Z to see that he's hurt me. I don't want Z to see how weak I can still be. I am so embarrassed, I could die. Not that I want to die, but I think this embarrassment just may kill me.

"Suzanne, wait!" Z says while grabbing me around my waist. "Wait! *Please...* I *can* have sex with you- *make love with you.* I *want* to make love with you, but I just need to talk a little first. I can't be with you before I talk to you about what we were like before. I have to talk to you, that's all. Please, just give me a minute."

"Okay," I breathe on an exhale.

I can hear the defeat in my own voice. I can hear the embarrassment, and I can hear the pain. This is awful. I can't believe I've thrown myself at two men in as many months, and both have turned me down. This is so humiliating.

Extracting myself from Z's lap, I move to the chair beside him. Breathing as best as I can, I find it hard to turn to him. I don't want to make eye contact. I don't want to see Z struggling to *not* hurt my feelings. I can't stand to see pity on his face.

"Suzanne, please stop thinking. This isn't about you not being what I want. This is about you being *everything* I want." Oh! That's sounded so beautiful. "I'm just trying to talk to you first before sex clouds us. I know what sex with you is like. I've been there. I know the intensity, and I know how it changed me. I don't want us clouded by the sex, by the *love-making* when we need to talk first. That's all this is, I promise. You are still the most beautiful woman I have ever known. You are still the woman I want, the woman I have wanted from the first phone call 9 months ago. Please Suzanne, trust me when I tell you, I do want you, *badly.*"

"Okay. What is it then? What do you have to say Z? I'm fine now, go ahead." And bracing myself, I raise my head, make eye contact and just wait for him to speak.

"Okay. First I want to apologize for all that happened to you as a child. I know my father had a major part in it, I know he hurt you, and though I know he isn't me, I still feel somehow responsible for his deplorable actions."

"Z, I know..."

"Let me finish please." And when I shut my mouth, he continues. "You had a horrendous childhood, I know that. Some days I can't believe you made it through your breakdown and all the revelations you had to endure. I know it was a strength in you, that maybe even you're unaware of, but I know it was a strength that got you through this last 9 months.

It had to be. Everyone is astounded by your survival, and by your ability to want to live again, not to just *exist.* You are amazing to me...

"...When I met you, I knew nothing of your past, obviously. But I know I pushed you. See, I thought you were like this bored wife- a woman who was married to a man who couldn't pleasure her, that's all. I believed you just needed a little push. I've done that before with some women, and I've known women like that who thrived with a little push. I thought you were just a sexually inexperienced woman who needed to be *taught* how to receive and how to *enjoy* pleasure. And you were that inexperienced woman. You, as *Suzanne* have NO experience with sex- I know that. I know you were violated and abused as that young girl, but SUZANNE knew nothing of pleasure. I wanted to be that man for you, and I think I was. I wanted to see you experience orgasm and pleasure. I wanted you to be sexually awakened, if you will. And I think I did that..."

"You did..."

"But at a very heavy price. I helped push you into your nervous breakdown. It was because of my actions, that you were pushed *over the edge*, I guess. And I can't really get over that- I've tried. I've spoke with Mack endlessly about it, but I just can't seem to make myself accept anything other than *I hurt you.*"

"But you didn't hurt me! Yes, you were intense with me, and yes, I had never had a lover like you before, but Z, I had never *HAD* a lover before. That's the point. I was already screwed up when we met. I was already losing it. I was on my way. And maybe your intensity pushed me over the edge, or maybe it didn't. I was going to *break* anyway, so whether you pushed me or didn't, *really* doesn't matter. You didn't hurt me on purpose. *That's* the point! You weren't cruel to me, and you weren't abusive. You were kind, and supportive, and loving, and sexy as hell, actually. You were like this awesome little interlude in the middle of a breakdown. You didn't do this to me. You had NO part in what happened 9 months ago, just as you had NO PART in what was done to me when I was young. All you were to me was a wonderful, beautiful experience that helped me get through the tragedy and the nightmare that became my life. You were an amazing memory of passion and love when I could barely stand to breathe, or even open my eyes some days."

"Suzanne..."

And grabbing me up into his arms, Z actually bursts out crying. Jesus *Christ!* He's crying like a man, all hiccupping coughs, and throat clearing, trying to hide it, and trying to be *manly* about it. Z is crying in my arms, and I'm just devastated for him. So much guilt he's had, so much sadness, for nothing.

"Z, you have to stop this. *Today.* It's over. You didn't do anything wrong to me. You helped me. Every single thing you did from our first phone call HELPED me. You set in motion everything I would need to be helped. Between you and Mack, I'm better. I'm not great, and I'm nowhere near ready to jump fully into life, but I'm better and that is solely because of your actions and because of Mack...

"...Please let this go now. I *need* you to let this go. I can't try to be something with you, if I fear you aren't well enough to handle all the

stuff that comes with me. I don't want you to hide from me, but I can't have you carrying around needless guilt all the time. It'll destroy me. Please Z, let this go. You didn't hurt me. You were everything to me then, and you kind of still are...." Ooops. Too much pressure.

"Suzanne, I *want* to be everything for you, I really do. I know it must seem crazy... Oh! Sorry..."

"Nope. You can say crazy. I know where I am, and sadly I know where I've been. I'm fine Z- just speak freely," I grin at him.

"Okay. I love you Suzanne. And I know it must seem CRAZY to you, and to Mack, and to anyone else who has ever known me, but *honest to god*, I love you. I don't know if it's one of those 'love at first sight' things, or if it's because I've watched how hard you fought to make it through the breakdown... I really don't know. I do know that I *honestly* love you. I am *in love* with you. Just having you this close to me after so much time spent apart, has left me shaken, and excited, and nervous, and actually kind of pathetic really, I mean look at me, I'm crying over here..."

Bursting out laughing, I just take his face in my hands and kiss his lips. That's all I need. I just want to kiss him. I have wanted to kiss Z forever it seems.

"Z, can we please talk about everything... *later*. I really *need* to be with you now. I know it's you, and I know we will be together- *together*. I know the difference now. I know you had sex with me because you cared for me. I know now that you didn't *do* sex to me to hurt me. I know that, and I'm *dying over here*. *Please* take me to bed."

"Suzanne... Are you sure?"

"Oh god yes! I have thought of little else but being with you again."

"Okay. But we stop the SECOND you feel anything bad, or scary, or overwhelming. Promise me, Suzanne. Please? I need you to know that you *can* tell me to stop if you need to. And I need you to understand that I WILL stop the second you ask me to. Suzanne, please?"

"Yes, Z, I understand that. But I won't stop and I won't be scared, and I won't hurt, or get confused about anything when I'm with you. I know it. Can we *please* stop talking now though, I'm, ah, kinda horny..." *BLUSH!* I can't believe I just said that!!

Pausing for a second, Z stares at me and then starts grinning.

"*Horny* Suzanne? Well, you certainly have come a long way. I guess I better catch up, shouldn't I?"

Holy *Shit!* He has his dirty-sexy-flirty-smile going on. This is awesome! Kissing my lips gently, Z takes my hand, rises from his own chair and walks me toward his bedroom. Oh, *thank god...*

CHAPTER 43

Once we enter Z's bedroom, I am struck motionless by the difference. My memories of his room are so clouded that I'm almost unsure if we ARE in Z's bedroom. Everything is gone. Everything has changed. It's no longer a boudoir- it's now a bedroom.

There is no red. Breathing in deeply, I hadn't realized how afraid I actually was about the red, but since it's no longer here I realize I'm free of it. There is no red, and therefore there are no bad memories. This bedroom is our *start*.

"It's so different..." I whisper.

"Yes. There is no one in here anymore, and no past. There are no memories of them for me. They've been wiped clean. I wanted them wiped clean for us."

"It's stunning. I love the colors. Blacks and beiges, and even that burst of teal looks perfect. It's just so lovely now."

"I'm glad you like it. I wanted this space to be a fresh start for us... I *hoped* it could be a fresh start for us."

"Oh, it is. There's no more red. I can't really handle red, Z. I'm trying, but it's still really hard sometimes. I take baby steps with red."

"I know. That's the one thing Mack ever told me- red was an issue. And I wanted you to be free of any issues when you were here again- *IF* you were ever here again... so the red is gone, *forever.*"

"Thank you..." I whisper once more.

"Please, Suzanne? Please tell me why you're crying. Are you sad? Is this too much? We can go back to the table if you'd like?"

"NO! I'm fine. I want to be here. I really want to be here with you. I love it here now, and I know I'm going to love it here with you. I *want* to be with you here."

"Okay. Do you want to talk? Would you like to sit and just talk a while?"

"God no. We can talk forever. Please, Z... just kiss me."

Exhaling, Z takes my face in his hands and just leans his forehead against my own. "Suzanne. You are the most beautiful woman I have ever laid eyes on. There were some days I couldn't breathe for wanting you so badly."

"I feel the same way about you. I always felt that way with you. During and especially *after,* I could barely breathe for wanting you back in my life. I just didn't know what kind of life I could give you. I had to figure out what kind of life I wanted before I could ask you, or allow you to be a part of the horror that I was in at the time."

"It's okay. You're here now. I want you here. Please be here with me Suzanne."

"I'm here now- I'm *her* now. I'm finally Suzanne. And now I can give myself to you completely. Thank you for waiting Z. Thank you for waiting for me, for *Suzanne* to finally come get you. Thank you for not leaving."

"Suzanne, we will stop if you..."

"Z. Please stop talking and just kiss me. *Please,*" I smile.

Grinning in return, Z lowers his mouth to mine and kisses me. Oh! His lips are so soft. His lips are strong, but not overwhelming. He's still amazing. Again, I feel his kiss *everywhere*- all over my body and everywhere *inside* my body. Z is all I feel.

Moaning into his mouth, I feel his fingers start unbuttoning my blouse. I feel his cool fingers graze against my breasts and I moan again. Pulling him harder to my mouth, I tingle with excitement and want.

Releasing his shoulders, I begin removing his jacket and shirt. I've *never* undressed a man before, *ever.* I didn't know how sexy and powerful it felt. Tugging his shirt from his waistband, Z's body is still, though he continues kissing me. Dropping his jacket to the floor, and spreading his shirt wide, my hands slide down his chest to his slacks.

Pulling his belt buckle open is, like, *awesome.* It's so empowering. I want to do this. I *need* to do this. After unzipping his slacks, I move my hands around him again, and push his pants down, as Z steps out of them. With only his boxer-briefs between us, I stop and just look at him with a little dirty grin I can't help.

"My turn..." he whispers with a return grin.

Stepping back a foot, Z pushes my blouse open, letting it also fall to the floor. Reaching around my back, Z lowers the zipper on my skirt and pushes it to the floor. Standing in only my bra and panties, I have an instant of insecurity, but fight covering myself.

"Suzanne you are *so* beautiful. All lush curves, and pale, smooth, soft skin. I've dreamt about kissing every inch of you for months. I've been haunted by the memory of your eyes. I have never loved or seen such beautiful eyes in my life. And your lips are perhaps the most sensual lips I have ever kissed. You are everything to me. You are every flaw and every mark you carry. And yet you are flawless and unmarked *to* me. You are absolutely beautiful in my eyes."

With tears flowing, I whisper, "Thank you for saying that. You're the only one who has ever acknowledged the marks and scars. You're the only one who loved my body, even when I couldn't."

"Oh, I'm going to love your body, I promise you that." Wow! That was so sexy!

Taking my hand, Z leads me to his bed. Pushing the duvet aside, Z once again, lifts my body onto his bed. I am weightless in this moment. I have no thoughts, or fears. I know nothing but anticipation. So rising to my knees, I kiss Z with everything I have. I want him to feel how special he is to me. I want him to feel my past and our future. I want him to feel my love.

"Suzanne. It's you. It will always be only you for me. I need to hold you. I need to love your body, so you know how much I love *you.* Please Suzanne. Please let me love you."

"I want that. I want to be with you. I want to love you Z, I really do."

As Z crawls toward me, I lie back on his bed. Leaning over me, Z settles into the space my thighs provide, takes my face into his hands, and kisses me with such sweetness, I once again cry from the immense love I feel.

Pulling from my lips, Z slips his hands behind my back, unhooks my bra, and slowly pulls it down my body. Watching me closely, as he always seems to do, I smile to reassure him. *I'm here* and I'm good. I'm *very* good.

"Touch me Z. Take me into your mouth again. I love you touching me."

Bending his head, Z takes my breast and slowly nibbles, and licks, and suckles me. Writhing against his body, I pull his head closer to me. Turning slightly, Z moves with me to our sides. I love this. This position is new for me. This is the *new* Suzanne. This is our new love. Turning me onto my stomach, Z begins kissing my neck and shoulders.

Moving down my body, I feel his hands under my panties, touching and caressing, while slowly removing them. Kissing down my body Z breathes, "Turn over for me Suzanne."

Once I turn over, Z moves further down my body as I shake with anticipation. God, I want his mouth on me. I want to feel his mouth again.

"*Please...* Z," I beg.

Moving between my thighs again, Z takes me into his mouth. Oh *GOD!* This is so amazing. My whole body lights up. Every nerve ending is stimulated. Writhing against his mouth, I moan loudly. When I feel the slow impale of his fingers, I'm done. Gasping, I grab his head and force him deeper into me.

This is incredible, even better than I remember. As his tongue and fingers work me, I find I mimic his movements with my hips. My thighs are wide and my feet seem to push me into his mouth as deeply as I can. I couldn't stop this if I tried.

Suddenly, I'm struck with the thought that there is no shame or embarrassment. And there is no pain. There is only this; Z and I loving *together*. The passion and the pleasure are so great, I'm overwhelmed by sensation.

"Z... I'm almost, I, oh *GOD!*"

What did he do? I don't care! **Oh. My. God.** My whole body burns with the need to release.

"Z? Oh *god.* I'm going to cum!" I can't believe I said that word *OUT LOUD*, and *I don't care!*

"Be with me, Suzanne. Right now, love."

Screaming, my whole body tenses and then... I release. My whole body burns with release. My tears flow and my gasps continue. I am with Z, and he is giving to me again.

"OH GOD! I'm free, Z. I'm free. There's nothing else but you and I. I can't feel anything or *anyone* but you..." Sobbing, I reach for him to pull him to my mouth.

Kissing him hard, I'm desperate to feel him inside me. I want him to have my pleasure. I want him to have all the love I can give him. I actually want to be *his* pleasure.

"Z come into me. Make love with me. I want you and I want this. I never thought I could have you again, I never thought you would *want* me again. Z, please be inside me."

"I have to grab a condom."

"No! I'm okay. It's fine. Come into me; be with me just like this, right now."

"Suzanne... I love you so much."

"Please don't talk, just *be* with me."

Kissing my lips once more, pressing his weight against my body, Z moves slowly into place. Gently against my body, Z pauses at my crest, and wraps his arms under my shoulders, holding me closer to him. I can barely breathe, but I feel so free, so safe. There is no panic. There is no pain.

"Suzanne, when was the last time? Ah, you're so tight. I don't want to hurt you."

"It was you, Z. My last time was with you. For months and months you were my last memory, my *only* good memory. I have never had sex with anyone since you. I've never made love with anyone *but you*, my whole life," I whisper.

"Oh, Suzanne..." Z moans.

Moving once more, Z finally begins his slow rocking into me. There is a tugging feeling, but no pain. He isn't hurting me at all. I'm actually enjoying the tugging and the pull. Finally, he is seated deep inside me. Finally, we both exhale.

"Suzanne? Will you stay with me? I want to marry you, and have a life with you. I *need* to have a life with you. Will you please stay with me?"

"Yes..."

Kissing my lips again, I feel Z's smile against my mouth. I feel his pleasure in his movements. I feel his love all around me, inside me, and outside our little haven. I have Z, completely.

For hours we seem to move in a steady rhythm of enter, retreat, lift, and move. We move sideways, and back and forth. We move together. I even seem to know what he likes, and he knows *exactly* what I like.

When I'm exhausted and building toward another climax, Z finally increases our movements. The speed is never overwhelming to me, but it's absolutely *desired* by me. I need him slightly harder and definitely faster. I need more. I want this to be complete between is.

"Z, I need more. Please finish this. Please touch me and take me over with you. I want to climax with you. *Please.*"

"Suzanne, I'm dying to finish inside you. You're my first, *ever.*"

Speeding up the movements, Z touches me that one amazing touch, and my whole body tightens. Oh my *GOD!* It's time. Panting, I feel the rising pressure. I'm suffering the tightening of everything inside me. I'm ready, but I just need... And then he does that other touch-thing to me...

"OH. MY GOD! Z!" I'm screaming, and actually kind of grunting. Jesus *Christ! Grunting?*

"*Shit! Suzanne...* " And grabbing me up into his arms, kissing my lips hard, I feel Z erupt inside me.

Turning us, I land again on Z's chest, with him still inside me. Once again, I am weightless, and boneless. I can't think clearly. I can barely breathe.

"That was *AWESOME!*" I giggle at my own stupidity.

"It really was, Suzanne. You're amazing and I love you. I really do,

you know? It's always going to be you Suzanne. Forever. Please don't ever push me away again, I won't survive it. Tell me when you need space. Tell me when you need a break. Tell me anything and everything, but please Suzanne, I'm begging you, don't ever push me away again. We can move slow. I'll talk to Mack. I'll do anything and everything to make this work, but please don't push me out of your life again."

"Okay." And that's it. That's all I can say.

Tucking me into his chest, Z wraps us in his duvet, and I feel myself being pulled into sleep. I want to fight it but I'm just so tired, and like, *free.* I'm safe, and weightless in Z's arms.

"Sleep Suzanne. When you wake up, I'll feed you, and we can talk about all the details later. Okay?"

"Okay. Good Night, Z."

"Good Night, Suzanne." And there it is. I hear his smile-voice.

===========

When I wake up, it's nearly midnight. Z is still holding me, while playing with a strand of my hair.

"Hi."

"Hi, back," I croak. Jeez, it must've been that back-arching scream of mine.

"Let's go to the kitchen and scrounge up some food."

"Yes, please. I'm starving."

Handing me his robe, I quickly cover up and tie the sash tight. Old habits die hard. I'm much better, but *as if* I'm going to walk around *naked.* Z's robe is huge on me but I'm covered, and it carries his scent, which I love, so I don't really care what I look like.

In the kitchen, Z makes us grilled cheese sandwiches. We didn't put away any of the food before we, ah, went to the bedroom, so nothing is really edible. Smiling, this is the absolute best grilled cheese I've ever had in my life.

"You're smiling."

"I am. This is the tastiest grilled cheese I've ever eaten."

"Oh, that's the only reason you're smiling?"

"Ah huh. Why? Should there be some other reason?"

"Are you teasing me, Suzanne?"

"Yup. I like teasing you, and Mack has given me lots of ammunition, so prepare yourself. This new and improved Suzanne is much more relaxed, and *much* cheekier. Do you think you can handle that?"

"Bring it on, love. I'm sure I could teach you a thing or two..."

"Um, you already have, Z. Some of your bedroom tricks could actually cause my filthy authors to blush, I think."

"Are you grinning at me Suzanne?"

"Ah huh."

"Can you say much more than 'Ah huh'?"

"Yes... But I'm just remembering a particularly interesting bedroom trick from earlier, so you'll have to excuse my distraction."

"I see. Well then, I'll ask one simple question, so you can get back to your memories. Would you like to live here with me or would you like to move into another apartment? Or, if you want, we can move to Chicago, but I thought you might be more comfortable away from Chicago. But the choice is yours. I'll go wherever you want. Or we can live separately until you're ready for more. I can be as slow as you need, or we can start today. *I'm* ready for today, but I can give you time and space, if you need it."

"Yes, I'd like to live here with you, if that's okay. But I need a few days. Maybe I'll just stay at Kayla's for a few days, just so I don't become too overwhelmed. Is that okay?"

"It's more than okay. Stay with me when you're ready. I can wait. Once we live together, we can move whenever, or *if ever* you change your mind and need to move from here. I really don't care. I need you to understand that. This is just an apartment to me now. I have no emotional attachment to it, other than its attachment to you."

"Okay." And finishing my grilled cheese, I try to think of what my first step should be. What my first *baby* step should be.

"Suzanne?"

"Yes?"

"Do you love me?"

"Desperately."

"Do you think you will desperately love me for a long, *long* time?"

"Absolutely. And you? Can you love me for a long, *long* time, Z?"

"Absolutely."

"What do we do now?"

"We go back to bed. And in the morning, we have coffee, and breakfast, maybe make love again, and then we talk about some of the bigger issues."

"Like?"

"Marcus."

"That's no longer an issue. I've said my goodbye. I said it in Chicago, before I fled for Kayla's, and then I wrote a letter earlier which Mack will give to him. Marcus and I are over, and we would have been over whether you and I had been together or not."

"*Been together?* I think the proper term is called *engaged,* but *are* together works just as well, I suppose."

"Did you propose to me, Z?"

"Don't you remember my proposal, Suzanne?"

"*Vaguely.* I was quite distracted at the time with the other things you were doing to my body. I could barely focus on listening to you speak."

"I see. Well then, I guess I'll have to propose again when you're not quite so distracted."

"Okay."

"Good."

"Z? If I *did* agree to some future hypothetical proposal, do I have to become Mrs. *Zinfandel?*" I smile.

"That's your choice. I wouldn't subject my name on anyone. Whatever you want Suzanne- you choose your name."

"Okay, *Mr. Zinfandel...*"

===========

In the morning, after a wonderful breakfast, and a tedious clean up of all last night's dishes, Z and I remain remarkably relaxed with each other. We're happy and very much like a new couple, with a definite excitement in the air. I catch myself grinning and smiling all the time. I actually look like a bit of a dork, another Mack trade off, I think. Actually, I really should call Mack.

"I'm just going to go give Mack a call. Is that alright?"

"Suzanne, shy of running away from me, you never have to ask my permission for anything, *ever*. And regarding Mack, there is nothing you ever need to explain, or tell me. I know what he means to you, and I know what you mean to him. Mack has made no secret of the fact that he loves you very much, and would move mountains to help you. I could never, *ever*, begrudge anything between you two. Mack gave you *Suzanne* back and he helped give *me* Suzanne. I can never thank Mack enough for all he's done."

"Me either. I tell him all the time how much I love him, and how wonderful and special he is, and he just grins and shrugs. He takes everything I say as if it doesn't matter; when to me, it matters immensely. I *love* him, Z... platonically of course- But I love him dearly and I think I will always need Mack in my life, separate from you. Can you handle that? Will it ever be too much for you?"

"No. I know he doesn't have *romantic* feelings for you, and that's the only thing that stopped me from going crazy myself when you would only see him and not me. But I understand it. I'm glad you found that with Mack. He's been my best friend for 25 years, and there is no one I trust more with your life or even with my own life. So go talk to Mack. Do whatever you need to do. I only ask that if you *can* talk to me, or if issues arise for you *regarding* me, I beg that you try to talk to me as well, so you and I can work things out together."

"I will talk to you about anything 'us'. I only talk to Mack about the other *stuff.* The stuff no one else knows, the stuff I don't want anyone else to know, *especially* you. I'm afraid you'll feel differently about me or something. Um, I'm still afraid of that."

"That won't happen, whether I know explicit details or not. Suzanne there is nothing that happened in your past that could change the way I feel for you presently *and* in our future. There is NO horror you could tell me that would change the way I feel for you. Trust me, please?"

"I'm working on it. I trust you with my body now, and I'm working on trusting you with my life, Z. The trust is coming, and I want it to come. I want you to be the person I trust most."

"Good enough. I love you, Suzanne. Go ahead, go call Mack."

"I'll be right back," and placing a kiss on his soft lips, I leave for the spare room to talk to *my* Mack.

===========

An hour later when I join Z in his study, he instantly spots the tell-tale signs of my crying. I've never been able to hide crying, and I always look hideous after a good bawling session. Jumping from his chair he begins walking toward me.

Raising my hands in the 'stop panicking' sort of way, I tell Z, "It's okay. I'm good. They were mostly happy tears, and I'm absolutely fine. You have to get used to this though. Some days I cry a lot, and other days not at all. This is my life for now, Z. I am a work in progress, and I'm going to be better and stronger for you one day. But you have to understand that I'm going to cry, and sometimes I *can* talk to you about my tears, and other days I can barely speak at all. This is part of me. Do you think you can handle it all? It's a lot to take on, Z. And we can move slower if you'd like. I just want you *in* my life; as little, or as much as you can give me. It doesn't matter to me, as long as I have you in *some* way."

"I'll take the tears, and the nightmares, and the upset, and the happy, Suzanne. I'll even take the *Mack*. It'll just take some time for me to stop trying to fix everything *for* you, because I'm a work in progress as well. But I can say this… I'm going to love you like you've never known love could be, and I'm going to make you the happiest you have ever imagined being."

Standing, Z walks to me and gives me a long, deep, beautiful kiss. Breathless, I pull away and just stare at his face. He truly is breathtaking, and apparently *mine* to love. It's a little overwhelming, but I'm going to make sure I work hard to keep Z.

"I want you to be happy *with* me, not *for* me. I want to share *your* happiness as well."

"Suzanne…"

"Just please think about what you want Z. Then really think about me and us. I need you to be sure that I will be what it is *you* need as well."

"I know what I want, and we'll work through all the details, until we each feel what we want to feel. Good enough?"

"Okay, good enough. But I really do have to go now. I'm meeting New York Kayla for lunch, and she's demanding all the details of our 'sex-fest', as she calls it. I promise to only give her enough to satisfy her, without giving her enough to torture you with later."

"She doesn't scare me, Suzanne," he grins.

"Well, she should. Mack is absolutely terrified of her, as he should be. Don't ever mess with my two Kaylas, Z. Individually, they could hurt you, but together, they could crush you," I say in my best, most stern voice.

"I'll keep that in mind."

"Smart man. But I really have to go. I'll call you later, okay?"

"Please do. I love you very much, Suzanne. We're going to *build* a wonderful life together, I'm sure if it."

"Ugh, you're going to make me cry again. I love you, and I'll call you after Kayla runs me over during lunch." He nods, placing a kiss on my lips before I leave him.

CHAPTER 44

Leaving the study, I'm struck again by how different Z's apartment is. Not just the decor has changed. The very air is different. The feeling in the apartment is lighter, and hopeful, and *new*. It's a new start here, just like Z and I. Everything is new.

This Suzanne is new. I can be any Suzanne I want to be, and this is the Suzanne I'm happiest being. I have 2 Kaylas, and a Mack. And I have Z in my life. I have said a proper goodbye to Marcus. And I am slowly saying goodbye to the nightmare that was my past.

This is a new Suzanne. Maybe I *can* have the life I always wanted. Maybe I *was* meant to have love. Maybe I'm not as horrible as I was always led to believe by the monsters in my past. Maybe they were wrong, and I am now a wonderful, new, *happy* Suzanne.

===========

Driving to the restaurant to meet Kayla, I can't stop thinking and smiling... *well,* like a crazy person, actually.

God, Z is so easy to love. He will always make me feel special. He will always make me *feel*. Z will be the happiest my life can ever be.

I know deep down that this will happen for us, and I honestly believe Z when he says he wants this, just as much as I do.

Thinking about loving Z makes me feel such happiness and pleasure, it's like I'm light, or elated, or whole, or something that resembles all those words put together. I can't even describe it properly.

I just know that in this moment of my life when I love Z so completely, I want to live in this exact moment of pure bliss and completion... *forever.*

And then I see the truck and my new Suzanne just stops.

===========

This is it. It's too late. But I have Z's love. I have his love in this precious moment of time. Right NOW, I have his love.

Oh, *GOD!* This is my **TEN**. This agony is *unbearable*. I have to close my eyes now, because I don't want to see this happen to me.

Unlike Porphyria's lover, I don't want Z to die, and *I* don't want to die. I want to *live* with this love. I was wrong! Oh, god, I was *so* wrong. I DO want to live with him in this love.

In this precise moment of complete love and adoration, my last memory of Z will be of him loving me completely, of him being mine... *forever.*

In this moment, I leave this earth with only the feeling of my true, healthy, beautiful love for Z... surrounded by the only happiness I have ever known.

There will never be anything more or less than Z's love, to stay with me *forever*.

Dammit.
With a long last exhale I whisper,
 "I *love* you, Z...
  But I am gone."

THE END

Sarah Ann Walker

ABOUT THE AUTHOR

Sarah Walker lives in Hamilton, Ontario with her American husband and their son.
Sarah left her career as an Office Administrator in the summer of 2011 after 9 years, and decided it was time to work on her dreams a little.

Sarah can be found on Facebook, Amazon.com, and Goodreads.com.

24501167R00195

Made in the USA
Lexington, KY
20 July 2013